For a Mother's Sins

Diane Allen was born in Leeds, but raised at her family's farm deep in the Yorkshire Dales. After working as a glass engraver, raising a family, and looking after an ill father, she found her true niche in life, joining a large-print publishing firm in 1990. Having risen through the firm, she is now the general manager and has recently been made honorary vice president of the Romantic Novelists' Association.

Diane and her husband Ronnie live in Long Preston, in the Yorkshire Dales, and have two children and four beautiful grandchildren. *For a Mother's Sins* is her second novel.

Also by Diane Allen

For the Sake of Her Family

DIANE ALLEN

For a Mother's Sins

PAN BOOKS

First published 2013 by Pan Books,
an imprint of Pan Macmillan
20 New Wharf Road, London N1 9RR
Associated companies throughout the world
www.panmacmillan.com

ISBN 978-1-5098-9555-7

1 3 5 7 9 8 6 4 2

A CIP catalogue record for this book is available from the British Library.

Typeset by Ellipsis Digital Limited, Glasgow
Printed and bound by CPI Group (UK) Ltd, Croydon, CR0 4YY

Visit www.panmacmillan.com to read more about all our books
and to buy them. You will also find features, author interviews and
news of any author events, and you can sign up for e-newsletters
so that you're always first to hear about our new releases.

1

'Is that baby never going to shut its gob? Take it out of here, Lizzie. Drown it if you want – I'm past caring.'

'But, Mam, he's only hungry, poor little man. Can't you give him a quick feed?'

'No, I bloody well can't! I've all this washing to do and then I need to hang it out to dry while the sun's shining. If I don't get some money in my pocket before the end of the day, that baby's not the only one who'll go hungry. He'll just have to wait.'

Molly Mason, soapsuds up to her elbows and face red and sweating from the steam filling the wooden hut that she called home, was in no mood for a bawling baby. Piles of workmen's washing beckoned and the sun was shining and the wind blowing – such fine drying weather was a rare event on the bleak moors at Ribblehead and she intended to take advantage of it.

Lizzie cradled her baby brother protectively in her

1

arms. How could her mother be so hard, leaving her youngest to cry his heart out with hunger?

'Give him a drop of gin with a bit of sugar mixed in, that'll keep him quiet until I've done.' Molly swiped an ample arm across her brow, cuffing away the sweat that was running down her forehead and dripping from the tip of her nose. 'Do something, Lizzie, just shut him up till I've got this done.'

Knowing that her mother would only lose her temper if they stayed, Lizzie wrapped little Tommy in a railway-issue blanket and took him out into the early summer sun. Clutching the tiny screaming bundle close to her, she used her body to shield him from the blustery wind. These days, her mother seemed to be angry all the time. Truth be told, she'd not been herself since Dad died. Tears sprang to Lizzie's eyes as she thought back to the terrible day last winter when her world had stopped with the death of her father. Her heart still hurt, indeed she thought it would never mend, she missed her loving father so much.

'By 'eck, Lizzie, that little brother of yours can make a fair din. What's to do with him?' Old Mrs Pratt stopped and pulled down the corners of the coarse grey blanket and peered at the screaming red face within.

'He's hungry, but me ma hasn't got time to feed him. She's loads of washing to get out.' Lizzie tried to hush Tommy, but he only screamed louder. She was on the verge of bursting into tears herself, desperate to quiet him but not knowing what to do. 'Ma says to give him

2

a drop of gin, but I don't like it, so I'm sure Tommy won't.'

Rose Pratt looked from the baby to the bedraggled fourteen-year-old. From beneath an unkempt mop of curly black hair, worried eyes peered out at her. 'Aye,' said Rose, taking pity, 'I think we can do a bit better than that, lass. Come on, bring him into mine and we'll give him a drink of cow's milk – that'll fill his belly.'

Thankful for the offer, Lizzie followed the plump form of her neighbour as she shuffled along the furrowed ruts of the cart tracks that passed for a road in Batty Green. Though the rough shanties that made up the settlement all appeared bent and worn, they had been standing only a short time. Thrown together in haste to provide shelter for the families of the men building the railways, their tin roofs had been lashed by the westerly winds, and what little paintwork there was had been stripped by the driving rain. In this unforgiving wilderness high on the moors, churned to mud by the numerous residents that now made it their home, the wild elements prematurely aged buildings and occupants alike.

Folk didn't settle in Batty Green to live like kings. The menfolk were there to build the railway and viaduct, while their families did their best to scratch out a living and survive in this remote and hostile place. Ingleton, the nearest market town, was a good five miles away down an exposed moorland track. Few in Batty Green could even name the nearest city.

Rose Pratt opened the door to her home and beckoned for Lizzie to enter. Eyes wide with awe, the girl hesitated on the threshold, taking it all in. Although the Pratts' shanty was built of the same shoddy materials and stood only a little way down the rutted furrow that divided the camp in two, it was a world apart from the one Lizzie called home. There were curtains at the windows and it was tidy and spotless, with separate sleeping and living quarters. Most of all, it was cosy, lit by a small blazing stove in the corner of the living area.

'Right, I've put the milk on the stove top to warm,' said Mrs Pratt, pushing a grey curl away from her rough red cheeks. 'Now let's see what we can find to give him it in.' She rattled about in a cupboard and came out with an empty bottle, then began rummaging in a drawer. 'Somewhere in here there's a teat our Jim used for nursing a couple of orphan lambs the other year. That ought to do the job, if I can find the blessed thing.'

Muttering under her breath, she carried on pulling out various bits of string and odds and ends that her husband kept in the drawer until at last she gave a triumphant cry and held up the teat. 'There, that'll do. We'll soon have him quiet.'

She fitted the teat to the bottle of warm milk and handed it to Lizzie. The moment the teat was thrust into the baby's eager mouth, his screaming stopped. Soon he was sucking contentedly at the warm liquid.

'There now, that's better. Poor little devil was starving!' Rose Pratt smiled at the tiny bundle as Lizzie fed him. 'Do you want a drink of tea, Lizzie? And I've

4

got some freshly baked biscuits, I bet you won't say no to one of those?'

Lizzie eagerly said yes to biscuits. At home, such things were a luxury only to be had at Christmas or birthdays. She had heard that the Pratts wanted for nothing; with four of her menfolk working on the railway line and none of them allowed to drink, Rose Pratt's home was always warm and the occupants well fed. Unlike the rest of the navvies' huts, where fires went unlit and mouths unfed as everyone struggled to live from day to day.

Rose poured the tea into a gilt-rimmed china cup decorated with violets and set it down on the table in front of her. It was so delicate compared to the plain earthenware mugs they drank from at home, Lizzie didn't know if she dared pick it up.

'Here, give me the baby,' said Rose. 'I'll hold him while you have your tea and biscuits.'

She leaned over and took Tommy, holding him close to her huge bosom. 'It's been a long time since my lads were this small,' she said with a smile. 'At least your mother knows where she's got him – not like my lads. Bye, they do take some keeping in order! I blame this place. Sins of the Devil are being nurtured out here, drinking and gambling. They'll all go to hell!'

Lizzie said nothing. She was too busy gazing around her at all the pots and decorations in the hut. Her mother reckoned Rose Pratt was an interfering old do-gooder who wanted her Bible throwing off the top of the viaduct. But Lizzie didn't mind the old woman –

though she didn't care for it when she started preaching from the 'good book', as she called it. Rose's talk of hellfire and damnation always made Lizzie think about her own life, wondering whether she was going to be eternally damned for some transgressions she'd unknowingly committed in her short life.

'Is your mother keeping all right? I was only saying to Jim the other night, I don't know how your mother does it, bringing up two children alone in this place. She must be thankful that you're getting old enough to help her. It's no place for a woman on her own. She'd be better off back in Bradford. At least there you'd be able to find work in the mills or in service, then it would be one less mouth for her to feed. Have another biscuit, there's plenty left for my boys.' Rose rattled the brightly decorated biscuit tin under Lizzie's nose, tempting her to a biscuit and hoping to elicit some gossip in return.

'My mam likes it here,' said Lizzie. 'She says it's wild and untamed, just like her. And she's near my father here. We couldn't leave him all by himself in the graveyard and us go back to Bradford.' Lizzie's thoughts flitted back to the grimy streets of Bradford and the smoking mill chimneys. She'd hated it there, living in a crowded house where they'd had to share an outside lavvy with the rest of the street.

'Aye, well it's certainly wild and untamed. I've never known gales like it, and the winters are bitter enough to freeze a body to the ground. No doubt there'll be a lot more joining your father in that graveyard before

6

the tunnel and viaduct are finished.' Rocking baby Tommy in her arms, Rose watched as Lizzie nibbled the edges of her biscuit, savouring every mouthful. 'Does your mother keep company with anybody, now you've no father?' she pried, pushing the biscuit barrel towards the child in the hope of teasing information from her in return.

'Na, me ma says there was only one for her, and no one will ever replace him. I hear her crying of a night when she's had a drop to drink. I think she gets lonely.'

'Aye well, that'll be the demon drink. Better your mother kept away from that stuff,' Rose sniffed disdainfully. 'It makes women wanton and men lustful – I'll not have it in my home. All I need is the good book to give me solace.' Realizing that she was rocking the baby a little too violently, Rose got up and began pacing the floor with the dozing Tommy clasped to her.

Lizzie's eyes followed Mrs Pratt for a moment and then returned to the biscuit barrel. Just one more biscuit, and then she'd better go. Otherwise she'd have to listen to the old woman going on about her Sunday School again. The last thing Lizzie wanted was to join the holier-than-thou band of Methodists that sang outside pubs, trying to save souls. Their children always looked as if they'd been scrubbed to within an inch of their life with carbolic soap. From what she'd heard, they even washed their mouths out with soap.

Wincing at the thought, Lizzie crammed the biscuit into her mouth. Barely able to speak through the crumbs, she thanked Mrs Pratt before taking possession of her baby brother, hurriedly making good her escape before she was cornered.

Stepping out into the sun and wind with Tommy fast asleep in her arms, Lizzie made her way home. In the distance she could see her mother pegging out washing on the lines that she had erected across the moorland on the edge of the shantytown. Molly Mason was battling against the cold spring wind, clothes pegs clamped in her grimly set mouth and long auburn hair whipping across her face. Lizzie knew her mother hated it when she had a mix of washing, especially when people sent her their whites for laundering. Then the work was even harder than usual, because the women of Batty Green wanted their whites washed in Dolly Blue – a whitener to keep the white sharp and clean – instead of just being scrubbed with the usual carbolic soap.

The empty dolly tub had been put back in its usual place under the eaves of the hut, along with her scrubbing board, mangle and posser. They'd be back in use again tomorrow when the next lot of laundry would have to be tackled. Before Dad died, doing the washing was a once-a-week chore, but now it seemed to take up all Ma's time because she did other people's things as well as their own. 'I've got to make a living somehow,' she'd say. Lizzie had tried to lend a hand, fetching water to fill the copper, plunging the posser into the dolly tub to churn up the soapy water, turning the mangle to wring out the water before hanging the clothes on the line, but it was exhausting work and her mother would soon lose patience with her feeble efforts. So Molly soldiered on alone, pounding the posser and bending over the scrubbing board until her back ached and her hands were chapped and raw from the bleach and strong soap.

Her arms aching from carrying Tommy, Lizzie opened the door and stepped into a hut that seemed very unwelcoming after the plush surrounds of the Pratts' home. Here there were no ornaments, no delicate pieces of china, no curtains at the windows. The nearest thing to a curtain was the sheet hanging from a wire strung across the room to screen off their sleeping quarters. The stove had been lit to boil the water for the laundry, so the place was warm at least, but it was sparsely furnished with only the bare necessities. Since her dad died, the hut had lost the homely feel it once had. They'd not had much, even in those days, but Dad had always made the little hut feel like a proper home. When he came home of an evening the house would be filled with laughter as he told funny stories or played jokes on them. With him gone, it was as if the heart had been ripped out of their home.

Lizzie placed her baby brother in the packing carton that doubled as his cot, wrapping him up tight in his blanket. He was still fast asleep; now that he had a full stomach he'd probably sleep for an hour or two.

She picked up the kettle and filled it up from the big wooden butt outside the hut. She had to make several trips to the spring in order to top it up each day. That was Lizzie's job: fetching and carrying water so they'd have enough for drinking and their daily ablutions. Not to mention the dozens of trips back and forth to keep the butt replenished on laundry days. Her arms and legs would ache from carrying the heavy buckets, until it was all she could do to lift them.

While the kettle heated on the stove she went to check on Tommy. At the sight of the red-cheeked baby sleeping contentedly she let out a yawn. It had been a long day already, she'd been up since six and the biscuits and drink had made her sleepy. She curled up in the Windsor chair, pulling her shawl around her. Soon her eyelids were drooping and her head lolling on the armrest as she dozed off.

The screams awoke her. In the first hazy moments between sleep and being awake, she wasn't sure whether she was having a nightmare or if the screams were real. Lizzie rubbed her eyes and peered through the gloom until she could make out her mother, standing over the makeshift cot and clutching baby Tommy.

'What have you done, Lizzie?' she wailed. 'What have you done to Tommy? He's not breathing.'

Her face was contorted with fear as she held the tiny body in her arms. As she clutched him tighter to her breast, Tommy's little white arm dropped lifeless out of the shawl.

Lizzie leapt from the chair, her heart pounding. 'I didn't do nothing, Ma, honest. He was fine when I put him down, he was right content, 'cause he'd had some milk off Mrs Pratt.' A lump formed in her throat and

10

her breath was coming in ragged gasps. 'I didn't hurt him, Mam. It wasn't me, I swear. I would never do anything to hurt our Tommy – I love him,' she sobbed, tears streaming down her face.

Rocking Tommy back and forth as if this would somehow restore life to his cold, still body, Molly tried to fight the panic rising within her. Her heart felt as if it would burst with grief. She looked from her son's face to her sobbing daughter. 'Stop blubbing!' she screeched. 'Fetch Doctor Thistlethwaite – he'll be in the hospital on the green. Go on, run! Fetch him now. Can I trust you to do that?'

As the door banged shut and the sound of Lizzie's running footsteps faded, Molly Mason sank into the chair her daughter had just vacated. Hugging the lifeless bundle to her, she rocked back and forth, trying not to give vent to the grief, knowing that if she did she would howl and scream and cry, unable to stop. What had Lizzie done? What was she thinking of, taking her precious baby boy to Mrs Pratt's? Leaving her to find him dead in his cot? Deep down, she was blaming herself for being too busy. Over and over again, the words she'd spoken only that morning kept repeating in her head as she clutched the silent baby to her breast: *Drown it if you want . . . just shut him up.* It had been the drink from the previous night talking. Her hangover had made her say things she didn't mean. All she'd wanted was to make enough money to feed them all, with perhaps enough left over for another gill of gin to dull the pain. It wasn't her fault. She'd done her best to make a good life in this world, but death was always lurking at her shoulder, especially in this godforsaken place.

All the gin in the world couldn't numb the raw pain she was feeling now.

Lizzie raced along the rutted track through the shanties, tears coursing down her cheeks, lungs burning and a pain in her chest so bad she thought she would burst. She ran as she had never run before, desperate to reach the crossroads and the Midland Railway Hospital. Like the workers' housing it was built of wood, but its sturdy walls and imposing size set it apart from the hastily erected shanties. The planners had known that this building would see lots of use, but they had situated it far enough away from the dwellings to prevent residents being disturbed by the screams of injured workers as their limbs were amputated. Even though the railway construction was still in its early stages, amputees were a common sight in Batty Green and Lizzie knew that this was where the men were operated on. It was also the place where her dad had been taken when he got hurt. The place where he died.

On reaching the door, Lizzie hesitated. The last time she'd crossed this threshold was the day her father was brought here. She didn't want to go in there ever again, but if little Tommy's life depended on it she had no choice. Wiping her eyes, leaving tracks of her tears down her cheeks, she gathered up every ounce of courage she could summon and opened the door.

Doctor Thistlethwaite was stooped over the end bed at the far end of the building. Hardly able to breathe, and careful not to look to either side of her at the groaning men in the beds, she walked the length of the ward.

'Please, sir, my ma says can you come quickly – my baby brother's died.'

Doctor Thistlethwaite paused, needle in hand, and turned to face her. Lizzie couldn't suppress a gasp of horror. The front of his apron was covered in blood.

'For God's sake, child, it's the living I'm bothered about. Can't you see I'm sewing this man up to stop him from dying?' He waved a hand at his patient, groaning in agony on the pallet bed. 'Tell your mother I'll be over as soon as I can. If the baby's dead there's nothing I can do anyway.' With that he turned away, intent on getting back to his work.

He was interrupted by a tug on his coat.

'Please, please come and look at my brother. Ma will kill me if I don't bring you back with—'

There was a curse from the doctor as a jet of blood spurted from the injured man, spattering the walls and ceiling. 'Now, look what you've made me do!' the doctor roared, desperately trying to staunch the flow.

Two nurses came running from the other end of the ward. While one went to help the doctor, the other grabbed Lizzie by the shoulder, wheeled her around and started to march her out of the ward. The doctor, still focusing on his patient, shouted, 'Go with her and see if there's anything that can be done. Tell the mother I'll

13

be along later today with a death certificate. I suppose it's been hungered to death.'

It was all the chubby nurse could do to keep up with Lizzie. She puffed and panted behind the girl as she sped homeward, muttering curses all the way. If there was one thing she hated it was having to set foot in the shanties of Batty Green. How these people could bear to live in such conditions, lost in filth and sin, was beyond Nurse Gladys Thompson. No wonder the baby had died, she thought. It was probably best out of the world it had entered.

'What have you been doing with this, Ma?' A frown creased John Pratt's fair mud-streaked brow as he lifted the bottle with the teat still attached to it from next to the fire where he was warming his toes while his mother bustled about making tea. 'You've not fed anything with it, I hope. This is the bottle I keep the rat poison in.'

'Oh my Lord, it isn't, is it?' There was a clatter as Rose Pratt dropped the milk jug, her hand flying to her chest. For a moment she stood frozen in place, blood draining from her face as an image flashed in her mind's eye: little Lizzie feeding her brother as she sat next to the fire.

'Where you going, Ma?' called John, as his mother hurriedly threw on her shawl and bustled out of the front door.

But Rose was too distracted to hear his question. Slamming the door behind her, she set off as fast as her legs would carry her, hurrying along the track in the direction of the Masons' shanty.

She was almost there when she saw a lamp approaching from the opposite direction. It was the carpenter. Rose slowed down and waited in the shadows; she would prefer not to encounter the man if she could avoid it. She despised the way he profited from others' misfortunes, doing a roaring trade in shoddily built coffins made of the cheapest wood. Then she realized he was carrying a coffin now. A small one, just big enough for a baby.

Rose clapped a hand over her mouth to suppress a cry of anguish and looked on from the shadows as the carpenter delivered the tiny coffin to the Masons' hut. When the door opened, Molly Mason's cries seemed to split the night. Rose turned away, sick with guilt. The next thing she knew, she was back at her own front door, having walked all the way home without realizing what she was doing. But what else could she have done? What could she have said? It was too late to do anything for little Tommy Mason now. Poor mite probably wouldn't have survived another winter anyway. The way things were going, he'd have died of starvation.

Burying her guilt deep within her, Rose resolved to remain silent. God would forgive her, she told herself. She hadn't meant to kill the poor little soul, He would know that.

Three days after Tommy's death his little coffin was carried down the dappled glade to the burial ground.

15

The air was filled with the smell of the wild white garlic and the delicate bluebells that lined the path to the ancient church of St Leonard's. For centuries the small church had served the dale's dwindling farming community, but since construction started on the railway it had seen an alarming number of funeral services as the navvy population buried their dead.

Tommy was laid to rest alongside the remains of his father. Lizzie watched as the vicar gave a blessing over the tiny coffin. Then the gravedigger hurriedly filled in the small hole before moving on to the next grave, where mourners wept for the man the doctor had been operating on when Lizzie went to the hospital the night Tommy died.

Numb with grief, Lizzie tried to smile through her tears as members of the community hugged her or squeezed her shoulder, at a loss as to what they might say to comfort her. She wouldn't have heard them anyway; ever since her brother died it was as if all other sounds had been drowned out by her mother's cries echoing over and over in her head: *What have you done, Lizzie? What have you done to Tommy? He's not breathing.*

While her mother lingered to shake the vicar's hand and thank him for his blessing, Lizzie wandered on to the bridge. On the river a small bird was hopping about on the mossy wet stones, dipping up and down with a beakful of worms for its young. For a few moments she lost herself, watching its progress, before her mother brought her back to reality by shaking her shoulder.

'Come on with you,' she said, her voice hard and devoid of emotion. 'The Welcome Inn's put a bit of a tea on in remembrance of Tommy. Any excuse to make money out of us hard-working souls. Still, I shouldn't complain. They've not asked for anything towards it, so we might as well get fed for nothing.'

'But I don't want to go in there,' complained Lizzie. 'Everyone smells of beer and they talk loud.'

Ignoring her protests, Molly dragged her daughter up the winding path from the church and to the rutted road that led from Ingleton to Ribblehead. It was all Lizzie could do to keep up with her.

When they got to the Welcome Inn and she caught a whiff of the beer and tobacco smoke billowing out from inside, Lizzie sat on the steps and refused to go any further. Molly's response was to cuff her on the ear and snarl, 'Now listen here, my girl, if it wasn't for you, we wouldn't have had to go through that today and I'd still have my son. So shut up and get in here with me.'

Reluctantly, Lizzie let herself be shoved into the dark, low-ceilinged inn. 'Go sit in the snug,' ordered Molly. 'I'm only going to have an odd one and a bite to eat – show my thanks, like – and then we'll toddle off home. We've got to have a wake for our Tommy, it's expected of us.'

Lizzie did as she was told and took a seat in the corner of the snug. It was a dark spot; even on the brightest summer's day the sun would never penetrate the thick glass of the windows, which were stained a

17

brownish colour. The inn, a solid squat building of weathered limestone, seemed as old as time itself. Nestling
in the lee of the fellside, its thick walls kept out the
blasts of freezing wind that blew down the dale, offering
the drinkers some respite from the harsh conditions.

Alone and forgotten, Lizzie watched as people came
forward to console her mother, buying her drinks in a
show of respect. Then the singing began. All other voices
in the room fell quiet as one of the gangers sang 'Danny
Boy' in a lilting Irish accent. After the final verse there
was a hush in the inn as the mourners remembered the
little soul that they had buried.

'Are you his sister then? Me mam says I've to make
sure you get something to eat.'

Lizzie looked up to see a plump girl with red rosy
cheeks.

'Well, are you going to have a bite of something?'

Lizzie shook her head.

Refusing to take no for an answer, the girl continued
in her dry Yorkshire accent: 'It's no good me and my
ma cooking all day if the thinnest one in the bar isn't
having any. Move up a bit and I'll bring us both a
plateful. I'm blinking starving myself. I've been rushing
about all day, helping out.'

With that the plump figure turned and bustled off
through the tall figures of the navvies lining the bar,
leaving Lizzie to shuffle deeper into the corner, making
space for her new friend.

A moment later the landlady's daughter was back,
carrying two plates piled high with sandwiches, pie and

cake. She plonked them down on the table in front of Lizzie.

'Tuck in. I can soon sneak back into the kitchen for more if you finish that lot.' She took a mouthful of brawn sandwich, then held out her hand. 'I'm Florrie, what's your name?'

'Lizzie.'

It was hard not to gawp as Florrie carried on tucking into her food, smiling as she chewed.

'Are you not going to eat that?' Florrie paused mid-mouthful to scrutinize Lizzie with concern.

'I'm not right hungry.' Lizzie looked at the plate of food, which on a normal day she would have relished. 'I'm missing my baby brother. My mam blames me for his death, but I swear it wasn't my fault.'

'Aye, well, there's nowt you can do now. My twin brother died when I was little, but you just have to get on with it. Not much else you can do.'

Lizzie was impressed. Florrie looked to be no older than she was, but there was an air of confidence about her. She wished she had that kind of self-assurance.

Chatting away like an old wise woman, Florrie reached across to help herself to one of Lizzie's sandwiches. 'Go on, they're good,' she urged. 'Me and Ma made 'em this morning. You can't bring him back by not eating.'

Lizzie took a tentative bite and Florrie nodded approvingly, then gulped down a mouthful of ale.

'Here, you need a drop of this and all, to calm the nerves.'

Despite herself, Lizzie savoured the meaty sandwich and followed it with a swig of ale. She didn't enjoy the first mouthful, but gradually she began to get used to the bitter iron taste.

'See, I told you, there's got to be some perks to being the landlady's daughter,' Florrie laughed, then added conspiratorially: 'Don't tell me ma, though – she'd kill me if she knew I'd got us both a gill.' Her blue eyes twinkled with delight at getting away with the theft of two drinks.

Before Lizzie knew it, she and Florrie were talking like long-lost friends. Hidden away in the snug, away from the smoke and noise of the funeral wake, they were soon comparing their lives and discovering they had a lot in common.

'I think I like you, Lizzie Mason,' Florrie beamed, gathering up the empty plates. 'See you next week sometime? How about Tuesday – one o'clock, on the bridge?'

Lizzie nodded happily. For the first time in ages, she felt warm and content, knowing that in Florrie Parker she'd finally found a friend.

2

'Oh my Lord, can't folk have a minute's peace? My poor bloody head is killing me.' Molly raised her head from her striped pillow and cursed the roaring boom of a dynamite blast as work continued on building the connecting tunnel between Blea Moor and Dent, a quarter of a mile away across the moorland.

'Happen you shouldn't have had so much to drink, Mam. Me and Cloggie had all on to get you back home.' Lizzie handed her mother a cup of tea as she sat on the edge of the bed pulling her stays tight, her long ginger hair hanging over her shoulder.

'Don't you start lecturing me, Lizzie Mason. You are in no position to— Did you say *Cloggie* brought me home? I didn't let him in, did I? It'd be just like him to take his chance. He's been hanging around this hut for weeks.' She gave a shudder. 'Creepy little bastard.'

Lizzie shook her head disapprovingly. Her mother was obviously still suffering from drink; she'd never normally swear. 'No. Soon as we got you into bed I thanked him and sent him on his way. He could hardly stand up himself.'

'Give us another cuppa, lass, I could drink a beck dry this morning.' Molly passed Lizzie her empty cup and pulled her top on. 'I'm going to have to pass on any washing today, I'd probably be sick if I tried leaning over the dolly tub. God knows what we'll eat tonight.'

'You don't have to bother about that, Mam. Mrs Pratt called earlier and left us a meat pie. Said she thought you'd appreciate it.'

'Nosy old bag. There's only one reason she'd be coming here, and that's to lecture me about the demon drink. It isn't as if I drink every day. If I couldn't bury my troubles yesterday, then when can I?'

Molly rose from the bed and opened the door, letting the breeze from the fell enter the hut. 'A bit of fresh air and I'll soon feel better,' she said, sipping her tea and looking across the shantytown towards the place where they were building the new viaduct. She leaned against the doorway. 'I don't know, Lizzie, perhaps we should go back to Bradford. I don't think this trainline will ever get built – at the inn last night there was talk of the investors having run out of money. I don't know what we'd do if that happened. We've already lost so much since we came here.'

Lizzie came to stand beside her, wrapping her arms tightly around her mother's waist. Molly laid a hand on her head and absent-mindedly stroked her fingers through Lizzie's long black hair. 'At least in Bradford we'd have a house to live in, not a bloody wood hut,' she said. 'Another month or two and you'd be old enough to go into service. We could both earn a living in Bradford.'

'But I like it here, Mam,' said Lizzie. 'I made a new friend yesterday. Her name's Florrie Parker and her mother runs the Welcome Inn. I'm going to see her again next week. I don't want to go back to Bradford. It's a horrible grimy place and I'm used to all this now.' Lizzie waved her arms, taking in the panoramic view of Great Whernside and Ingleborough, two of the great peaks that rose out of the wild moorland that surrounded Batty Green.

'Aye, and I'd have to leave my two men behind in the churchyard,' sighed Molly. 'All right. We'll see if we can stick it out until Christmas. If we can't, then it's back to Bradford. Your uncle Bertie will soon fix us up with lodgings and jobs.'

Lizzie hugged Molly tight. 'We'll be all right here, Mam. I'll help more, honest I will.'

'Aye well, not today. I'm not doing anything – my head won't stand it. I'll have to do double tomorrow and hope for good weather.'

Lizzie watched as her mother sank wearily into the chair by the fire. Molly Mason had never been one to give in, but losing Tommy so soon after Dad had been a terrible blow for her. But in spite of the hard times they'd been through, Lizzie had grown to love this place. She resolved to do whatever she could to make sure they stayed here.

*

Florrie was sitting on the small road bridge, hands tucked into the pockets of her smock apron, beaming happily as she watched all the comings and goings on the new viaduct. The building works were swarming with navvies and navigators, and the air was filled with the thud of their picks hitting earth and the occasional rumble of what sounded like thunder as another bundle of dynamite went off, blasting a way through the mountainside of Blea Moor.

'I could sit here all day,' Florrie said with a grin as Lizzie sat down alongside her on the bridge edge. 'I love to see how fast it's coming along. Look, the scaffolding's nearly up for the first arch. I wouldn't want to be the fellas at the top, mind. They're almost touching the sky.'

'My dad worked on the scaffolding. That's how he died – the wind whipped up behind him and his hands were so cold he lost his grip and fell.' Lizzie spoke in a quiet, matter-of-fact voice, her eyes gazing at the point where the scaffolding met the sky.

'God, I'm sorry, Lizzie. I didn't mean to upset you.'

'You didn't. It's like you said yesterday, there's nowt to do but get on with it.' Lizzie shrugged. 'All the same, life's not been the same since he died. But I'm still here, so I suppose that's all that matters.'

'Come on, let's go and have a look underneath it.' Florrie sprang to her feet and tugged on Lizzie's hand. 'They've made a track down there alongside the beck – you can follow it all the way to the other side of the valley.'

The two girls ran across the moorland, giggling with mischief as they darted between the carts ferrying stone and wood to the site. The carts made slow progress, with the horses struggling to haul their heavy loads up the muddy slope, urged on by the shouts of their drivers.

'Mind where you tread,' warned one of the drivers. 'You could sink into one of these bog holes and we'd never see you again.'

Others were less friendly. As they reached the gap in the moorland where the viaduct was to run, a burly foreman waved his arm at them and yelled, 'This is no place for women – bugger off home, out of the way.'

'He called us women!' said Lizzie once they had managed to dodge the angry foreman and get a safe distance away.

'Well, we nearly are. Bet you can't say that you haven't been having . . . feelings. I know I do, seeing some of the men that come into the pub.' Florrie laughed and gave a wicked grin: 'We should have shown him our fannies and charged him for the pleasure!'

Lizzie could feel her cheeks blushing crimson. 'Me mam says it's wrong to talk about such things,' she said, horrified.

'You big softie,' Florrie teased.

'I'm not. It's just that it's unladylike to talk of these things.'

'Ooh, hark to Lady Jane!' said Florrie, putting on a la-di-da voice. 'Lives in a wood hut with no money but *lovely* manners.' She nudged Lizzie in the ribs. 'Aye,

25

that'll keep you fed and warm at night. Come on – race you to that barn.'

She took off along the track, her heels kicking up dust, leaving Lizzie to ponder her words. Better to have manners, she decided, than to be easy prey for dirty old men. She'd been aware for a while that her body was beginning to change, and she'd seen the looks men gave her. But there didn't seem to be any reason to go rushing into womanhood. From what she'd seen, Lizzie didn't want any of it.

By the time she caught up with Florrie, her friend was sitting on one of the horse mounting blocks next to the barn. She was puffing and panting, and her cheeks were so red she reminded Lizzie of a red berry about to burst.

'Hey, slowcoach – you're not sulking, are you?' Florrie gasped, peering intently at Lizzie's face.

'No, I'm taking my time, that's all. Do you fancy walking the full length of this lane? I think it comes out not far from the church. I'd like to pay my respects to my dad and baby Tommy.' As she spoke, Lizzie was studying her new friend, wondering what to make of her. Much as she liked Florrie, there was something about her that made Lizzie uneasy, though she couldn't quite put her finger on it.

Florrie got to her feet and brushed the dust from her skirts. 'Why not? I sometimes walk there myself.' Then she added cryptically, 'Some days it can be quite rewarding.'

Lizzie frowned to herself. What did she mean by

'rewarding'? It sounded like something Old Mrs Pratt would say. Was Florrie religious and not letting on? It hardly seemed likely, given the conversation they'd just had.

Though the sun was shining there was a sneaky wind blowing down the valley, tunnelling between the two peaks that rose either side of Chapel-le-Dale. Lizzie gazed at the shadows of clouds scurrying across the great flanks of Whernside and the sleeping-lion form of Ingleborough. She still couldn't believe how lucky she was to be living in such beautiful countryside; it was so different from the first thirteen years of her life, which had been spent amidst the grime and smog of Bradford and its wool mills.

'What's up, cat got your tongue?'

Jolted out of her reverie, Lizzie turned to her companion. 'No, I was just taking it all in, reminding myself that, no matter what's happened, I'm lucky to live here.'

'*Lucky?* You must be joking!' Florrie gave a toss of her head. 'Soon as I'm old enough, I'll be off. When this railway line's built I'm going to get on the first train out of here and find myself a rich fella in Leeds. I've no intention of hanging about like the rest of my family.' Florrie picked up a stone from the path and threw it as far as she could. 'Waste of bloody time, living here. There's never anything to do.' Then her eyes darkened as she added, 'Besides, I want to get out of the way of my dad. I've had enough of him.'

Lizzie, who had worshipped her father, turned to

her friend in astonishment. 'Why? What's up with him?'

'He likes his women, that's what's up with him. Even my ma reckons he's a bastard – not that she'd say it to his face, mind. He's handy with his fists, especially on Ma. She's forever telling people that her face got bruised 'cause she fell over or banged her head on a door.' Florrie might like to pretend she was a toughie, swearing like a trooper and talking hard, but Lizzie could see the tears welling up in her eyes. 'That's why I'm off: I don't want to end up with a fella like my dad.'

The pair lapsed into silence as they walked down the glade to the little church of St Leonard's. Lizzie made her way over the grassy bank of the graveyard to where she had stood the previous day. A mound of earth and some square sods were the only witness to her baby brother's resting place underneath the wall by the riverside. Her father's unmarked grave was already covered over by a carpet of grass and daisies. Lizzie wondered how many more would be laid in the ground before the railway was finished. She only hoped that she would not be joining them; there was too much life to embrace. One thing was for sure: she would not give in easily.

There was a tug on her skirt. 'Come on, let's go into the church – we might be lucky!' Florrie gave a wink and ran off giggling towards the church entrance.

Lucky? What on earth could she mean? Intrigued, Lizzie followed her friend, casting several backward glances at the graves as she said a silent prayer for lost souls. By the time she got to the porch, Florrie had already entered the church.

Today it was empty. Without the distraction of mourners paying their respects, Lizzie was able to take in the plain whitewashed walls and the wooden pews that smelled of polish. She shivered as she gazed up at the altar, remembering the way the vicar had stood looking down at them while her mother sat beside her, sobbing into a handkerchief.

'Come on, Lizzie – give us a tune on the organ,' giggled Florrie. She tugged on the lid of the church organ, only to find it was locked. 'Damn! He sometimes forgets to lock it and then I can have a play. I right enjoy myself, too.' She moved off down the aisle towards the final pew. 'Still, never mind. Let's have a look in the collection plate – somebody might have left a penny or two to save their souls.' She winked. 'It can save my soul instead.'

'You can't take money from the church, that's wicked!' Lizzie remonstrated, appalled. 'I may not go to church but I know what's wrong.'

Florrie paid no heed. She was too busy collecting the pennies.

'Stop it, Florrie – you'll never go to heaven if you do that. Put it back!' Lizzie rushed over and grabbed at Florrie's hand, sending the coins flying. As they rained down on to the wooden floor, Lizzie fell to her knees and began picking up the rolling pennies. She was so busy trying to rectify Florrie's theft that she didn't realize that her wayward friend had darted out of the church.

A dark shadow loomed over her. 'Get up, you thieving child! How dare you steal from the Lord's house? God will smite you down with a great blow, for there is no greater sin than stealing from Him.'

Lizzie raised her eyes and saw the long black cassock of the vicar. Head bowed, she scrambled to her feet, clutching the bronze pennies in her hand.

'But I . . .' she stammered, too shocked to get her words out. Hurriedly she placed the coins back on the collection plate, shaking with fear as the vicar loomed over her.

He raised his hand and brought it down hard on her ear, making her head spin. Tears sprang to her eyes and she wiped her nose on the sleeve of her dress. Her face burning with shame at the wrongful accusation, she raised her eyes fearfully to meet the vicar's implacable glare and tried to stammer out an explanation.

'Quiet, you terrible child. You think I haven't noticed that you've been stealing from my church for weeks? But then, what should one expect of a navvy's brat – you people are like a pestilence infesting the dale!' He leaned forward, scrutinizing her face. 'Wait – didn't I bury your brother only yesterday? Hah! You would do well to bear in mind that the Lord giveth and the Lord taketh away – and in your case he's taken your brother, all because of *your* sins.' The vicar grabbed Lizzie by the scruff of the neck and shook her.

'I haven't done anything, it's her,' Lizzie sobbed, pointing to the empty porch. Florrie must have heard the vicar coming and made herself scarce. 'I loved my brother. I didn't do anything to hurt him.' Her head was throbbing where the vicar had hit her and tears and snot were running down her face. She tried to clean herself up using the sleeve of her dress, but the vicar had tightened his grip on her neck and was steering her out of the church, her feet tripping over themselves in an effort to keep up.

'Enough!' he roared. 'This will be the last time you steal from my church – I'm taking you back to that forsaken place they call Batty Green and we'll see what the local magistrate has to say.'

As soon as they were out of sight, Florrie crept from her hiding place behind the church wall. Seeing the few remaining coins in the collection plate, she grabbed them and made good her escape. Too bad the vicar had showed up, she thought. It would be too risky, helping herself from that plate again.

The vicar hammered on the weathered wooden door of Lizzie's shanty with such force that the whole building shook. Lizzie's eyes were red and she couldn't stop sobbing even to draw breath. He'd finally released his hold on her neck, which felt bruised where he'd gripped it as he marched her all the way up the hill to Batty Green, but now he had her arm clamped in his fist. The pain was nothing compared to the humiliation and terror she'd endured as he ranted at her throughout the long walk, accusing her of being in league with the Devil and telling her that she would burn in eternal hell along with the rest of her vile family.

'It's no good repenting now – tears won't wash your soul clean,' the vicar hissed in her face, giving her another violent shake.

Then he pounded on the door again, determined to gain admittance. The response from inside the hut was a muffled 'All right, all right, I'm coming!' Not satisfied with this, the impatient vicar hammered on the door with his fist again, as if he was trying to break it down by brute force.

At last the door opened, to reveal Molly Mason, squinting in the daylight, her hair uncombed and alcohol on her breath. Beyond her, in the rear of the hut, a half-naked Cloggie could be seen, sitting on the edge of Molly's bed.

The vicar was all too familiar with Cloggie, who was a regular in the local drinking establishments and a shameless whoremonger. Clearly, the child's mother was another of his whores.

'Fornicators – ye shall have thy part in the lake which burneth with fire and brimstone!' he roared. Faces were appearing in other doorways now, curious to see what all the commotion was about. 'You disgust me, woman!' he told Molly. 'I see now where this wretch gets it from – a prostitute for a mother and no father. The child doesn't stand a chance. No wonder she was thieving from the church. I saw her with my own eyes. It was my intention to take her before the magistrate, but under the circumstances I think the workhouse at Sedbergh would be more fitting. At least there she will find holy guidance and be put to good honest work.'

'No, no, I won't go to the workhouse, you can't make me,' Lizzie screamed, trying to pull free of his grip. 'Tell him, Ma! Tell him he can't take me there!'

But the once-proud Molly Mason had no fight left in her. Swaying unsteadily, she shrank from the overbearing man of God. Avoiding her daughter's pleading eyes, her voice dull and listless, she said, 'Do with her what you want. Maybe she'll be better off at the workhouse – I can't feed and dress her any more, I can't even look after myself.' And with that she closed the door.

Even the vicar was sufficiently taken aback to release his grip on the child, who now fell to her knees, sobbing and screaming. 'Now then, now then, what's all this about?' demanded Rose Pratt, shuffling through the gathering crowd. 'What's all this about, Vicar? I could hear the racket from over in my hut. What's up, Lizzie pet?' she asked, stooping to clasp Lizzie's hand, but instead of bringing comfort this only succeeded in making Lizzie cry all the harder.

'You may well ask, Mrs Pratt,' said the vicar to Lizzie's neighbour, a prominent member of the local Methodist congregation. 'I found this wretch thieving from my church. Far from castigating the child, the wanton slut of a mother has just disowned her. I am left with no option but to take her to the workhouse.'

'Now, Vicar, don't be so hasty.' Mrs Pratt laid a protective arm around the sobbing girl's shoulders. 'Our Lizzie's a good lass, she'd not steal. And her poor mother's not herself – burying a baby within six months of losing her husband has taken a terrible toll on her.'

Lizzie sniffed and tried to stop the tears. 'I wasn't pinching, Mrs Pratt, honest. I was only picking up the pennies to put them back.' She turned her pockets out to demonstrate that she hadn't been trying to make off with the collection money.

'See, Vicar? I think you'll find it's all a misunderstanding. And as you can see, Lizzie doesn't have anything in her pockets, so she's not really pinched anything, has she?' Laying a hand on the vicar's arm, she said, 'Why don't you come and have a nice cup of tea at mine – and bring Lizzie with you? I'm sure we can sort this out.' Then she lowered her voice conspiratorially and added, 'Why, if I were to tell you the things that go on in this godforsaken place . . . well, let's just say your pennies would seem of no consequence.'

His interest piqued, the vicar allowed himself to be led away in the direction of Rose's home.

'Well, that's worked out grand, Vicar. Lizzie will stop with us until her mother finds her feet again. I'm so glad we're all in agreement. I've always wanted a daughter, and Lizzie will have a good home here, never fear. So that's that then, eh. Mind how you go, Vicar.'

Rose Pratt practically had to push the vicar out of the hut, but finally she closed the door behind him with an enormous sigh of relief. Even she had heard enough of his pompous sermonizing. 'I thought he was never going to go! My word, he could talk the legs off a donkey, that one.'

Lizzie, who had been sitting in the corner, too afraid to breathe a word while the vicar was present, peered anxiously at Mrs Pratt. She couldn't for the life of her understand why the old lady had come to her rescue, but she was grateful that she had. She'd heard terrible stories about the workhouse and what happened to people who went there.

'I didn't take that money, Mrs Pratt, I swear. I'd never do a thing like that. I'm much obliged to you for standing up for me – and for letting me stay.'

'Aye well, let's say I owe you a favour and least said about it the better. Only thing that worries me is how do I explain to my lads that you're stopping? Two of them are going to have to sleep head to toe for a night or two until we sort you a bed of your own. Still, it'll not hurt 'em.' She began clearing the table, gathering up cups and plates, then lifting the lid of the biscuit barrel to check the contents. Empty – the vicar had eaten his way through the entire lot, greedy so-and-so.

Seeing Lizzie still sitting in the corner, she said briskly, 'Come on, young Lizzie, time to earn your keep. The lads'll be home soon and wanting something to eat, so come over here and peel me these potatoes.' Rose emptied a dozen potatoes into an enamel dish and gave Lizzie a knife. 'Get a move on, lass, they'll not peel themselves.' Then she shuffled off to rearrange their sleeping quarters to accommodate her new guest.

As Lizzie peeled the potatoes the day's events kept running through her mind over and over. Never had she known a day like it: accused of thieving, dragged

35

home by that horrible vicar only to be confronted with the sight of her mother, drunk in the middle of the day and with a naked man in her bed . . . That was almost the worst part of all. Had she no respect for herself? And then telling the vicar to go ahead and put her daughter in the workhouse. How could she?

And as for Florrie Parker: just wait until Lizzie got her hands on that little troublemaker. She was going to wish she had never been born.

3

Lizzie lay uneasily in the wooden bed that was her new resting place. She'd hardly slept a wink all night and now she was wondering how she would adapt to the early morning routine of the Pratt household. She screwed her eyes tight, pretending to be asleep as she heard the men of the house rising and getting ready for another day's work on the railway. Coughs, grunts and the sound of the Pratt men relieving themselves made her curl under the bedclothes in embarrassment. The only man she'd ever shared a house with was her dad, and that was different because he was kin. Although it was only six in the morning the sun shone through the window, promising a good day, but in Ribblehead such promises meant little. At any moment a change in the wind could bring dark clouds that would envelop the great peaks and deliver a downpour that would go on for hours.

'What were you thinking of, Mam, when you took that one in?'

Lizzie could hear the Pratt family discussing her, even though they'd lowered their voices.

'I'd no choice, the poor lass. That dry old vicar was going to put her in the workhouse for the sake of his collection plate. I don't think she'd taken anything anyway, the miserable old devil. They're all the same, that C of E lot.'

'But we haven't the room, Mam,' John, the eldest, protested.

'If we haven't room for a soul in trouble then what are we worth? Look at what we've got: a warm home, food on the table and the five of us content and well fed.' Rose emphasized the last two words by plonking a ladleful of porridge in her son's bowl. 'Stop your moaning, John. We'll soon knock up a bed and sort out quarters for her. By the end of the week you two lads will be back to normal. In the meantime it won't hurt you to share for a night or two. Now, I'll not have another word said. Besides, she'll be a good hand for me around this spot. I'm not getting any younger and you four men take some looking after.'

'But, Rose . . .' Jim, her worn-down husband, started to protest.

'No, not a word, Father. I've made her welcome and it's here she'll stay. That is, until her mother wants her back – shameful hussy that she is at the moment.'

Rose banged the black pot on the stove top, signifying an end to conversation. The men bowed their heads and ate their breakfast in silence. They knew better than to argue.

*

John and Mike left the family home a few seconds later than their father and younger brother, Bob. Mike took the time to check himself in the small mirror that hung next to the door while John was busy tying his spotted neckerchief at a jaunty angle. They were both proud, good-looking men who took pride in their appearance, unlike the rest of the navvies, most of whom worked and slept in the same clothes day after day. Their mother had taught them well: 'Respect yourself and folk will respect you' was a favourite adage of hers, and she'd drummed it into them from the time they were small.

'I don't know what's got into Ma,' John Pratt growled to his younger brother, keeping his voice low so Rose wouldn't hear. 'She's been acting funny the last few days, and now she's taking in thieving orphans.'

'But she's not an orphan. She's still got a mother and it should be up to her to sort the lass out,' Mike said as he tapped his clay pipe empty before putting it into his jacket pocket.

'The mother's in no fit state, from what I hear. That worthless case Cloggie's been taking advantage of her grief, plying her with drink since the baby's funeral in the hope of having his way with her. Useless sod – she's too good for him, if she only realized it.'

'Aye, she's a fair woman, all right. Not bad for someone who's got a lass that old. I've seen her hanging the washing out. When the wind takes her hair, she looks like something out of a painting . . .' Mike lost track of his thoughts for a moment, picturing a windswept Molly pegging washing on the line.

'She's too much about her for you!' John laughed, throwing a light punch at Mike's shoulder. 'Best let your older brother show how it's done.'

'Keep your bloody voice down! Ma would hit us into next week if she knew what we were thinking. She hasn't a good word for the woman.'

'You're right there, lad,' John laughed. 'There would be hell to pay if one of us were ever to walk out with her!' He nodded at the door. 'Come on, time we were off.'

The men left the house, hurrying to catch up with their father and younger brother, both sporting a twinkle in their eye as they considered what good sport a night with Molly would be if they dared risk incurring their mother's wrath and disappointment.

Ahead of them they could see the huge banks of soil that were being heaped up either side of the scaffolding, covering the valley floor of peat moss and cotton grass. Men were busy putting harnesses on the horses that would tow the heavy carts loaded with construction materials, and two carts pulled by pit ponies were standing by to take the dyno men and their explosive cargo into the tunnels below Blea Moor, where they were blasting their way through to Dentdale.

As they waited for John and Mike to catch them up, Jim Pratt took the opportunity to point out the latest developments on the construction site, explaining to his youngest son how the various parts of the viaduct would eventually connect together and the vast distance it would cover. To his dismay, Bob seemed completely unimpressed. Unlike his older brothers, the boy showed little interest in improving himself. He was a dark and moody lad who didn't seem to care about his work or his appearance, or even his family. His mother put it down to Bob being the 'afterthought', as she called it. Most days they just left him to it, ignoring his surly manner, but this morning he was even grumpier than usual. Jim gave up trying to educate him, removed his pocket watch from his waistcoat and checked the time. They were running late. He shouted at his lads to get a move on.

The brisk pace left them breathless, so no words were exchanged until they reached the point where their paths separated, John heading for Blea Moor and the others for the foundations of the viaduct.

'See you tonight,' John called cheerfully, turning away from them.

'You might,' said Mike. 'I've something in mind.'

He grinned as his brother wheeled around and hurried back to him.

'And what might that be?' said John, raising an eyebrow. 'Does it involve a certain widow?'

Mike looked anxiously at Jim and Bob, who had carried on walking. 'Keep your bloody voice down.'

'I tell you what, our lad, let's have a bet on who can win the Widow Mason over. How about a week's wages to the one who beds her first?' John winked, certain of his own prowess in these matters.

'You're on – but not a word in front of Father or our Bob. They'll only blab to Mam and there'll be hell to pay if she gets wind of it.'

Mike spat in his hand and held it out. John did the same and they shook hands.

'May the best man win,' said Mike.

'No contest!' John laughed. Then he took off at a run, having noticed that his ride was leaving without him. As he jumped on the back of the cart, he shouted down the valley: 'You haven't a chance, mate. Besides, what would Jenny say?'

Shaking his head, Mike hurried to catch up with his father and Bob.

Jim Pratt gave him a curious glance. 'What was that all about?'

'Nay, nothing, Pa. Our mad John up to his usual tricks, that's all.'

'Now then, Lizzie, soon as you've washed them pots up we'd better go and see your mother, make things right with her. While we're there, we can pick up a few of your clothes.' Rose looked across at the girl, who was standing with her back to her, scrubbing the porridge pot. 'Are you still all right about stopping with us, pet?' she asked.

'I'm fine, Mrs Pratt.' Lizzie kept her face turned away so that the tears wouldn't show. The last thing she wanted was to seem ungrateful to the elderly neighbour who had saved her from ending up in the workhouse. 'But I'm going to miss my mam. I can still go and see her, can't I? She didn't mean what she said yesterday. I bet if you ask her this morning she won't even remember what she said.'

42

'Course you can, darling.' Rose came and stood beside her, running her fingers through Lizzie's unkempt hair and studying her troubled face. 'Tell you what – come Saturday, after the lads have got paid, I'll have Bob take us to Ingleton in the trap. There's a shop there where we can pick out some lovely ribbons for this hair. I always wanted to buy ribbons and pretties for a little girl, but it wasn't to be.' She gave a heavy sigh.

Lizzie said nothing, but far from being cheered by the promise her heart sank at the prospect. Ribbons, indeed! She was fourteen, not four. If she had to stick something in her hair she'd much prefer a hair slide.

No point worrying about it, though. Saturday was four whole days away, and the way her life was going at the moment anything could happen between now and then.

'What do you want?' demanded Molly Mason, opening her front door to find Rose Pratt on her doorstep.

'Now, Molly,' said Rose, pushing Lizzie in front of her so that Molly could see the girl. 'I've brought Lizzie with me so we can get this sorted out. You can't just ignore—'

'Ignore what? I haven't got time to be messing about with you – and what do you think you're doing with our Lizzie? I've been calling her the last hour. She should be filling my boiler up, ready for today's washing.' Molly scowled and reached out her arm to pull Lizzie inside the hut.

'Surely you remember something of yesterday, Molly?

Have you forgotten what happened when the vicar called on you? The things you said?' Rose stepped between mother and daughter, holding Lizzie back.

Pulled between the two women, Lizzie didn't know which way to go.

Molly squinted at Mrs Pratt in confusion. 'Vicar? A bloody vicar, here, in this house? That'll be the day!' She released Lizzie and planted her hands on her hips defiantly. 'Did I offer him my soul? Because that's about the only damn thing I've got left to trade.'

'Now, Molly, there's no cause for blasphemy. Why don't you let us both come in and I'll tell you what we're going to do.' Rose stepped forward, trying to edge her way into the hut.

'Lizzie, get your bloody self in here! As for you – ' Molly pushed Rose Pratt on the shoulder, nearly pushing her over – 'you can jigger off.'

'Mam, stop it! You told the vicar he could take me to the workhouse – and he would have done, too, if it wasn't for Mrs Pratt. You were drunk again, don't you remember?'

It was the first time Lizzie had stood up to her mother, but she knew she had backing and for the first time since Dad died her stomach was full and she felt clean and she hadn't had to listen to her mother's alcoholic slumbers.

'You cheeky brat! Don't you tell me when I'm drunk – you're too much like your father. He was always lecturing me.' Molly spat the words out like venom. She hated anyone knowing that she drank, but most of all she hated herself for drinking. But how else could she have survived these last six months? Without a tipple to numb the pain, her grief would have killed her.

'I'm sorry to say it, but she's right, Molly.' Rose drew herself up to her full height and said in a firm voice, 'I'm going to take your daughter home with me now. When you've straightened yourself up, you know where to find us. Lizzie won't be going anywhere, will you, pet?'

Lizzie shook her head, angry and ashamed of her mother. Molly used to be such a good mother. When Dad was alive, the shanty hut was always full of laughter and talk about what they would do with all the money he'd make building the greatest railway in England. All that ended when he fell to his death from the top of the viaduct. Lizzie could still hear the horn they used to sound the alarm that there had been an accident; she could see the crowd of workmen surrounding his crumpled body as it lay on the ground. His legs had been broken in the fall and his face was deathly white against the pool of red blood that surrounded his head. And she remembered the screams of her mother as she ran as fast as she could with an unborn baby in her belly, collapsing beside her husband's body, refusing to let go when they tried to drag her away. She'd heard those same screams again the other night when Tommy died. That night when their entire world had finally fallen apart.

'Come on, pet,' said Rose gently. 'Let's leave your mother with her thoughts. We'll go and make some bait for my boys. They usually have a drink and a bite to eat mid-morning. You can take John his, up at Blea Moor. He usually misses out because my old legs won't take me up there, but yours will.'

'Aye, bugger off, the pair of you! I can manage without you, Lizzie Mason. You'll soon come running back when she's dragging you to Sunday School and chapel.'

The door slammed shut in their faces, but through the thin wood they could hear Molly's body slide into a crumpled heap, sobbing for her lass, the only one she had left in the world, and asking what she had done to deserve such a hard hand.

As Molly sat drying her tears on her apron, a moan sounded from behind the sacking curtains that divided the room and the ragged form of Cloggie stumbled from the bed. Molly sniffed, pulled herself together and rose to her full height.

'You can bloody well get out as well!' she said, marching across the room. She dragged the hungover navvy to the door, hauled it open and shoved him outside. 'Go on, bugger off! And don't come back. You've had me now, but by God that'll be your one and only time.'

Then she leaned on the closed door, vowing that never again would she allow herself to get in such a state. She'd clean her act up and make sure that Lizzie knew she was loved. As for Rose Pratt, she'd show that interfering old bag. Nobody walked over Molly Mason. Surely, with all the people and money in Batty Green, there was a way to make a decent living. Now that she

46

was a free woman, no baby, no family, the world was her oyster. If she couldn't make it now, she never would.

Lizzie turned at the sound of the commotion. Her cheeks flushed red with humiliation when she saw her mother's lover being pushed out of the front door in a state of undress. Even at her tender age, Lizzie could spot a loser – and Cloggie was definitely that. Her dad used to say that Cloggie viewed life through the bottom of a glass; she hadn't known what it meant back then, but she did now.

'Never you mind, pet. You're with me now. At least your mother has had the sense to throw him out. It's a step in the right direction. Now let's get them sandwiches made and you can take them up to our John.'

Lizzie bowed her head, ashamed of her mother. Molly obviously didn't love her, else she wouldn't carry on that way. It was as if, when Tommy died, she'd given up caring about her daughter, blaming her for the baby's death. She probably thought Lizzie was guilty of stealing from the church, too. It was so unfair. None of it was Lizzie's fault: she'd just been in the wrong place at the wrong time, and there was nothing she could do to make things right again.

The track up to Blea Moor was lined with navvies hacking their way into the peaty soil of the Yorkshire fell, building the foundations for the railway. One day this track would be buried beneath great banks of earth topped by iron rails, with the steam trains thundering through on their way to Carlisle. Lizzie tried to imagine the sound of the train engines chuffing along and their whistles echoing off the fells, but for now there was only the sound of the navvies grunting as they swung their picks, and the singing of the skylarks above her. Now and then there'd be the clop of horses and the jingle of their harnesses, and she'd have to step off the track to get out of the way of the heavy carts loaded with supplies. No one acknowledged her presence. The navvies ignored her as they went about their work or took a break from their labours, puffing on their clay pipes and giving their aching backs a rest.

By the time she reached the gaping hole that had been blasted into the fellside, which was now known as Blea Moor tunnel, Lizzie thought her lungs would burst from the effort of the long climb. Pausing to take a breath, she turned around and looked out over the Ribble Valley. The green fields and rolling fells stretched out before her, with the sun glittering on the River Ribble as it wound its way down the valley on its journey to the Irish Sea. Never had she seen such a beautiful view. Despite all the things that had happened to her, she would never willingly trade this place for the smoky mill chimneys of Bradford.

She could have stood there all day, transfixed by the white cotton grass blowing in the wind, but the spell was broken by the sounding of the hooter. This was followed by shouts from the dyno men, warning fellow workers of the impending blast. Lizzie was standing a few hundred yards from the gaping tunnel when the dynamite exploded. She had never been so close to a blast: the noise was ear-shattering and the ground beneath her shook as another section of the mountain's innards disintegrated. A great cloud of dust and debris came roaring out of the mouth of the tunnel, completely enveloping the scaffolding and the entrance to the tunnel. Lizzie turned away, shielding her eyes from the grit flying through the air, covering her mouth and nose with her sleeve. When she looked back, men were emerging from the places where they'd been sheltering around the works. There was an eerie silence, as if they were all saying a prayer before resuming their assault on the tunnel.

Lizzie sat down in the brown wiry grass and looked on as the men scurried about like ants, clearing up the debris. She was so engrossed, she didn't notice John Pratt's approach. She gave a start when a shadow fell across her and he spoke.

'What are you doing up here? Is something wrong – did Ma send you? She's all right, isn't she?'

'Your mam sent me up with your sandwiches. She said you usually miss out.'

The worry on his face was replaced by relief. 'You shouldn't be up here on your own. It's not safe with this blasting.'

He took the package she held out to him and sat down on the grass beside her. Lizzie studied his face as he bit into his sandwich. She'd never been that close to him before. His blond hair and fair-skinned face were plastered with dust from the blast and a knuckle on his left hand was bleeding slightly where he'd cut it.

'Aye, well she should have known better than to send

you. It's no place for a young girl. There's some funny buggers up here that wouldn't ask twice about your age. I'll have to have a word with Ma tonight. Trouble is, she always thinks the best of everybody.' John fixed her with his forget-me-not-blue eyes as he said this, then ran a hand through his dusty hair. 'Seems she thinks she's got to provide a home for waifs and strays too.' He finished his mouthful of sandwich and took his pipe out. 'She's always wanted a lass, but she ended up with us three lads. Even so, it's a rum do, taking on another woman's lass – especially at her time in life.' He lit his pipe and drew hard on it before standing up. 'Get yourself back home and don't talk to anyone,' he admonished her before turning away. 'And mind the sinkholes – if you're not careful you'll find yourself on top of them before you know it.'

Lizzie remained where she was, gazing after him as he walked down the fellside towards the gaping hole. He didn't look back at her once, pausing only to pat a man on the back before disappearing into the dark cavity.

Slowly she got to her feet and brushed her skirt down, musing over what he had said as she started to make her way down the fell. John wasn't the only one mystified by his mother's decision to offer Lizzie a home. Grateful as she was that Rose had saved her from the workhouse, Lizzie had no idea why she'd stepped in to save her. She was puzzled too by his talk of folk who wouldn't ask her age. She'd soon tell them she was fourteen if they wanted to know.

The bumps in the grassy fellside meant she had to

keep constant vigil else she'd turn her ankle, but Lizzie enjoyed her walk back down into the valley. She hummed a tune to herself, a secret smile playing about her lips as she thought about how blue John Pratt's eyes were and what a lovely laugh he had, but then she recalled what her so-called friend Florrie had said about feeling things and her face turned crimson with embarrassment. The blush faded as she told herself it was all right for her to like John Pratt, but then she began thinking of liking him in more than a friendly way and the blush returned, ashamed at the direction her thoughts were taking. He was too old and she was too young. It was that Florrie who was to blame. Lizzie had never entertained such thoughts before she met that little thief. As if it wasn't bad enough that the crafty little minx had almost got her thrown in the workhouse for stealing! Now here she was, having lustful thoughts about men. No wonder the vicar said she'd burn in hell – she probably deserved to.

'I'll tell you what we'll do: you can pay me a shilling a month and then I'll let you keep my lass. You're not having her for nothing – I know your game. You only want her so she can run around after you, fetching and carrying and cleaning the house. Well, you're welcome to her – but it'll cost you.'

Having hatched her plan, Molly had made her way to the Pratts' hut, keeping out of sight until she saw Lizzie emerge with the package of sandwiches in her hand and set off up the hill. With four men earning, the Pratts could surely afford a shilling a month. And why shouldn't she profit, especially since she'd have to do without Lizzie's help, thanks to them.

'You're wrong, Molly,' protested Rose. 'I only took her in to save her from the workhouse – and you know it. I was doing you a favour.' She kept her voice low, not wanting any attention being drawn to her doorstep. The last thing she wanted was Molly making a scene. If she wasn't careful, others might start asking why Rose Pratt had taken in the Mason girl, and they wouldn't be satisfied with the explanation that she did it to keep the girl out of the workhouse. After all, it wasn't as if Lizzie was kin to her. No, if she was to keep her guilty secret, the best thing might be to go along with Molly. So in a resigned voice she said, 'All right, Molly, if that's what you want we'll strike a deal. If you promise not to spend it on drink, I'll give you your shilling a month and Lizzie can work for me. Lord knows I could do with another pair of hands.'

'Done.' Molly spat in her hand and offered it to Rose.

'Fine.' Rose turned without shaking the outstretched hand. 'I'll go and get you her first month's wages.'

Molly stood on the steps, unable to hide her grin of delight. So far everything was going to plan. Rose Pratt might think she was hard and uncaring, but she'd show her. That money was going to be put away for Lizzie, though she'd be none the wiser until the time came to hand it over. In the meantime, Molly didn't care what anyone thought of her. She was going to see to it that things changed for the better, and then she'd show the lot of them.

4

Molly stretched and yawned, gazing up at the tarred roof above her and then turning her head to the scrap of sacking that served as a curtain, screening her bed. The shanty was nothing to brag about at the best of times. In the cold light of day, especially when viewed through sober eyes, it was a sorry sight. She eased her legs out of the bed and pulled back the curtain. The sun shone through the murky windows, illuminating her squalid surroundings. Had she really come to this? Pain filled her heart as she took in the empty packing crate that had been baby Tommy's cot. She hadn't moved it since that horrible moment when she touched his little cheek and found it stone cold. A wave of sorrow hit her, making her long for a glass of gin to deaden the pain, but she reminded herself that drink had only made things worse. It might temporarily help her forget, but ultimately it was taking over her life, and she was better than that.

She staggered out of bed and went to the mirror, recoiling with shock when she saw her reflection. Grief had certainly taken its toll on her. She pushed her hair off her face and examined the wrinkles that were beginning to creep like thin spider webs across her brow. Wincing as her chapped fingers snagged in her hair, she lifted a strand and inspected it. Her long silky auburn hair had always been her crowning glory, but now it felt like straw and hung lank and greasy. Cursing herself for allowing things to deteriorate to this state, she boiled a kettle and filled a bowl with boiling water, adding a little cold water from the butt before immersing her hair and scrubbing it clean with soap. When she was done, she gave it a final rinse with vinegar so that it would have a lovely sheen.

Wrapping her damp hair in a towel, she set about cleaning the rest of her body, lathering a flannel and washing the places where Cloggie had put his dirty hands, trying not to think about how much she had enjoyed it after a bottle or two of gin. She threw her dirty skirt and bodice in a corner of the room and delved in her trunk until she found a dress that she hadn't worn in months. She breathed in deep as she pulled it over her head, muttering, 'Time to get your pride back, lass,' as she buttoned it up the front. Twisting her still-damp hair into a plait, she fastened it at the back of her head with a pin. It would be more practical that way than hanging loose around her shoulders.

Once she had finished cleaning herself, she filled the copper and lit the fire under it. While she waited for the water to boil she gathered up all the rubbish and empty bottles, shook out the mats and swept the floors. By this time the water was hot enough to wash the clothes and sheets and curtains. And then she scrubbed the table and cleaned the filthy windows till they sparkled.

It was well into the afternoon, with nearly all the jobs done, when she turned to discover she had a visitor.

'Mrs Pratt's sent you some dinner.' Lizzie stood on the step, quietly studying her mother. It had been months since she'd seen Molly looking this way.

'Oh, she did, did she? Probably checking up on me, making sure I hadn't hit the bottle, seeing as you all think I'm so dependent on it.'

'No, she just noticed that every time she looked out of the window you were hard at work. She thought you wouldn't have anything in, so she sent you this fresh bread and some slices of ham. There's enough for supper as well.' Lizzie walked into her old home, placed her basket down on the table and began emptying the contents out.

'I don't live on charity, Lizzie Mason – you know that. Put that stuff back in your basket and take it straight to her.'

'Mrs Pratt said you'd say that. She also said to tell you that was what good neighbours were for, helping one another out. She's all right, Mam, honestly. She's not said a bad word about you.' Lizzie chewed her lip nervously, waiting for her mother to explode into one of her fits of temper.

'I'm sorry,' said Molly, registering the fear in her

daughter's eyes and understanding the cause. 'That's the trouble with me: I've a terrible spiteful tongue in my head sometimes, but you know how hard life's been lately. I am grateful that she's kept you from the workhouse and given you a roof over your head. Only until I get back on my feet, mind!'

Molly pulled a chair up to the table and patted the one next to it, inviting Lizzie to sit down next to her.

'Do you want a brew, our Liz? I can run to a cup of tea, you know.'

Lizzie smiled and sat down on the wooden chair, eyes following her mother's every move as she poured the tea and removed the crocheted cotton doily from the top of the milk jug, the heavy weighted beads clanging against the side of the milk jug as she lifted it up to pour.

'What do you reckon, our Lizzie, does it look cleaner? I've been at it since first thing this morning. By God, there was some muck! I can't believe how lost I'd let it get.' She stared at her feet, unable to meet her daughter's eyes. 'Seems that up-his-own-arse vicar's done me some good after all. Not that I wouldn't like to knock his block off, mind. Fancy trying to tell me my daughter is a thief – and us with young Tommy still warm in his grave. I know better of you, Lizzie, and I'm sorry I let you down.' She reached for her daughter's hand. 'Tell Rose Pratt she can have your bed – but only for the time being, because you'll be back with me soon. She must be struggling to fit you in with all that lot, so get her to send one of her lads for it later on.'

Lizzie looked at her mother through tear-filled eyes. She was so relieved to see signs that her mother had come to her senses and was getting back to her old self.

'I'll tell her, Mam. I'm sure she'll be glad of the bed – two of her lads were sleeping head to toe last night. I don't think they like me much for that.'

Molly smiled. 'Mind you look after yourself. Don't go letting her fill your head with all that Bible rubbish. Remember the old saying: them that go to church usually need church.'

Lizzie grinned. 'Don't worry, Mam, I'll be fine. I know I'm going to have to work for my keep, but I don't mind. At least it'll be better than working in service, and I'll still be near you. She says I can come across and see you any time I like.' Lizzie pushed her chair back and stood up. She moved towards her mother, wanting to give her a hug before she went, but hesitated, still uncertain of how things stood between them.

'You know I love you, don't you, our Liz? I've been unwell, that's all. You've got to forget all those hard words I said. I didn't mean any of it. Tommy was a sickly baby, he could have gone any time, it wasn't your fault.' Molly held out her arms and hugged her daughter, her eyes brimming with tears. Though Lizzie would only be living across the way it felt as though she might as well be a million miles away. It was obvious that the cruel words she'd spoken had caused a hurt that would be slow to heal, and as a result she'd lost a part of her daughter's heart for ever.

As soon as her mother released her from the embrace,

57

Lizzie was gone. She badly wanted to believe Molly's promises, but she'd fallen for such promises before, only to find that her mother had abandoned all her good intentions the minute she started drowning her sorrows in gin.

Alone once more, Molly sat and opened the packages Lizzie had left on the table. There was a newly baked loaf and five slices of home-cured ham, all carefully wrapped in greased paper. The smell of the fresh bread made her mouth water and her stomach rumble, as she suddenly realized how long it had been since she'd eaten. She made herself a sandwich and then went to stand in the doorway while she ate it. The view of the bleak moorland and the bare bones of the viaduct that would stretch from one side of the valley to the other inspired mixed feelings in her. She took a mouthful of her sandwich and chewed on it wistfully. It was going to be a fair piece of engineering, that viaduct – assuming it ever got built. It must be costing the wool merchants in Bradford and Leeds a small fortune; she'd heard folk say that it was built on bales of wool. Molly knew better. It was being built on the lives of the navvies, with no compensation for their grieving families. While she would always be proud of the part her husband had played in building it, the sight would always remind her of the loss she'd suffered.

Molly set aside her sandwich, wrapping the remainder up for later in the day. Checking her appearance in the battered old wooden mirror, she draped her shawl over her shoulders and put on her boots. It was time to make a change in her life. What she had in mind wouldn't be easy, but now that she had no children to look after there was nothing to do but give it a try.

She walked along the rutted track through the shanties until it joined the main road leading to Hawes and Ingleton. On one corner of the junction stood the hospital. Molly had been so busy staring at the hospital that she didn't notice Cloggie sitting by an open fire with three of his mates until she was level with them. God, she really didn't want to walk past him, especially when he was in the company of his Scouser cronies. The four of them had worked on the docks together, until they came to Ribblehead in the hope of making more money for fewer hours working on the railway. They'd work four days and then spend the next three drinking away their earnings. They were passing around a bottle now. Cloggie was just raising it to his mouth when he spotted her.

'Hey, Moll,' he yelled, gesturing her over with the bottle. 'Come and join us. I've been telling the lads all about you.'

His friends immediately staggered to their feet, calling, 'Come on, girl – come and have a drink, we won't bite!'

Mollie walked on, wrapping the shawl more tightly around her.

'Hey up, girl, sit here,' said Cloggie, moving his wiry form along the fallen tree they were using for a bench.

'No, I'm not stopping. I want nothing more to do with you, Cloggie McFarland. Now let me be.'

'What do you mean?' Cloggie jumped to his feet and hurried towards her. 'Come and sit down – have a drink, you know you want to.' He grabbed her arm, leering at her and offering her the bottle in his other hand. Though short in stature, Cloggie had a reputation as a dirty fighter. Most of the navvies gave him a wide berth, knowing how dangerous he could be when his temper flared.

'Leave me be, Cloggie. I don't want to have anything more to do with you.' Though inwardly she was petrified, Molly yanked her arm free and carried on walking.

'You've changed your tune. I didn't hear you complaining when I spread your legs,' roared Cloggie, grabbing at her shawl. He brought his face close to hers, the reek of his foul alcoholic breath wafting under her nose.

'Let go of me, I wish I'd never let you touch me.' Molly glared at him without flinching, even though she feared for her life.

'Why you stuck-up bitch!' Cloggie lifted his hand to hit her.

'Go on then, what's stopping you?' Molly stared him in the eye.

'Ah, fuck off! You weren't up to much anyway.' Cloggie let go of her and wandered back to his mates, who were gawping at her, their filthy faces split in toothless grins. A cry of laughter rang out and Molly heard her name and a string of filthy comments, but she walked away, her legs shaking with fear as she crossed the road to the hospital.

When she reached the hospital doorway, she paused to take a deep breath, trying to gather her thoughts and calm her pounding heart. 'Well, Moll, you've nailed that one dead, and made an enemy into the bargain,' she told herself. But she had no doubt that she'd done the right thing. Cloggie was nothing but a chancer. Even under the influence of a gin-fuelled haze, it was hard to understand what she'd ever seen in him.

'Is there something I can do for you, or have you just come begging?' asked Doctor Thistlethwaite briskly, looking up from a patient to inspect the woman standing in the open doorway. It took him a moment to recognize Molly Mason: she'd tidied herself up since the last time he had seen her, on the day he called at her house to write a death certificate for her baby. When her face wasn't twisted in grief, she was quite a good-looking woman.

Molly was trying hard not to lose her nerve. The sight of the hospital interior, the groans of the patients and the overpowering smell of carbolic soap mingled with ether had brought back painful memories. She tried to focus on the doctor and shut out the surroundings. He was a dapper gent with penetrating almond eyes that seemed capable of reading into your soul. 'I was wondering what you do with your dirty bedding. I thought maybe I could wash it for you. Say a farthing a sheet . . . ?' The speech Molly had been rehearsing during her walk to the hospital had failed her. Faced with the doctor's stern gaze, her words came out in a faltering, almost incoherent jumble.

'My good woman, the Midland Railway Company ensures that hospital laundry is collected once a week. And besides, with the best will in the world, you would never be able to cope with the demands. A few days of bad weather and you'd be unable to deliver.' He stepped forward, intending to wish her good day and close the door firmly behind her, but at the last moment it occurred to him that the hospital might yet have a use for her services.

'Tell me, does the sight of blood bother you? I could do with an assistant, but you'll be no use to me if you swoon whenever you see a spot of blood. I'm looking for a jack of all trades, someone willing to turn their hand to anything – there are lots of menial tasks around the ward that the nurses don't have time for, as well as little jobs like writing letters for patients. I assume you can write?'

'Yes, sir, I can write.' Molly bobbed a curtsy and smiled, sensing that there was a job within her grasp.

'Show me your hands.' He gestured for her to step into the light so he could scrutinize her hands, which were spotlessly clean. She thanked the Lord that she had scrubbed under her nails after she finished cleaning the house earlier. Satisfied with their condition, Doctor Thistlethwaite gave a nod of approval and beckoned her to follow him to his desk. 'Now write your name on this piece of paper.' He handed Molly an ink pen and writing paper, on which she dutifully wrote her name.

'Excellent. The job is yours. I'll see you here, first

thing on Monday morning. There's no way of knowing how many hours you will be required each day – much will depend on events beyond our control. In the event of an accident at the construction site, we have no option but to work on until our patients have been attended to. We can discuss the matter of your pay when I've had a chance to see how well you manage. You will be under Nurse Gladys's supervision – I'll introduce you to her on Monday. Report here at six a.m., not a moment later. We run a tight ship – can't afford to do otherwise.'

He escorted Molly out and briskly shook her hand before closing the door behind her. She stood on the step, head reeling, wondering what she had let herself in for. Still, a job was a job. Soon she'd be earning money and proving to everyone that she'd turned the corner. It wouldn't be long before she'd be on top of her life again.

'Now then, Lizzie, don't forget – tomorrow's Saturday, the day when my men get paid and we all go into Ingleton for supplies. I expect your mam used the provision hut run by the Midland.' Rose couldn't resist a sniff of disdain at this, but quickly recovered herself: 'Of course, there's nothing wrong with the provision hut, but I like to go and get myself something decent, and there's a right good butcher's in Ingleton. Plus you never know what you might pick up at the market. But whatever you do, keep clear of them hostelries.' This was accompanied by a shudder of disapproval and shake of the head. 'Such drunkenness, you wouldn't believe! Why the sinful goings-on in those places on a Saturday evening . . . Well, you won't see any of *my* men indulging.'

'Not for want of trying,' mumbled Jim Pratt under his breath.

'What was that, Father?'

'I said, Aye, it can be very trying.' Old Jim winked at Lizzie, knowing that she'd heard his original response. He found the religion a bit wearing at times, and always turned a blind eye when his lads slipped away for a quick gill while Rose was shopping, only wishing that he could escape her watchful gaze occasionally.

'You won't get any of mine spending their wages on liquor, like most of them do around here. I blame that Henry Parker, him as runs the Welcome Inn. The railway never should have given him the job of doling out the wages. He picks the money up on a Friday night from Ingleton and then he pays the men on a Saturday morning – and by Saturday night most of their earnings have been spent in his establishment. The man's not daft.' Rose sighed and cleared the table of breadcrumbs.

'Leave him be, Mother. Henry's only making a living like the rest of us.' Jim kept his head down, puffing on his pipe and reading his paper, not bothering to look up.

'And why aren't you working today? We'll not have as much coming in this week if you've only worked four days.' Rose stood with her hands on her hips, face red with annoyance at her husband's defence of a man she considered to be a denizen of the bowels of hell.

'I'm fifty-two, woman, with three grown lads. Let them keep us for a while.' Jim folded his paper down and defiantly met Rose's gaze.

'Aye, well, I can't be doing with you getting underfoot when we're trying to get on with our work. Clear off while Lizzie sweeps the floor. And then we're going to set to and do some baking – them lads will expect summat good for their supper.' She wiped her hands on her pinny and subjected Jim to her steeliest glare.

'I'm off!' he said, conceding defeat. 'Reckon I'll go and read my paper in the earth closet, where I won't be disturbed. It's a devil when a man can't get peace in his own home.'

'Well, you'll be thanking me when we're back in Durham in a nice little cottage with everything we could ever want. Maybe then you'll admit it was worth coming here to make some brass.'

Lizzie and Rose watched Jim skulk out of the hut, his braces hanging off his shoulders as he made his way to the small lean-to that served as a toilet. Lizzie couldn't for the life of her understand why anyone would want to spend more than a minute in there, let alone the time it took to read the paper, but she kept her thoughts to herself.

'That's it, use the tips of your fingers, don't get it on to your palms – pastry doesn't like getting warm. It'll be worth nothing if it gets too hot.' Rose was leaning over Lizzie, teaching her to bake. 'Keep going until it gets like bread crumbs and then add your water bit by bit. Don't get it too wet, mind. You just want it to hold together enough for you to roll it out.'

Rose was proud of her baking skills and had always longed to pass them on. She'd leapt at the opportunity to train Lizzie in the art.

'Aye, not too rough, it needs to be handled gently.' She nodded approvingly as Lizzie rolled out the bottom layer of the pie. 'Now put your rhubarb in and a good cup and a half of sugar, blackcurrants and gooseberries. You can never add enough sugar with that lot – tart, they are, a bit like your mother on a bad day! But all it needs is a bit of sweetening and then they're grand.' Rose tousled Lizzie's hair, joking with her pupil. 'Now put its lid on and crimp the edges with your thumb. You don't want any of it spilling out in the oven bottom. That's the way – then give it a wash with this spare milk. Grand, that's your first pie done! I can leave it all to you next time.'

Lizzie stood back and admired her handiwork.

'Did your mother never bake?' Rose asked.

'We've no oven at home, only the stove top. She used to bake when we lived in Bradford, but I was too young to learn then.'

'Your mother must miss her city ways. I expect it's been hard for her, leaving it all behind to come here. The things us women do for our men – and then they go and leave us,' Rose sighed, bending down and putting the pie in her small oven. 'We'll make her a cake and then you can take it to her on Sunday while we're at chapel. She'll not want you coming with us, of that I'm sure. If you want, you could pop over and visit her tonight. Our John's going across to pick your bed up – it'll fit nice and snug in that corner we've cleared. Do you want to go with him? I'm sure your mam will be glad to see you.'

'No, I'll not bother, Mrs Pratt.' Lizzie's eyes were downcast.

'Whyever not, pet?'

'I saw her walking down the track towards Ingleton.' Lizzie's voice trembled. 'I don't want to see her if she's drunk.' She looked up at Rose with tears in her eyes.

'Aye, pet, she'll be fine. She knows she's too much to lose. Our John will tell you what she's like when he comes back. I bet you've nothing to worry about. Now come here and give this old woman a hug.' She clasped Lizzie in a tight embrace, wishing she could ease the lass's worries. 'We'll get some ribbons for you tomorrow – red 'uns, I think, for this bonny black hair. What do you think of that?'

Lizzie smiled and kissed her on the cheek. For the first time in ages, she felt loved.

John Pratt knocked on Molly's door, having double-checked that his neckerchief was tidy and his hair brushed. His brother Mike might have been joking about making a play for Molly Mason, but he definitely wasn't. John had had his eye on her for a while. All right, she was a few years older than him, but so what? Better an experienced woman than a slip of a lass, and she was still a looker even after having two children.

67

He waited for some time, knocked again, and was on the verge of giving up when Molly finally came to the door.

'I thought I heard something,' she said. 'I was busy sorting through Lizzie's clothes – I thought your mother would want them.' She stepped aside and waved him in, noticing how shy and uncertain he was in her presence. 'Sorry, I know you're one of the Pratt boys, but I don't know your first name.'

'I'm John, the eldest. My mother's sent me for Lizzie's bed. She says Lizzie made it right with you this morning.' It was all he could do to look at Molly. She'd let her long auburn hair down and it was cascading over her shoulders, but it was her eyes that had him spellbound. He'd never been close enough before to notice the colour: they were the deepest shade of green. She was a good looker, that was for sure. He was gazing at her, lost in admiration, when he realized that she'd been asking him a question and he hadn't heard a word.

'Cat got your tongue?' she laughed. 'I said you take the frame and I'll bring the slats and bedding.'

'Oh! Sorry, I must have been daydreaming,' he stammered. 'No, don't you lift that. I'll come back for the rest, you shouldn't be carrying it.' He picked up the wooden frame and moved it across the room, lifting it on its end before carefully easing it through the doorway.

'Do you want a drink, John, on your return journey?' Molly asked as he struggled to manoeuvre it.

'I don't drink. I thought you'd know.' John stood struggling to hold the frame clear of the muck and dirt.

Wishing that for once in his life he could confess to liking the odd gill.

'I didn't mean a drink drink, I meant a cup of tea. The kettle's boiling and I could do with some company.'

Molly tried not to smile as the young man turned a rosy shade of red.

'Aye, I knew that really. And yes, go on then, I'll have a cup of tea with you.'

John set off homeward barely conscious of the weight of the bed frame, a broad grin plastered across his face. A cup of tea with Molly Mason – now that was something.

When he returned he found Molly securing a bundle of bedding. 'There, I've rolled the mattress and bedclothes together and Lizzie's clothes are in the middle of it all. I thought if I tied it up with string then it wouldn't get dragged in the muck out there.' She waved him to the table. 'Here, sit down. I'm just letting the tea brew for a minute or two.'

As she took two mugs down from the shelf above her stove Molly cast a sly glance at her guest. He's a bonny lad, all right, she thought to herself. Then it struck her that this 'lad' must be somewhere in his mid twenties, so in truth he was a man. She put the mugs on the table next to where John sat. 'Sorry, I've no sugar – can't afford it. Are you all right without?' she asked, pouring the tea.

John, who had been watching her every move, mumbled that without sugar was fine.

'Tell me, which bit of the railway are you on? I don't

recall hearing my late husband mention you, so you can't have been on the viaduct.'

'I'm with the blasters, up at Blea Moor. I drill the bore holes for the dynamite – and hope to God I don't get blown up with it.' John stirred his mug of tea wistfully. It was dangerous work, and he had witnessed a number of accidents in his time there. He went to work each day never knowing whether it would be his last, whether it would be his turn to end up in the hospital. But he knew his job and went about it carefully, and over time he'd grown used to living with the danger.

'Ah, so it's you I've to blame for the constant rumble of thunder!' said Molly with a smile. She knew he had one of the most dangerous jobs on the line.

'Aye, me and a few other fellows. It keeps us on our toes.' Not wanting to spend his precious free time talking about work, John changed the subject: 'My mother's taken up with your Lizzie. She's had her baking today. I dare say she'll be telling you all about it when she comes across on Sunday.' He smiled at Molly and then lowered his eyes, pretending to gaze into his mug. Much as he wanted to look at Molly, he was too nervous to make eye contact with her.

'I thought she'd be off to the chapel with your family,' said Molly, surprised.

'No. Me mother says we've to respect the way you've brought her up. She's not a Methodist, so we'll not be forcing it on her. I know Ma can be a bit over the top with her religion. Sometimes it's as if she doesn't know the real world.' John took a long sip from his mug.

'And what about you? Do you know the real world?' Molly asked coyly.

'I know more than some of them in this godforsaken hole. I know by the time this railway's built I should have enough money under my belt to start my own business.' He put his mug down hard. 'Right, I think I'd better get myself back home before they wonder where I'm at.' He lifted the bedding bail on his back. 'Thanks for the tea.' He lowered his head and walked out of the door. She was a wick one, that Molly. Happen he'd have to go back for another tea some time.

Molly watched John's progress down the track and didn't go back inside until he disappeared into his home. Dusk was falling and lamps were being placed in windows. It was turning chilly now the sun had gone in and the smell of wood fires filled the air. In the distance a lone sheep bleated as if to signal the end of the day. Somewhere in the distance she could hear someone playing a mouth organ, the melancholy aria seeping into her soul, making her feel lonely.

Here she was in this desolate place, completely and utterly alone for the first time in her life. No husband, no son, no daughter. Nothing but the shilling that Mrs Pratt had given her in payment for Lizzie's services. Feeling a lump forming in her throat, she gave herself a good talking to. It was no good crying for baby Tommy and her much-loved late husband. She needed to look to the future, concentrate on getting through the weekend, and then starting her new job. But in the meantime, at least she knew Lizzie was being looked after well. Better than she could have cared for her.

The thought of Lizzie living with the Pratts made her thoughts turn back to John. Molly wondered whether she might have made a friend there. Too bad she spoiled it by teasing him – that had been unkind of her. Next time she saw him, she would have to apologize.

5

'Right, lads, give Mother your pay. Let's be seeing what you've made this week.'

Rose Pratt sat at her table with notebook open. Each son had a dedicated page with their contribution to family living written on it and each had his own savings account, leaving them with a few shillings and pence in their own pockets to spend as they wished. Young Bob was the last to hand over his pay. Being only seventeen and an unskilled general labourer, he earned the least.

'Ma, can't I have a shilling more for myself? The other fellows laugh at me, giving you all my earnings.' Bob was fed up with never having any money on him while his mates were free to spend their earnings as they saw fit. His face darkened as his mother launched into one of her lectures about the importance of saving.

'Don't you look at me like that, young man. You are watered and fed well, you've a roof over your head, and by the time this line's built you'll have money in the bank. So hold your noise and go fetch the horse and cart to take us all into Ingleton.' Rose wasn't having any truck with one of her boys turning into a waster.

Bob mumbled something under his breath. Face like thunder, he jammed his hands into his pockets and gave the table leg a kick on his way out.

'And you needn't act like that, my lad! If you don't stop sulking, I'll take what you've got in your pocket as well,' said Rose as she finished counting the money and putting it into the battered biscuit tin that held the Pratt family savings.

'You could let him have a bit more, Ma,' John said quietly.

'Aye, and you can mind your own business,' snapped Rose, putting the tin away. 'He won't miss what he hasn't had. Now, are we all ready? Lizzie, have you banked that stove up with coal slack? I don't want to come back to a cold hovel, my bones are fair chilled by the time I climb down out of that trap.'

'Mike and me are off on our own today, Ma,' said John. 'There'll be more room in the trap for Lizzie and Dad if we don't go. We thought we'd spend the day with some of the work lads, take a trip into Ingleton. Our Mike has a liking to visit the waterfalls, seeing as it's such a grand day.' John smirked at his brother, kicked him on the shin out of sight of their mother.

'Waterfalls? What do you want to go there for? Don't you see enough water in this forsaken place?'

'They're opening a walk around the falls, Ma. I thought I'd ask Jenny Burton to take a stroll with me.' Mike could have killed his brother for dropping him

74

in it, but decided to make the best of it by taking the opportunity to break the news about Jenny. He was going to have to tell her sometime. There'd be hell to pay if she found out from someone else. She hated it when anyone kept things secret from her.

'And who might Jenny Burton be?' Rose, who had been standing in front of the mirror tying on her bonnet, wheeled around to face her son. 'Where's she from and what does her father do? She'd better not be one of them trollops from round here – you can do better than that, lad.'

'I'll not have you calling Jenny a trollop. Anyway she's not from here, she lives at Gearstones Lodge. Her father runs the boarding house there.' Mike was cringing as he spoke. He knew Rose was dreading the moment when one of her sons brought another woman into the family.

'Not the doss-house where all the Paddies board? No wonder she's set her cap at you, lad – she'll be after your brass!' Molly's face was red with indignation. 'Lizzie, go and tell our Bob to wait outside with horse and trap. Father, you and John make yourself scarce. I need to talk to my lad.'

There was a scramble for the door as Lizzie, John and Jim beat a hasty retreat, leaving poor Mike to face his mother's wrath.

'So how long have you known this floozy, and is it serious?'

'We met about six months ago. You'll like her, Ma. Jenny's not a floozy, she's a grand Dale's lass.' It was all Mike could do to keep a civil tongue in his head, faced with his mother's uncalled-for remarks. He thought the world of Jenny.

'I'll be the judge of that. Ask her to come to tea with us tomorrow, and then I can see what I think of her. I'm not having my lads led astray by just anyone.' With that, Rose picked up her basket and marched out of the door. She'd soon see what she was made of, this Jenny Burton, the 'grand Dale's lass'.

Not a word was said as Mother Pratt climbed into the trap, assisted by John, who was much relieved that he wouldn't be going with them to Ingleton. Bob, still smarting over his mother's refusal to give him a few pennies extra, whipped the team into motion and the cart trundled off up the road with the occupants sitting in awkward silence.

The road was busy, with many of the residents of Batty Green heading off to market or to the Welcome Inn. As they passed the inn it was clear the place was jammed to the rafters with men spending the wages that Henry Parker had just handed to them. As they continued along the road down Chapel-le-Dale, Lizzie breathed in the smell of peat and flowers wafting on the breeze and gazed at the curlews and lapwings twisting and diving overhead. She felt awkward in the silence of the trap; she wasn't part of this family quarrel and she would rather have stopped behind than have to endure sitting next to the sullen Bob. When they got to the top of the rocky outcrop above Ingleton, the Irish Sea came into view in the distance, glinting in the sunshine, and Lizzie wished she were on there on a boat, sailing off to another world.

'Well, Mother, are you going to talk to us or are we supposed to read your thoughts today?' said Jim as they began the descent into Ingleton. He hoped she'd simmered long enough and that his words wouldn't prompt an explosion. When she didn't reply, Jim lit his pipe, coughed nervously and ventured to add: 'It had to happen one day, lass. You can't keep them under your wings for ever.'

Rose, still seething, shuffled in her seat. 'Gearstones, Father! Gearstones – of all the places! They sell ale there, you know. A farm lass, I could understand. But a doss-house owner's lass? What's our Mike thinking?'

'You can't help who you fall for. Good Lord, I should know,' sighed Jim as they pulled up outside the Ingleborough Hotel. While Bob held the horses steady, his father hopped from the cart and slipped his arm around Rose's waist as he helped her down. 'Just look who I ended up with – and my mother said you were no good for me. So don't you be too quick to judge, Mrs Pratt. If Mike loves her, she'll not be a bad 'un.'

This failed to mollify Rose, who stood brushing the dust from her clothes, scowling and muttering under her breath.

As if oblivious to his wife's mood, Jim continued in a cheery tone: 'Now go and get those ribbons bought for Lizzie here. The pair of you have been talking about it ever since she came. You might have lost one, Mother, but you've gained another with this 'un, eh?'

He gave a broad wink to Lizzie, who smiled, not knowing what to say.

'We'll see,' huffed Rose, finally deigning to respond. 'I'll know better after tea tomorrow, when I've finally met her.' She fixed a stern gaze on her menfolk. 'Now don't forget to pick up the flour and paraffin – and mind you don't get up to anything you shouldn't, the pair of you. Lizzie and me will meet you back here at two.'

Wishing she could spend the next few hours with Jim and Bob, Lizzie allowed herself to be steered into the bustling market. Thankfully, the prospect of a couple of hours' shopping soon distracted Rose from her bad mood, especially now she had a young protégée to instruct in the art of driving a bargain.

'Right, young Lizzie, let's go to the butcher first. A lot of folk go to Ivor Sunters, but not me. I'm fussy about my meat and I reckon nothing of him. I once got some pig's trotters off Ivor and by the time I'd got them home, they already smelled bad. We'll go to Ben Lawson's. Ben's always pleasant and he's reasonable with his prices – you must remember to tell your mother.'

As soon as they were out of the butcher's, Rose resumed her monologue, leaving Lizzie with no chance to get a word in as she was dragged through the market. 'Next we need some candles and after that I want to buy some cotton, so we'll get your ribbons then. And after that we can go to the new-fangled teashop that's just opened. I bet you'd like to sit in and have one of those fancy cakes before we go home? Lord knows I need something to calm my nerves.'

Their progress was slow, with Rose constantly running into people she knew and stopping to exchange all the latest gossip. Invariably there would be curious glances at Lizzie, which would lead to whispered questions and explanations until curiosity was satisfied and everyone resumed speaking in a normal voice so that Lizzie could hear. But there was no whispering when they encountered a small man with dark, slicked-back hair, a sharp nose and rounded ears, who stood surveying Lizzie in a manner that reminded her of an inquisitive rat.

'Good morning, Reverend Tiplady,' gushed Rose. 'And how are you this morning?'

'A good morning indeed, Mrs Pratt,' beamed the Reverend. 'Has the Lord not blessed us with a beautiful day?'

'Indeed he has.' Rose was putting on her poshest voice and best manners. 'Tell me, Reverend, are you visiting us with your missionary brothers?'

'Yes, we travelled up from Bradford yesterday. As soon as I have attended to the needs of the navigators in Ingleton, I'll be making my way up the valley to Ribblehead.' His dark, beady eyes shifted from Mrs Pratt to Lizzie, peering at her so intently she could have sworn he was reading her every thought. 'And who might this young lady be? I've not seen her in chapel on any of my visits.'

'This is Lizzie. She's staying with us for a while, just until her mother gets back on her feet.'

'I see. And what is wrong with her mother?' Reverend

Tiplady's lips twisted into an insincere smile that revealed his black, rotting teeth.

'She lost her husband and her baby, and I regret to say it but she took to the bottle to drown her grief, poor soul.'

'Ah, the Devil's in the drink! He finds our weak spot and tempts us with his evil ways,' roared the Reverend. Fixing his beady eyes on Lizzie, he added: 'Take care, Mrs Pratt, that you've not invited him over your threshold.'

'No, Reverend Tiplady, Lizzie's a grand lass. She's been a great help to me. In fact, we're on our way to buy some hair ribbons as a little present from me.'

'Vanity, Mrs Pratt! Beware of vanity.' He smiled his rotting grin and told them, 'I'll bid you good-day, ladies,' then wandered on his way down the cobbled street.

Rose waited until he was out of sight before speaking. 'If it were up to him, Lizzie, we'd not dare to breathe. Thankfully him and the rest of his brethren don't make it up from Bradford too often. I'm sure I don't know why they bother coming at all – you'd think there'd be far more souls to save there than here.' She tutted indignantly, then took Lizzie's elbow and began steering her towards the haberdashery shop. 'The Reverend's got a lot of fingers in a lot of pies, so we've got to keep the right side of him, pet. I know there's wild ways to be avoided, and I want to meet my maker with a clear conscience, but I swear there's something about that man that makes you feel like going the other way! Vanity, indeed. Since when did a few ribbons make anyone vain? Why, I've a mind to buy you the best ones in the shop.'

Deciding that now might be a good time to tell Mrs Pratt how she felt about ribbons, Lizzie piped up, 'I'm not bothered, Mrs Pratt. Honestly, I'm too old for ribbons.'

'Nonsense! Don't let that old fool worry you, dear,' admonished Rose, opening the door to the shop. 'Come on, I've been wanting to do this for years.'

'Well, don't you look a tuttle! What has she done to your hair, our Lizzie?' laughed Maggie when she opened her door and saw her daughter all decked out in her new finery.

'Don't, Mam. I blinking hate them. As soon as they've gone to chapel, I'm taking these plaits out. I swear she thinks I'm four, not fourteen.' Lizzie batted her two long plaits away, wishing she could rip out the huge red bows that tied them at both ends. 'I'd never have let her put them in, but she's in a right mood today. I daren't offend her for fear of making it worse.'

'Why, what's up, lass? Has she caught one of her lads drinking? Everyone in Batty Green knows they have a crafty one down the road when Rose isn't looking.'

'It's worse than that. Mike, the middle brother, is bringing his sweetheart to tea today. His ma only found out about her yesterday. From what's been said, I don't think she's suited.'

Intrigued at this latest development, Molly was eager to hear more. 'Who is she? Come on, lass, you've only told me half a story – let's hear the rest. If Mike is anything like his older brother then she's got herself a good catch.' Molly winked at her daughter.

'Mam, stop it. Don't embarrass me. All I know is that she's from Gearstones Lodge. Her father runs the boarding house there.'

'Does he now? That'll not go down well with the old Bible basher! She'll be having a fit, I expect. I can't see that lasting.' Molly laughed with delight, knowing that such a match would be the worst thing a religious woman like Rose Pratt could imagine. Seeing the unhappy expression on her daughter's face, she reluctantly abandoned the topic and tried to think of something that would cheer her up. 'How about I put some food in a knapsack and we take a walk below Ingleborough? It's a grand day for a picnic, and I want to see what this limestone pavement looks like. Besides, I've something to tell you. Your mother's been busy while you've been getting dressed up like a doll.' Molly tugged on one of Lizzie's plaits. For all her teasing, she was glad to see her daughter looking well and cared for.

'Mam, stop it! I can't help it – you've to do as you're told over there.'

'Well, see you do, miss. I'll not say anything of the sort to Rose Pratt, but I'm fair thankful that she saved you from the workhouse. I'd not have been able to live with myself if I'd lost you an' all.' She looked into Lizzie's eyes and confided: 'I wasn't going to tell you this, but I came to an agreement with Rose. She's paying me a shilling a week for your help and I'm putting it all away for you.' She reached under her bed and pulled out a jar, rattling it so Lizzie could hear the coins. 'See, it's right here. If anything ever happens to me, this is yours, d'you hear?'

'But, Mam, how are you going to get by? You don't make enough from taking in washing, especially when the weather's bad.' Lizzie couldn't believe that she was being rented out for a shilling a month and her mother was setting it all aside for her.

'Don't you worry about me, I've got it all sorted. I'll tell you about it on our walk,' said Molly gaily. 'So come on, what are you waiting for? Everybody keeps telling me how bonny this limestone pavement is and I've never had chance to see it.'

'What's so special about limestone pavement?' asked Lizzie, unconvinced. 'We walked on many a pavement in Bradford.'

'No, lass, don't be silly. This is a different sort of pavement. It's years old, made by Mother Nature and her best friend, the weather. It's where the earth has worn all sorts of different patterns into the limestone. It's terrible to walk on, so just you mind yourself when we get there.'

The walk up to the pavement was a tough one and both mother and daughter were out of breath by the time they reached the limestone escarpment. The tangled weathered forms of white limestone stretched out in front of them for miles with the odd hawthorn tree, twisted and shaped by the wild north winds, clinging to the precarious crags for dear life. In the far distance, they could see a man on his knees, peering into the crevices between the rocks.

'Your father said the holes and stones were called clints and grikes. He was going to bring us up here and show us all the rare plants that grow in these parts.' Molly's voice fell and she gazed sadly around her. 'What with your dad and Tommy dying, and then getting into a state, I've been looking on the black side of things of late. But it's time to move on – right, love?' She took a deep breath of the fresh air and waved a hand at the landscape in front of them. 'Bye, this land's wild. Smell that peat, and look at them clouds scurrying across the flank of Whernside. Mind, it's a shame they're making that blinking great hole in the side of the fell there.'

Lizzie knew how her mother felt. She felt the same way: there was something about this place. It made you want to fill your lungs with mountain air until they burst. She'd happily sit and gaze at this view for hours, never feeling bored because the mood seemed to change with every movement of the clouds and sun. She never wanted to go back to Bradford and she could tell her mother felt the same.

'Go on then, Ma,' she said, moving to a spot at the edge of the pavement where there was a smooth piece of rock for them both to sit on. 'Tell me your news. What have you got planned?'

Molly sat down next to her, placing their unopened picnic at her feet. 'Well, after I'd come to a deal with Ma Pratt, I decided it was no use me feeling sorry for myself – you don't get anywhere if you start doing that.

84

So I gave myself a good dressing down and told myself, "Molly Mason, you've two legs and two arms and a brain that's not too coddled. It's time you shifted yourself and found a way to make ends meet." So off I went to the hospital to ask if they'd send me their laundry. At first it looked as if Doctor Thistlethwaite was going to send me packing, but as I was heading out the door he called me back. To cut a long story short, he's given me a job. I start in the morning.' Molly gazed triumphantly at her daughter.

'What are you going to be doing, Ma? You don't know anything about nursing.' Lizzie was horrified at the thought of her mother working at the hospital. To her, it was a place of death. An image flashed into her mind of the night she'd gone there to fetch the doctor for Tommy, the fountain of blood spurting out of the man on the bed. She couldn't think of anything worse than spending your days working there.

'I'll be helping out with anything that needs doing: changing bedding, cleaning the floors, writing letters for them who can't.' Seeing the scepticism in her daughter's face, she said firmly, 'It's a job, our Lizzie. Beggars can't be choosers. If they ask me to stand on my head, I'll do it, as long as it makes us some money. Now, let's open these sandwiches – I'm starving. It's been a long time since breakfast.'

'But they all die in the hospital,' said Lizzie, watching as her mother unpacked the food.

'No, they don't, Liz. There's George Thoroughgood – he's mended now. Granted, he lost his leg. But he can fairly move on that peg-leg when he wants to. And there's the fellow that lost his hand that sits outside Gearstones sharpening knives. He was in the hospital a long time, but he's making a living now.'

'Then why couldn't they save Dad? Why couldn't the hospital make him better?' Lizzie's eyes filled with tears.

'He'd fallen too far, pet, he didn't stand a chance. It was his turn to go, like it was little Tommy's. Life can be cruel sometimes.' Molly put her arm around Lizzie and squeezed her tight, kissing her gently on her furrowed brow. 'But you know what, our Lizzie, you can't let it beat you. You have to be like that piece of cotton grass over there, bending with the wind instead of letting it snap you in two. It took me a while to realize that, but now I'm going to start acting like that grass, weathering all the storms, clinging on regardless. Believe me, life's going to be a whole lot better for you and me from now on, pet.' She smiled at her daughter. 'I've thrown all the bottles out, stopped trying to drown my sorrows and faced up to them instead. I've made a fresh start. As old Ma Pratt would say, I've seen the light. Happen it's not the same light as she sees, but it's a light all the same. Now tuck in and then we'll have a look for these fancy flowers that grow up here.'

They fell into a companionable silence as they tucked into their lunch and were lost in admiring the view when they were interrupted by a soft-spoken male voice coming from behind them.

'Afternoon, ladies.'

Molly turned to face the man who was walking towards them.

'Oh, afternoon, Doctor Thistlethwaite. I didn't expect to see you up here in the wilds.'

'Weather permitting, I often come up here to find a bit of peace and to indulge in my secret pleasure.' He shrugged off the bag he was carrying over his shoulder and sat down beside Lizzie.

Unaccustomed to the company of gentry, Lizzie felt uneasy sitting next to this refined gentleman in his smart tweed suit.

'And what is your secret pleasure – if it's not too bold of me to ask?' said Molly, surprised at her own daring.

'I'm a secret botanist in my spare time.'

Molly had no idea what a botanist might be, but it sounded grand.

Seeing their nonplussed expressions, the doctor hurried to explain. 'Forgive me, a botanist is a collector of plants. I take them home and draw them, studying their properties in minute detail. I find them fascinating.' He opened his shoulder bag and pulled out some foliage. 'Take my crowning glory today, for example. Isn't she glorious? There are people in Kensington who would pay a fortune to have a hart's tongue fern growing in their gardens. And how about this little beauty – it's an orchid. They like the limestone, but I'm not quite sure the name of the species. I'll have to look it up when I get home.' He held the delicate pink plant in his fingers, extending his hand so Lizzie could inspect it.

Lizzie smiled, not knowing quite what to say.

'You know, when I was doctoring in the Crimea, plants proved the saviour of many a patient. That squelchy moss that grows at the bottom of these great fells? It's called sphagnum moss. If you have a patient with an open wound and no bandages to hand, you can apply sphagnum to soak the blood up. And yarrow – the ferny white flower that grows in the hedgerows – that stops bleeding. I could go on for ever, but I fear I'd bore you.' He gently placed his precious plants back into his bag. 'It's a good job I'm not married, else my wife would constantly be bored to tears.'

'No, no, it's fascinating. In fact, that's why we came up here today, to see the flowers. And to take the air. We just stopped for a bite to eat – would you like a sandwich? Lizzie, pass Doctor Thistlethwaite that sandwich.'

Molly nudged Lizzie, making her offer him their last sandwich.

'So you were in the Crimea, Doctor? That must have been terrible for you. My husband's brother died out there.'

'It wasn't pleasant. I can't for the life of me understand why they've taken to naming places after some of the worst battles. You'd think the men who served in that war would want to forget about the horrors they'd witnessed, but when I walked under the viaduct to the new huts that have just gone up I saw they'd put up a sign saying Sebastopol. I could only shake my head in dismay.'

'The men are proud to have served there, Doctor Thistlethwaite. Those navvies may spend their days knee-deep in peat and bog, but they are proud men and patriotic,' said Molly.

Lizzie remained silent, watching the doctor eating her sandwich.

'Are you ready to join us tomorrow, Mrs Mason? I warn you, it will be hard work, and there will be times when the stench will make you want to be sick. Are you sure you can stand that?'

'It'll be nothing I can't deal with – will it, Lizzie? We're used to hard work.'

Lizzie shook her head. She was nervous of speaking in front of Doctor Thistlethwaite. She recalled how sharp he'd been with her the night she'd begged him to come to her brother. Now he'd just eaten their last sandwich and her mother was going to be working for him.

'In that case, I'll see you in the morning.' Doctor Thistlethwaite rose and brushed the crumbs off his suit. 'I look forward to working with you, Mrs Mason. Mind you don't go fainting on me, that's all I ask.'

'Don't worry, I won't,' Molly called after him as he set off down the fellside.

'I don't like him, Ma. He talks sharp,' Lizzie whispered.

'Liz, there is one thing you need to remember in life: no matter how posh folk talk, no matter what they wear, they all look the same with no clothes on and they all have to go to the toilet like we do. Even the

Queen of blooming England does the same as us every morning, so we are just as good as any of them, my girl.'

Molly smiled at her daughter. Her father had said those same words to her when she was young. It was funny how the world turned.

6

'Hold him down, woman! I'm never going to get his leg off if you don't keep him still.'

Molly leaned all her weight into holding down the tunnel builder, who was screaming and thrashing about in agony, despite the dose of morphine he'd been given. Trying to avert her eyes from the man's ruined leg, she looked at Doctor Thistlethwaite. His brow was covered in beads of sweat as he sawed through the smashed limb. Beside him, the nurse was white-faced. Despite her years of experience, the woman looked as if she might pass out.

It was quite an initiation into her new job at the hospital. Her first morning had barely begun when there was a clamour at the door and six strong navvies entered, carrying their injured colleague on a stretcher. The doctor had ordered them to place him on the scrubbed pine slab that served as the operating table, then he had sent the navvies packing and summoned Molly to cut away the man's torn trousers. Seeing the smashed bone sticking through holes in the blood-soaked cloth, she had been afraid to touch the patient for fear of causing him more pain. But Doctor Thistlethwaite had shouted at her to pull herself together and get on with it. Hands slick with the blood pouring out of the man's wounds, she had done as she was told and cut away the clothing to reveal the full extent of the damage. Trembling and fighting the urge to be sick, she stood back to let the doctor examine the injury. It took him only a moment to assess the damage and then he began instructing the nurse which instruments to fetch and which drugs to administer. To Molly's dismay, he'd announced that there was nothing for it but to amputate the leg, and it would be her job to hold the poor soul down while the doctor did his work.

The smashed leg with the boot still on the foot was now lying on the sawdust-covered floor. It was more like working in a slaughterhouse than a hospital, thought Molly. She gritted her teeth and watched as the doctor made sure the bandage was secure before stitching up what was left of the limb. When he was done, he mopped his brow and turned to her.

'Molly, wrap that leg up in a sheet, tag it and take it to the outside mortuary. He'll want it burying with him if he dies – and if he lives he'll want to know where we've buried it.' Then he turned back to the nurse and instructed her to thread another needle so he could finish sewing up the wound.

For a moment, Molly stood frozen. She looked at the leg on the floor, feeling her stomach lurch at the thought of picking it up. The doctor must have heard the retching sound that escaped her lips.

'Go on, get out! I don't want you being sick in here – there's enough to clean and scrub already,' the doctor yelled.

Molly glanced towards the operating table and caught the satisfied smirk on the nurse's lips. She took a deep breath and told herself she could do this. After all, it was no worse than handling meat.

'I'm fine,' she said. 'I'll fetch a sheet from the storeroom to wrap it in, then I'll take the leg out.' Gulping back the acid bile that rose into her mouth, she walked unsteadily to the storeroom. After picking up the sheet she seized the opportunity to grab a few lungfuls of clean air, then she re-entered the ward, making her way past the other patients in their beds. Hearing the man's screams had forced them all to relive their own time under the surgeon's knife. Some lay with their faces turned away or buried under the covers, trying to shut out the horror. But one man was sitting up in bed, looking at her anxiously.

'Nurse, is Bill going to be all right?' he asked. 'He looked in a bad way. I worked with him on the Ingleton line before we came up here. He's got five children to feed.'

'The doctor's doing all that he can,' Molly told him. 'Don't worry, I'm sure Bill will be fine.' She was lying through her teeth. How could he be fine after this? Even if he lived, how was he going to support a wife and five children?

Molly drew back the curtain that separated the operating table from the rest of the ward. As she did, the patient moaned. At least he'd survived the surgery.

'Right, let's get him into a bed,' said the doctor, satisfied with his handiwork. 'If we're lucky, he might just survive.' The nurse nodded and set down the tray of medical instruments. Doctor Thistlethwaite was reaching back to untie his bloodstained apron when he caught sight of Molly. 'Get that leg moved,' he barked.

Molly bent down, partly closing her eyes as she wrapped the leg in the cotton sheet. It was heavier than she had anticipated and she struggled with the weight for a moment, then began making her way back through the ward past the other patients. She heard one of them say, 'Bad sign that – poor bugger, they must have taken his leg off.' Then she was outside in the sunshine and clear fresh air.

Once inside the mortuary hut she set the leg down on a shelf, tied a label on it and wrote: *Left leg, 1 May 1870. Bill . . . ?* The doctor's words echoed in her head: 'He'll want it burying with him if he dies.' She couldn't help wondering whether it would be better for Bill and his family if he died. At least then he'd be reunited with his lost leg as he entered the gates of heaven. Better that than be left legless and with no income to feed his family.

She leaned against the mortuary door for a moment, trying to compose herself. People were busily going about their business as if it were an ordinary day: a tinker was shouting for people to bring him any knives that needed sharpening or pans that needed mending, and the baker from Ingleton was leading his donkey, laden with freshly baked bread, selling loaves from door to door. Molly reminded herself that life went on, mouths needed to be fed, wages earned. She wiped her hands on her apron and turned to go back into the hospital.

'You did well, Mrs Mason,' said Doctor Thistle-thwaite, who had been watching her from the doorway. 'Not a pleasant start to your first day, but you seem to have passed the test. Most women would have taken fright and walked out.' He smiled at her. 'His name is Bill Beecroft. Would you mind writing that on the leg tag, please.'

Molly smiled at him and nodded. When she'd finished writing the tag, she re-entered the hospital, filled with a new sense of pride. Though she still felt nervous about facing up to the brutality of hospital life, she was more confident now of her ability to cope.

'I thought for sure you were going to faint,' sneered the dark-haired nurse. 'Doctor Thistlethwaite doesn't like women who faint at the sight of blood. He always compliments me on my nerves. By the way, the oper-ating table needs scrubbing and the floor needs washing down. You'll find a mop and bucket in the corner over there.'

Molly shot her a look. Snotty cow! She might be a nurse, but there was no need for her to take that atti-tude. 'Actually,' she said, 'the doctor just complimented me on keeping my nerve. Next time I'll know what to expect and will take more notice.'

'We have a special relationship, Doctor Thistlethwaite

and I,' preened the nurse, giving her hat a tweak before turning to walk away.

'You mean, he sleeps with you when he's desperate.' Molly couldn't stop herself. Obviously the woman saw her as a threat. Well, if she wanted to play that game she'd give her a run for her money. One thing was for certain: she wasn't about to let herself be bullied by this little upstart.

'I don't know what he was doing, hiring someone as common as you! You're just a drunk who can't even take care of her own daughter.' The nurse glared at her with hatred in her eyes.

'Aye, I've got my faults,' said Molly, 'but at least I treat folk like humans and don't look down my nose on folk that are not as privileged as myself. Don't worry, I'm not after your doctor.' And with that she grabbed the bucket and mop and stormed out before she said something she might regret. She wasn't about to risk losing her job over a falling out with some stuck-up nurse. Better to shut up and get on with the job; she'd let her actions prove her worth.

Lizzie lay in her bed, pretending to be asleep but listening to Rose and Jim's whispered conversation.

'He's not home yet, Father,' said Rose anxiously. 'He's out gallivanting with that lass, I know it. That boy will be the death of me.'

'Now shush, Mother. Our Mike's a grown man, you've got to let him make his own way in life. Besides, she seemed all right to me.'

'Aye, well she would, all that blonde hair and big doe eyes. I saw you looking at her, Jim Pratt. It doesn't alter the fact that she's a landlord's daughter, not good Methodist stock like us.'

Rose had always dreaded the thought of her boys leaving home, but this scenario was worse than anything she could have dreamt up. Imagine if Mike were to do the unthinkable and marry this girl.

'What will be, will be. You can't alter life, Ma.' Jim put his arm around his wife, comforting her. 'Now let's go to bed and stop thinking about it.'

But Rose couldn't stop thinking about it. As her husband's heavy breathing subsided into snores she lay staring up at the ceiling, listening for the sound of the door and Mike returning. It was all right for Jim to talk, but Mike was her lad. Sons and mothers were supposed to be close, but now she was going to lose him to a floozy.

'Where did you get to last night?' Rose banged Mike's mug of tea down.

The breakfast table went quiet. Lizzie stirred the porridge, thankful that she wasn't sitting at the table with the family.

'Don't start, Mam. I stopped at Gearstones, all right. I'm twenty, I don't have to tell you everything.'

'I hear the mice play dominoes a lot at Gearstones. They're always knocking on the walls,' said John, spluttering a mouthful of tea over the table as he laughed at his own joke.

Rose cuffed him over the ear. 'Wash your mouth out, John Pratt! I may be old but I know what you're saying – and we'll have none of that before *any* of you are wed.'

There was a uncomfortable pause and then Mike dropped the bombshell. 'Well, Ma, now you've mentioned weddings, I've something to tell you. I asked Jenny for her hand in marriage last night, and her mother and father agreed to it.' Mike watched his mother anxiously, knowing that this would not get a favourable response.

'Congratulations, lad,' said Jim, getting to his feet and reaching across to shake his son's hand. 'She seems a right grand lass.' He turned to his wife: 'Mother, what do you say?'

For a moment there was silence as Rose slumped in her chair, handkerchief pressed to her face. 'I knew it! I knew when she was here on Sunday that I'd be losing my lad. Oh my dear God, I'm losing one of my boys.' Her voice rose into a hysterical wail. 'Lizzie, bring me a drink of water. I feel faint.'

'Now, Mam, don't take on so. I'll only be half a mile down the road. And you won't be losing me, you'll be gaining Jenny – she'll be the daughter you always wanted.'

'She'll never be my daughter – never, do you hear me! And you might as well leave today. Go on, go – now that you've broken your mother's heart.' She broke off to sip from the glass of water that Lizzie had quietly placed in her hand. 'Oh my poor heart, I think I'm having a heart attack.' Rose's face went red and she clutched her chest as if struggling to breathe.

'Mother, you stop this at once! There's nothing wrong

with you, nothing whatsoever. You do this every time you don't get your own way, and I won't have it any more. Do you hear me? It stops now. Pull yourself together and wish the lad the best.' Jim was a man of few words, but he'd finally had enough of Rose's hysterics. He was right glad that one of the lads had enough go in him to walk away from his mother's apron strings. 'It's time our John started looking for a woman and all – he's nearly an old fellow now. And you, young Bob – high time you started talking to folk, else they'll think you're thick.' As if astonished at his own outburst, Jim sat down without another word.

The room fell into a stunned silence, broken only by the occasional muffled sob from Rose, still sitting with her hankie pressed to her face. Embarrassed, and feeling this was no place for anyone who wasn't part of the family, Lizzie crept outside. With nowhere else to go, she sat down on the steps. The shantytown was just beginning to wake and the smell of woodsmoke hung in the morning air. The sun was slowly rising over Cam Fell, its rays filtering down like fingers from heaven, catching the flight of thousands of moorland insects going about their business. It looked as if it was going to be a lovely day. Lizzie made up her mind to go for a walk later. Perhaps when Rose took her afternoon nap she could sneak an hour away, stroll down to Nether Hall and sit on the bridge. The view down the Ribble Valley was spectacular on a good day.

The sound of the door sneck being raised jolted Lizzie from her mind's wanderings.

John tugged on one of her plaits. 'Coast's clear, Liz. You can go back in – we've all had our lecture. Look after Ma today, will you? She's bound to be a bit down. Our Mike's packing his stuff – he's decided to leave the happy family home right away.' He patted his cap before setting it on his blond hair. 'If you see your mother, tell her I'll bring your bed back at the end of the week. Seems we have one too many now.' He grinned at Lizzie, shoved his hands in his pockets and set off down the street, kicking the dirt up as he went.

Lizzie made her way back in just as Jim and Bob were emerging on their way to work.

'I hope you have a good day, Lizzie,' Bob said quietly, blushing from the top of his head to his toes.

Lizzie was amazed: Bob had never spoken to her, he'd barely even acknowledged her. Jim's words must have hit home.

'You will take care of yourself, won't you? I know I've said some harsh things, but I was only thinking of you, Mike.' Rose was standing by the stove watching Mike pack his few belongings.

'I'll take care, Ma, but I've got to go. I'm stifled here.' He looked up at her. 'You just don't understand, do you? We're not children any more.' Tying his things in a bundle, he slung it over his back then went to kiss his weeping mother on the cheek. 'Bye, Ma. You know I still love you, but I've got to move on.' He ducked his head as he walked out of the hut, then turned back to wink at Lizzie. 'Take care of her, Lizzie Mason.' And then he was gone.

'All my life, I've looked after my lads. I've gone without, making sure they were fed and clothed. I've not slept nights when they were ill, I've wiped their bums and dried their tears . . . And after all that, they just up and leave.' Rose sank into the pine rocking chair, clutching the tea towel to her and staring fixedly at the stove, as if she were looking back into the past, back to a time when her lads were young and the world was less complicated. 'It's a hard job, being a mother. Mark my words, Lizzie – if you have any children, they'll break your heart. They always do.'

Lizzie stood watching her for a minute, then began clearing the table. There seemed nothing else she could do, and she didn't feel comfortable giving the old woman a hug.

'I know now how your mother must have felt when your brother died. At least my lad is only down the road. I'm so sorry, so very sorry. I feel terrible about what happened. Oh, that poor little mite, I can't stop thinking about him.' Rose held the cloth to her eyes and sobbed.

Lizzie went over and laid her arm on Rose's shoulder. She seemed to have aged overnight; her lads were her world, the thought of being parted from them was devastating to her. 'You mustn't upset yourself. Tommy was sickly. Mam said so.' Lizzie swiped away the tear that was running down the side of her nose and tried to dispel the memory of Tommy's lifeless little arm falling out of his blanket as her mother clasped him to her. Crying only made matters worse; you had to get on with life. 'Come on,' she said brightly. 'I'll put the kettle on and make us a pot of tea while I wash up.'

'You're a good lass,' said Rose, wiping her nose. 'I bet your mother's missing you. You must be her only comfort now her boy is gone.'

While Rose sat rocking in her chair to the rhythm of the big old clock, Lizzie got to work washing the pots and breakfast things. And as she worked she couldn't help wondering why Rose kept harking on about baby Tommy. She couldn't see that his dying had anything in common with Mike leaving home, yet to hear Mrs Pratt talk you'd have thought she was responsible for both.

'Just put it back in that corner. And you can leave the bedding, I'll make it up after you've gone.' Molly stood with her hands on her hips, giving instructions on where to place the bed frame that seemed to have been constantly shunted between huts over the last few days.

'Ma said it may be of use to you, now our Mike's left home. In case Lizzie ever wants to stop over, now you're getting back on your feet.' John shifted the bed close to the wall with the force of his leg. 'I hear you're working at the hospital. How are you doing there?' He stood straight and wiped his brow with his cap before sitting at the dining table.

Molly sat down in the chair opposite him. 'I'm absolutely off my legs. I don't think I've ever worked so hard in my life, but in a strange way I like it.'

'And how do you get on with Starchy Drawers? I

bet she has a caustic tongue in her.' John grinned wickedly.

'You can't possibly mean Nurse Gladys Thompson,' grinned Molly sarcastically. 'Oh, she's got a lovely manner about her, that one. We get along very well when she's not watching my every move, frightened that I'm after stealing her precious doctor's affections. How do you know her? She doesn't seem the sort who'd dirty her shoes visiting Batty Green.'

'All us lads know her. We've a bet on at the works – the lad who gets her to walk out with him will pick up a tidy sum. But nobody's been brave enough yet to ask her. She's a bit of a tartar, isn't she. I know she's always been after Doctor Thistlethwaite, but I can't believe he'd give her a second glance. He's too busy with his plants to even notice the stupid woman.' John stretched his legs out and made himself more comfortable.

'Do you fancy a brew or will your mother be wanting you back home?' Molly rose and placed the kettle on to the stovetop, trying not to stare at the good-looking young man who had been on her mind constantly of late.

'Ah, Ma can wait. She's looks like she's chewed a wasp at the moment, and she's not talking to my dad, so it isn't right pleasant at home at present. Between you and me, I'm bloody fed up of sitting around looking at their two long faces and our odd Bob. Your Lizzie's the only one with a smile.'

'What's up? That doesn't sound like your mam. It isn't our Lizzie getting under her feet, is it?' said Molly, secretly annoyed to hear that her daughter smiled at John, and that he'd noticed. 'Because if it is, she can move back here. I'm settled at the hospital and she's old enough to look after herself while I'm at work. She could still go across to help your mam with anything that needed doing.'

'No, it isn't Lizzie, it's our daft Mike. He's gone and proposed to Jenny Burton. They're getting married a week on Sunday, but no one's dared tell Mam that. She's in enough of a huff at him as it is, just for leaving home.'

'He's getting married and your mam and dad don't know! That'll break their hearts.' Molly turned from the stove and looked at him, appalled. 'They'll have to be told, John. It isn't right.' She placed a steaming cup of tea under his nose.

'Aye, but they're going to be even more upset when they find out they're going to be grandparents. Our Mike's gone and got Jenny in the family way. That's why everything's happened so fast – the poor lad's over a barrel. Either he marries Jenny and upsets our lot. Or he drags his heels and gets the living daylights kicked out of him by her brothers. Either way, I wouldn't want to be in his shoes.' John took a long slurp of tea.

'Well, at least he's thinking of the baby. All the same, he should tell your parents. I'm sure they'd understand. In fact, I bet your mother can't wait to be a grand-mother. Children always bring families together.' Molly couldn't help blushing as she caught John's blue eyes studying her.

104

'You don't know them like I do. My mam'll be preaching about how he'll burn in hell for the pleasures of the flesh. Poor bugger, he's been caught out good and proper.' John set down his cup and gazed around the hut, taking in the sparseness of the furnishings and lack of decoration. 'Do you want me to put a pot rail up for you? Then you can hang all your cups up, like at Ma's.'

'That'd be grand, if you've got the time. I've always wanted a Welsh dresser but I've never been able to afford one. A pot rail would be the next best thing,' said Molly.

'Right, I'll see what I can do. I'll try to come over one night next week,' said John, suddenly conscious that this was a woman his mother had called wanton, not to mention a few other things. He got to his feet, eager to be away. 'You'll not say anything about our Mike, will you? Best let him get married in peace. They'll all come round soon enough once they know there's a baby involved.'

'I'll not say a word.' Molly opened the door for him. 'And thanks for the offer of a shelf, that'll be most useful.'

John tugged his cap and set off for home, a spring in his step.

Molly closed the door behind him and picked up the two dirty cups. It had been good to have a bit of male company. Already she was looking forward to his return. As she did the washing up she found herself humming, stopping in her tracks at the realization. Her heart hadn't felt this light in a long time.

'Lizzie, be a love and pop outside for a minute, I want a word with our John.'

Lizzie, who'd been sitting at the kitchen table, polishing the brass pans, wiped her hands and obediently made her way out. Curious as to why Rose suddenly wanted her out of the way, having made her way outside she immediately sat down beneath the open window to eavesdrop on the conversation.

'Now, our John, what's going on? It should have taken you five minutes to deliver that bed, not an hour. I don't want you getting too familiar with that Mason woman. You know she's not our sort. I've enough on, what with watching our Mike. I don't need to be wondering what you're getting up to as well.'

'Mother, she made me a cup of tea and we exchanged pleasantries, that's all. For the love of God, get off my back. You've more to bother about than me.' John was fuming. He'd had enough of being tied to his mother's apron strings, never being allowed out of her sight except to earn money or do her chores. Truth be told, he was also feeling guilty about his attraction to Molly Mason.

'Aye, I've your stupid brother to bother about. And I don't want to see you going down the same road.'

'It'll be a cold day in hell before I get married and become a father,' he lashed out.

'What do you mean get married – who's getting married? Is our Mike getting married? Is she in the family way?' Rose's voice was becoming louder. 'John, tell me – is that what's going on?'

'Aye,' mumbled John, cursing himself for letting his brother's secret out. 'He's getting married on Sunday. And she's expecting. That's why he left – he'd no option.'

Rose let out a wail. Her lad was getting married and she knew nowt about it. And she was to be a grandmother! A baby, a wedding – why hadn't the vicar told her about the banns being read. Surely even in this heathen hole they had to be read three Sundays in a row? She'd have to have words with that boy of hers, but in the meantime there was a wedding to prepare for. The baby made all the difference. At least her lad was doing the decent thing, but he should have told her. A wave of mixed emotions washed over her and a faint smile came on her lips at the thought of a new life coming into the world.

'Go and get the horse and trap, John – and be quick about it. I want you to take me to Gearstones.'

Angrier with himself than ever, John slapped his flat cap across his knee and cursed under his breath. His mother had hurried across the room and was now on her knees, rummaging under her bed for something. 'You'll not cause any bother, will you, Ma?' John pleaded. 'Promise me you won't.'

'What do you think I am!' said Rose, indignant. 'I didn't know I was going to be a grandmother. This changes everything, no matter who or what she is.' She got up from her knees, the family money box in her hands. 'He'll need his cut if he's going to give that bairn

107

the start-off it should have in life. I'll not let the little mite end up like poor Tommy Mason.' Opening the box, she removed the linen bag with Mike's name written on it and put it in her pocket. 'He can count us in for this wedding and all. I'm not missing one of my lads getting married. Tell Lizzie to come back in and finish these pans and to put us a bit of supper on for when we come back. Go on, get a move on, don't stand gawping like a big lump.'

John closed the door behind him, still shaking his head at the turn of events. He was dreading his mother entering Gearstones. Even hardened navvies gave the place a wide berth; it was an unsavoury neighbourhood and definitely not the kind of place his mother was used to. He only hoped that on their arrival they would find Mike and his bride-to-be in the big house where her family lived and not the doss-house where they made their money. He wouldn't put it past Mike to make out that was where they were going to live, purely to have his revenge. He knew that his mother would keep well away from that den of drunken lechery.

Spotting Lizzie sitting under the window, he told her: 'Ma says you can go in now.' And then, realizing that she was in a position to have heard everything that had been said, he added, 'Don't take any notice of Mam. Your mother's a grand woman.'

Lizzie kept her face turned away so he wouldn't see her tears. It had hurt to hear Rose declare that her mother was not one of their sort. She'd barely heard a word that followed, her mind was in such turmoil. If Lizzie's mother wasn't their sort, what did that make her? No matter how long she stopped with the Pratts, she'd never be one of them. Come to think of it, she really didn't want to be one of them. As soon as she could, she was going home. She could still help out doing chores for Ma Pratt, but she'd move back in with her mother. After all, Molly was back to normal and probably missing her company.

'Never in all my days have I seen such a place! Not one person was sober, the language was fearful, and as for her father . . . Well! He's the roughest man I've ever come across. I told our Mike he'd be better off getting a navvy hut from the Midland. At least then the baby would be brought up clean.'

Rose was in a state of high dudgeon by the time she got home. As the rest of the family pulled pillows over their heads in an effort to shut out her ranting, Jim lay in the bed beside her waiting for a chance to get a word in.

'You should have seen the dust, Father! I came out itching all over. The place was lousy. I can't bear to think of my lad living in that muck and filth. Why, if we didn't have Lizzie stopping with us, happen they could move in here.'

Finally seeing an opening, Jim ventured an opinion: 'And how long do you think that'd last? Mike's got to be his own man. He's got responsibilities, and his bride'll not take kindly to you interfering, Mother.'

Rose, who'd not listened to a word he'd said, continued: 'I'll have a word with him tomorrow. They'll need all the help they can get. You always do, with your first one. And then I'll sort it with Lizzie and her mother.'

'Do what you want, woman,' sighed Jim, rolling on to his side. 'I'm off to sleep. Some of us have to work in the morning.'

Lizzie, too, turned in her bed. This would definitely be her last night in this house. Clearly she was no longer wanted here.

7

Rose watched as Lizzie made her way to her mother's hut. She had been so thankful when the girl had suddenly announced in the middle of breakfast that she wanted to go home, it was all she could do not to let out a great sigh of relief. It wasn't that Lizzie wasn't wanted – her help would be needed more than ever when the baby was born, so that shilling a month would turn out to be a good investment – but they simply didn't have room for her.

The hut was empty when Lizzie arrived. She knew that Molly left early to go to her job in the hospital, and she'd planned to prepare a nice surprise for her to come home to. Rose had agreed to give her the day off so she could clean her mother's place from top to bottom, but the place was spotless. At a loss, Lizzie sat next to the stove and gazed around the room, wondering what to do. Finally she came to the conclusion that she might as well make the most of her day off and have a wander down the dale. What with all the upset the other day, she never had made it down to Nether

Hall to sit on the bridge and take in the view of the valley.

Cheered by the prospect, Lizzie set off. The sun hadn't stopped shining this past week, allowing work on the viaduct to progress without the constant delays caused by rain and wind and fog. The scaffolding had gradually been extended until it spread right along the valley floor. The huge man-made embankments were growing too, ascending from the boggy land at the base of the fell like a huge black snake weaving its way up towards the dark empty hole of Blea Moor tunnel.

The railway had brought in more workers and new shantytowns had sprung up to accommodate them. On the far side of the viaduct was Sebastopol; a little further along was Jericho; while Jerusalem, the collection of huts that housed the tunnel diggers, was located right next to the tunnel entrance. It was easy to spot the men who worked the tunnel because they wore tighter breeches than ordinary labourers, enabling them to run unhindered when they set the explosives.

To the south, the line was almost complete. Workmen were now building the station house and a row of workmen's dwellings that had been given the name Salt Lake Cottages. Lizzie thought how grand it would be to live in one of those cottages. She tried to picture herself gazing out of a window overlooking the Ribble Valley. There was nothing she would like better than to wake every morning to the mountainous flanks of Pen-y-ghent every morning.

'Hey, what you up to?' a voice called as Lizzie walked

down the track to Horton village. Lizzie didn't turn around. She knew that voice.

'Don't you talk to me, Florrie Parker. I'm having nothing more to do with you.'

'Come on, you're all right. You're still here, aren't you?' Florrie tried to catch her up, but Lizzie kept her head down and strode on as fast as she could, not wanting to have anything to do with her.

Florrie grabbed her arm and pulled her to a halt. 'Wait a minute, Lizzie, I want to say sorry. I didn't mean to get you into trouble.'

Lizzie turned, intending to give Florrie a piece of her mind, but instead she gasped in horror, her anger forgotten as she took in the damage to her friend's face. One eye was all swollen and black and blue, making it hard for Florrie to see out of it, and her nose appeared to have been broken. 'My God, Florrie, what have you been up to?'

'Oh this? Just an "accident", as my mother would say. In truth, I got in the way of my mum and dad arguing. I should have known better really. It happens that often.'

'Your dad did this?' Lizzie was horrified. Her father would never have raised a hand to her or her mother. 'But that's terrible. A man shouldn't hit a woman.'

'You try telling him that when he's in one of his moods. He doesn't understand that my mother only flirts with customers to get them to spend their money. Dad gets jealous, uses his fists and then feels guilty afterwards.' Florrie looked at Lizzie with her half-closed eye.

'Have you been to see the doctor? My ma works at the hospital now. We can turn around and go see her – she'll sort you out.'

'Nah, doctors cost money. Besides, I'll be all right, it's only a knock. Looks worse than it is.' Florrie smiled. 'So are we friends, then? Good.' She turned to head homewards. 'Got to go back – I'm supposed to be helping out in the kitchen. Don't want them to notice I'm missing, else I'll end up with another to match the other.' She smiled, showing that she had also sustained a chipped front tooth.

'Friends!' called Lizzie. 'And just you mind what you're doing.' She didn't have the heart not to accept Florrie's offer of friendship, not now she'd seen how her father treated her. Poor thing, no wonder she was so wild. The Welcome Inn seemed anything but welcoming: Florrie obviously had no home life, no guiding light in her life. Lizzie smiled at the memory of her own father, the nights when he'd come home and sit her on his knee and sing to her while her mother made supper. She'd always felt so safe with his arms wrapped around her, knowing that he would never let anyone or anything hurt her. He might be dead now, but at least she would always have the warm glow of his memory in her heart, whereas Florrie would always carry with her the legacy of her father's fists. Poor Florrie. Lizzie vowed she'd stand by her friend, no matter what.

Deep in thought, she wandered on down the track

to Nether Hall. The once-grand house was now in a state of decay, its mullion windows covered with ivy and the masonry crumbling and in need of repair. Lizzie tried to imagine all the grand balls and soirees that would have taken place in the building's heyday. Nights when the ladies and lords of Ribblesdale and the surrounding area would have pulled up in their horse-drawn carriages, dressed in all their finery. It must have been quite a sight.

She walked on through the yard and down to the widening stream of the River Ribble, until she found a spot where she could sit admiring the view, which extended all the way down the valley, and breathing in the clear peaty air of the Yorkshire fells. Sand martins swooped and glided above the lapping waters, catching flies to feed their young, who waited, screeching hungrily, in nesting holes burrowed into the sandy riverbanks.

Lizzie leaned back and enjoyed the sun's rays. Winter in the fells was hard. The river froze over and everything was buried in deep layers of snow. It was so bitterly cold that your breath froze whenever you ventured outside and drifts of snow built up against the hut, making it difficult to open the door. Last winter it had been so cold that she'd thought they would all freeze to death in their sleep. But she had survived. And now the sun was shining and she was taking advantage of her day off.

Molly's eyes followed Doctor Thistlethwaite as he moved from bed to bed, doing his rounds. She'd forgotten all about the patient she was supposed to be writing a letter for.

'Are you listening to me?' The Irish accent of the railway's latest victim brought her back to the present. 'Have you written down what I said?'

'Sorry, I got distracted. Now what did you say?' Molly put pen to paper and finished the letter to his loved ones back in Ireland, telling them of his plight. But her thoughts remained with Roger Thistlethwaite. His manner could be abrupt at times, and she'd always thought that he didn't care about his patients, that he had more in common with a horse doctor than a professional medic. Watching him at work these last few days, she realized that her assessment of him couldn't have been further from the truth.

'If you've finished that, Mrs Mason, the chamber pots need emptying. Please do it at once.' Starchy Drawers, as Molly now thought of her, marched past, nose in the air as usual.

'God, she's a snooty one!' The Irishman laughed. 'Go on now, best know your place. *She'll* not be emptying chamber pots – that's far too lowly a job for herself.' He winked as Molly rose to tackle the chore nobody else wanted.

'I'd like to empty one over her head,' Molly whispered, making him roar with laughter.

'Go on, girl, get them pots emptied!'

A broad grin on her face, Molly walked to the end of the hut to collect the slop bucket. On the way, she passed Doctor Thistlethwaite, who was making notes about his last patient. He paused in his work to peer over his spectacles at her.

'And how are you today, Mrs Mason? I must say, the patients have taken a great liking to you. They tell me you are very kind to them.'

'I'm fine, thank you. Bill Beecroft seems to be making a good recovery.' Molly still felt a little queasy when she thought back to her first experience of surgery. She hoped she would make as good a recovery as the patient.

'Yes, we might have looked like we were butchering him at the time, but believe me it was the only way to save his life. Are you enjoying your work here?'

Molly paused, struck by the eyes that were peering enquiringly at her. She'd never noticed what an unusual colour they were, a sort of rich almond shade. In fact, she realized that she'd never paid him much attention at all until this moment. It struck her that he was actually quite an attractive man.

'Yes, I am enjoying the work,' she replied, trying to play down her West Yorkshire accent. 'I find it quite rewarding. I go home tired, but that's to be expected, I suppose. I'm sure it will get easier as the days progress.'

'Good, I'm glad. You're an asset to the team.' And with that Doctor Thistlethwaite put his head down and continued writing.

As she set about emptying the chamber pots, Molly told herself it might be a mucky job but it was worth it to have those almond eyes smile at her and to hear his words of approval.

Who knew, she might yet give Starchy Drawers a run for her money.

'What are you doing here, pet?' said Molly, surprised to find her home occupied by Lizzie. There was a welcoming smell of stew wafting from a pan on the stove; Lizzie had just taken the lid off to give it a stir when her mother walked in.

Throwing her apron over the back of the chair, Molly sat herself down, kicked her shoes off and began rubbing her weary feet. 'Aye, I'm fair jiggered.'

'Mrs Pratt was worrying where to put her Mike and his bride, and baby when it's born. I decided that rather than wait for her to ask me to leave, I'd tell her I wanted to come home.' Lizzie poured a steaming ladleful of stew into a bowl and set it down in front of her mother.

'Oh, so she's found out, has she? That'll keep her sneck out of other people's business for a while. She can't talk about other folk when her own flesh and blood have fallen by the wayside. A baby on the way and a publican's daughter in the family, by 'eck it's a corker!' Molly laughed as she tucked into the stew. 'Good job her John brought your bed back the other night, you're going to need it.'

'Mother, have some sympathy, the woman's beside herself. Mike hadn't even told her he was to be married on Sunday.' Lizzie paused, struck by a sudden thought. 'And how did you know all about it?' She sat down next to her mother and tasted a spoonful of the warm beef stew. It was something Mrs Pratt had shown her how to make and she was quite proud of her first attempt.

'John mentioned it, when he came with your bed. I told him he should let his mother know about the wedding and the baby.' She took another bite of her stew. 'This is right good, lass. Make me this once a week and I'll be happy as a lark!' She grinned at Lizzie. Her little girl had grown up these last few months and she'd been too preoccupied with her grief to notice. It had done them both good to be apart for a little while, but now she was glad that her daughter was home.

'I'm still going across and helping her every day, Mam. I don't mind, it'll come in useful having her show me how to cook and sew and run a house.' Lizzie looked over the edge of her spoon as she drained her dish.

'You can do that, Liz, no problem. Your shillings can go in the kitty, and I'll be content knowing you're with somebody while I'm at the hospital, so it'll work out well.' She hesitated for a moment, debating whether to confide in her daughter, then said, 'John's coming over next week – but don't you go telling his mother. She'll not be suited that he's made friends with me.'

'I'll not say anything, but what's he coming for?' Lizzie eyed her mother curiously, recalling John's words to his mother that night Rose told him Molly wasn't their sort.

'He's offered to make me a pot rack. I think he felt a bit sorry for me, looking around our sparse cabin, and I wasn't going to say no. Besides, he's good company.'

'I'll not say anything. I like John.' Lizzie took her

mother's plate away and put it in the sink with the other dishes. When she looked back, a question on her lips, she saw that Molly's eyes were closed and her head was lolling against the armrest. Lizzie picked up a blanket and draped it over her mother, then set to work scrubbing the stew pan.

8

The grey clouds hung low over Whernside and Ingleborough, threatening rain at any moment as the wedding party gathered at the little church.

Rose sobbed in her hankie as her son waited in the aisle for his young bride to appear. The atmosphere could have been cut with a knife as the two families glared at one another.

'Just look at them, Father. You'd think they'd make an effort. The shame of it, my Mike marrying into that family.'

'Quiet, Mother. As long as they're happy, there's nothing you can do but wish them well.' Jim leaned on the pew as the bride-to-be entered the church, giving his arm to the sobbing Rose.

The vicar stood before the couple, the ring on his prayer book.

'Do you, Michael Bernard Pratt, take this wom—'

'He better bloody had do, else I'll break his bloody legs!' boomed across the pews.

The vicar hesitated. 'Do you promise to love her, cherish her and be faithful unto her, for as long . . .'

Rose glanced at Jim as the service continued. 'What's he done, Father? Just listen to what he's married into.'

'He'll be all right, Rose. He's made his bed, now he must lie in it. There's nothing we can do.'

'I always brought them up better than this. I only hope that he'll bring her back to live with us, then happen I can see a bit of hope.' Rose watched as Mike slipped the ring on Jenny's finger and kissed her on the cheek. 'Well, that's that then. My Mike's lost to another.'

'Aye, don't take on so, Mother. He's only up the road, even if they don't move in with us.'

'You'll never get me crossing the threshold of Gearstones. If they don't move in with us, he'll have to come and see me.' Rose's face was red with indignation.

'Now, Mother, you know you don't mean that. Once that baby's landed, you'll never be away.' Jim smiled at her.

'We'll see, we'll see.' Rose was looking forward to the birth of her first grandchild. Whether it was born at Gearstones or Batty Green didn't make much difference to her, but she had to be seen to be keeping things to her standard. She'd never admit to Jim that she couldn't wait to cradle the newborn in her arms, no matter how lowly the surroundings.

John knocked on the door of Molly's hut. 'Come on, answer – you must be in,' he muttered under his breath.

The last thing he wanted was for his mother to see him hanging around outside Molly's hut. She'd been watching him like a hawk all week. Ever since the wedding she'd been in the mood from hell. Mike had turned down her invite for him and Jenny to live with them, making the atmosphere at home unbearable.

He was just about to climb down the steps and go back home when the door opened.

'John! Sorry, I thought I heard someone knocking.' Molly smiled at him, she'd heard the first knock but had wanted to make sure she looked all right for her handsome male visitor, checking her hair and appearance in the mirror before opening the door to him.

'Aye, well, you're here now.' John walked up the steps and entered the now-familiar hut. 'I've brought you this – ' he held out a two-tiered shelf. 'I've been sitting carving it in my dinner break up at the tunnel. It gave me something to do other than gossiping and playing cards with the other men.'

'John, it's beautiful! And you made this yourself?' Molly admired the wood, carved with curls and rustic leaves and then covered with dark varnish.

'Aye, well, it's only made with dynamite-crate wood. It looks better for a coat of varnish. It will hold a fair few cups and I've put you some brass hooks on it so they can hang down and look bonny like my mother's. I know you women like these things.' John blushed as Molly enthused about his handiwork. 'I've brought my hammer and some nails, I thought I could put it up for you, if that's all right?'

'You hang it up and I'll make us a drink,' said Molly.

She put the kettle on, watching from the corner of her eye as John took hammer and nails out of his back pocket and levelled the rail on the wall.

'I hear the wedding went ahead on Sunday,' she said.

'That it did. But it was not one I'd ever want to attend again. I don't know what our lad thinks he's doing, marrying into that lot. My mother's going mad and taking it out on the rest of us. By God, you should have seen her face when someone threatened to break our lad's legs if he didn't say "I do"! It was a bloody picture!' John laughed and turned to look at Molly. She was pouring boiling water from the kettle, and he noticed the slight flush on her cheeks and a dimple on her left cheek as she smiled at his words.

The conversation stopped while four nails were banged into the wall to hold the prized possession in place.

'That looks lovely. I'll have to treat myself to some new cups to show it off. Now how much do I owe you?' Molly put the two cups of tea on the table and stood with her hands on her hips admiring the new shelf, but also slyly admiring John, who had taken her fancy with his easy ways and openness.

'You owe me nothing, except perhaps a listening ear from time to time. I get a bit fed up with the company at home and the rough talk of some of them that work on the line. I could do with a bit of refined company occasionally.' He sat and took a long drink of his tea, peering over the edge of his cup for a sign of interest from Molly.

'Well, you're in the wrong spot for refinement here, John lad!' Molly laughed. 'The only thing that's refined here is the bloody tea that you're drinking!'

'I don't know, you seem pretty refined to me: an independent woman with a near grown-up daughter and a decent home. And a good looker too. Couldn't get much better, I don't think.' He gave Molly a cheeky wink, his eyes twinkling with mischief.

'John Pratt! And there was me thinking you were a shy, bashful lad. What would your mother say?' Molly egged him on over the table.

'What she doesn't know won't hurt her. And I'm not telling her if you don't.'

'Right, you can come across any time, but no funny business. Friends, yes, but that's as far as it goes. I've still my late husband to think of.' Molly looked stern.

'Course, I hadn't anything else in mind. You don't even have to say it.' John smiled at her, remembering the gossip and scandal that had surrounded her and Cloggie. He was secretly hoping that one day it would be him she was bedding. 'I'll fetch you some cups from Ingleton on Saturday. I know some that will go just right on that shelf.' He made for the door. 'See you next week then.' He lingered in the doorway and smiled as she touched his hand gently before he pulled it to.

Molly closed the door behind him and listened as he started whistling a cheery tune on his way home. Here she was, a woman in her early thirties, yet her heart was beating like a teenager's. She felt a smile creeping on to her face and butterflies in her stomach. How daft, to feel that way over a man again. She scolded herself for thinking that way, and then smiled as she mused over this young man who seemed to have feelings for her. Happen, there was a reason to keep at Batty Green after all. Things were certainly looking up.

'Are you not coming with us today, Lizzie?' Rose shouted to her young employee, who was busy scrubbing the pine table.

'No thanks, Mrs Pratt. I'm going to do a few more jobs for you and then I'll be heading home.' Lizzie stopped scrubbing for a moment, the grey frothy water mixed with soda crystals dripping down her arm as she pushed a loose piece of hair out of her eyes.

'You needn't make us any supper. I'll fetch something cooked back from Ingleton, so once you've finished you have the rest of the weekend off. Don't bother with the door, our Bob's stopping home and all. He says he needs some time to himself. Why he says that, I don't know . . .'

Rose carried on muttering and complaining under her breath as she closed the door behind her and went to join John and Jim in the trap for the weekly shop.

Lizzie scrubbed hard at the table, till the pine almost looked white as she washed the suds off with cold water.

'She's enough to make you leave home.' Bob came from behind his bedroom curtain. 'I just need a bit of peace. "Our Mike this, our Mike that . . ." I'm bloody sick of hearing about our bloody Mike!' Bob scratched his head and yawned and sat in the chair next to the stove.

Lizzie pretended not to hear him. Out of the three brothers, Bob was the one she knew the least. He always kept himself to himself and sulked around the house without saying much.

'What do you make of my ma? Isn't she enough to send you doolally?' Bob asked, watching her through sleepy eyes.

'She's always been right good with me. I don't know where I'd have been without her.'

'That's her good Christian values that we get drummed into us all the time.' Bob spat a mouthful of saliva into the stove.

'Well, I think I'm about done now.' Lizzie untied her apron. She didn't want to be left in Bob's company. She felt uneasy with him when he was sulking.

'Aye, you bugger off and leave me to myself. I've plenty to do while they're away,' said Bob, getting up from the stove to come and lean by the door as Lizzie lifted the latch. 'See you tomorrow,' he whispered as she closed the door behind her.

Lizzie was thankful she'd finished for the week. Usually she enjoyed Rose's company most of the time, but this week Bob had been right when he said it was all Mike this and Mike that. Lizzie had never seen anyone carry on the way Rose had after the newly-weds turned down her offer of letting them share the hut. Never.

John told her it had taken Jim all night to calm his mother down.

When Lizzie got home the hut was empty. Since she'd started at the hospital her mother seemed to spend all her time there, working long hours and coming back shattered. At least it was keeping the wolves from the door; between them they were making enough to stay well fed with a roof over their heads.

Outside, there were clouds on the horizon, threatening rain later in the day. Lizzie decided she'd make the most of it and go for a walk while the sun shone. There'd be plenty of time to tidy up later.

Lifting her skirts clear of the muddy ground, she walked up the rutted track, heading away from the viaduct and on to the fells between Gearstones and Ribblehead. Along the way she passed abandoned spoil wagons and the earthworks and sinkholes made by the navvies. There were one or two workers labouring even though it was Saturday, making an extra shilling or two for their families. Lizzie watched as a wagon driver whipped his horses into action, dragging their heavy load of stone behind them as they leaned into their harnesses. These great stone blocks would form the towering pillars of the viaduct.

The wind started to whip up, sending clouds scudding over the high peaks of Whernside and Ingleborough. Further down the fell, grey looming wisps of cloud seemed to cling to the hillsides. Deciding it would be best not to go too far, Lizzie stopped when she came to the outcrop of limestone where the spoil-wagon tracks ended. She climbed up the grey limestone, grazing her hands on its rough surface, and sat on one of the crags high above the fell floor. The wind was picking up now, and large drops of rain were staining the light grey limestone. A small rowan tree, struggling to survive in the harsh environment of the limestone pavement, bent in the force of the wind, its leaves rustling. Lizzie pulled her shawl around her tightly and gazed up at the viaduct. A spot of rain landed on her face as she turned it heavenwards.

'Admiring the view?' said a voice from behind her. 'Cause I know I am.'

Lizzie jumped up. She hadn't realized there was someone behind her.

'Now don't be like that – sit back down. You know we're friends. I've watched you out walking.'

Strong arms pushed her back down on to the limestone, the harsh rock scraping her skin and making it bleed. He must have followed her over the moorland and come around the back of the outcrop to creep up on her.

Lizzie tried to stand up but his arm was wrapped tight around her and she couldn't move. Fear gripped her. She could tell by the look in his eye and the smell on his breath that she was in trouble. He ran his tongue down the side of her neck, licking her and smelling her body.

'Now don't be silly, I only want a kiss and a bit of a fondle. Don't you make a noise, or it will be the worse for you.' He ran his hand the length of Lizzie's leg underneath her skirt and she started to scream. 'You stop that, else I'll have to hurt you, to be sure I will.' His hand went over her mouth, while he fumbled with his trousers. 'You've asked for this, looking at me with those big eyes. You've practically begged me for it.'

Lizzie freed her hand as he fumbled with his breeches and desperately reached out for something she could use to beat him off. Her fingers found a loose stone, and she grabbed it and swung her arm, hitting him on the head. The blow dazed him sufficiently to make him loosen his grip for a moment. She looked at the blood running down into his eyes and jumped to her feet, but she wasn't fast enough. He caught her arm and pulled her back towards the edge of the limestone.

'No you don't, you bloody vixen!' He was holding her right over the edge of the crag. Lizzie bit his hand to make him release her. Her heart was pounding in her chest as she struggled to break free, knowing she was fighting for her virginity and her life. Suddenly her feet slithered on the crumbling limestone and she felt the stones give way under her feet. Unable to save herself, she toppled over the edge, bouncing off the rockface until her body came to rest in the bracken below.

Barely conscious, her limbs twisted at unnatural angles to her body, she lay motionless at the bottom of the cliff as the rain and mist rolled down from the fells, enshrouding her. Incapable of moving, she heard shuffling in the bracken, and then the sound of her molester breathing heavily as he approached. Lizzie closed her eyes and pretended to be dead as he leaned down, his rank breath in her face. She tried not to scream as he kicked her in her ribs and growled, 'Best end to you, lil' bitch.' Then as he walked away she prayed that he wouldn't return. Better to die here alone than endure that.

As the shock of the fall began to subside, the feeling in her limbs gradually returned. Every muscle, every nerve, every bone in her body was in agony. She could not move her left leg or arm. She tried to use her right arm to drag herself under the overhang of the limestone, but the pain was so intense that the last thing she remembered was the piercing scream that erupted from her lungs before blackness fell all around her.

Molly opened the door to a cold, dark hut. She'd been looking forward to coming home to a warm meal and Lizzie's company, but there was no sign of either. She lit the oil lamp and put it on the table, then got the stove going so she could boil a kettle for tea. All the while she was thinking of what she'd say to that daughter of hers when she got home. She spent enough hours at the Pratts' place all week, you'd think come the weekend she'd spare a few hours to prepare a meal for her mother. Instead it looked as if it was down to Molly to cook supper and have it ready for when Lizzie eventually decided to come home.

It was a dark, miserable evening. The fog that had rolled in during the afternoon had turned to rain. It was coming down in sheets, turning the tracks between the navvy huts to a quagmire. Days like these, you had to wonder what on earth you were doing, making a life at Batty Green. Molly turned the bacon and went to the door, peering through the dark towards the Pratts' hut. She'd hoped to see Lizzie hurrying through the rain towards her, but there was no sign of her. There was a light in the Pratts' window, so they must be home. All cosy and warm and fed, no doubt.

Fuming, Molly returned to the stove, put the spitting bacon and egg on to two plates and placed them on the stovetop to keep warm. A shilling a month or not, this was really not on, keeping her lass at work until all hours, and on a Saturday night too. Determined to give Rose Pratt a piece of her mind, Molly grabbed her shawl and marched out into the rainy night.

'What time do you call this?' she demanded the moment Jim opened the door. 'Could you not at least have the decency to send Lizzie home before dark, instead of working her all hours?'

Jim looked at her in surprise. 'Nay, lass, she's not with us. Mother told her to go home soon as she finished her chores this morning, afore we even left for market.'

'That I did,' said Rose, drying her hands on her pinny and hurrying to the door. 'Molly, is she not with you? It's not like her to stray from home.' She looked from Molly to her husband, her brow creased with worry. 'I haven't seen her since this morning. She said she didn't want to come to Ingleton with us, so we left her here with our Bob.' She turned back inside the house. 'Bob, do you know where Lizzie went?'

A muffled 'No' came from behind the curtain.

Rose shook her head. 'I can't get any sense out of that lad at the moment. You'd think he'd get off his bed and come out here to give me an answer.'

'She never goes out, she's always either here or home,' said Molly, frantic now that she knew Lizzie wasn't at the Pratts'. 'It's not fit for a dog to be out on a night like this.'

Rose ushered her inside. 'We'll find her, lass. John, put your coat on and go knock on some doors. Try that blasted Welcome Inn, she might be there – I know she's friends with that good-for-nothing Florrie Parker.'

As he pulled on his jacket and boots, John tried to catch Molly's eye without his mother noticing. He wanted to say something, offer some words of comfort, but knew he daren't do anything that would alert his mother to their friendship. In the end he gave up and hurried out into the wild wet night, hoping that Lizzie had simply lost track of time and was safe and sound in a friend's home.

'Now then, pet, sit yourself down. Jim, make a drink of tea for her while I have a word with our Bob, see if she told him where she was going.'

'She's all I've got left. I know we've had our ups and downs, but I love my lass,' said Molly, clutching her head in her hands, her long hair hanging damp over her shoulders. Tears were welling in her eyes. Something must have happened to Lizzie, she could think of no other explanation.

Rose drew back the curtain that screened her son's bed. Bob was lying with his face to the wall.

'Did Lizzie tell you where she was going when she left here?' she asked. When he failed to respond, she nudged the bed and demanded, 'Look at me when I'm talking to you, lad. Did Lizzie—'

'No! For the second time! Now leave me alone,' said Bob, still keeping his face turned away from her.

'Are you sure?' Rose insisted. 'Her mother's worried sick about her. Anything could have happened to the poor girl.' Enraged by his refusal to turn and face her, she grabbed hold of his shoulder and pulled with all her might.

'I've bloody well not seen her! Leave me alone!' cried Bob, shaking himself free and trying to pull the covers over him.

'There's no need to swear, not in my house!' said Rose, then the significance of what she'd seen hit home. There were blood spots on her immaculate white pillow. 'Bob! Is that blood? Did you hurt your head? What happened?'

'I slipped on the mud and banged my head.' He burrowed deeper under the covers. 'Leave me alone, I'm trying to sleep.'

Rose withdrew, pulling the curtain closed behind her.

'He knows nothing, Molly,' she said apologetically. 'Our Bob doesn't say much at the best of times. I sometimes wonder what I've done to deserve him.' She pulled her chair next to Molly and laid a comforting hand on her arm.

'Where can she be? Lizzie never goes anywhere. It's my fault – I shouldn't be working at that hospital. I should have more time for her. She's been through just as much as me.' Molly's eyes looked into Rose's, pleading for sympathy.

'Now then, pet, don't talk that way. We'll soon find her, she'll not be far.' But the anxious glance she cast at her husband betrayed her. She too was beginning to fear the worst.

Jim put on his coat and went out to join the search. It was all Rose could do to dissuade Molly from going out too. Instead the two women sat and waited, Rose saying over and over that her lads would bring Lizzie home safe, repeating it so often that she almost believed it. But when the men returned, the door slamming open from the gale that was now raging outside, they were alone.

'No one's seen her,' said Jim. 'She's not with Florrie. We've tried all the huts and nobody's seen her.'

John knelt beside Molly. 'It's not fit to look for her tonight – we'll never find her in this weather and dark – but it'll be light by five. I'm going to get a search party organized and we'll set out first thing.' Then he went back out into the night, leaving Molly crying inconsolably.

9

By dawn the rain had eased and the wind was clearing any remaining clouds from the valley. John had found plenty of recruits willing to give up their Sunday lie-in to scour the countryside for Lizzie. They might be rough, hard-drinking navvies, but when trouble befell their community they all stood together. To cover the ground more quickly they divided into three teams, with John leading one, Jim another and Bob tagging along with the third.

'I should go with them,' said Molly, standing in the Pratts' doorway as the teams set off in different directions.

Rose laid a restraining hand on her arm. 'Your place is here, pet. When they find her, this is where they'll bring her – and the first thing she'll be wanting is her mother.' She pulled Molly inside. 'Come on, lass, come and wait. That's all we can do for now.'

John strode out upon the fell, scanning the horizon for a sign of movement, a skirt blowing in the wind, Lizzie's wild dark hair trailing behind her as she ran. But the only humans in this landscape were the men of the search party, spread out in a line extending from the viaduct and searching behind every rock and shrub. They had brought along a sturdy bog cart with thick wide wheels, capable of carrying a load over the rough moorland. John hoped that it would not be needed, but he had decided it was as well to be prepared for the worst. If Lizzie had come to harm, she would have to be transported home.

Slowly the men made their way up the valley towards Gearstones, their feet sinking into the boggy ground, the sphagnum moss that grew on the fell bottom squelching underfoot as they waded through the peaty mire. Though it had stopped raining, the air felt damp and the mist hung around the high peaks with only a glint of sunshine trying to break through. It played on the raindrops clinging to the cotton grass, making rainbow hues shine on the bowing grasses.

All of a sudden a shout went up. John's heartbeat quickened as he saw one of the men run forward and pick something up. He lifted it above his head, and even from a distance John could tell that it was one of Lizzie's red ribbons, twisting in the wind. Galvanized by the confirmation that she was out here somewhere, the men redoubled their efforts. John only hoped they would find her alive. While conditions were nowhere near as bad as they would have been in winter, last night's storm had brought an unseasonal chill to the valley. She would need to have found shelter if she was to stand a chance of lasting the night.

As they climbed the valley and the grassland started to give way to bracken, their progress slowed. The men had to sweep back and forth with their sticks to see through the dense growth. Ahead of them was the great outcrop of limestone. John branched off from the search party and made his way through the bracken towards the base of the rockface. There, in the hollow at the bottom of the outcrop, he spotted a hand and arm.

John shouted to the rest of the men and raced to her side. She was lying face down in the peat. He dropped to his knees beside her and took her hand in his. It was icy cold. But when he gave it a tug, trying to turn her over, he heard a soft moan. He crouched and peered into her face and saw her eyelids flicker. She was alive, but only just.

'Lizzie, Lizzie, it's me,' he said, stripping his jacket off and covering her with it. 'You're safe now, we'll get you back to your ma.'

As he cradled her head tenderly in his lap, Lizzie groaned, muttered a few words and then passed out again. By this time the men had arrived, dragging the bog cart. Gently they lifted her frail body on to it. The navvies looked on, anxious but relieved to have found her. They'd not wanted to take bad news home to her mother.

John walked by the side of the cart all the way back down the fell. He could see Lizzie's leg was broken, and her arm. It looked as if she must have fallen from the top of the outcrop and pulled herself under the rocks. He only hoped that she would survive her ordeal.

Molly ran out to meet the bog cart, her shawl and hair flowing in the wind, calling Lizzie's name. Some of the men had hurried back with the news that Lizzie had been found alive and they were bringing her home, and she'd set off up the track before they had finished speaking.

John watched as she grabbed the side of the wagon, tears running down her cheeks, anxious eyes on her daughter's pale form. 'We'll take her to the hospital, Moll. The Doc will soon fix her up – she'll be all right, stop worrying.' He wished he felt as optimistic as he sounded. If Lizzie died, it would hit Molly hard. The girl was all she had left.

'Not the hospital! She doesn't like the hospital, she thinks everyone dies there!' Molly screamed as the wagon went past her home.

'She'll have to, Molly.' John had to hold her back to prevent her trying to stop the cart. 'She's broken her leg and arm, Doctor Thistlethwaite will have to—'

'She'll lose her leg! She can't live like that!' Molly screamed.

'No, it's a clean break, it's not smashed – the doctor will save it. Same with her arm. But she's in a bad way, Molly.' He gripped her by the shoulders and looked deep into her eyes. 'If she's to get better, she's going to need you. You have to be strong for her sake, Molly, no hiding in the drink. I know you can do it. And this time I'll be here to help.'

Distraught, Molly pulled away from him and looked on as two of the navvies carried her daughter into the hospital hut. Then she ran after them, taking her place right beside Lizzie's limp, broken body as Doctor Thistlethwaite examined her.

John turned away from the hospital door, wet and exhausted. The fear in Molly's eyes had chilled him to the bone. Head down, he dragged his boots homeward through the mud. When he got to the hut, instead of going in, he slumped on the steps outside.

'You've found her then? Thank the Lord for that,' said Rose Pratt, coming to stand beside him.

'Aye, well, I wouldn't be thanking your God just yet. She's as near heaven as I'll ever get.' John eased his mud-covered boots off and followed his mother inside. 'Are Bob and Dad back yet?'

'No, but someone's gone to tell them that she's been found, so they'll be back soon.' Rose put a mug of tea in front of him. 'How is she? What was the poor lass doing, climbing up there?' She pulled up a chair and looked into her son's troubled eyes. 'What's up, lad? Was she in a terrible mess?'

John nodded. 'She kept drifting in and out, but she managed to whisper a few words to me . . .' He shook his head and looked helplessly at his mother. 'You're not going to like this.'

'Go on, tell me, son. What did she say?'

'I could barely make it out, her voice was so weak, but as I carried her to the cart she said, "It was Bob. Bob pushed me."'

Rose let out a gasp and clasped a hand to her mouth. 'She could only manage a whisper, but she said it all right. I couldn't believe it, but then I got to thinking about the way he's been sulking around lately . . .' John took a sip of his tea and looked at his mother.

'No, not my lad.' Rose was shaking her head adamantly. 'He'd have nothing to do with her falling. He wouldn't lay a finger on anyone, not my baby. She's making it up. She's just like her mother, that one. I should never have taken her in! She's been trouble since day one.' Rose got up and began to poke the fire in the stove, turning her face away from her son in an effort to hide her anguish. She knew, she'd always known, that something was not quite right with her youngest offspring. Ever since he was little there had been days when it seemed he was wrestling with dark thoughts, but she'd clung to the hope it was just a phase, that the difficult years between boyhood and manhood would eventually pass and he'd emerge on the other side as normal as his brothers and father.

Shaking her head violently, she turned to John with the kindling stick still alight in her hand. 'You're not to say a word of this to your father or to Bob. I'll have a word with him when we're on our own. Don't you breathe a word of this to anyone, you hear?'

John finished his tea in silence. He too had watched his brother wrestling with the black moods that came over him, but he had never thought that it would come to this.

'I'll talk to him,' Rose insisted. 'When you and your father get the trap ready to take us to chapel, I'll have a word with him and get to the bottom of this.' She threw the stick into the fire. 'Oh, I can't stand thinking about this another minute. You lads will be the death of me!' An image flashed into her mind: the blood on the pillow, the cut on Bob's head and the feeble explanation he had given her. She clutched at her chest, her voice shrill with panic: 'If he's done it, they'll hang him. Oh my Lord, he'll end up at Lancaster Assizes! Oh, the shame of it, and after I've brought you all up to be good honest men. First our Mike and now this – what next, what have I done to deserve this?'

'Ma, calm down. I wish I'd never told you.' John put an arm around his mother. 'He mightn't have done it, I might not have heard right.'

'No, John. You and I both know that our Bob's not that bright. Something happened yesterday – he's got a cut on his head and bruises on his hands. If he'd been at work, I'd think nothing of it, but he stopped at home all day yesterday.' Rose was tugging on her damp handkerchief as if she would tear it into shreds. 'There's nothing else for it: he'll have to go your aunt Nancy's in Durham. Yes, that's the best thing, get him out of the way until everything calms down. With a bit of luck, the lass will not live. That way no one'll be any the wiser and he can come back home soon as the fuss has died down.'

John stared at her, horrified. 'Ma, how can you say that? Hasn't Molly been through enough without your wishing poor Lizzie dead?'

'Better hers than one of mine. When you've had children, you'll know how I feel. I'd die for you lads,' Rose sobbed.

'Ma, stop it. You need to calm down before Father gets home. There's no sense in upsetting him with this until we know it's right.'

John turned away from his mother, wishing he hadn't told her what Lizzie had said. The events of this weekend had shown him a side to his family that he had never seen before. For the first time in his life, he was ashamed to be a member of this household.

'Now, Bob, before we go to the chapel I want to ask you a question and I want you to answer me truthfully, else the Good Lord will have his vengeance upon you.' Rose peered intently into her son's eyes as she said this. She could tell that he knew what was coming. 'Did you have anything to do with Lizzie falling off the limestone edge near Gearstones? I'm not going to get angry if you did, but you've got to tell me.'

Having put her question, Rose sat back, hands trembling in her lap, eyes downcast. Secretly she was praying that he'd say no and she'd believe him.

'Don't know what you're on about. Silly bitch must have fallen.' Bob glared at his mother and then turned to look out of the window as if he'd lost interest in the conversation.

'There's no need for navvy talk in this house. We made Lizzie welcome and she's been a good help. Now tell me, how did you get them bruises on your hand and that cut on your head – truthful, mind. No lying, else I'll know and the Lord himself will know, this being His Sabbath day.'

'I fell, I told you.' Bob was becoming agitated, the way he always did when he was lying.

'I don't believe you, my love. I think you were with Lizzie.' Rose reached out for his hand.

'You don't understand – none of you do! Nobody listens to me! It's like I'm not here, and since she came I might as well not be.' Bob clenched his fist and banged it on the table.

'What do you mean, love? We're always here for anything you want and need.'

'No you're not. I've never any money, I've never any mates. I listen to our Mike and John, always talking about women and what they get up to, but they never include me. I've never had a girl, not like them. So when I saw her there, I thought of the way she had you eating out of her hand and . . . I thought maybe I'd get some attention from you, if she were my girl.'

Rose came round and put her arm around him. 'Oh, Bob, my Bob, what have you done? Did you deliberately push her off the cliff?'

'All I wanted was to touch her, but she fought me. She hit me with a rock and I lost my temper, like I do, Ma. Then I kicked her hard, 'cause it was all her fault. It was her fault, Ma. She kept smiling at me when she was working here.' Bob broke down and cried like a baby, his mother stroking his hair and rocking him to and fro.

'Hush, now. We'll see you right, lad. She might not come round again, and then nobody will know. To be on the safe side, it's best you go away for a bit, my pet.

After chapel, John will take you to Skipton station and you must take the train to Durham. I'll give you a note for your aunt Nancy, telling her you've not been well and need a rest. Give it to her and she'll see you right. I've packed your things already and put your share of the savings in there – mind you keep it to yourself.' Rose held her son's face in her hands and kissed him on the brow. 'Whatever made you think we loved you less? You're my baby, you're my special one.' She held him tight in her arms as tears dropped down her cheeks. Her last-born; would she ever see him again? God protect him, she prayed, and keep the Mason girl quiet. Please, God, let her be quiet.

10

Molly held Lizzie's limp white hand while the doctor examined her broken limbs and inspected her cuts and bruises.

'How is she, Doctor? Is she going to live? You're not going to operate, are you?' Molly's voice was full of fear as she watched the doctor run his hands over her daughter's limbs and open her eyelids, looking into her pupils.

'Stop worrying, Mrs Mason. She's taken a nasty fall, but I think her breaks are repairable. It's the knock on the head I'm not too sure of. She appears to be suffering with that and the cold more than anything. Nurse, pass me those splints and let's set this leg and arm while she's out for the count and can't feel much pain.'

Assisted by the nurse, Doctor Thistlethwaite pushed and pulled the left leg until the broken bone was in position, then he bound it tight with bandages and wooden splints. Even though she was under the influence of morphine and asleep, Lizzie winced and moaned in pain, but she didn't come to even when he moved on to her arm and repeated the whole procedure.

All the while, Molly stroked her brow and whispered to her, tears rolling down her cheeks as she felt the pain with her.

'Nurse, wash her cuts and bruises and then cover her with a layer or two of blankets – she's got to get some warmth into that frozen body of hers.'

Beckoning for Molly to follow, Doctor Thistlethwaite stepped away from the bed. 'I've done the best I can, but she might have a limp when that break heals. She's lucky they found her when they did. A few more hours out there on the fell and the shock from her injuries would have killed her.'

The nurse reappeared with a bowl of warm water and cloth, but as she approached the bed Molly stepped in.

'I'll do it. She's my daughter, I'll wash and tidy her.'

As she reached for the bowl, the nurse gave the doctor a questioning look. He nodded for her to hand it over.

'Very well, Mrs Mason. Carry on. But make sure you get her warm.' He patted Molly on the shoulder as she set about cleaning her daughter's wounds. 'Sit with her all day, if you wish – I know you'll only worry about her if you go home. We'll keep an eye on her and see what she's like when she regains consciousness.'

'Do you think you should let her, Doctor? She's not qualified,' sniffed the nurse, looking down her nose at Molly.

'Sometimes a mother's love can heal things that we have no hope of curing, Nurse. Besides, I've been

147

watching Mrs Mason – she's got a way with the patients. I think she needs nurturing, she could well be an asset to us.' Doctor Thistlethwaite smiled as Molly tenderly swaddled Lizzie in blankets. 'There's nothing like kindness to make a good nurse.'

'More like a common slut,' the nurse muttered under her breath as the doctor turned and went about his business. She could see that Molly Mason was beginning to worm her way into her world and she wasn't going to stand for that.

'Well, has he got away then?' Rose covered a sniffle as John closed the door behind him and sat down at the table.

'Aye, he's gone. Looked a bit fretful, but he climbed on board and waved at me as the train set off.' John leaned forward and put his head in his hands.

'I can't understand what good our Bob will be to Nancy,' said Jim, in the dark about the real purpose of his son's visit. 'The last person I'd want about the place would be our Bob. He's neither use nor ornament most of the time.'

'She wanted someone to light her fire and get her shopping, that's all. Besides it'll do him good to live in a city for a while.' Rose looked at John, hoping he wasn't about to expose her lies.

'Aye, but our Bob?' Jim picked up his newspaper and began to read.

While Jim smoked his pipe and lost himself in his paper, Rose beckoned for her son to follow her outside.

When he proved reluctant, she grabbed his shirtsleeve and tugged until he got up and went with her.

'Was he all right, my lad – he wasn't too upset, was he?' she asked, as soon as Jim was out of earshot. 'Do you think he understood that there was nothing else we could do?'

'He was fine, Ma. He was more excited about going on a train than anything else. You'd swear he'd hadn't a clue what he'd done or how serious it was. When the whistle blew and steam started coming out of the engine, he was so excited you'd have thought he was five years old not seventeen. I suppose it's the first time he's seen a train up close.'

'As long as he's all right,' fretted Rose. 'I'll bother myself to death until I hear from him.' She peeked through the window to make sure that Jim was still reading by the fire, then whispered, 'You'd better get down to that hospital and see if Lizzie is still with us. I know I shouldn't say it, but I rather hope she's gone to a better place. God have mercy on both our souls, but at least she'd take her secret with her and my lad would be safe.'

John bit his lip, not trusting himself to reply.

'Say nothing to her mother,' Rose continued. 'If anyone asks, just say we were concerned about Lizzie.' Then she turned away and went back indoors.

John was desperate to return to the hospital, not to do his mother's bidding but because he wanted to tell Molly how sorry he was and to make sure Lizzie was all right. He couldn't understand his mother wishing the poor lass dead. After all it was Bob who had done her wrong and, if it was up to John, he would suffer the consequences.

It was only as he entered the hospital that it struck him: if Lizzie had awoken and repeated her accusation, what sort of reception could he expect? He stepped into the ward with some trepidation.

'You all right, John lad?' came a voice from one of the beds. It was a workmate of his from the tunnel, who'd recently been admitted as a patient.

'Aye, grand,' said John, nervously continuing to the far end of the hut where he could see Molly sitting by Lizzie's bedside.

'Where do you think you're going? You can't come in here!'

It was Starchy Drawers. John was in no mood for being told what to do.

'Oh aye? And who's going to stop me, 'cause it'll not be thee,' muttered John, who was in no mood for the flibbertigibbet of a nurse with all her airs and graces. He strode to Molly's side and touched her on the shoulder. 'How is she?'

The small white figure underneath the blankets looked more frail than ever, and when she turned her face towards him he could see the pain in Molly's eyes.

'She's so ill, John, it's touch and go. Doctor's done all he can, now we've just to wait to see if she pulls through.' Molly patted her daughter's hand and looked sorrowfully at him.

'Has she spoken yet? Has she told you what hap-

150

pened?' He felt bad asking, but if he went back to his mother's without an answer it'd be the worse for him.

'Not a word. She's not come to since you carried her in.' Molly broke down, her body shaking with grief.

'Aye, come here, pet, stop your worrying. She's a strong one, is Lizzie. She'll not give in without a fight.' John held her shaking body in his arms and tried to comfort her.

'You see, Doctor Thistlethwaite! This is what happens when you let these types into the hospital. Fornication! I can't believe my eyes.' The nurse was screeching her views at the poor doctor as they approached.

'I don't think I'd go as far as that, Nurse. I'd say this gentleman is consoling Mrs Mason. Indeed, I would have done the same myself had I been given the time.' Doctor Thistlethwaite looked at John as if he was weighing up the opposition.

The nurse glared enviously at Molly, who stared back at her, not giving her an inch even though she was upset.

'Is she going to be all right, Doctor?' asked John, loosening his grip on Molly as she sat back down next to Lizzie's side.

'We'll see. It's the blow to the head I'm concerned with, but her colour's coming back, so that's a good sign.' Doctor Thistlethwaite smiled at Molly as he felt Lizzie's head. 'She's in good hands. With God's help, she'll survive.'

*

'Well? How is she?' No sooner had John walked through the door than his mother was asking.

'She's in a bad way, but her colour's coming back, so there's hope.'

'Is she talking, lad? That's all I want to know.' Rose was so agitated she'd forgotten that Jim was in the room.

'Nay, Mother, she's hardly going to have a conversation with him if she's that poorly.' Jim put his paper down on his knee and looked at his distraught wife.

'She's not said a word since she was taken in.' John was seething. His mother's behaviour was despicable. How could she wish another woman's child dead, just so her own could go unpunished?

Rose heaved a sigh of relief, 'Let the Lord protect her – and others.'

John was still standing in the doorway. With Mike and Bob gone, it was just him and his parents, meaning he'd have Rose's undivided attention. He looked at his father, smoking his pipe and reading his paper, oblivious to his scheming, manipulative wife. How could he be so content with his lot?

'I'm off out,' John announced, turning to leave. As he closed the door behind him he heard his mother calling after him not to be late for his supper.

It was nearly dusk and there was a chill in the air. John buttoned his jacket up. He hadn't changed out of his Sunday best, but there was no way he could face going back into the house now. He set off walking, and kept going until he found himself under one of the few completed arches of the viaduct. He looked up at the

152

scaffolding and, beyond it, the darkening sky. You could get dizzy just looking up there, never mind climbing up the scaffolding and perching up there while you worked. The great blocks of granite used to build the viaduct were so heavy that he'd seen many a horse break a leg trying to pull the heavy loads through the mire. All for the sake of some rich businessmen, wanting to build a line that could compete with the West Coast and East Coast lines. Surely, they must have looked at a map and seen the mountains and mires and fells that the line would have to cross on its journey between Settle and Appleby? He'd seen them in their fancy suits and hats, when the foreman of the works took them to inspect the tunnel. They'd stood there, in everyone's hearing, complaining that the tunnelling wasn't proceeding fast enough. That bloody railway was their only concern. The welfare of their employees meant nothing to them. They didn't care how many workers died.

John leaned his back against the scaffolding and gazed down the valley towards Gearstones. He could just make out the twinkling of oil lamps being lit in the lodge's windows. He wondered how his brother Mike was doing with his new bride. He hadn't had a chance to catch up with him since he moved out. He'd try and seek him out tomorrow before work. He lit his pipe and breathed in the tobacco while thinking about Molly. She was a bonny woman, and he'd been impressed by the way she'd set about bettering herself, landing the job at the hospital and restoring her pride and self-respect. He could do worse, he told himself. Yes, she was a widow and a mother and older than him. It seemed only the other day he'd joked about it as he put a bet on with Mike as to who'd be first to woo her, but now he was starting to think he could do a lot worse than to court Molly Mason – to hell with his mother and her opinion on the matter.

11

Autumn came quickly to Ribblehead. Gales swept the navvy settlements on Batty Green, the strong gusts blowing men off the viaduct and making work impossible. The hospital was busier than ever, with accidents a daily occurrence.

Lizzie sat up in bed, trying to shut out the screams of the latest patient to be admitted. She'd been looking forward to this day. After seven long weeks, the wooden splints on her leg and arm were going to be removed.

'Are you all right, my love?' Molly appeared by her bedside, anxious lest her daughter had been upset by screams from the latest victim of the railway.

'I'm fine, Ma. When's Doctor Thistlethwaite going to come and take my splints off? I want to go home.'

'Hush now, pet. The doctor has to attend to that poor man first. Besides, what's the hurry to get home? You'll only get bored – don't forget you're going to need to take it easy for a while. No doing anything silly, else you'll be back in here.' Molly ruffled her daughter's hair fondly.

'Molly, can you help me see to this patient?' called Doctor Thistlethwaite.

She immediately hurried to his side, happy to oblige. She'd learned a lot about nursing in the days and nights she'd kept vigil over Lizzie, hoping and praying that she'd live through her ordeal, watching as she fought for her life. And then one morning Lizzie had suddenly come round and it was as if nothing had happened. Aside from the fact that her arm and leg remained in splints and she had no recollection of how she had been injured, Lizzie showed no ill effects. It was a miracle, and Molly had been so overwhelmed with joy that she'd planted a kiss on Doctor Thistlethwaite's cheek. Ever since then, they had been on first-name terms – to the obvious displeasure of Nurse Starchy Drawers.

'Now, Lizzie, today is the day.' Doctor Thistlethwaite leaned over his patient. 'Pass me those scissors, Molly. Let's get these splints off and see what we are left with. Arm first, Lizzie.'

He snipped away at the bandages that had been in place since the day Lizzie was admitted to hospital, revealing a white shrivelled stick of an arm.

'Don't worry,' he said, seeing the dismay on her face. 'It'll only take a week or two for the muscle to build up. Before you know it, that arm will match the other one. Bend it for me, please, Lizzie.'

She moved it tentatively. The limb felt stiff and delicate, and she was frightened it would snap.

'Excellent! Keep moving it and everything will be fine.' Doctor Thistlethwaite felt the length of the arm and beamed with satisfaction. 'Now the leg. You'll not be able to run straight away, young lady. I warn you, it will be a long process, but at least you've got two legs – not like old George over there.'

Despite his jolly demeanour, the doctor was far from confident that he'd been successful in setting the bone correctly. It had been a bad break, and as always in such cases there was a risk the limb would be permanently deformed. Still he smiled and kept the conversation light and breezy as he removed the splints and bandages, and ran his fingers along the bone.

'Stand up for me,' he said. 'Put your weight on your mother, because your leg will be too weak at the moment.'

Lizzie looked uncertainly at her mother. She didn't want to put her foot down, it felt too strange and she didn't dare.

'Come on, Lizzie, you can do it. Hold on to me.' Molly held her hand out and helped her daughter to her feet.

'Well done! Now, ladies, let's see you walk all the way to the door.' Doctor Thistlethwaite stood back and watched as Lizzie and her mother slowly walked to the door and back, limping slightly but walking all the same.

'Excellent! I'm delighted to say it looks as though you've come through your misfortune virtually unscathed, Lizzie.' Doctor Thistlethwaite turned to Molly, whose eyes were brimming with tears, and added, 'I can see your mother is delighted too. Now then, it's about time you went home, isn't it? I'm sure you've had enough of this place.'

'John promised to come for me, didn't he, Ma? He said he'd come after work. He promised to carry me – just until I get stronger.' Lizzie's eyes lit up, knowing that she would be leaving the hospital. She'd hated every minute, stuck there with no escape from the smell of blood and urine, and the moans and groans of injured and dying men. Especially those nights when she was on her own after her mother had finished work.

'Yes, he'll be here. I spoke to him this morning.' Molly laughed and ran her fingers through Lizzie's long black hair.

'I can take her if you want, Molly. It's no problem,' volunteered Doctor Thistlethwaite.

'Thank you, Doctor, but John promised. Besides, you're needed here.' Molly smiled warmly at him. He couldn't have been kinder these last few weeks. Since Lizzie's accident, the two of them had become close friends.

'If you're sure?'

'Yes, I'm sure. Lizzie is no lightweight and John's used to carrying awkward loads.' Molly grinned as Lizzie pulled a face at hearing herself described as an awkward load.

As the doctor walked away, Molly sat on the bed next to Lizzie and began encouraging her to move her leg and arm.

'Two grown men, fighting over a woman her age!' sniffed Nurse Starchy Drawers, unimpressed by what she had just witnessed.

'Why not?' piped up the elderly patient whose temperature she was supposed to be taking. 'At least she's a proper woman – unlike some I could mention!'

And as she stuck her nose in the air and stormed off in a huff, the old man roared with laughter.

'What's that you're reading, Ma?' John had just finished washing himself down with warm water from the jug and was drying himself with the coarse towel before pulling his shirt on.

'It's a letter that came this morning from our Bob. He's wanting to come home. It seems he's got fed up, being with Nancy. He's such a bad writer, I've all on to make out what he's written here.' Rose sighed and sat with the letter in her palm. 'What are you getting dressed up for? And how come you're home so early? Has something happened at the tunnel?'

'No, I promised Molly I'd carry her Lizzie home today. I left work early because we don't want her to be out in the damp night air.' John smoothed his hair and checked himself in the battered mirror.

'Oh, so it's "Molly" now, is it? The woman's your elder – she should be Mrs Mason. What's more, she's a widow – just you think on!'

'Oh, Mother, them days are on their way out. She's a neighbour – a neighbour who's in need of help. For God's sake, leave it be.' John slipped his jacket on and pulled his cap down, then reached for the door. 'Don't wait up for me, I might be a while. I was thinking of having a game of dominoes with the lads after I get

Lizzie home.' Without waiting for a reply, he banged the door shut behind him.

Rose sighed and looked at the crumpled letter in her hand. She couldn't risk Bob coming home yet awhile. Like it or not, he'd have to stop a bit longer with his aunt – at least until they could be certain that Lizzie didn't remember what had happened to her. She got out pen and ink and replied to his begging letter. Better that he was safe and bored in Durham than locked up in Lancaster Gaol. She'd write and tell him no. He'd be all right with Nancy.

'Right, young lady, are you ready for home?' John smiled at the beaming Lizzie.

'I am. My ma says you're going to carry me home – I can't wait!' Lizzie grinned and stood up shakily on her weak leg. 'Look, John, I can stand on my own! I can even walk a few steps. I'm going to be fine.'

'Don't you be doing too much, my girl. You heard what the doctor said – slowly does it.' Molly tried to calm her excited daughter.

'Come on then, let's be away.' John put one arm around Lizzie's waist and the other under her legs, and lifted her into the air. She wrapped her good arm around his neck and rested the weak one in her lap as he carried her through the ward, the injured navvies wishing her well as she bade farewell to them all, sad to leave the kindly faces.

Florrie was waiting at the hospital doorway and she

skipped along beside them as John carried her best friend across the furrowed tracks. She was glad that that Lizzie had survived. Since the accident, she had gone to the hospital every day. At first they wouldn't let her in, but she'd waited outside, refusing to leave until someone came and told her how Lizzie was doing. Then, when Lizzie was feeling a little better, she'd been allowed to keep her company. She'd take in books and sit listening as Lizzie read aloud, wishing that she had half the brains that her friend did.

Molly had gone ahead to make sure the hut was ready to receive them. As they approached the front door, Florrie announced, 'I can't stop, Lizzie. My ma wants me back at the inn to help. But I was determined to see you home.' She held out a bunch of wildflowers: 'Here – I've picked you some flowers. Ain't they lovely?' As Lizzie took the now-drooping flowers and sniffed the bouquet her friend had thoughtfully picked for her, Florrie gave a cheerful wave and trotted off home. Bless her, she was a good friend. The flowers would soon revive in a glass of water and then she could have them by her bedside to cheer her up.

When John set Lizzie down in the chair next to the stove, Molly took one look at her daughter's pale face and announced, 'Right then, miss, let's get some supper in you and then it'll be an early night for you. I bet you can't wait to be back in your own bed again.'

Lizzie was too busy gazing at the shelves adorned with shiny plates and cups to hear what was being said. The place had changed a lot while she'd been away.

There was even matting on the floor. 'It looks right cosy,' she declared. 'More like a home.'

'Aye, well, I've had a lot of help from this fella – not that he'll let on.' Molly smiled at John. 'I don't know what I'd have done without him.' She ladled stew into a bowl and set it in front of Lizzie.

'Give over, it's all your own doing,' said John. 'You've worked every hour God sends at that hospital. All I did was put things up where you wanted them.' He pulled his chair up to the table as Molly passed him some stew.

'You know how grateful I am.' She reached her hand out and touched John's, words not enough to convey her feelings. Wiping the tears from her eyes, she said, 'Would you look at me – sad old fool! What am I like? First hour home for my lass and I'm crying like a baby. We should be celebrating our Lizzie's return.' She wiped her nose on her pinny and put on her firm voice again: 'Come on, lady, get that eaten and then off to bed with you. I promised Doctor Thistlethwaite there'd be no excitement for a day or two, so I'd better do as I'm told.'

Molly sang softly to herself as she washed the dirty pots, content that her daughter was back with her and apparently none the worse for her ordeal. She'd been afraid that Lizzie would be tormented by nightmares about the fall and the long hours she'd spent lying out there in the wind and rain, but thankfully the child had no memory whatsoever of those terrible events.

She dried her hands and turned to look at John, who

was sitting in the chair next to the stove, lighting his pipe. 'I love the smell of a pipe,' she said. 'It reminds me of my old man. He used to do just what you're doing now. He'd stretch his legs out and puff on his pipe and look out of the window for hours.'

'Aye, except I wasn't looking out of the window. I was enjoying a far bonnier sight than anything out there.' John rose and walked over to Molly, placing his hands tight around her waist.

'Will you be quiet and behave yourself, John Pratt? You'll wake our Lizzie, and I don't want to upset her on her first day back home.' Molly tried not to giggle for fear it would spoil her pretence of being cross with John as he gently kissed her and playfully bit her neck.

'You're a fine woman, Molly Mason.' He ran his fingers down the side of her face and cupped her face in his hands, kissing her tenderly on the lips. 'You're enough to make a poor Methodist lad go off the road of good intentions and into the fires of hell.' He grinned as his hands wandered up Molly's skirts.

'Give over.' Molly closed her eyes and swooned in his arms. 'We shouldn't, Lizzie might hear.'

'Shh, come down here, woman. Come on, stop your fretting – I'll be quiet.' He took Molly's hand, pulling her down on to the warm matting where he laid next to her, kissing her on the mouth and stroking her hair. 'I love you, Molly. I don't know what it is, I don't know how it's happened, but I know I want you so badly.' He kissed her neck and bosom and pulled her skirts up as he laid on top of her and entered her.

Molly gasped as she wrapped her legs around him and looked into his eyes as he clenched her hands above her head and made love to her with easy natural motions. Both of them forgetting the world around them, their passions fully aroused.

'I shouldn't have let you.' Molly lay next to an exhausted John, looking up at the hut's roof and feeling the hard floorboards through the matting. 'You'll think you can always do that to me, and I wanted you as a friend.'

John reached over, wrapping his arm around her. 'Moll, did you not hear me? I love you. I'd never take advantage if I didn't love you.' He kissed her gently on the neck to reassure her.

'No, I shouldn't have done it.' She shook her head and closed her eyes. 'I've too much history behind me. And what would your family say? Their lad going with the whore across the way. I can just see your mother now.' Molly sat up and pulled her skirts down.

'It's nowt to do with her. Anyway, she's got bigger things to worry about. There's our Mike, living with the family from hell and a baby on the way, not to mention our Bob. Besides, she's no angel herself.'

'Your Bob's all right, isn't he? What's up with him?' Molly turned her head to look at John.

'Nay, he's got himself into a bit of bother, that's all.' Realizing it was a subject best left alone, he steered clear of it. 'Moll, you know it's right, I love you.'

Both of them stood up and Molly gazed out of the window rather than face him.

164

'I think you'd better go, give me time to think.' She leaned on the wooden cupboards, still avoiding his eyes.

John picked his cap up and said nothing as he went out of the door into the crisp night air, his thoughts in turmoil.

Molly turned and walked over to where Lizzie was asleep, pulling the curtain back and looking at her dark-haired daughter asleep in her bed. She'd known for a while that her feelings for John had moved beyond friendship, but rather than face up to what was going on she'd tried to focus on her work and Lizzie, hoping that the attraction she felt for him would subside.

Planting a kiss on Lizzie's forehead, she drew the curtain to screen her bed and went to sit by the fire, her thoughts still taken up with John.

12

The snow came down thick and fast, dazzling the eyes and making people feel light-headed as they watched the huge flakes falling down. It had snowed for over a week, off and on, leaving drifts the height of a man all across Ribblehead and the shantytowns. Ingleborough, Whernside and Pen-y-ghent were like white sleeping giants wrapped up in a blanket of snow. Construction of the railway had ground to a halt and the navvies were getting cabin fever with no work to do and no means to get out of the valley. The pipes of the chimneys belched out dark grey smoke against the heavy winter's sky while residents of Batty Green huddled around their stoves.

'I can hardly keep warm, our Lizzie, it's so bloody cold.' Molly wrapped her shawl around her as she put her breakfast down in front of her daughter. 'I'm going to have to get some more coal from up near the track today. At least we don't have to pay to keep warm – that's one of the few perks of working for the railway. I don't know what it's going to be like in December if

166

it's this cold when we're not even out of October. We'll probably all freeze to death in this godforsaken spot.'

Lizzie crouched over the stove, resting her bottom on the top of it to get some heat through her bones while she ate her porridge.

'Don't you block all that heat off! Your mother's frozen and all, you know. Right, I'd better see if I can get someone to carry me a sack down from the coal yard. I dare say it'll be frozen solid and too heavy for me to manage.' Molly pulled her shawl over her head and stepped out into the blizzard, her skirt dragging in the snow. She held her shawl tight to her as the wind blew cruelly through it, and the snow caught on her eyelashes and hair as she trudged up the hill to the coal yard.

'Bye, am I glad to have got here.'

Molly lifted her head to see who was greeting her.

'I'm frozen to the bone – I can't feel my feet and my fingers are blue.' The red-faced postman from Ingleton puffed and panted as he stopped to get his breath. Molly was the only human he'd seen on his five-mile trek from Ingleton and he was desperate for a bit of conversation. 'I had to get through – I've a letter marked urgent and it's been staring at me these last five days from the mantelpiece. Where do the Pratts live? Can you tell me which hut it is?' He blew on his mittened hands as he waited for a reply.

'If you give me a hand with a sack of coal, I'll take you there.'

'I'll help you with it – if I can have a warm-up and

a brew before I set off back to Ingleton.' The postman put his head on one side, looking at Molly like an inquisitive robin.

'Deal.' Molly stomped off with the postman hard on her heels.

Jim Pratt opened the door to find a three-foot snow-drift blown against the steps and a weary postman.

'Letter for the Pratts,' he said, doffing his cap. 'I've come as soon as I could. This weather's held me up.' And before Jim had a chance to respond he was off, look-ing forward to some warmth and hospitality at Molly's.

'What is it, Father?' Rose wiped her hands and peered at the letter in her husband's hand.

'It's the postman from Ingleton. He's come out in this weather to deliver us a letter. Must be because it's got "urgent" written on it.' Jim ran his finger over the seal and then passed it to Rose to open.

'It's from our Nancy, I know her handwriting.' Rose ripped it open and began to read.

A moment later, hands trembling and eyes filling with tears, she slumped into the chair next to the table.

'What's up, Ma?' John rushed to her side.

Tears ran down her face as she waved the letter for them to read.

John lifted it from her shaking hand and read:

My Dearest Sister,
    I really don't know how to start and tell you the news I have to break to you and I fear

that there is no easier way than to tell you straight out. I'm afraid that last night I came home from a friend's home only to find Bob missing. It wasn't until the following morning when I went into the outhouse that I found the poor lad's body. I'm sorry to say he had taken his own life by hanging himself from one of the beams. I'm so dreadfully sorry for your loss and I know no amount of words will help you with your sorrow.

He'd not been himself since your last letter. I think that he'd taken it hard when you told him to stay a bit longer with me. He was finding it difficult to fit in up here, tending to be bullied a bit by his workmates. You know how it is: they always pick on the weakest. Bob, bless his soul, was easy prey.

I've arranged for the funeral to take place this coming Thursday. Everything is in hand and I presume I will see you on the Wednesday, so I'll air the spare room. The vicar says he can't be buried in the churchyard, so he's to be laid to rest on a bit of spare land next to the cemetery with the other suicides.

I'm so sorry to be sending you this awful news. God be with you and your family.

Your ever-loving sister,
Nancy

John screwed the letter up in his hand as he looked at his ashen-faced father and his wailing mother.

'This is your bloody fault – if you hadn't sent him away, he'd still be alive.' Words spewed out of his mouth. 'You're a bloody hypocrite, Mother!' John stamped about the room, unable to contain his grief and anger.

'Enough, lad,' said Jim. 'We're all upset. Your mother's not to blame for his death. She didn't know he was down.' Jim put a comforting arm around Rose as she sobbed uncontrollably.

'Tell him, Ma. For once in your life, practise what you preach: tell my father the truth. It's time he knew what Bob got up to and how you've covered for him ever since!' John banged his hand down on the table.

Rose sobbed into her apron, unable to look at her furious son.

'I said that's enough! Stop your bellowing, I know why he was sent away. You may think I sit in that chair and don't take anything in, but I'm not daft. It didn't take a genius to see the way Bob looked at that Mason lass. Then on the day she goes missing, he comes home with a cut on his head and sulking for the Devil. Oh aye, there's not a lot gets past me. And don't you look at me like that, Rose – our John's right: you're too devious for your own good. Maybe now our Bob's dead, you'll see what you've done and mend your ways. It's time the pair of you squared yourselves up. Remember who's head of this household.' Having said his piece, Jim sat in his chair next to the fire and lit his pipe. 'Now, when does she say the funeral is?'

170

John unscrewed the letter, this time reading it more carefully. 'Thursday. She says Thursday, but that was yesterday. We've even missed his bloody funeral.' John slumped in the chair next to his mother's. 'I'm sorry, Ma, I shouldn't have lost my temper. You did what you thought best.'

Rose lifted her head and tried to smile at her son, her eyes red and puffy. 'I only did what I thought was right for him. I loved him – he was my baby. You're all my babies.'

John held her in his arms and rocked her. 'I know, Ma, but we're all grown-up. We can stand on our own two feet. You can't look after us for ever.'

Jim spat a mouthful of saliva into the fire, making it hiss. 'I'm off to the Welcome Inn for a bloody gill – and don't any bugger try and stop me or lecture me. A man should be able to have a drink in time of sorrow.'

He'd no sooner left the house than he came across the postman, about to embark on the return journey.

'Good day to you!' the postman shouted.

'Good day, my arse!' Jim shouted back.

'Now you're sure you'll be all right if I go back to work? Promise you'll keep warm and not do anything daft.' Molly looked at her daughter lying in bed.

'Mam, just go. It'll be grand to have some time to myself, and besides I can read this book that Doctor Thistlethwaite gave me. He says Charles Dickens is really good and he writes about our sort.'

'How would he know about our sort? He's never

known what it is to go hungry. He likes to think he understands us, but he never will.' Molly laughed at her book-loving daughter. She could read herself but never had the luxury of time to devote to reading a book from cover to cover.

'Right, I'm off then. Coal's by the stove, dinner's on the table – and you mind what you're doing till I get home!'

Molly closed the door and set off along the track. The snow had melted, leaving behind a muddy slush that seeped into her boots and left the hem of her skirt soaked. When she got to the hospital she stood in the doorway stamping her feet to clear them of the icy mush before entering.

'Ah, Molly, I was wondering if you were going to be joining us today,' said Doctor Thistlethwaite, hurrying to the door to greet her. 'I've no work, I'm afraid. Since this weather has put a stop to work on the railway we've had no new casualties and Nurse Thompson is able to manage those patients already on the ward. However, I'm glad to see you as. there's a matter I would like to discuss with you . . .'

Noticing Nurse Gladys Thompson creeping closer to the door in an effort to eavesdrop, Doctor Thistlethwaite took Molly's arm and said, 'Perhaps you'd care to step outside for a moment, so we can talk more freely.'

The two of them walked around to the side of the hospital until they reached a place where they could shelter from the wind. Turning to face her, Doctor Thistlethwaite said, 'I've watched you with the patients and with Lizzie. You have a way with people, putting them at their ease even when they are in great pain. It occurred to me that your talents should be put to use nursing patients, and to that end I would like to offer you a position as my aide. I could then instruct you in care of patients and administering drugs to them. It would require hard work and dedication, but the skills you learn would always stand you in good stead.' His almond eyes studied Molly over the top of his spectacles, searching her face for an answer.

'I don't know what to say, Doctor,' said Molly, blushing. 'I'm flattered that you have faith in me, but I'm not that quick to learn and I'm not the strongest reader. I don't know if I'd be up to the responsibility.'

'Nonsense. I wouldn't ask if I didn't believe you were capable. Report for work at seven o'clock sharp tomorrow and we'll make a start. Nurse Thompson can do your duties while you accompany me on my rounds. This is the ideal time to learn, when we're not run off our feet.' He smiled and took her hand in his. 'And how's Lizzie doing? Delighted to be home, I expect.'

'She couldn't wait for me to get out of the house and leave her in peace so she could start reading that book you gave her, Doctor Thistlethwaite.'

'Ah, Dickens! Now there's a chap that knows about the working classes. Oh, and you can stop calling me "Doctor Thistlethwaite" – when we're alone, I'd prefer you to call me Roger.' He opened the door. 'Seven o'clock, remember. Don't be late.'

Molly set off for home, mulling over her new position and smiling at the thought of Starchy Drawers' reaction when she found out she'd be doing Molly's job for a while. Before she knew it, she was back at her own door.

'I'm back, Lizzie love,' she called happily, hanging her shawl by the door. 'Turns out they don't need—' She broke off at the sight of Lizzie, huddled up in the chair next to the stove, tears pouring down her face. 'Whatever's up, pet?'

'I've remembered, Ma – I've remembered what happened to me that day. I didn't fall off the outcrop – I was pushed!' Sobbing into her mother's apron, Lizzie recounted all the memories that had come flooding back of Bob's attack on her. The forgotten details were all vividly recalled now, and she described every move he had made, every word he had said, how she had fought to keep her virginity and how he had come to the place where she lay and kicked her. She sobbed and cried until she could cry no more and Molly cradled her all the while, trying not to cry herself, whispering comforts and rocking her in her arms until she finally cried herself to sleep.

'Come on, you bastards! I know you're in there, and I know what you've done. Thought you could send him away and cover up for him, did you? Well, I hope he rots in hell! I promise you, he will when I get hold of him.'

Molly banged and hammered on the Pratts' door,

174

shouting abuse until neighbouring doors began to open and the other navvies came out of their huts to see what the commotion was about. 'You bloody hypocrites! She could have died! John, you bastard, the whole time I was with you, you knew what that brother of yours had done! You knew!' She banged her fists on the door and kicked it till it rattled. 'He should bloody well hang for what he did to my Lizzie!'

Finally the door opened and John stepped out, grabbing Molly's fists as she pounded them against his chest.

'Hold your noise, woman. Your wish has come true – our lad hanged himself last week. He couldn't live with the guilt and being away from home, so he took his own life. Justice has been done, lass. Now let it be.' John's grip loosened as Molly stopped her screaming.

She peered suspiciously at him through her hair, which was hanging tangled across her face, giving her the look of a wild banshee. 'I don't believe you. You've been covering for him all along. That time you laid with me – you could have told me then, but you didn't. All the time I thought you were being nice, doing things around the house, you were just covering your brother's tracks. You think nowt of me.' Molly looked into John's cool blue eyes and saw the pain in them. 'I'm sorry for your loss, but after what he did to my lass – it was the best end for him.' Molly hung her head and turned to walk away.

'I love you, Molly Mason. That's the truth. I want to marry you!' John shouted after her as she walked home, not so much as turning her head in recognition. 'Are you listening? I said, I want to marry you.' His

175

voice boomed around the navvy huts, cutting the air with his declaration of love. Lifting his arms to the skies, he yelled again, but it was in vain.

'Get yourself in here now!' said Rose, pulling at his shirt. 'What a thing to shout, with your brother still warm in his grave. How could you?'

'Be quiet, Mother. I've just lost the woman I love – all because of you. Are you satisfied?'

'Shut your mouth, you stupid boy! She's not fit for the likes of us. Why, Molly Mason's as common as muck, and you should think yourself lucky that this happened, else she'd have been a weight around your neck all your life.'

John wasn't listening. Hanging his head dejectedly, he walked away.

Molly sat in her chair, thoughts running through her head. Had she been too hard? She'd stood there yelling that he should be hanged and all the while the lad was dead. But what did they expect her to do? He'd tried to rape Lizzie, and then he'd walked away, leaving her for dead. It was no thanks to him that she'd survived. And what did his family do? Bloody hypocrites! Never again would she have anything to do with the Pratts.

She looked around her at the shelves John had put up and the cups and plates that he'd bought. Was it his way of paying her off, easing his guilt, or had he actually done it all for love? The words he'd shouted after her were ringing in her ears. Had he really wanted to marry her? She remembered the night their bodies entangled with passion on the floor of the hut, the way he'd kissed her and looked at her. That couldn't be false, surely? Molly felt sick, torn between hatred for one brother and the love she'd felt for the other. How could she walk away from the man she loved for the sake of his brother's sins? But she had to be right by Lizzie and she couldn't court a man whose face would be a constant reminder of the terrible wrong that had been done to her. She put her thoughts away as she heard Lizzie stirring from her bed.

'You all right, Ma?' Lizzie slowly walked towards her mother.

'Aye, I'm all right, pet. It's you we've to look after. That bastard Bob – he'll not be harming anyone ever again.' Molly wanted to tell her that he'd hanged himself, but Lizzie had endured enough revelations for one day. 'How about I make us a brew and some drop scones?' She got up and placed the griddle pan on the stovetop and went to the store cupboard to gather the ingredients. 'Your ma's got a bit of news, lass: I'm going to be training as a proper nurse from tomorrow.' Molly grinned at her daughter. 'Let's get you mended and walking better, then I'll give Nurse Starchy Drawers a run for her money, eh?'

Lizzie gazed tearfully at her mother. 'I don't want to go back to help Mrs Pratt again, Mam.'

'You'll not be going back there, pet, don't you worry. Those hyprocrites'll have to find themselves another skivvy.' Molly took her anger out on the scone batter, beating it for all she was worth.

'I'm sorry, Mam. Happen it was my fault – I did used to smile at him, but he always looked miserable so I thought it would cheer him up.' Lizzie's eyes filled with tears once more.

'Lizzie Mason, you did nothing to be ashamed of! Nothing! You didn't encourage him – that lad never was quite the full shilling. And as for his mother, well . . . I just don't know what to say. Here, pass me the butter and let's forget them, we've some scones to eat.'

Lizzie passed her mother the butter and hugged her at the same time. 'I love you, Mam. I'm sorry.'

'Nowt to be sorry for, lass. It's them buggers over there that should be sorry.'

Molly bit her lip in concentration, it was the first time she had dressed a broken arm and she didn't want to cause her patient pain. She stepped back and scrutinized her efforts. It was a bit scruffy, but it seemed to be keeping the bones tight and in place, and that was what mattered.

'Well done, Mrs Mason. I couldn't have done it better myself!' Doctor Thistlethwaite congratulated her. 'Don't you think she's done a neat job, Nurse Thompson? I knew she was a natural!' Roger Thistlethwaite smiled and moved on to his next patient, proud of his teaching skills.

Molly bent to tuck her patient back into bed and found Nurse Thompson's face glaring at her as she stooped to tuck in the covers on the other side.

'Don't you think you can worm yourself in that fast,'

hissed Nurse Thompson, pulling the sheets tight over the injured man. 'Bandaging an arm's nothing!'

'Ah, go boil your head!' said Molly, wondering what the poor man in the middle was making of finding himself stuck between two warring nurses. From the grin on his face, he appeared to be revelling in it. 'For goodness' sake, Gladys,' she said, 'can't you see there's room for two of us here?'

Nurse Thompson's only response was to stick her nose in the air and turn away.

'Right,' muttered Molly. 'If that's what you're wanting, I'll give you a run for your money.' She'd had enough of Starchy Drawers accusing her of flirting with the doctor. Since nothing she could say would put a stop to the jealousy, she might as well go ahead and flirt.

'Roger – oh, I'm sorry, I meant Doctor Thistlethwaite – what would you like me to do next?' Molly winked at her patient and wiggled her bottom as she walked over to where the doctor stood. She knew Nurse Thompson would be apoplectic with rage, hearing her address him by his first name.

'This patient came in with frostbite. Stand here next to me and I'll show you how to dress his feet,' said Doctor Thistlethwaite, leaning over and carefully wiping the navvy's feet, before talking Molly through the procedures that he was undertaking.

Moving as close to him as she could, Molly bent over, her tight-fitting bodice revealing her plump breasts as she pretended to be interested in the man's frozen feet. Roger Thistlethwaite found himself losing track of what he was saying as his eyes kept wandering to Molly's cleavage. 'Perhaps I should have Nurse Thompson help me,' he stammered. 'My mind is not quite on my job today. Nurse Thompson, come and see to this patient, would you please? I need some fresh air.'

Doctor Thistlethwaite rose and walked out of the ward, leaving Molly smiling and Nurse Thompson fuming at having to take over the unsavoury task.

'There you go, Gladys – *that's* flirting. If you don't want me doing that all the time, stop your jealous ways and give me a chance.' She bent and picked up the navvy's discarded socks. 'These are threadbare. He needs some decent socks before he goes back outside again – I'll see if we have any.'

Molly walked away smiling to herself. With luck, she'd have no more trouble from Nurse Thompson. Her only concern was that Roger Thistlethwaite might have taken her advances to heart.

October changed into November and work on the viaduct remained at a standstill, thanks to the snow. The dale was buried in snow, freezing winds blew through the partly built viaduct and the railway navvies barely ventured out of their huts. The Pratt family appeared to have turned their backs on the world. Since the day Molly had hammered on their door, the only time they'd been seen out was when they attended church. Even John had elected to stay indoors. A handful of his fellow tunnel builders still made their way up to

Blea Moor, blasting their way through the rock, the tough little fell ponies emerging from the gaping entrance with loads of dark frozen earth which was deposited on spoil heaps either side of the line. The work was hard and cold and the navvies spent their time either getting chilled to the bone outside the tunnel or working up a sweat inside. Pneumonia was rife, keeping Molly and Nurse Thompson so busy that they finally called a truce and devoted their energies to combating the spread of the disease.

By the end of the day, Molly was so exhausted she could barely stand, but she looked forward to getting home to her daughter. Undaunted by the snow, Lizzie spent her days getting out and about as much as possible, with the result that both her leg and arm seemed to be healing well. She was standing by the stove, stirring a pot as Molly staggered in from the cold, her legs heavy with tiredness and a gnawing pain in her stomach that seemed to be getting worse as the day went on.

'Are you all right, Ma?' asked Lizzie. 'You don't look too good.'

'I'm all right lass, just tired. We lost two to pneumonia today. I hate the sound of a man drawing his last breath.' She winced, her face grey with pain and fatigue. 'Oh, my Lord, my stomach's bad tonight.'

'Here, Mam, I've made us some potato soup. That'll soon warm you up.' Lizzie placed a steaming bowl of soup in front of her mother with a hearty slice of bread.

'You're a good lass, our Lizzie. I'll try a mouthful, but then I'm away to my bed.' She managed only a few sips and a nibble of the bread before setting down her spoon. 'I'm sorry, pet, but I can't eat any more – I just want to lie down.' Molly dragged her tired body across to her bed and started to change into her nightie. 'I know it's hard on you, love, being on your own all day. I wish I could sit up and keep you company for a bit, but I'm really not up to it tonight.'

'Don't worry about me, Mam. I've been busy reading.'

'You and them books! I'll have a scholar on my hands, if I'm not careful. You'll end up like Doctor Thistlethwaite.' Molly gave a wan grin as she undid her stays, pulling her nightie over her head and drawing the covers around her. 'Don't you go reading all night,' she muttered as a pain gripped her. She closed her eyes tight, wishing sleep would come upon her.

Lizzie put the pan of soup to one side; they could heat up the leftovers for dinner tomorrow. She pulled her chair up next to the stove and got her latest book out, leaving her mother in darkness as she took the oil lamp to read by. Soon she was lost in the adventure written on the pages.

It was dark and silent when Molly woke up, a terrible pain ripping through her body, so bad it almost made her scream. Her nightdress was damp, and when she ran her hands over the mattress beneath her, it felt damp and sticky. It was too dark to see, but when she put her damp fingers to her face she could smell the iron tang of blood. Trying not to disturb Lizzie, she fumbled to light a candle. Her bedding and nightdress were saturated in blood, so much blood that Molly had to fight off a wave of nausea. She gulped hard and sat on the edge of the bed, totting up how many weeks had passed since she slept with John. There was no doubt in her mind: she'd lost a baby, a baby that would have been loved by both its parents. Tears ran down her cheeks. If only Bob hadn't laid a finger on Lizzie, things would have been fine. She held the pillow to her face and sobbed into it. Two babies in one year: the world could be so cruel.

'Lizzie told me you were ill and unable to work today. I feel so guilty. I've been asking too much of you lately.' Roger Thistlethwaite looked at Molly with concern.

'I told Lizzie to let you know it was only something I ate that didn't agree with me. You needn't have come all the way up here. There's worse cases than me to worry about.' Molly stood up from her chair, trying to prove that she was fine. 'It was that pork I had the other night. I never could stomach the stuff. Now stop fussing, both of you.'

'Are you sure there's nothing else wrong – no pain or fever? You're looking extremely pale,' said Roger.

'I'm all right, for God's sake. Give me a day or two to shake off this belly ache and I'll be back with you.' Molly knew she shouldn't be so sharp with him, but she was desperate for Roger to leave before he pieced together enough clues to suspect her secret.

'Right then, if you're certain, I'll go. Lizzie, you're to come straight to me if your mother gets any worse.' Roger Thistlethwaite reached for his hat, but then paused to look at her one last time before making for the door. 'How about tea at my hut on Sunday? Lizzie, you could choose another book and it would give me a chance to make sure your mother's well enough for work.'

'Can we, Ma? Please? Go on, Ma, I've nearly finished the one I'm reading and I'd love to have tea with Doctor Thistlethwaite.' Lizzie couldn't contain herself. The one good thing about being in hospital had been the books that Roger had given her to read. She'd never dared hope that he would go on lending her books now that she was home.

'We'll see,' said Molly. 'After all, we might be snowed in by then. I've never known weather like this.' She smiled and took Lizzie by the shoulder, surreptitiously leaning on her to say her goodbyes to the doctor.

'Three-ish, all right?' Roger Thistlethwaite tipped his hat and closed the door.

They stood in silence for a moment, listening to him whistling as he made his way back to the hospital.

'Let me get back into bed, our Liz. I need to lie down,' said Molly weakly. 'Don't you tell anyone how badly I am. I'll be back on my feet by Sunday, you mark my words.' Molly struggled back into her bed, more broken-hearted than in pain, and lay listening to Lizzie singing. At least Lizzie was happy; she was glad that she had kept the miscarriage from her, managing to change the bloody sheets and hide the evidence while Lizzie slept. It would have been too awkward, trying to explain to her.

Molly felt as if her heart would burst with pain.

Both the pain of losing another baby and the pain of losing John, the man she thought she had truly loved but now couldn't stand the sight of. She missed him so much, that smile and the easy way he had with her and Lizzie. She had felt so comfortable in his presence – how could he not have told her about his bastard of a brother? How could he have kept that from her?

Molly hugged her pillow and wept into it, stifling her cries so that Lizzie wouldn't hear.

13

'Are you feeling any better, Molly? I must say, your colour has improved. I was rather concerned when I called in to see you the other day.' Roger Thistlethwaite took a long sip of his tea and studied Molly. 'I'm so glad you decided to come, you've made an old man happy.' He watched Lizzie inspecting his book-laden shelves, the smile on her face answering his question: 'You like reading and writing, Lizzie?'

Lizzie nodded, too engrossed to answer him.

'Lizzie, answer Doctor Thistlethwaite properly.' Molly pulled her daughter up sharp. 'Manners cost nothing.'

Molly put her cup down and continued to take in the doctor's hut. The array of plants, trying to live in the bleak conditions, the rows of potions and bottles mixed in with the library of books. There were good pieces of best china on display, but they seemed neglected as they jostled for prominence amongst the literature and decaying plants. The hut was definitely missing a woman's touch, Molly decided as she listened to Lizzie, not believing how easily her daughter talked to a man of education.

'I do, Doctor Thistlethwaite, I love it.' Lizzie dropped on the stool next to him. Her first impressions of him had not been favourable, but she had since found out that he was a good man. She had grown very fond of him during her time in the hospital.

'Well, I had dinner with James Ashwell, the contractor for the Midland, and he's looking for a junior clerk. I know it's highly irregular for a girl to be in an office, but you've got brains and you can read and write, which is a lot more than some can do here at Batty Green. I think it would be an ideal job for you. It's only at the contractor's hut, but they are a better class of people for you to mix with.'

'You must be joking!' Molly laughed. 'That's a lad's job. Our Lizzie would be a laughing stock. Women can't work in offices.'

'She can here. There's no one in these parts as clever as Lizzie and she'd be safe and warm. And it's paperwork, there'd not be much physical work to do.' Roger Thistlethwaite looked at Lizzie. 'What do you think? Shall I have a word?'

'No, Roger, I can't have her showing herself up.' Molly shook her head.

'But she wouldn't be. She takes after her mother and is a quick learner. Even you can't say you've not enjoyed being shown the nursing I've taught you. Now it's Lizzie's chance to shine.'

Lizzie lifted her head up. 'Let me have a go, Ma. I

can at least try, and it'll be better than cleaning up for a living. I'm nearly fifteen, I can do it.'

'You'll be the death of me, Lizzie Mason. I'll only agree if I can see this Ashwell man and where you'll be working. I'm not having you in any danger, not again.' Molly couldn't believe what she was saying. It wasn't done, the girl should know her place.

'Right, I'll talk to him, see what he says. But I did happen to mention it the other evening, so I know his response already.' Roger Thistlethwaite smiled and finished his tea. 'On a different note, I believe we have missionaries amongst us. I understand they originate from Bradford, but at the moment they're living in rented accommodation at Ingleton prior to coming to live in our midst. A Reverend Tiplady, I believe, here to save our souls.' He smirked.

'Oh my Lord, that's all we need – Bible preachers amongst us. The world's gone mad!' Molly threw her hands up in disgust.

'My thoughts entirely, Molly. I've no time for religion, having seen what I've seen. However, I make an exception at Christmas. I know it's a few weeks away yet, but I've been thinking and . . . may I invite you both to my humble abode on Christmas Day? It would be a privilege to have you as my guests.'

Molly was shocked. To be asked to Christmas dinner at the doctor's was a huge step up from sitting around a near-empty table in her hut.

'Oh, Ma, can we? Please, Ma? It'd be lovely here and we wouldn't be on our own.' Lizzie's eyes pleaded with her mother while Molly weighed the pros and cons of being seen to have Christmas dinner with the doctor.

'I don't know, Lizzie.' Molly struggled with the notion of sharing Christmas with an unmarried man and one way above her class.

'Please . . .' Lizzie pulled on her mother's skirts.

'My intentions are honourable. I'd welcome the company. Life can be lonely, when you are getting on in years and unmarried.' Roger Thistlethwaite smiled and waited for a response.

'Go on then, we'll come. Lizzie will enjoy it. And if it means you not being on your own at Christmas, I can see no harm in that,' Molly succumbed. In honesty, she was quite looking forward to it herself.

'Now then, Mr Ashwell. I want to know will you be right with my lass? No taking advantage, no working her to the bone, she's already been through enough without being messed about again.' Molly looked around the contractor's hut. Plans of the railway lay everywhere and two men were concentrating on studying the path the line was taking while a young lad sat gazing out of the window. It was a lot larger than most of the huts and had the benefit of two stoves to keep the occupants warm. She knew the men that worked there were renting accommodation with local farmers; not for them the cold of a Batty Green shanty. This hut was purely for business, not for living in, as the only sign of domesticity was a kettle boiling on one of the stoves.

'Mrs Mason, Lizzie will be doing small errands for

me, perhaps writing the odd letter or two when I haven't time, and just helping keep the clutter down. As you can see, us men are not the most organized. I haven't time because I'm too busy trying to see this blasted project stays on time.' James Ashwell was well spoken, clean-shaven and a man of principles. He'd little time for some of the hard-drinking navvies and the tricks they got up to. He walked away and studied some plans, his tall lean body bending as he read the papers by the light of the window, giving instructions to the men he was obviously in charge of.

'Right, as long as you know how it's to be.' Molly turned to leave. She couldn't believe she'd stood up to the main man of the Midland, and now her nerve was beginning to falter. 'Monday, eight o'clock, a shilling a week and we'll see how we go.'

James Ashwell lifted his head and watched the determined woman bustle her way outside. It took some nerve to lay down the law to him. He could understand now what his friend Roger Thistlethwaite saw in her.

'I'll make sure she's on time,' said Molly, and closed the door behind her. He seemed a decent man. A bit sharp, but then he was in charge of the whole shebang so he'd every right to be.

Molly hummed a tune as she walked along the path home. That was Lizzie sorted with a good job, and she was content with nursing. Things were taking a turn for the better. She'd pop into Ingleton next weekend on the new train-tram that the Midland had rigged up running along the temporary train lines along the valley bottom. Now that she could afford it, it would be good to visit the market and pick up a few bits for Christmas. Perhaps a length of cloth to make a new frock for Lizzie; she'd like that.

Her thoughts were of Christmas and presents as she rounded the corner of the huts, her head down, concentrating on putting together a list of wants.

'Oof! Not so fast, look where you are going.' She bumped head-on into a man coming from the opposite direction, knocking her hat askew.

It was John Pratt. She quickly set her hat straight and tied it firmly under her chin, giving him a curt glance as she walked on.

'Molly, Molly, wait, wait. Talk to me.' John ran after her and pulled on her sleeve. 'I've missed you so much these weeks.'

'Leave me alone, John Pratt. Go back to your mam, like a good lad.' Molly pulled her sleeve away from him. She was about to walk away but the sight of his sorrowful face stopped her.

'Molly, stop it. You know I love you. I couldn't help it. You don't understand how it was. I'd have given anything to tell you, but our Bob was the baby of the family, I had to keep quiet for his sake.' John stood in the rain that had started to fall.

'Aye, and how do you think I feel? Lizzie's the only one I've got left and your lot lie and try to kill her. You don't love me, John Pratt, you're too busy looking after your own.' Molly stomped off, leaving John standing in the pouring rain and watching her.

*

It had been raining all week, but Molly and Lizzie didn't care about the miserable weather as they climbed into the wagon of the train-tram. Each of the three canvas-covered wagons that made up the tram was packed with navvies and their families. Just like a real train, the tram engine blew its whistle to signal it was time to depart, and the excited Christmas shoppers were off. Babies screamed and children pulled on their mothers' skirts as the excitement grew over the prospect of a shopping spree in Ingleton.

'So, what are you going to buy with your first week's wage? Don't go thinking you can spend it all every week, mind. I'm only making an exception this week with it being Christmas.' Molly sat next to Lizzie on the cramped wooden plank that sufficed as a seat on the short trip. 'You'd think they'd clean these wagons out a bit better before using them for us.' Molly peered at her laced-up boots, now covered in the mud that was at the bottom of the wagon.

'I'm going to get Doctor Thistlethwaite an ounce of Kendal Twist for his pipe. I know he smokes that because I saw him unwrapping some the other day, when we were at his house. And of course I'll get you some-thing, Mam, but that's a secret. And some sweets and some . . .' Molly paused for breath, thinking what she could do with her shilling.

'It's going to have to go a long way, is that shilling. Here, I'd better give you another sixpence – mind you don't lose it.' Molly handed Lizzie a silver sixpence from out of her draw-string bag. 'I'll leave you to shop on your own, but we'll meet up for dinner at the pie shop at one, all right?'

'Oh, thanks, Mam. I didn't know how I was going to buy your Christmas present without you seeing and now I can buy Mr Ashwell some snuff. He's been so good with me this week. At times I've felt daft when he's had to show me what to do, but he says I'll soon get used to his ways.'

'I'm glad he's all right with you, but I still think you're in a funny job for a lass.' Molly pulled her skirt from under the bottom of a well-endowed woman and gave her a glare as she did so. 'Some folk have no manners,' she whispered to Lizzie as they both giggled.

The Christmas market at Ingleton was heaving with locals, tradesmen, navvies and their families all buying that little bit extra for the two holiday days. The butcher's stall had unplucked geese hanging by their feet, or if you wanted a live one there were some in a pen behind the stall. There was a display of carcases and joints, with rabbits, pigs' heads and trotters and shoulders of mutton – all tempting fare for Christmas dinner.

It was hard to make yourself heard above the sound of tradesmen touting their wares with shouts of 'Fresh Bread and Cakes for your sweetheart' from the baker competing with local farmers' wives yelling about the quality of their milk, eggs, butter and cheese.

'Remember, I'll meet you at one, outside the pie shop. Lizzie, are you listening? Mind what you're doing – don't talk to anyone you don't know.' Molly pulled her hat tight around her head. 'This blooming weather, you'd think it could stop dry just until we get our shopping. Are you all right then?' She looked at her daughter, who was absorbed in taking in the market scene.

'Yes, I'll meet you at one, I'll keep an eye on the church clock.' Lizzie couldn't wait to go shopping on her own.

Molly watched as she walked away, still dragging her leg a little. But a bit of a limp was nothing; it was a miracle that she was alive. She sighed, it had been quite a year – one she'd rather forget. The sooner Christmas was over and the New Year started, the better. Happen, it would bring better luck with it.

She went over to the butcher and haggled over a piece of ham she intended to cook and share with Roger Thistlethwaite. He'd assured her that Christmas dinner was all in hand and she wasn't to worry, but she felt she had to make some contribution. Then she went on to the draper's and picked out a length of material for Lizzie: a purple woollen fabric that would be both practical and warm. She could soon stitch something together, once she'd convinced her daughter to stand still long enough for measurements.

The shopkeeper wrapped her purchase and she put it in her canvas bag to keep it out of the rain. The bag was getting full now; another few bits and that would be Christmas taken care of. She was smiling at the prospect of lunch with Lizzie as she stepped out of the shop doorway and found herself face to face with Rose Pratt.

Rose put her head down and pretended not to see her.

'Go on then, pretend I'm not here. Trouble is, I am – and whenever you see me or my lass you're going to remember what your lad did to us!' Molly lashed out, still angry at the lengths Rose had gone to, covering her lad's tracks.

Lizzie ran up to her mother, her leg impeding her slightly. 'Sorry I'm late, Mam, I had to wait for my mistletoe. There was a courting couple trying it out and the stallholder got cross with them.'

'I should think so too! They should know better and be decent.' Molly pulled a disapproving face and looked shocked, just to please her daughter, but really she was thinking back to when she was younger and courting Lizzie's dad. The first Christmas they spent together they had shared a loving clinch under the mistletoe.

'I wish I had a beau. No one ever gives me a second glance.' Lizzie gazed wistfully at a couple passing by.

'There'll be time enough for that, my girl. You're only fourteen, the less you know about men the better. They use and abuse you – most of them are only good for one thing, and sometimes they're not any good at that!' Molly snapped at her daughter.

Lizzie had no idea what her mother meant, but she judged now was not the time to ask for an explanation. Instead she followed her mother into the pie shop in silence.

'Pie and mushy peas twice, and two pots of tea – and there had better be a decent bit of meat in them pies, not all tattie and turnip.' Molly gave the young serving girl her instructions and peered out of the steamed-up window. 'This rain's never going to stop. No doubt the beck'll be flooded.'

Lizzie was unwrapping her gifts to show her mother – all bar one, which she kept hidden under the table. 'I've got Doctor Thistlethwaite his baccie . . .' Lizzie placed the long twisted length of brown, almost black Kendal Twist on the table. 'Mr Ashwell his snuff . . . Florrie some sweets, 'cause her dad never buys her anything. And of course I didn't forget you, Mam, but that one's a secret.'

'You've been busy. I think I've got all I need so we'll head home on the next tram. The day's worsening and I want to get home while it's still light, stoke the fire up and put this ham on to boil.' Molly stopped talking as the young lass came back with their dinners, nervously placing the plates in front of Molly as if waiting for a caustic comment. 'Well, it looks all right, so let's get it eaten. It makes a right good change to have something made for you that you've not done anything with yourself.'

Lizzie grinned as her mother tucked into her dinner. She'd never eaten pie like it, the taste was so good. Then again, it was her first time in an eating house with her mother, and that was the biggest thrill.

'We've only just made it back in time, Liz. Look at that water – any deeper and we'd not have made it through.' Molly peered from under the canvas covers at the waters of the River Doe lapping at the wheels and rails of the

196

tram. 'And look up there – that's a new waterfall coming out of that cave's mouth. That'll be all the melted snow.'

Lizzie peered through the lacing of the wagon at the many gushing streams turning into waterfalls as they cascaded down the sides of Whernside and Ingleborough.

'There'll be some damage done if this keeps this up.' Molly shook her head and held on tight as the wagon lurched. 'I'm blinking glad to see that viaduct and journey's end.'

The tram jolted to a halt and the relieved passengers clambered out with their shopping and ran to their homes to find refuge from the rain.

'Put the kettle on, Liz, I'm fair parched. That pie must have had a lot of salt in it. I suppose it was to disguise the old meat.' Molly grinned, she knew damn well that the pie had been excellent, but she needed a ruse to get Lizzie out of the way while she hid her precious parcel of cloth. 'You'll have to go and fill the kettle from the water butt outside.'

Lizzie slung her shawl over her head and scowled as she grabbed the kettle off the top of the stove and went out into the wet again. While the kettle was filling she happened to glance up. What she saw made her drop the kettle and let out a scream.

Molly flew out of the door in a panic. 'What's up? What are you screaming for?' She threw her arms around her daughter, anxiously looking around to see the cause.

'Mam, the lines are moving – all the banking is sliding down.'

Both women stood mesmerized as with a huge rumble the newly formed banks of spoil disintegrated. Within minutes the line had completely disappeared, taking trees, scaffolding and men with it.

The two women stood trembling and holding each other.

'Another few minutes and we'd have been under that, Lizzie. That would have been the end of us. Thank God we're safe – we must be being kept safe for something, me and you.' She kissed her daughter on the head and squeezed her tight.

Others were emerging from their shanties to see what the noise was, and as they registered what had happened and the scale of the disaster, navvies began running through the shanties, shouting for wagons and carts to be brought. Oblivious to the danger and the raging elements, they raced towards the mudslide. The race was on to save those who were trapped underneath it.

'I'd better go to the hospital, Lizzie. There's bound to be lots of casualties coming in after this.' Molly ducked into the hut and grabbed her shawl. 'Will you be all right on your own, pet?'

'Course I will, Mam.' Lizzie smiled bravely. 'And, Mam, I love you.'

'I love you too, pet.' Molly brushed a tear from her cheek. At long last she had won her daughter back.

The smell of the cooking ham had filled the hut all Christmas Eve and now it lay on a plate ready to take over to Doctor Thistlethwaite's.

'It smells good, Mam.' Lizzie picked a little loose bit from the side of the resting ham before her mother slapped her hand.

'You can stop picking at it, Lizzie Mason. There's little enough to go round, without you chewing your way through it.' Molly stoked the stove and grinned at her daughter. 'I don't know what to expect in the morning. I've never had Christmas dinner outside my own family. I hope it's not too posh, like. It can't be, can it? He's only in a hut like us.' Molly pulled her long hair back before pulling her nightclothes over her head. 'Time to get to bed now, else Father Christmas won't come,' she laughed.

'Mam, I'm too old for Father Christmas. There's no such person and you know it.' Lizzie nearly jumped out of her skin as her words were followed by a knock on the door.

'See, you were wrong – he's come early!' Molly joked as she picked up the candle and moved to open the door in her long nightdress. She opened it slightly and shouted out into the night, asking who was there.

A quiet voice answered. 'Sorry, Moll. I thought you were both still up – I saw a light and I just wanted to wish you a happy Christmas.' John was standing on the steps to the hut, a Christmas card in his hand and his face glowing by the light of the storm lantern he was holding.

Molly fell silent. At the sound of his voice her heart missed a beat. No matter how hard she had tried, she couldn't forget the affection and the passion that they had felt for each other. 'Aye, well, you've said it. Now we're away to our beds.' She tried to close the door, but John's foot jammed it open, making her slam it against his foot.

'Please, Molly, it's Christmas. I only want to give you this card and tell you how much I miss you.' John leaned against the door and pleaded with her.

Inside the hut, Lizzie watched her mother leaning against the wooden boards of the door, candle in hand, obviously battling with her feelings.

'Let him in, Ma,' she urged. 'I want to say happy Christmas. It wasn't John's fault what Bob did.' Lizzie wasn't just asking for herself. She wanted to get her mother's feelings out in the open. 'It's Christmas, Ma. Please.'

Molly stepped away from the door and stood quiet as John entered the room.

'Happy Christmas, Lizzie.' He walked over and gave her his Christmas card as she sat on the edge of her bed. 'Happy Christmas, Molly. I miss you. Can't you forgive me? Please.' He strode over to Molly, who didn't flinch as he laid his hand on her arm. He looked into her eyes and saw that she was not going to give him quarter. Then he bowed his head and left.

Molly quietly closed the door after him and said nothing as she blew the candle out and climbed into bed.

'I like John, Ma,' Lizzie whispered into the darkness.

Molly didn't say anything to her daughter but her heart was beating fast. She closed her eyes and thought of his blue eyes and the soft blond hair and the loving smile. She liked him too, but it was her pride that was the problem. Molly had her principles, she'd said what had to be said, and there was no going back. She stared into the darkness of the hut. From outside came the faint sound of carols being sung. Tomorrow would be Christmas Day. This time last year, she had been a happily married woman with a good future to look forward to. Now she didn't know what life held from one day to the next. Fate had been cruel to her, but it was up to her to put things right – and she'd do that for her lass, no matter what.

The rain had finally stopped as Molly and Lizzie made their way to Doctor Thistlethwaite's hut. It stood on the far side of the stream from the workers' shanties, in a little enclave of huts constructed for foremen and other staff deemed important by the Midland Railway, though most of those who could afford to preferred to rent lodgings in the dale. Smoke was rising out of the chimney as the two women knocked shyly on the door, not knowing what to expect.

'Merry Christmas!' Roger Thistlethwaite opened his door and urged them to come in out of the bitter weather. 'Please, sit down, make yourselves comfortable. Here, let me take your shawls.'

Molly and Lizzie smiled at one another as he fussed over them, trying to put them at their ease.

'May I say what a beautiful brooch that is, Molly.' Roger Thistlethwaite admired the little black kitten with paws hanging over a silver horseshoe adorned with white heather as he helped her out of her shawl.

'Lizzie gave me it for Christmas. It's supposed to bring me luck.' Molly smiled and sat down next to the stove, quietly admiring the table that he had laid for dinner.

'Ma got me some material for a new dress. She's going to make it for me – it's purple and lovely.' Lizzie couldn't wait. 'And I've got you this – ' She handed her precious gift of tobacco to him. 'I know you smoke it because I've seen you in the hospital.'

'Why thank you, Lizzie, that's very kind. And thank you, Molly, for the cooked ham – it looks delicious. I'm afraid today I've cheated. You can't really cook in these huts, so Mrs Parker is bringing me all the trimmings that make Christmas from the alehouse. You can see I've managed the goose, but for the rest I'm afraid I'm just a useless man, so I had to rely on someone else's time and expertise.'

Molly and Lizzie looked at the goose. That alone would have been enough for them, so they couldn't imagine what else Mrs Parker might be bringing. The poor woman, carrying things down the wet path to the doctor's. You'd have thought she'd have enough to do, without cooking dinner for them.

'Now, let me see, I think I have a little something for you both.' Roger Thistlethwaite handed Lizzie a package and watched as she ripped it open. 'For my little bookworm, a book. I'm sure you'll enjoy *Wuthering Heights*. It's set in the fells, tells of a heartbreaking love affair.' Roger watched as Lizzie flicked to the first page after caressing the leather-bound edition with love. 'And for my new nurse, a small present with my utmost gratitude for all her help.'

Molly opened the thin box to reveal some white embroidered handkerchiefs with the initial M delicately embroidered on them.

'I can't . . . I can't accept these. They must have cost the earth!' Molly held them in her hand and looked at Roger Thistlethwaite.

'My dear, you must. You are worth so much more to me. Besides, it's just a token at Christmas.' He patted her hand gently. 'A gift from a lonely old man who's glad of the company.' He rose and started to pour out two glasses of sherry. 'Is Lizzie allowed one?' he asked, reaching for a third glass.

Molly looked up from admiring the fine hankies. 'Yes, a small one. It's Christmas, after all.' She smiled fondly at Lizzie, whose nose was buried in her book already. 'Not that she'll notice. Look at her!'

'There's nothing like a good book,' said Roger. 'Reading's to be encouraged.' He sat down and relaxed as the sherry warmed his throat and the view of Molly and her daughter warmed his heart. This was what Christmas was about, sharing it with the people you cared for.

A knock on the door broke the silence that had descended. A moment later Mrs Parker came bustling in with steaming dishes of potatoes and carrots, and to round it all off a huge figgy pudding with sherry sauce. Having placed everything on the table, she thanked the doctor for his payment and hurried away, pulling her damp skirts up around her ankles as she went down the hut steps.

'She's a good woman, is Helen Parker. Pity her husband doesn't realize it. The times she's told me she's bumped into something, when I know he's used her as a punch bag. He's nothing but a brute. One day he'll get his comeuppance.' Doctor Thistlethwaite turned away from the window and waved his guests to take a seat at the table. Then he picked up the carving knife and began slicing the goose as Lizzie and Molly looked on in wonder at all the festive fare laid out in front of them.

'He hits Florrie as well,' said Lizzie. 'I've seen her with a black eye. And he broke her tooth.' Lizzie held her plate out for a slice of goose.

'If it weren't for Helen, nothing would get done. It's her that keeps the Welcome Inn going. She's a good cook and folk like her. Henry's too busy being cock-of-the-midden, handing out pay to the navvies only to take it off them in his bar.' Molly tried not to drool as she helped herself to roast potatoes.

'Mr Ashwell doesn't like him. He reckons he's up to something. I heard him saying so to Fred that works on the plans.' Lizzie added her four-penn'orth, helping herself to pickled cabbage as she did so.

'Now, Lizzie, you shouldn't repeat what goes on at work. It's none of our business.' Molly stopped her in her tracks, not wanting the doctor to think they gossiped.

'It'll not go any further than these four walls, so don't you worry, Lizzie. Mr Ashwell is a good judge of character, and he's probably right about Henry Parker.' Roger Thistlethwaite refilled Molly's glass and smiled. 'But Mrs Parker has done us proud and is to be congratulated.' He lifted his glass up. 'To Mrs Parker and my clever new nurse, Molly.' He smiled as Molly blushed and Lizzie giggled. It was so good to spend Christmas with a family he would dearly like to make his own.

14

The New Year blasted its way in with icy winds from the north and biting sleet that stung the cheeks with its icy fingers.

Between the squalling showers workmen for the Midland had been busy all week erecting a new hut for the Bradford missionaries to come and show the heathen navvies the error of their unholy ways.

'Bye, they look half-frozen.' Molly watched the workmen through the frosted windows of the hospital. 'We must be badly in need of some religion for the Midland to be building a hut in this weather.'

'Some of us might be,' Starchy Drawers commented as she walked past with bandages. 'Have you seen to Mr Bibby? He needs his bandages changing.'

The thaw in her attitude towards Molly had not lasted long. The news that Roger and his new nurse had dined together on Christmas Day had not gone down well.

'Yes, and I've emptied the pee-pots, so you needn't ask me to do that.' Molly folded her arms and glared at her would-be rival. 'Look, madam, I told you when

I first came: I'm not interested in the doctor. He's too old and I'm not clever enough for the likes of him. He's a nice man, but I don't want a man in my life. I'm happy as I am, independent.'

The snooty nurse merely put her nose up and walked away scowling. Molly shook her head and went over to check the paraffin heater at the end of the hut. She was hoping to find it in need of refilling: she'd have welcomed an excuse to go outside for some respite from the atmosphere on the ward.

'Morning, ladies. How are my patients this morning?' said Doctor Thistlethwaite cheerily. The smell of his pipe gave his presence away before he was through the door.

'Morning, Roger. Let me take your coat.' Nurse Thompson grabbed the doctor's coat, but he barely noticed as he set off down the ward in Molly's direction. Instead of coming out with a caustic comment, as she would if the doctor hadn't been there, Nurse Thompson smiled insincerely, took some clean sheets from the pile and followed.

Knowing that if she stayed she'd probably say something she'd regret, Molly put on a saintly smile of her own and informed the doctor she was stepping outside for a breath of fresh air. Outside slushy heavy flakes of sleet were falling, covering every surface with a grey sludge that seeped into boots and clung to clothes, leaving you chilled to the bone. She sheltered under the eaves and watched as a little man dressed in black from head to foot, with a sharp-featured face peeking out from under a wide-brimmed hat, made his way over the stone packhorse bridge. His feet skidded from under him a time or two as he trudged through the snow, and each time he'd pause and look in the direction of the hospital, as if exasperated at the effort required to reach his goal. Molly grinned wickedly at the sight: if the Reverend Tiplady was to survive in Batty Green, he'd do well to buy himself a pair of strong boots. Those polished town shoes wouldn't last a minute in these conditions.

Finally he made it to the hospital and stood panting, trying to catch his breath and regain his dignity – no easy feat with his shoes scrabbling for purchase on the icy wooden steps.

'Is this the hospital, my child?' The words seemed to burst out of his chest as if he was delivering a sermon from the pulpit.

'It is, sir. You must be the Reverend Tiplady – we're expecting you.' Molly bobbed and stood her ground as he climbed the steps.

'Well, lead on then! Get me out of this Devil-sent weather.' He held on to the banister of the top step for dear life as Molly opened the door to the hospital and ushered him in.

'This weather is foul,' the Reverend muttered as he stamped his shoes free of slush and shook the sleet from his hat. 'I never thought I'd say it, but I'm missing the smoking mill chimneys of Bradford. At least they offered some shelter and raised the temperature a few degrees.' Having salvaged his Bible from the pocket, he thrust his coat into Molly's hands.

She stifled a snigger as, in his haste to greet Doctor Thistlethwaite, he almost slipped on the wet wooden floor.

'Reverend Tiplady, I presume.' Doctor Thistlethwaite shook hands with the little man.

'May God be with you, sir. I've come to save souls – and it appears I'm not a minute too soon, judging from the look of some of these men in the camps. It's a hot-bed of sin and vice from what I see, and the women are no better: swilling gin with babes on their hips. The Devil is a fearful tempter.'

Doctor Thistlethwaite frowned. The Reverend's preaching had only served to remind him why he had no time for religion. 'I'd be grateful if you could bear in mind that this is a hospital and we like to keep the patients calm and quiet. If you could just say a few words of hope and healing to each of them, I'm sure they would appreciate that. We only have the five patients at the moment and Frank Bibby might be grateful for a blessing – he's rather too ill for a sermon.'

Having issued his instructions, Roger Thistlethwaite returned to writing up his notes, politely disregarding the fire-breathing preacher.

'I'll show you around, Reverend,' simpered Nurse Thompson.

Molly was only too happy not to be lumbered with the task. She'd come across the Reverend's sort before: too quick by half to judge a person at first sight.

'Where are you staying? I do hope that you're not travelling every day from Ingleton in this weather?' Nurse

209

Thompson enquired as she took his arm to guide him to the first patient.

'I'm staying with the God-fearing family of Rose Pratt – wonderful woman, has a heart of gold, and so upset over the loss of her selfish son, despite his having carried out the worst sin of all by committing suicide.'

Molly had to bite her tongue. She wanted to scream at the pompous preacher, tell him that the worst sin Bob Pratt committed was not hanging himself but trying to rape and kill her Lizzie. She was stopped by Roger Thistlethwaite shooting her a warning glance. He'd heard the gossip about Bob Pratt. Laying his hand gently on her arm, he whispered, 'They only hear what they want to hear.' She could only nod and turn away, busying herself checking the medicines.

'Bugger off, you bloody black omen of death! I don't want your Protestant hands on me! I'm not one of yours so you needn't come near me!' Irish Tam shouted at the approaching minister. 'I'd rather rot in hell than have you lay hands on me, you bastard.'

Molly went over to Tam and said a few quiet words to calm him down, then positioned herself at the end of his bed to prevent the Reverend coming any closer. 'Mr Shaughnessy's Catholic, as you may have gathered. I don't think he'll appreciate your visit. As a matter of fact, a lot of the navvies that work on the line are Catholics who've come here from Ireland or Scotland to find work building the railways. They're good people with their own religion, so I know you'll respect them for it.' She pushed her auburn hair back defiantly, as if daring the Reverend to come anywhere near her patient or argue with her defence of the navvies who worked on the line. Her eyes twinkled at the prospect of a run-in with this loud-mouthed preacher. She'd have been only too happy to tell him that the hard-drinking navvies' sins paled into insignificance compared with the sins that had been committed in the 'God-fearing' house he was staying in.

'All of us will meet our maker eventually, regardless of which house we worship in. Then we will have to admit to our sins,' Reverend Tiplady intoned. He eyed Molly with suspicion. Here was one who was in need of salvation, no question. Silently resolving to find out more about this outspoken nurse who didn't know her place, he turned to Nurse Thompson and demanded his coat and hat. Then he walked out into the bitter day, as best his shiny shoes would let him, without so much as a backward glance.

15

Lizzie approached the house whistling and with a smile on her face. The whistling stopped when she opened the door and found her mother home.

'Hello, Mam. I didn't think you'd be back yet,' she said coyly.

'You seem happy. Had a good day?' Molly peeled the last potato and dropped it into the pan on the top of the stove, wiped the knife on her apron and pulled a chair up to the table.

'I like my job, Ma. It's interesting, there's always something new going on and everyone's so nice to me. Especially George. George is always saying nice things. He says I'm good at spotting mistakes. George reckons I've brightened up the office since I started.'

'And who might George be?' Molly smiled, noticing how Lizzie's face lit up at the mention of George.

'He's Mr Ashwell's son. He's eighteen, Mam.' Lizzie would have liked to tell her mother how her stomach filled with butterflies when he looked at her and how she couldn't wait to go to work in a morning, just so she could see his smile, and that little frown of concentration he wore when he was studying the plans.

'Well, mind you make sure George behaves himself.' Molly looked stern for a second and then smiled. Her precious daughter was growing up so fast. Clearly George was her first sweetheart. 'It's nice to have a special friend.'

The mention of special friends jogged Lizzie's memory: 'John came in today, Mam. He said I was to tell you that his Mike has had a little girl.'

'Does he think I care? I've washed my hands of that family.' Molly cast her eyes around the table, as if trying to find something else to do.

'Mam, you don't mean that! You know you like John, and I know you miss him.' She knew too that her mother would want to hear all the news she had to tell about John Pratt: 'He came in to order more dynamite. They've hit a hard patch in the tunnel and it's taking some blasting. He wanted rods as well, because he's been given the go-ahead to drill and place the blast. He says he'll make more money doing the drilling as well, now there's only two men at home.'

Molly went quiet. 'Next time he comes in, tell him to take care. He's just daft enough to blow himself up – not that he'll be missed.'

Lizzie knew her mother didn't mean it. John's cheery voice was missed by them both.

'Mam, you'd be in tears, you know you would. The two of you're best friends, but you're too stubborn to—'

'When I want your advice, I'll ask for it, Miss Know-

213

it-all.' Molly tasted the stew, seeing if it needed anything added. 'Did he say anything about his lodger? I bet the Reverend Tiplady isn't going down too well with him.'

'Oh, I know him! He's horrible. I met him once when I went to Ingleton with Ma Pratt. He frightened me, and even she didn't seem to like him much. He's not living across there, is he?'

'He is. That stupid woman has made her hut his home.' Molly shook her head. 'Rose Pratt and her bloody religion! Here, pass me two plates, Liz – let's get these tatties out and have supper.'

'Tell me, Rose, who's the ginger-haired nurse that works at the hospital? She seems very wilful and opinionated.' The Reverend Tiplady broke off tucking into his mutton and cabbage, gravy dribbling down his chin, to interrogate his host.

Both John and Jim sent warning glances in Rose's direction. Both knew that once she started telling him her views, she'd never shut up.

'That would be Molly Mason. She lives in a hut across the way. She's—'

'Have another piece of meat, Reverend,' John butted in, desperate to stop her gossiping.

'I don't mind if I do. Now, this Molly, why is she living in this place?'

'Her husband worked on the viaduct until he had an accident and died. Now she's managed to talk herself into a job in the hospital. She's a bit—' Rose stopped in her tracks as both her men glared at her. 'She's a bit rough and ready, but a lovely woman once you get to know her.' Rose daren't say what she really thought. She knew by the looks John and Jim were giving her that there would be hell to pay if she did.

'Hmmph,' snorted the Reverend, unconvinced. 'Well, the Lord works in mysterious ways. She must have some qualities else the good doctor would not have her working in the hospital.' He belched loudly and mopped the greasy gravy up with the crusty bread that was left.

'We all have our weaknesses, Reverend,' said John, forcing a polite smile to his face. Eager to escape the preaching of his mother and their guest, he excused himself from the table and went to put on his coat. He couldn't stand being locked in the house with all that hypocrisy a minute longer.

He walked aimlessly until he came to the small bridge that crossed the source of the River Ribble. At this stage it was no more than a stream that gurgled over the flat limestone bedrock, a far cry from the swollen river that made its way out to the sea at Preston. It was a frosty night and the stars were twinkling bright and sharp in the clear sky. John made out the shape of the Plough and the Great Bear, and took a long drag on his pipe as he leaned back against the wall contemplating his life.

He badly wanted to win back Molly's love. Ever since the first day he'd seen her, that wild hair blowing in the wind as she hung the washing out, she'd been the only woman for him. Yet here he was, the only son left at home, when all he wanted to do was escape the confines of the nest and fly to the arms of the woman he loved. Trouble was, she refused to believe that he loved her. Somehow he had to find a way to prove to her that they were meant for each other. In the meantime, he would go on loving her as long as those stars in the sky kept twinkling. He would not give up. Whatever it took, by God one day she would be his.

'Mrs Mason, could I ask you to work a few extra hours this evening?'

Molly and Nurse Thompson were busily rolling bandages. There were a lot of them to get through, and Molly was so intent on finishing the task that she didn't even look up at the sound of Doctor Thistlethwaite's voice. 'Of course, Doctor,' she said, not registering anything unusual about the request and oblivious to Roger hovering nervously as he awaited her response. 'Was there anything particular you wanted me to do?'

'No, no. I just wanted to ask you some questions to see if you are up to scratch.' He coughed awkwardly. 'Nurse Thompson, there's no need for you to stay.' Having said what he had come to say, Doctor Thistlethwaite hurried away, leaving them to their work.

'Molly, forgive me: I had to make up an excuse so that I could catch you on your own.' Roger Thistlethwaite paced the floorboards as he addressed her. 'You see, I'm not getting any younger, I've led a selfish life and I suppose I'm still being selfish in what I'm doing now . . .' He hesitated, struggling to find the right words.

'What I'm trying to say is that time is running out on me and I've realized that plants and books are no substitute for the finer things in life.'

'Roger, what's this about?' asked Molly. She had never seen Roger Thistlethwaite so flustered.

'You see, when Lizzie and yourself came and shared Christmas with me, I realized what I'd been missing all my life. What I'm trying to say is . . . Molly Mason, will you be my wife?' He turned, his almond eyes pleading with her over his glasses.

'I . . . don't know what to say. Did I hear you right? Did you ask me to marry you?' Molly was shocked, the last thing she'd expected was to be asked for her hand in marriage.

'Yes, I did. I know it's a shock for you, but I can't stand looking at you any longer and you not being mine. I used to see you laughing with that John Pratt and I wished that you would look at me the way you looked at him. Now that he's no longer around, I'm taking my chance and asking you to marry me.'

'I don't . . . I can't . . . I can't marry you, I'm not your sort – I'm a navvy's woman, not a doctor's wife. Folk would laugh at you. I'm not refined enough for your sort.' Molly rose from her chair, sending it tipping back on to the wooden floorboards with a clatter that woke one of the patients, who moaned quietly in protest.

'What would we care? I love you, and I'd be a good father to Lizzie. She's a bright girl, we'd make the perfect family.' Roger Thistlethwaite pulled on her sleeve, urging her to reconsider.

'Roger, there's just one thing wrong: I don't love you. I could never love you, you're not my kind. I'm sorry if I'm hurting you, but it would never work. I'm too independent in my ways to become a lady that takes high tea. I'm sorry, it wouldn't be right. I'm truly, truly sorry but you're not for me.' She patted his hand and looked at him twiddling his glasses in his hands, avoiding meeting her eyes. Then she picked up her shawl and turned away.

Doctor Thistlethwaite gazed after her as she walked the length of the ward, through the door and out into the night. He should have known better. What would a spirited woman like that want with a crusty old bachelor like him? He hung his head and turned to blow out the oil lamp at his desk.

From out of the dark, a voice whispered: 'Never mind, Doc. You couldn't have kept up with her anyway – she'd have killed you in the first week!'

The doctor shook his head. That Dan Oversby was definitely on the mend.

16

The snow that had blighted the early winter months had disappeared with the coming of the New Year. Under pressure to make up for lost time, the navvies were hard at work, wrapped up in several layers of clothes as they defied the bitter wind and damp conditions to complete construction of the viaduct and tunnel. The line of scaffolding now extended even further across the valley, and gangs of men worked to heave into place the huge foundation blocks, hewn from the granite of Littledale.

John made his way up to Blea Moor tunnel following a path that ran alongside an icy stream fringed by icicle fingers of frozen grass and bracken. Occasionally the stream fed into pools that reflected the clear blue of the sky; beautiful to look at, but breathtakingly freezing if you fell in. The clanking of picks and shovels followed him along the cutting as track gangs shovelled soil and ballast for the rails to be laid on.

'Another bloody day!' a work colleague greeted John as he half-ran down the steep face of the banking into the tunnel entrance.

The small cluster of huts known as Jerusalem was just visible. It was here that the tunnel men lived, the ones who built the airshafts and the blasters who set the charges. John had joined this elite group. The work was dangerous, but he was hell-bent on making enough money to break free of his mother. He'd put up with being treated like a child and forced to live a life of hypocrisy long enough.

As he entered the tunnel he nodded to his work-mates, most of whom were gathered around a brazier. It was the best place to be on a day like today, with the clouds moving in around the tunnel head, threatening to obscure the newly built huts from view.

'Watch what you're doing with that dynamite!' John shouted at the youngest member of the crew. 'Don't put it too near that bloody fire, else we'll all know about it.' He shook his head as the young man stood cursing him under his breath. Frozen dynamite wasn't the easiest stuff to handle, but trying to thaw it out by placing it near the fire was a dangerous practice that might result in the explosives becoming unstable. 'Don't stand there cursing me – do as I bloody well say!' John roared as he entered the lantern-lit hole.

'Now then, John, we've a bit of bother this morning,' said the ganger. 'We've hit a right bad patch of granite, it's taking some getting through.' The two of them walked over to where men were shovelling debris into a cart that was sinking lower and lower as the stones and rubble were piled in. The horses, standing in harness ready to haul the back-breaking load, looked around with wild eyes. They knew it wouldn't be long before they were whipped into action. The ganger indicated a seam of rock: 'I think if we drill in deep here and here, and place a large charge here at this junction of rocks, we should crack it.'

'Aye, I think I can do that,' said John. 'But it'll take a bit of doing. Best empty the tunnel first – I don't mind blowing myself up, but I'm not taking anyone with me.' He lifted up his pick and started hacking at a crevice, widening it so that he could drill a hole deep into the seam.

'Right, I'll clear them out now and leave you to it.' With that the ganger began ordering the crew to leave, slapping the horses' haunches to get them to move out too.

'Everyone out! And keep out!' he bellowed, making his way to the entrance where the men were warming themselves.

'Need we shift, boss?' said the men, reluctant to leave the warmth of their fire. 'We're far enough away here, right?'

'Nay, you'll be all right here, lads. If it blows all the way back here, the whole mountain'll come down!' He walked away, the sound of their laughter echoing in his ears as he carried on up the banking side.

John drilled the hole deep into the granite face, then carefully padded it with dynamite. When he was done, he set the fuse, running it half the length of the tunnel. His fingers trembled as he used a burning candle wick to light it, and as the spark flared and hissed its way along the ruse he took off, running as fast as his feet would carry him in the direction of daylight.

Lungs bursting, wincing from the pain of running on her bad leg, Lizzie tore along the track to the hospital. She'd flown out of the surveying hut as soon as she heard his name mentioned, knowing that she must tell her mother immediately.

'Mam! Mam!' she yelled as she climbed the steps to the hospital. Still yelling, she burst through the door and stumbled the length of the ward until she reached her mother. Gasping for breath, she told her, 'Mam, one of the runners just came down from the tunnel – there's been an accident, they think John's dead!'

Molly dropped the tray she was carrying. The blood drained from her face and her hands flew to her mouth. Not again, not again, not John, not when she hadn't told him how she truly felt. She tore off her apron and head covering, thrusting them into Lizzie's hand without a word as she ran out of the hospital. Stumbling on the uneven ground, she ran on past the shanties, past the scaffolding, past navvies making their way to the tunnel to join the rescue effort. On and on she ran, even though every breath hurt her lungs, desperate to get to the man she loved. Tears were streaming down her face as she neared the tunnel entrance and half-fell down the banking to the place where they were bringing out the dead and injured.

She walked past bodies covered with coats or whatever else the men could find to cover the damage done by the blast. She passed men drenched in blood and crying out in pain. She walked between them, pulling on the sleeves of the men who were bringing out the victims, the ones who were attending the wounded, asking them if they had seen John. Their only response was a sad shake of the head. Then she went back to where the corpses lay, lifting the covers and checking their faces. The last body was so badly damaged it was unrecognizable, just a tuft of blond hair remained. She got down by the side of the corpse and wailed, doubled up with the pain of her loss. He was gone, her true love, her one hope of happiness. On her knees in the dust, past caring what kind of spectacle she made of herself, she used her sleeve to dry her eyes and wipe her nose.

'Now if that had been Lizzie doing that, there would have been hell to pay!' said a familiar voice above her.

She looked up, her tear-filled eyes widening as she saw the man coming out of the tunnel. 'You're alive! I thought you were dead – I thought this was you!' Molly didn't know whether to laugh or cry. All she knew was that John was here, alive. And now she knew just how much she loved him.

'Aye, I'm here, but that silly bugger isn't. I told him not to warm his dynamite next to the fire and now look what's happened. My bloody charge didn't go off, but his certainly did. What are you doing here anyway? You'll be needed in the hospital when these poor devils are taken back down.' John came and put his arm around her.

'What do you think I'm here for? I thought you were dead.' Molly wiped her eyes, angry at the question and angry at herself being caught shedding tears. Then she smiled, overcome with relief. 'I thought I'd lost you.'

'So I do mean something to you.' John grinned back at her.

'I thought you were dead. I could never have lived with myself if this had been you. And Lizzie would have been so upset – she worships you.' She lifted her sleeve again to wipe her eyes.

'Here, borrow my hankie, for pity's sake. Nurses shouldn't wipe their noses on their sleeves.' John pulled his hankie out of his pocket and passed it to her. 'I take it we're back to being mates then? You know I've done nothing else but think of you all these months.' He pulled her to him and looked deep into her eyes. 'Molly, listen – just listen for once. This is all because of my bloody mother, she's always to be in control whether she's right or wrong. I'm standing up to her now. I've been saving up so I can make it on my own. I can't get out fast enough, especially with that bloody preacher hanging around.' Taking her by the hand, he led her to the side of the workings, pulling her down to sit next to him on the damp grass.

Molly wiped her eyes with his grey hankie, sniffling as she replied, 'You've got to get away from your mother, John. She rules that house. Even your father won't stand up to her.'

'Oh, I don't know about my father, he can stand his ground. You should have seen him the night we found

224

out our Bob had died. He could hardly stand, he hit the bottle so hard. My mother didn't dare say a word.'

He broke off to light his pipe. The rescuers were now loading the bodies on to a cart. He watched in silence for a moment and then said, 'That churchyard's going to be full with us lot before this is done. But in a few years we'll have been forgotten, and there'll be only the railway to remind folk that we were ever here.'

'I'd better go. I'll be needed at the hospital.' Molly sniffed and stood up. 'Will you come and see us? Lizzie really misses you, and in all honesty, she's not the only one. It's been a bloody long winter and I could do with a bit of sun to creep back into my life.' Molly blushed. She couldn't bring herself to say that she loved him – it wasn't her way.

'I'll come around. I've missed Lizzie, too. I see her sometimes in the boss's office, but she daren't talk.'

Molly nodded, reached out as if to touch him but seemed uncertain, almost shy. Picking up her skirts, she turned and hurried back down the path to Batty Green.

He watched her for a good ten minutes until she was out of sight. It felt good to have her back. She might be a bit of a rough diamond, but he loved that woman. She was kind and good-hearted and would fight for those she loved. One day he'd marry her – and to hell with his mother!

'You see, Mrs Pratt – or may I call you Rose? After all, I'm beginning to feel like one of the family.'

Jim Pratt lifted his eyebrows at the over-familiarity

of the minister. In Jim's opinion it was high time the bugger cleared off to a home of his own.

'There's no structure to the living up here. It's a free-for-all of drinking and gambling, not to mention fornication and children being born out of wedlock. Batty Green is a veritable breeding ground of sin – the Devil's own playground!' Tobias Tiplady thumped his fist hard on to the table, making the spoons and forks rattle with the force.

'Is your hut nearly ready, Reverend?' Jim Pratt lowered his paper and glared at his wife as he put the question. It was high time he had a bit of peace in his own home, instead of having to put up with the feverish lecturing of this overzealous preacher.

'Mr Ashwell says it will be complete by the end of the week. However the brethren and I will need someone to cook for us while we go about God's work. You can't fight the Devil on an empty stomach! So my brothers won't join me until I've employed a cook. I was thinking I might find someone suitable by asking at the market in Ingleton this Saturday.'

'You needn't do that, Reverend – I'll cook for you all. It would be my privilege to keep you all fed. After all, there's only Jim and me now. Our John's hardly ever here. So don't you be hiring any young bit of a thing – lasses today can't cook.' Ignoring the thunderous expression on her husband's face, Rose continued: 'What's another few tatties and dumplings in the pot, Father, when they are going to such good, God-fearing people?'

Jim shook his paper yet again. 'What indeed?' he muttered sarcastically.

'Splendid! Splendid! I'll pay you, of course, although the ministry doesn't provide a vast allowance to support our well-being, I'm afraid.' His rat-like features twitched in a smirk at the thought of getting a full stomach for a minimal outlay.

'Don't you worry about that,' said Rose. 'Money will not come into it. I'll be doing the Lord's bidding in my own way. Another cup of tea, Reverend?' She waddled over to the kettle and filled the teapot.

Jim closed his newspaper and folded it noisily. He'd be having words with Rose later. The saying 'poor as a church mouse' did not ring true where Tobias Tiplady was concerned. If Rose insisted on cooking for him and his followers, then this 'mouse' had better pay, else he'd get flattened like the squeaking rat that he was. He got to his feet, put on his jacket and muffler and announced, 'I'm off out.'

'Now then, Father, what are you doing out here in t' dark?' John, arriving home at the end of a long day, was surprised to find Jim Pratt sitting on the steps to their hut.

'I've had enough, lad. That bloody Tiplady, why if he's a man of God then I'm the man in the moon. He's nothing but a self-serving, sanctimonious leech, taking advantage of folk in need. And your mother's too blind to see it.' Jim kicked the step, swearing under his breath.

'Aye, you'll get no argument from me. But he can't

be here much longer, surely. His hut's nearly finished. Come away, let's go and have a pint together – Mother will never know, she's too busy saving souls.'

'Aye, well, it'll be her soul that takes the most saving out of the lot of us,' sighed Jim, reaching for John's hand and allowing himself to be helped up off the steps. 'She's always up to something, is your mother. You'll not believe this: she's only gone and wangled herself the job of feeding Tiplady and his brethren, without so much as a by your leave from me – not that I have any say in owt nowadays. But I'll tell her in the morning that they can pay for their own bloody food. I'll not have her spending my hard-earned money on that bugger and his cronies, even if it means I burn in hell. At least it'll be bloody warm there, not like this dump.' Jim slapped his son on the back. 'Come on, let's make it a pint or two, we'll soon shift the little bugger if we come home drunk – he'll not like that!'

By the time they got to the Welcome Inn, Jim and his eldest were laughing and chatting the way they used to before the business with Bob soured things.

They took their pints to the snug and settled themselves in, looking around contentedly. 'Do you know, Father, when that railway's built I'd like a place like this. A good wife behind the bar, children running around my feet, and my own business,' said John, licking the froth off his lip.

'Then go for it, lad. Don't let your mother boss you – she's had her own way too long. Get yourself across to that Mason lass. Bye, she's a feisty one and will lead you a dance, but she's a good woman and fellows will always turn their heads when you've that on your arm. Besides, you've a ready-made family with that Lizzie. She's a grand one, is little Liz.' Jim pulled on his pipe and acknowledged a workmate across the bar.

'I didn't think you knew about Molly and me.' John looked at his father.

'Give over, lad! I wasn't born yesterday. You were always skulking across the way, and she was the talk of the viaduct gang yesterday after she ran all the way to the tunnel mouth to make sure you were alive. There wasn't a man up that scaffolding that didn't want to be you! Just be canny, though, and don't get her in the family way like your daft brother did with his lass. Between us, we'll manage to talk your mother around.' Jim raised his glass at his son and got up from his seat. 'Just off to catch up with Ginger over there. Let me know when you're off home.'

John watched as his father patted his mate on the back and sat down for a natter. Jim never ceased to amaze him. He barely said two words to anyone at home, yet he noticed everything and never let on. If it weren't for the fact he'd been born in Durham, he'd have been the very epitome of a true Yorkshireman: 'Hear all, see all – and say nowt.'

17

'John!' Lizzie ran to the door and threw her arms around his waist.

'Now don't let young George Ashwell see you doing that, else he'll be having words with me. He's set his cap at you good and true, if you ask me.' John could hardly get through the doorway, Lizzie's grip on him was so tight.

'You're only joshing, he doesn't think anything of me.' Lizzie blushed and pretended to be coy as she pulled on John's hand, leading him to a seat next to the fire. 'Mam said we had a visitor tonight but she wouldn't tell me who it was.' She took John's cap and hung it on the sneck behind the door.

'If I'd told you, there'd have been no end to it.' Molly laid the table and smiled at John, back in his rightful place next to the fire. 'Pour John a drink then, I didn't get a jug of ale from the inn for nothing.' Molly stepped back from the table, making sure everything was perfect.

Lizzie poured from the heavy jug into the earthenware beaker and watched as John took a long sip.

'That's grand, been looking forward to that all day – and your mother's cooking.' He beamed at both women. 'So, what've you two been up to today? Lizzie, what great plans have you been making for the building of this railway?'

'Well, Mr Ashwell says that the gradient's too—'

'Lizzie, what have I told you? What's said in that cabin stops there. It's not for us to know.' Molly pulled her up sharp.

'Moll, it was my fault, I shouldn't have asked her,' John cut in. 'I ought to have known better. What I meant to ask was: what's George had to say today?' John grinned, trying to tease Lizzie out of the sulk that was looming on her brow.

'Aye, well, that's not much better! The boss's son with his eye on my lass – I've told her to keep him at arm's length. None of them shenanigans, she's still only a bairn.' Molly mashed the potatoes with fervour and dished them out on to three plates, trying to hide the grey lumps that were always present in her mash and hoping that John would not notice.

'Molly Mason, I've missed your loving words and your winning ways, you miserable old woman.' John stood up and kissed her hard on the lips while she stood at the table with wooden spoon and potato pan in hand.

Taken completely by surprise, Molly gawped for a moment and then blustered: 'I'm only telling it as it is. And you can bloody well behave yourself, else you'll get them enamel dishes to wash.' Turning away, she smiled to herself, abandoning all pretence of being angry. It was good to have John back at her table.

'How come your mother let you out to play then?' Molly's sarcastic question made Lizzie splutter on a mouthful of potato.

'She doesn't know I'm here. She's too busy ordering them missionary do-gooders about. I doubt she's even had time to make my father a warm supper tonight. That'll not go down with my old fellow so well.' John scraped his plate clean, relishing the warm supper Molly had prepared for him. 'She's besotted by that black crow, Tiplady. Him and his entire hellfire-and-brimstone gang. I didn't think it could get any worse than having him living under the same roof, but me mam seems to be at his beck and call day and night now they've moved into their own lodgings. Father's about ready to throw a fit.'

'From what I see of Reverend Tiplady, he's an arrogant so-and-so who has no idea how tough it is to survive up here. Close your ears, our Lizzie, 'cause you haven't heard me say this so you don't repeat it, do you hear? I reckon the reason they're here is because the big bosses in Leeds think religion would do us good. Bloody cheek! They'd do better to look after our bodies instead of our bloody souls. They should see what it's like at the hospital on a bad day – one look at a man's arm hanging off or a mangled leg and they'd be running off with their tails between their legs,' Molly scowled.

'Mam, stop it. Mr Ashwell knows what happens,' said Lizzie, anxious to put in a good word for her employer.

'Happen he does. But does he tell them in charge? And do they give a damn? There's two sorts in this world, Lizzie: them that work and no matter what they do they'll never get no better, and them that sit on their backsides all day telling folk like us what to do. They'll never get their hands dirty nor have to scrimp and save for their next meal. They use folk for their advantage – don't you ever forget that, my lass. Just think on that when the young George is winking at you, because he's after something and he'll not be paying for it.'

'Molly, you're a hard woman. George is a grand lad. He might be the boss's son, but he's a good 'un. His father's brought him up well, and from what I hear, his mother is an ex-mill lass who's come from nothing. Your trouble, Molly Mason, is that you know far too much for a woman. You need a good fella to take you in hand.' John leaned back in his chair, balancing it on two legs while he ran his thumbs under his braces.

Molly, passing behind him with the dirty plates on her way to the sink, gave the chair a quick shove with her free hand, sending John sprawling on the floor.

'When I've found him, I'll let you know,' Molly chuckled and Lizzie joined in the laughter as John, nursing his wounded dignity, picked himself up.

'That wasn't fair, I was only sticking up for Lizzie.' John sat back down, his face red.

'Nay, you should know by now, Lizzie takes after her mother: we can stand our ground, it's the fellas in our lives that cause the bother.' Molly wiped her hands

233

on her pinny and kissed John softly on the top of his blond hair.

'Mam . . . do you have to? At least wait until I've gone to bed!'

'Hark at you, Lizzie Mason! Her as makes eyes at George over the desk all day! You should practise what you preach, missy. Why, you're no better that than Tiplady.'

All three laughed, glad to be in one another's company again. It had been too long since they'd laughed this way.

Nurse Thompson and Doctor Thistlethwaite were deep in conversation, heads bowed and whispering. Molly was too far away to hear what they were saying but she kept an eye on them as she tucked in the sheets around her patient. Nurse Thompson had been smiling all day, something that was highly unusual. Eyes still fixed on the couple, Molly tucked the bottom of the sheet in, lifting the mattress up and dropping it down heavily – causing the patient to let out a yelp of pain.

'Hey! Mind what you're bloody doing – I came in with my foot to be mended, not bloody broken again!'

Molly apologized to her upset patient and stood with arms folded at the bottom of his bed. That was it! She'd seen one flashy grin too many from Starchy Drawers. Unable to stand the suspense any longer, Molly walked up to the pair of them.

'Go on then, if I'm out of a job, get on with it. I can't do with all the whispering and smiles.' She glared at them, waiting for an answer.

'Sorry, Molly, what are you referring to? Nurse Thompson and I haven't mentioned you once. I'm sorry if we gave you that impression.' Doctor Thistlethwaite stumbled over his words and blushed.

'Tell her, Roger! Oh, tell her, please.' Gladys Thompson pulled on the doctor's sleeve and practically squealed the words.

'I don't think now is quite the right . . .' Roger Thistlethwaite stumbled.

'We're getting married! We're getting married in a month's time – isn't it wonderful?' Gladys Thompson was beside herself. She giggled like a schoolgirl and kissed the embarrassed Roger on the cheek. 'Yes, he's asked me to marry him. Of course, it was only to be expected. After all, we are of the same class,' she added, her snooty demeanour returning.

Molly smiled with relief. She'd been convinced that she was about to be dismissed.

'Congratulations, I'm sure you will both be very happy and that you'll make the perfect couple. You have so much in common.' Molly noticed that Roger couldn't look her in the eye. She would have dearly loved to tell Starchy Drawers that he'd asked her first and was only settling for second best because she'd turned down his proposal, but she didn't want to upset Roger, and even Nurse Gladys deserved to have a bit of happiness – a commodity that was in short supply in this godforsaken place.

Besides, she had her John back and that was all that mattered.

18

'Well, I suppose if your family is ill, you'll have to return to Bradford. It's unfortunate that you have only stayed with us such a short time. Of course, I'll have to inform the Missionary Society of your decision.' Reverend Tiplady scowled with displeasure at his assistant. If it were down to him, he'd have insisted that the man stay. It was most inconvenient his leaving now. He ought to be ashamed of himself, allowing a bout of winter influenza to stand in the way of his calling.

The young missionary, red-eyed and sneezing violently, thanked the Reverend for his consideration, picked up his few belongings and set off for the train station at Skipton.

'That's a shame, Reverend. He was such a nice young man.' Rose Pratt stopped sweeping and came to stand shoulder to shoulder with her idol, watching as the young missionary scurried out of the missionary hut and off down the track. In addition to cooking for the brethren, she'd taken on the role of Tobias Tiplady's housekeeper. After all, the hut had few furnishings and keeping it tidy didn't take too much of her time.

'God works in mysterious ways, Mrs Pratt. Perhaps his calling was not as strong as it should be.'

'I think he missed his family. It's not easy up here, if you're a good family man.' Rose plumped up the straw mattress that had been the young missionary's bed and rearranged the bedding. 'I'm not changing this bedding, he's only slept in it a week.'

Tobias Tiplady grunted and walked to his desk in the far corner of his new hut.

'It sounded as if he was coming down with something, the way he was sneezing. At least we'll not be catching it now he's gone,' said Rose. 'There's some broth on the stove for your supper and I'm going to be away now, before Jim starts grumbling again.' She picked up her empty dishes, jangling them into her basket before she threw her shawl on.

'Your husband doesn't know how lucky he is,' complained Tobias, looking up from the letter he was writing to the Missionary Society. 'Here am I, on my own again. The Lord's work can be fearfully lonely.'

'Now don't take on so, Reverend. I'll be back in the morning. Like you, I've to see to my flock. Mind you, it's rare I have the time nowadays to see Mike and his family. They may only be up the road, but my old legs won't carry me. Besides, it's a terrible place. That's where you ought to preach next, Reverend: Gearstones doss-house. Bye, they could do with a bit of religion up there.'

Rose wrapped her shawl around her head and made for home, not waiting for Reverend Tiplady's reply. Though the sinful doings up at Gearstones were a constant refrain of hers, the truth was she knew nothing of what went on up there. Her son offered no information whatsoever on what went on there, and as time went by she had convinced herself that she didn't care. Tonight, as she made her way back along the rutted track to her hut, her aching back and limbs were so painful that she hadn't the energy to worry about anything beyond getting home.

Jim was sitting reading his paper when she walked in. He looked up as she pulled off her shawl and placed her heavy basket down.

'It's been a long day, Father, and I'm fair worn out. That new preacher's gone back to Bradford already. Apparently, his family's badly. Tobias wasn't too happy about having to do without his help.'

'He should bloody well do without your help an' all,' said Jim, looking at his wife's tired face. 'Lord knows I've told you plenty of times: let him get a young lass in there to cook and clean. You're an old bird, our Rose. It's time you took it easy.'

'Happen you're right. I'll tell him to go and hire somebody at the end of the week. I thought I'd manage. Turns out the head's willing but my poor old body is on its last. I still think I'm sixteen, that's my trouble. It'll have to be a cold supper tonight, all right?'

Jim grunted. 'Aye, I suppose. That's the third night in a row, mind. There's only so much cured pork a man can eat, Rose. No wonder our John's found a new trough to eat from.'

'What do you mean?' Rose was suddenly alert. 'Is he out again?' She leaned forward, trying to decipher the expression on Jim's face.

'He told me he was at a mate's, having supper there. I think he's got pally with a lad that lives on top of Blea Moor. He seems to mention him a lot. Joe or Josh or something similar . . .'

'As long as he's not across the way with that hussy, I don't mind. It'll do him good to make a few new mates, broaden his horizon – provided they don't drink.' Rose carved the cold pork and got out the pickle jar and a loaf of bread and placed it on the table.

Jim prayed under his breath to the Almighty. He hoped he'd be forgiven for telling lies, in the circumstances. The lad was back with Molly and the pair of them seemed happy. He for one wasn't going to stand in their way.

He looked mournfully at the plate of cold meat in front of him. All day he'd been hoping for a warm meal like the one Reverend Tiplady was probably enjoying right now. Instead she'd served up the same fare as he'd endured last night and the night before. Thank God Rose had finally seen it was too much for her, looking after the Reverend and her own family. Hopefully by this time next week she'd be cooking for him alone.

'So is your ma going to be a bridesmaid at this wonderful wedding that's coming off in the dale?' John asked Lizzie.

Molly, who was standing just behind him, washing the dishes, had declared him a terrible tease and refused to say another word on the subject. 'I hear Starchy Drawers wants to get married at St Leonard's, and right quickly.'

'Ma says the wedding's next weekend and it'll be a quiet do, but we're invited. I think we'll be the only ones there. None of Doctor Thistlethwaite's family are still alive and she's from up Scotland. It's a good job Mam finished my new dress, else I'd have nothing to go in, but I think I look pretty enough in this. At least, George says I do.' Lizzie blushed and did a small twirl to show off her dress for John.

'Happen young George is right: you're pretty as a picture. The bonniest lass up the dale – apart from your ma, that is. She's the apple of my eye, but you come a close second. I'll treat you to a new hair comb next time I'm in Ingleton and then you'll look spot on.' John laughed as Lizzie kissed him on the cheek and then blushed.

'Hey, that's enough of that, young lady! He's my man, not yours,' Molly joked.

'I think you two should get married. Then John could be my dad.' Lizzie stopped twirling and looked at the couple. 'Why don't you? You've been friends for months – Doctor Thistlethwaite's only been walking out with Starchy Drawers a few weeks. Florrie reckons you'd make a perfect couple. She saw the pair of you kissing the other day.'

'That's enough. John and I are just good friends,

which is how it should be at the moment. And you can tell that Florrie Parker to keep her comments to herself.' Molly's voice was warm but stern. 'Now how about you go to bed – it's past ten o'clock and I don't want you twining in the morning when you've got to get up.'

'But, Mam . . . John's still here,' Lizzie whined.

'I'll be on my way.' John rose from his chair, embarrassed by Lizzie's suggestion and Molly's response.

'No, stop – I want you to stay. I need to talk to you. Lizzie, I'll pull the curtain across and then John can't see you undress. No more lip, all right? It's bed time and that's final.'

John sat back down in his chair as Molly drew the curtain that separated the sleeping quarters.

'Night, John,' Lizzie shouted from behind the curtain as she blew out the candle next to her bed, the smell of candle wax filling the air.

'Night, sweetheart. Sleep tight and mind the bed bugs don't bite,' John replied, watching Molly carry a bowl of water from behind the curtain. She gently put her hand on his shoulder and nodded her head in the direction of the doorway.

He followed her outside and watched as she threw the dirty washing water into the open drain that ran alongside the huts, then sat down on the hut steps alongside him. It was a cold evening and he put his arm around her, pulling her close.

'You know I didn't prompt her to say that.' Molly laid her hand on John's knee and looked into his eyes.

'In fact, little does she know it, but Starchy Drawers was Doctor Thistlethwaite's second choice. He was stupid enough to ask me first.' She smiled at the look of surprise that crossed John's face. 'Needless to say I said no. And now he's opted to marry Gladys. Poor man's desperate for company in his old age.'

'He'd have been a good catch, worth a pretty bob or two. You could have done worse.' John knew it would have broken his heart if she had accepted. He loved everything about her: the way her lips quivered when she was upset, the twinkle in those beautiful green eyes when she was happy . . .

'Oh aye, he's worth a bob or two, but I couldn't marry if there was no love there. You can't share your bed with a man you don't love.' Molly's eyes dropped.

'And do you love me, Molly Mason? Because every time I look at you, I want to sing. Sing so loud that even the bloody viaduct would tremble with the noise. I want to tell the world how much I love you. Most of all I want to marry you. So how about it? Marry me, Molly Mason; and we'll run away from all this. For God's sake, say yes and be mine.' John squeezed her tight and kissed her hard on the lips. So hard she couldn't reply for a second or two.

Molly stroked John's cheek and placed her finger on his lips. 'You know I love you, but it feels so wrong. For a start, you're younger than me. And then there's your mother. What would she say? She'd be heartbroken – two of her sons marrying trollops.'

'Bugger her! It's my life. I want you to be my wife

and Lizzie to be my daughter. I don't care about the rest.'

'Oh, John, I want to marry you so much. I never thought I'd feel this way again. After everything that happened, I'd become all bitter and twisted – and then you came along. May God strike me down dead if I'm wrong . . . but yes, I'll marry you. Only not yet. Let's be patient, my love, and wait a while. How about in the summer? But the answer's yes, John Pratt, I would love to marry you.'

19

It was a strange marriage that took place at St Leonard's that cold February Saturday. The groom was considerably older than his bride, and with no congregation bar Lizzie and Molly, the church was empty. The vicar blessed the couple and wished them well as they set off in the gig that they had hired for the day. Dark evening clouds enfolded the wedding party as they crossed the moss-covered bridge and climbed the steep hill back to Batty Green.

The vicar blew out the candles one by one and placed his surplice in the small vestibule before putting the church records in a place of safety. It had been a pleasant enough day, a change from the many funerals he'd been called upon to conduct since the railway came to the dale. Even baptisms were poignant affairs now; more often than not he would hold the tiny babe in his arms to enter the house of God one day, only for it to return a few months later in a coffin. It was a hard world and his faith was often tried, but the coming together of a couple made up for it. He was sure the doctor would be happy. Certainly, his new wife seemed overjoyed. But he thought he'd detected a slight pause in the vows and a glance at Molly Mason before Roger Thistlethwaite said, 'I do.' Nothing would surprise where that woman was concerned. He recalled all too well the day he caught her child stealing from the church and marched her home, only to find the mother drunk and in the company of a man who was not her husband.

With the final candle blown out, its wisps of smoke curling down the nave, he looked around the small plain church before closing the door behind him. He stood in the small porch and pulled his hat on. This infernal rain – could it not keep fine just long enough for the bride and groom to get home and for him to dash to the vicarage? He wrapped his cloak about him and stepped out of the porch, only to be stopped in his tracks by John Pratt. The lad was bent double, gasping for breath, his face red and sweaty, his jacket and breeches soaked from the rain.

'Is the doctor here? Is he bloody well here, man?' John summoned enough breath to speak between gasps. He shook the vicar roughly by the shoulder. 'Tell me, is he here? My mam, she's badly, she looks terrible.'

'No matter how ill she is, there's no call to speak to me in that manner, young man. Anyway they've gone, they're on their way home. You'll have to catch them there.' He wrapped his cloak tight around him and strutted up the path to the vicarage.

John bent over, still trying to get his breath, kicked the foot scraper next to the church's entrance. 'Shit, I knew I'd miss them if I came down by the gill,' he muttered. Then he wiped his forehead with his cap and set off on the long run home.

Rose Pratt had been shivering and shaking for a few days. She'd thought she was coming down with influenza: her body ached and she'd a raging temperature. But then the spots and blisters started to appear. At first, they just looked like spots, but now they had started oozing pus and they stank. No matter how she lay, she was in pain. She lay alone in her bed, her hair matted, her heaving bosom sticky and sweaty. It exhausted her even to hear the sounds of everyday life going on around her.

'Jim, Jim, fetch me a drink of water, this thirst is killing me,' Rose whispered, reaching out a feeble hand from underneath the blankets.

Jim lovingly wiped her brow, mindful of the scabs that had appeared on his bonny-faced wife. 'Here, love, just a sip. Don't want to chill your belly now, do we?' He gently lifted her head and watched her take a small sip, the movement almost too much for her. 'John's gone for the doctor. We should have had him sooner – and would have done if we hadn't listened to you. I know it's his wedding day but tha's more precious to me than his special day.'

He patted her hand lovingly, trying to fight back a tear in his eye. Hard northern fellas like him didn't cry. He sniffed loudly and walked away, trying to hide his feelings. He was standing over the sink, not wanting to look at his wife as she lay groaning in her bed, worry and fear overtaking him as the door flew open and John entered with the doctor by his side.

'How long has she been like this?' Doctor Thistle-thwaite turned white when he saw her condition. He put his hand on Rose's forehead. 'She's burning up.' He stepped back and looked at the two burly men. They seemed lost without their matriarch.

'She started complaining she was tired about a week ago. And then these blisters came out the other day.' John answered for his father, who had sunk into his chair. The old man knew all too well what his wife had. He'd seen it once before, when he was a child, and he'd never forgotten the devastation that it had caused.

'I'm sorry but she's going to have to come into the hospital. I believe she has smallpox. It's a fearful disease and I can't tell you what the outcome will be.'

'Tha don't have to tell me a thing, Doctor,' said Jim. 'I know what smallpox is about, I lost my mother to it when I was a little 'un. I caught it an' all – look at my neck and shoulders.' Jim rose from his seat, pulled back his shirt and lifted his long grey hair up to reveal the pits in his skin where the scabs had been. 'I was lucky – I don't have any on my face and I lived, but my Rose here looks in a bad way.'

'We'll take her into the hospital and try to make her comfortable. She'll need to be kept apart from the other patients – this is contagious, as you probably already know, Mr Pratt.'

'Aye, I know. It ripped through our little village, barely a family untouched. I'm sorry we've fetched it to your door.' Jim bowed his head and leaned against Rose's bed. 'You'll be all right, lass, Doctor here will look after you. Our John's going to carry you into hospital.'

He walked away and gazed into the night while John and the doctor carried Rose out. Her moans brought back to him the night he lost his mother and the pain and anxiety that followed. Wherever she had caught it from, this was only the beginning. Smallpox would cut through the railway camps like a thief in the night, breeding on the squalid conditions that most of the navvies lived in. God have mercy on all their souls – not that Jim placed much store in Him. After watching your mother die and most of your family, you gave over believing in such a cruel trickster.

'I'll wash everything in sight and burn the bedding. I remember that much from when I was a nipper,' Jim called after the doctor. 'Never thought I'd see it again, though.' He closed the door and went back into the empty cabin. Rose was so ill, he knew there was little hope she'd survive. He sat in his chair and looked at the unmade bed and the pots and hangings on the walls in the hut that they had made their home for the last eighteen months. The old biscuit box full of earnings was just visible under the bed. He'd give it all away if he could save his Rose. He put his head in his hands and sobbed. She was his rock – a bullying, stubborn rock, but no other woman could hold a light to her. She'd better bloody live, that feisty old bugger . . . else what was he to do?

*

'Put her here John, in the end bed. We'll move the rest of the patients into the other half of the hospital. We really need an isolation ward, but this will have to do. The next twenty-four hours will be crucial and I need to know where she's picked it up from – she must have been in contact with someone who had the symptoms.' Doctor Thistlethwaite took off his jacket, his wedding corsage still attached to the buttonhole. He washed his hands in the enamel dish that Molly held and then set about examining Rose.

Much as she had disliked the woman, Molly wouldn't have wished this on her. She'd never seen anything as bad as what the illness was doing to her body.

'Her hearts weak, the rhythm doesn't sound right.' Doctor Thistlethwaite turned to John. 'You'd better get your father – I don't think she'll last the night.'

Molly touched John's sleeve as he hurried past her, wiping his eyes. There were no words that would comfort him.

John walked homewards with heavy feet. As he rounded the corner of the track he saw the glow of a fire near the viaduct, the silhouette of his father outlined against the orange and gold dancing flames.

'Father, Father, come quick! The doctor says Ma mightn't last the night. She's bad, real . . .' He fell silent as his father poked the straw mattress and bedding into the flames.

'She's buggered, lad. She'll not be here in the morning. I've seen it before and I don't think I can take it again.' Jim didn't even turn round. He kept his eyes on the blaze and kicking any stray bits of mattress that fell out back on to the fire.

'That's why you've got to come. She needs you.' John turned, assuming that his father would follow him.

'I'm not coming, lad. She's got her God with her, and I want to remember her like she was. She'll be the first of many. There'll be a lot of tears yet.'

'You've got to come – she loves you.' John pulled on his father's sleeve. He desperately wanted to get back to his mother.

'Call that bloody preacher for her – she'll want him. Rose'll know why I'm not there.'

John looked at him. He didn't understand: his wife was dying, surely he wanted to be with her. His foot slipped in the mud, nearly making him fall as he made off towards the hut where Reverend Tiplady lived. He would call for him, she'd like that. His presence would give her solace.

Rose gasped for breath, the pain in her chest was increasing and every minute of life had to be fought for. She gazed around her at the people trying to make her last few hours on earth comfortable. She could just make out the form of Molly Mason; that ginger hair, she was the only one at Batty Green with that halo of burnished copper. She had to tell her, get her forgiveness before meeting her maker. She snatched her hand as she bent down beside her with her cooling cloth.

'I need . . . I need to tell you, it . . . it was an accident,' she whispered in a ghost of a voice.

'Rose, you need to rest. Never mind about the accident.' Molly mopped Rose's brow, taking no heed of the ramblings of a dying woman.

'I've got to tell you . . . I poisoned Tommy . . . by accident.' The grip on Molly's hand was so strong and her confession so terrible it stopped Molly in her tracks.

'Tommy? You're telling me you poisoned my baby – you killed my bonny lad?' Molly looked in horror at the woman who had caused her more pain than anyone else in her life.

'It was an accident . . . I gave him some milk . . . in a bottle. It was John's poison bottle . . . I didn't know. Forgive me . . . forgive a dying woman.' The words were like a shard of glass in Molly's heart and she watched as another shot of pain hit the pleading old woman.

'You nasty old bitch! I hope you rot in hell! No amount of praying will save you – and no, I'll not forgive you, nor any of your family.' Molly pulled her arm away from Rose's grip. Her eyes glazing with hatred at the old woman, she threw her dish and cloth down and stamped out of the hospital. Doctor Thistlethwaite shouted after her, but she was too consumed with rage to hear him. Her baby boy dead and her daughter only alive by a miracle – all because of that family. How could she ever look at John without being reminded of that? She stood on the steps of the hospital and caught sight of him making his way across the track with the preacher Tiplady.

'Aye, get her the preacher, because by hell she needs

251

one! No matter how she prays, she'll never get into heaven!' Molly spat the words out like venom.

'Moll, I haven't got time for this. I know you don't like my mother, but I thought you'd find some kindness in your heart for a dying woman.' John brushed past her with the Reverend Tiplady in pursuit.

'I'd be careful what you say, Mrs Mason – God has ears,' warned Reverend Tiplady, hurrying to the side of his parishioner.

'God has ears! That's bloody rich.' Molly pulled her apron off and left it on the hospital steps and started to make her way home. Her heart ached as she remembered the day she had found Tommy dead in his makeshift cot. The harsh words she had said to Lizzie, and how she'd been driven to drink to cope with her grief. Tears welled up in her eyes, till she could barely see where she was going. Why did she have to go and fall in love with that woman's son? That was the cruellest thing of all. Had he known? Would he ever have told her? She got to the bottom of the steps to her hut and looked across to where the Pratts lived. Beyond that, she could make out the bowed figure of Jim Pratt, standing next to some burning embers under the viaduct.

She'd go and give him a piece of her mind. Lifting her skirts, she marched across to the lonely figure.

'Now then, lass, you've crept up on me, that's a fact.' Jim turned and looked at the lass that his lad loved, the light from the fire catching the highlights of her hair.

Molly stared at him as he sniffed into his hankie. He'd been crying and he seemed to have lost height and shrunk into an old man.

'Well, did you know? Had she told you?' Molly blurted the words out. She'd always been quite fond of the old man, but she needed to know whether the whole family had been part of this conspiracy of silence.

'What are you on about? Know what?' Jim saw the anger in the young woman's eyes and realized that there was something wrong.

'My baby – your bloody wife killed my baby! Not enough that your son nearly killed my lass, your bloody wife killed my Tommy! Why? What have I done to you, except to be daft enough to be in love with your lad?'

'Nay, she'd not do that, not my Rose. She loves babies, she wouldn't hurt a hair on its head.' Jim was genuinely shocked, his whole world turned upside down.

'She poisoned him with milk in a bottle. She said it was an accident, but I'm beginning to wonder. She's always hated me!'

'Nay, she's not like that. It'd be an accident. She might be a stubborn old stick and protect her brood too much, but she's not spiteful or cruel.' Jim started to walk off.

'Don't you walk away from me, I need the truth,' Molly yelled.

'That's what I'm off to find out before it's too late. I'm off to hear it from her.' Jim spat out his chewing tobacco and strode out into the night towards the lights of the shanties and hospital.

Molly stood watching for a minute and then ran to catch up with the heartbroken old man.

When he reached the hospital steps, Jim hesitated. He didn't want to enter the hospital. He'd not set foot in one since his mother died. Now the memories came flooding back, the cries of the dying and the smell of death. He breathed in deep and climbed the steps, Molly right behind him. He walked down the rows of beds to where Doctor Thistlethwaite and the dark shape of Tiplady stood by the bed he knew to be his Rose's. John rushed forward and put his arm around his shaky father, glancing at Molly but not saying anything.

John urged his father to the bedside. The doctor put his arm around Jim's frail form and said quietly, 'I'm sorry, she passed away a few minutes ago. Reverend Tiplady is just giving her a blessing.'

Jim bent down, knocking the preacher out of the way and squeezed Rose's limp hand. Gazing into her white face, framed in long grey hair, he said, 'I'm sorry, old lass. I should have been here for you. You know I hate hospitals, vicars and doctors – can't stand 'em.' He bent over and kissed the pox-marked head of his beloved. 'I'll never know the truth now, will I? Can't tell this lass what you did or whether you meant it. Truth's gone with you, my love.' He gently kissed her once more and then rose. 'John, fetch her home. It's what she'd have wanted.' He patted his son's shoulder and dragged his feet slowly out of the hospital, leaving the group watching him on his lonely walk.

*

254

'Well, I'm glad the old bugger's dead, after what she did. She never did like me, always looked down her nose at all us lot. And what she's died of is going to wipe us all out – Doctor says it's infectious.' Molly banged her cup down on the table. 'Stop your snivelling, our Lizzie. What we've got to worry about is keeping you safe from harm. I don't want you getting this smallpox.'

'But she was all right, was Mrs Pratt. She looked after me and saved me from the workhouse. I remember that day she fed Tommy – she didn't mean to kill him, Ma, I know she didn't. I remember her searching for a bottle and Tommy was crying so much and upsetting her, she didn't bother washing it out. It was an accident, Ma, really. She was kind to us both that day.' Lizzie blew her nose and looked at her wild-eyed mother. 'John loves you, Ma, so don't turn your back on him, not when you've just got back together.'

'Tuh! Don't know what to make of that 'un. I hope he keeps away for a while, for more reasons than one. If he comes and you answer the door, keep him on the door step – I don't want any of his disease coming into my house. It'll be bad enough these next few weeks. Doctor Thistlethwaite says more folk will be catching it. Muggins here will be in the thick of it at the hospital, but we must keep you clear.'

Molly wasn't about to let Lizzie catch smallpox. What happened to her didn't matter, but not Lizzie. The girl was all she had left.

*

'Are you all right, Father?' Mike put his arm around his dad, he'd not seen him for a while and he was shocked at how small and fragile he had become. This was the man that had always been there for them, that in years past could wield a pick like Hercules himself and always took care of his family. Now he was so frail it was as if all the life had been sucked out of him. He sat with his hand on the corpse of Rose, which had been laid out in her best nightclothes with two pennies on her eyes to pay for her safe passage into the next world. The coffin was nothing fancy but would serve its purpose and was awaiting the passage to the church-yard of St Leonard's. Jim had argued with the doctor, insisting that he be allowed to keep vigil on Rose. He knew her body should be quarantined, but he'd nothing to lose now that the most precious thing in his life had been taken from him.

'Aye, I'm all right, lad. Life goes on – I've you and John to think about, and happen now I'll get to have a look at that granddaughter of mine.' He patted Mike's hand. He wasn't a bad lad, he'd come as soon as he'd heard his mother had died and now he'd taken over the funeral arrangements, insisting that the funeral tea would be held at Gearstones. Rose would probably have had something to say about that, but he'd insisted. At least they were keeping the cost within the family.

John beckoned Mike over to him. 'Have you heard what our mother confessed to on her deathbed?' John had wanted to talk to someone about it since his father told him, but didn't want his father to have more worry.

'Apart from trying to control all our lives?' Mike shrugged, but then paused when he saw the anguish on his older brother's face.

'She confessed to Moll that she'd killed her baby, Tommy. She fed him milk out of my rat-poison bottle.' John pulled on his brother's sleeve, urging him not to speak until he'd finished. 'Trouble is, our Mike, I think it's true. Lord knows it was an accident, but I remember coming home and seeing a teat stuck on the bottle. When I asked what she'd been doing with my rat bottle, I remember her going white and running out of the hut. It wasn't long after that she started doing all she could for Molly: taking Lizzie in, sending her to take food to her mother. I couldn't understand it at the time, but when I heard about Tommy I started to put two and two together.'

'Aye, God, why didn't she say?' said Mike, stunned by the news. 'She's been living with that guilt all this time! No wonder she didn't come and see our bairn, it would only have reminded her. And what with Gearstones being her idea of hell on earth, I bet that just put the top hat on it, the stubborn old fool. What does your Molly make of this?' It had been bad enough that Bob had turned out to be such a black sheep, but his mother . . .

'Haven't been near,' said John. 'I know Moll, she'll not want to see me yet. Best to let her calm down in her own time. I bloody well love the bones of that woman and if this has put space between us again I don't know what I'll do,' John sighed.

Mike, always the joker in the family, jostled his brother's arm and said, 'You mean you love bedding her, our John. I still owe you a shilling, don't I?' He laughed loudly, making his father stir.

'A bit of respect, lads! This is your mother lying here – and don't think I can't hear what you're talking about. As soon as your mother's in her grave I'll be away across to see Molly Mason. We've done her wrong twice and the poor lass doesn't deserve it. As for you, John – if you love her so much, best let her know it, else you'll lose her.'

The brothers exchanged glances. Their father had the ears of a bat, that was for sure, even if he looked nearly ready for the grave himself.

20

Rose's grave was the last plot but one in the tiny church-yard. The vicar prayed over her while worrying what would happen when that last grave was filled. He'd conducted more funerals in the eighteen months since the railway had arrived in the dale than in all the pre-ceding years put together. And now the doctor had warned him that, with the coming of smallpox, this burial would be the first of many.

'Ashes to ashes, dust to dust . . .' The vicar peered over his prayer book at the grieving family. The youngest member was screaming its head off in protest at the passing of a grandmother it had never known. One by one, Rose Pratt's nearest and dearest sprinkled soil on her coffin and paid their respects. If the iron-willed Rose Pratt had succumbed to illness, the poorer shanty dwellers, many of whom were malnourished and lived in squalid conditions, would stand no chance.

'Thank you, Vicar. That was a good service.' Jim Pratt came across and shook the vicar's hand. 'You're welcome to join us for a bite to eat up at Gearstones. My lad and his wife have laid a tea on.'

The vicar shook his hand and murmured a noncommittal response. Jim Pratt was a good man who had been dealt a hard deal in life, but Gearstones was not a place the vicar would frequent if he could avoid it.

Jim hoisted himself up into the back of the gig and took the seat opposite John. Jenny, who was sitting with his granddaughter fast asleep in her lap, smiled and put her free arm around him. Jim smiled back at her. Mike's wife was a good lass; Rose should have given her a chance. But then, that had always been Rose's way. If you weren't one of hers then you were lacking.

Mike urged the horses into action and they set off. As they passed the Welcome Inn, they saw the doctor heading through the door. Since he wasn't the sort to drink there, they assumed he'd been summoned to attend to some poor soul who'd had a few too many and got into a fight. It was a regular enough occurrence at Henry Parker's establishment.

Their route took them onward, past the shanty town at Ribblehead and the viaduct spanning Batty Moss, until finally they came in sight of Gearstones, the sprawling group of houses and the infamous doss-house that Rose had visited once in her life and sworn she would never return to.

'Come on, lass, let me help you down – that bairn needs her cot.' Jim held his hand out to help his daughter-in-law down.

'No you don't! I'll help her, Father.' John jumped

down quickly and eased his father aside. 'Get yourself in, Pa. The front door's that middle one.' John pointed at the largest of the doors in the imposing square house that backed on to the rough track over to Hawes. He lifted Jenny down and followed his father in, while Mike took the horse and trap down the bank to the stables.

'It's good of your family to do this for me,' Jim told Jenny as he waved her to go in first. 'You'll have to let me know how much I owe them.'

'You owe them nothing. We won't take it, even if you offer.' Jenny opened the door to reveal a beautiful hallway, lavishly decorated and immaculately clean.

Jim stared in wonder at the home that Rose had declared a den of iniquity. 'Your home's bonny. I thought you took boarders and sold ale in here.' Jim couldn't stop himself.

'Only down at the doss-house, where you came last time, and the ale house next door to it. This is our family home. I can't think of anything worse than having to live over the ale house!' Jenny untied her hat and hung it on the hall stand before walking into the parlour and laying the baby down in her crib.

The parlour was richly decorated and from the windows you could see right down the valley, with the new extending towards the huge peak of Pen-y-ghent in the distance. Jim could only imagine what Rose would have said if she'd known she was missing all this! A den of iniquity indeed! Clearly the Burton family lived well, for all their rough manners at the wedding.

'My brothers and parents will join us shortly. Don't

worry, they'll be right with you. The only reason they were unreasonable with Mike was that they were frightened he wouldn't stand by me. They were just being overprotective. I'm their baby sister and they wanted to make sure I was taken care of. Now they've gotten to know him, they think Mike is a grand fella, one of the family. And they all dote on this bundle of trouble.' Jenny rocked the cradle gently. 'Keep an eye on her for me, will you? I want to make sure everything's ready.'

As soon as she closed the door behind her, Jim turned to John. 'Did you know they lived like this?'

'Aye. Our Mike landed on his feet when he married Jenny. The doss-house is rough, but I always knew the Burtons were worth a bob or two.' John grinned at his father's expression.

'Your mother must be turning in her grave with envy! She'd no idea, else she'd have been coming up here every day, just to look at the carpet and wall coverings.' Jim sat down in one of the comfortable chairs and gazed out of the window at Ribblesdale.

'That's why I didn't tell her. She should have taken the time to get to know people before judging them. It was a fault of my mother's.'

Mike caught the last sentence as he came into the room. 'I know I shouldn't talk ill of her now she's in her grave,' he said, 'but she certainly liked to control us all. And John's right: she always did judge folk before getting to know them. Jenny's family own all the buildings you can see and most of the land up to Dent Head. Mind, it wasn't her money I was after, it was Jenny. If me ma hadn't been too blind to see how much I loved Jenny, I'd have invited you up here instead of to the doss-house, but the way she was carrying on made me so angry . . .' Mike sat down next to his father. 'Well, it's all water under the bridge now. The Burtons have laid out a cold tea for you and I'm to ask whether you both want to stop the night. I know it's not far to go back home, but we'd like you to stay.' Mike patted his father's hand while John stood behind his chair.

'Nay, lad, I'm not stopping. I've something to do before this day's over – another thing that your mother, God rest her soul, interfered in.' Jim twiddled his gold watch chain, a treasured possession he'd inherited from his father. 'I might as well tell you now, lads, while I've got you both together. I'm going back to Durham. There's nothing left for me here and you two are big enough to look after yourselves. Besides I can't live through another smallpox outbreak – I've too many memories of the last one. I just pray none of you catch it.'

John and Mike nodded. Neither of them wanted to see their father go, but it was obvious he was heart-broken. The last week had aged him and all his fight had gone. Without his Rose, he was lost.

'We understand, Father,' said John. 'We're both big enough and old enough to look after ourselves. But are you sure you'll be all right?'

'Aye, lad, I'll be grand. I'm going to lodge with your aunty Margaret, if she'll have me. It's where I should be now, helping out my older sister. She was good to me when we lost our mother. Now we're both widowed, we can help one another. I've been thinking about her, having to manage on her own since her husband died last year. Well, now I can do something about it.'

'We'll send you some money every so often, Father. It's the least we can do,' said Mike.

'I don't want any of your brass, lad. You have enough on your hands with this bonny little thing – and you never know, she might be the first of many. And you, our John, you need to look after that Molly and her little lass – although she's not that little nowadays. Moll's a good woman. A bit rough around the edges, but that's what you need standing alongside you in this hard world.' Jim's eyes filled with tears that he tried to hold back.

The drawing-room door opened and Jenny stuck her head in. 'Come through, you three. The tea table's set and there's some folk walked up from the funeral and Ribblehead to pay their respects. She was a popular lady, was Rose.'

Urged on by Jenny, they went through to the dining room, which was full of mourners and members of the Burton family. Spread out on a huge table was a funeral feast the likes of which Jim had never seen.

'Aye, lass, you've done us proud,' said Jim, tears rolling down his cheeks as he hugged his daughter-in-law.

'It's nothing, you're my family.' Jenny kissed him on the cheek.

'If only Rose was here to see it.' Jim's voice trailed off, realizing the irony of his words.

'She is. She's up there, looking down – and probably kicking herself for missing her own funeral tea.' Jenny squeezed her father-in-law's hand and led him through the throng of mourners to the feast.

'Is your mother in, lass?' Jim shouted through the hut door.

He was still warm after the exertion of walking all the way from Gearstones, but as soon as he stopped he could feel the cold beginning to creep in through his gloveless fingers.

'I'm sorry, Mr Pratt, Mam says I can't open the door to anyone when she's not here, and she's at the hospital.'

'Never mind, lass. I'll catch her tomorrow. You keep that door shut – your mother's right, keep safe.' Jim walked back to his empty hut alone. He'd left John behind having a drink in the ale house. Rose had been right: it was full of Irish navvies, the worse for drink – a completely different world from the Burtons' home. Still, if that was how they wanted to make their money, let a better man than him tell them that they were wrong. He bent down and lit the stove and put the old black kettle on it to boil, pulling up the Windsor chair that Rose had insisted she had to have brought down with them from Durham. He smiled as he ran his hand lovingly over the highly polished chair arm, remembering when they had bought it together and how he'd scrimped and saved to purchase it. She always did want the best.

He closed his eyes, thoughts of his Rose going through his mind, remembering days when they were courting, how bonny she was, her eyes twinkling as she kissed him. Knowing how wickedly she was leading him on as they frolicked in the hay loft at her father's farm.

'Come on then, what you waiting for?' her voice called to him and her laughter bewitched him – a faraway laughter, mocking but urging him to follow. And there she was, holding her hand out to him, surrounded by flowers in a beautiful daisy-filled meadow, exactly how he remembered her. Nay, he must be dreaming . . . but no, she called again.

'Come on, Jim, it's lovely here. There's nothing left for you there.' Her beaming smile drew him towards her, and she flirtatiously tossed the long blonde hair that she used to have all those years ago. 'Come on, trust me,' her voice called again.

'I'm coming, Rose, I'm coming.' Jim reached for Rose's hand. 'Where are we going?'

She giggled and whispered, 'You'll see, my love.'

And Jim felt no pain as he slipped without knowing from one world into the next.

'I'm sorry, John. Losing both parents within a week of one another can't be easy.' Doctor Thistlethwaite looked up from signing the death certificate. 'He seemed fit enough, but he simply couldn't live without your mother. He died of a broken heart – melancholia. I've seen it a few times in my life.'

John sat in the chair opposite the doctor. 'He said I'd to stop with Mike and drown my sorrows after the funeral. That he was all right and I didn't have to worry about him. I should have known. We even left him to walk home, because he insisted he wanted to be on his own.' John ran his hands through his sandy hair, unable to believe that he'd buried his mother yesterday and come home to find his father dead this morning.

'Don't feel guilty. I don't believe he suffered any pain. As I laid him out in our new mortuary hut he almost looked as if he was smiling.' The doctor rose and patted John on the back. 'You know where I am if you need me. And if I'm not being too presumptuous, Molly Mason will give you a shoulder to cry on. She was upset this morning when she saw your father's body come into the mortuary.' He picked up his hat and put it on. 'Well, I must get back. We had three new cases of smallpox this morning. I had to admit young Florrie from the Welcome Inn yesterday – it's touch and go whether she'll live.' He shook his head sadly. There's no rhyme or reason in this life, the grim reaper can appear at any time. Thankfully, the railway has rehoused the Reverend Tiplady and commandeered his residence as an isolation ward and mortuary. Lord knows, I'm going to need them.'

The doctor doffed his hat and left John with his head in his hands, wondering how he was going to break the news to Mike. He dreaded the thought of another funeral to arrange, especially when it meant dealing with that sanctimonious vicar. Soon both his parents would be in that churchyard. And from what the doctor had just said, many other residents of Batty Green would be following them as the smallpox continued to spread.

21

Molly cleared away the dinner things, only half-listening as Lizzie chatted away about the latest goings-on at her job. She too had come home with news, but it was not good. All through the meal she had wondered how to break it to Lizzie, knowing that she'd be devastated when she heard. So she held back, letting her daughter babble on about the forthcoming visit of the director of the Midland Railway.

'He's travelling from Leeds in the morning, and guess what – the last bit of track was laid today, so the train will bring him right to where the station is going to be, just above the hospital.' Lizzie was clearly brimming with excitement. 'Oh, I forgot to tell you! Even though the station's not built yet, the trains will be stopping there from Saturday onwards. So you can catch a train to Settle and beyond from Batty Green – except the station's going to be called Ribblehead.'

'Lizzie Mason, you witter on and forget to tell me the most important bit of gossip yet!' Molly forgot her worries momentarily and joined in her daughter's enthusiasm. 'This will open a whole new world to us. Just think, we can go to Settle for shopping! Or if I save up, we can even go visiting relations in Bradford – there's bound to be a connecting train.'

Lizzie's face lit up at the prospect, but she wasn't done with delivering all the details of the director's visit. 'Mr Ashwell's going to ask the director for money to make the graveyard bigger. That miserable old vicar came by this morning to say he'd only one grave left and that would be going to Jim Pratt. With smallpox rife he'll be needing lots more room but the church can't afford to buy the land. Mr Ashwell had to turn him away, but he's promised to have a word with the director about it. He told me he was devastated at the smallpox outbreak and that no decent boss would think twice about putting his hand in his pocket.'

Now that the subject had turned to smallpox, Molly saw her opening.

'Lizzie, I'm sorry, love, but I have bad news. Florrie was admitted to the hospital today. She's got smallpox.'

'No!' cried Lizzie. 'That's not possible. I talked to her only the other day. She said she was tired, but she always is. She can't be poorly, she just can't. We're best mates, I love her, Mam – what would I do without her?'

Molly wrapped her arm around her sobbing daughter. What she really wanted to ask was whether Lizzie had any idea whose baby Florrie was carrying. Both doctor and nurse had been shocked when they had removed her voluminous skirts and seen Florrie's extended stomach. Fourteen and already pregnant – who would have taken

269

advantage of such a young lass? Batty Green might be a wild place, but there was an unspoken code of honour among the navvies that prohibited such behaviour.

'She might be all right, love. The next few hours will tell. I've volunteered to sit with her tonight, 'cause her mother's having to serve behind the bar and her father doesn't want to know, uncaring bastard. When Doctor Thistlethwaite carried her out of the inn, all he said was that it'd be one less to care about. You'd have thought he wanted her to die.'

'He likes to hit her and her mother. Florrie was trying to save up and leave home. She'd do anything for money.'

'Lizzie, she wouldn't go with men for money, would she? She knew not to do that, I hope.'

'No, she's all talk. Flirts but runs a mile if anyone flirts back, she says her dad would kill her if she did.' Lizzie turned pleading eyes on her mother. 'Are you leaving me on my own? I don't want to be by myself, not tonight with Jim Pratt dead and Florrie dying. Please don't leave me on my own.'

'But, Lizzie, I promised. It's better that Florrie's got someone she knows with her.'

'Please, Mum, don't leave me . . .' Lizzie felt as if she was surrounded by death. And now all she could think about was the horrible vicar refusing to bury Florrie because he knew it was really her that had pinched the church money. 'Please . . .'

Molly shook her head in frustration. 'Lizzie, please, I'll be back before you wake up. Just bolt the door like you usually do.'

'I'll come with you. Florrie's my best friend, so I'll come with you.' Lizzie started to button her shoes up.

'You will not! I'm not having you anywhere near that hospital hut. It's bad enough that I work there, without you going courting death. Tell you what, I'll ask John if he'll sit in with you. I haven't had a chance to offer my condolences since his father's passing, so I ought to call by in any case.' She gathered up her shawl and wrapped it around her. 'I'm not that bitter over your baby brother to turn my back on the poor devil when he's in the thick of it. He'll need me now there's nobody at home. Stay here, and hopefully I'll be back with him.' She stopped in the doorway and fixed Lizzie with a stern gaze: 'I mean it, Lizzie: you're to stop here. No trailing off to see Florrie while I'm across the way!'

Lizzie nodded her head, relieved that she wasn't going to be on her own.

'I'll not be long, John. It's just till dawn, then Nurse Gladys will take over. I wouldn't ask, but I can't leave Florrie. She's in bad way and only a baby herself – and then there's the baby she's carrying. I'm afraid neither one of them will survive.' Molly knew John could be trusted with the news. Although if Florrie lived to give birth it would be common knowledge soon enough.

'She's having a baby? But she's even younger than your Lizzie! The bastard! Some fellas just want it cutting off.'

'I tried asking, but she was in no condition to talk

so I learned nowt. Listen, don't say anything to Lizzie about Florrie expecting a baby.'

'Don't worry, I won't.' John picked up his jacket. 'Away, Moll. I'll stay with Lizzie till you're back. Lord knows there's not much joy sitting in this hut on my own. I was beginning to feel maudlin.'

Molly touched John's sleeve and looked into his blue eyes, pausing for a moment to breathe in deep. She realized suddenly how much she had missed the smell of him. It was the smell of a true man.

'John, I know I was like a mad woman the night your mother died, but I couldn't cope with it. She'd already caused me so much pain and then for her to say that about Tommy, when she was dying . . . it wasn't fair.' Molly stood on the steps of the hut, tears springing to her eyes despite her efforts to hide her grief.

'She just wanted forgiveness. It was a mistake, a stupid mistake, that cost poor Tommy his life. Why she didn't say anything at the time, I don't know. I remember her running out that evening, and when she came back it was like she'd seen Lucifer himself. But she insisted she was all right and wouldn't tell what had upset her. I never connected it with her using my rat-poison bottle earlier in the day. Moll, I'm sorry we've caused you so much pain.' John hesitated, and then blurted out the decision he'd come to, sitting alone in the hut that he'd shared with his parents: 'I'd best tell you now, I'm off to lodge with the tunnel gang up at Jerusalem. I can't do with being on my own here. So you'll not have the sight of me to remind you of things. Best we move on, eh?'

As soon as the words were out, he ran down the steps, leaving Molly stunned. It took a few moments for her to recover and run after him.

'But, John, I need you,' she cried.

'You don't need me. You're the most spirited woman I've ever met – stronger than any fella I know. And Lizzie's turning into a bonny young woman; she'll soon have a lad whistling after her.'

Molly pulled hard on his sleeve, stopping him in his tracks and clasping his firm chin in her hands to make him face her straight on.

'But I love you, John. I can't live without you. I've no one except our Lizzie,' she pleaded.

'Aye, and I love you. But after all the harm that's been done, after the deceit and fighting, we've both lost the ones we love. I think we both need a bit of peace, at least for a month or two, to give us time to think.' John tore himself away from her grasp and walked on to the hut where Lizzie was waiting for him. Molly followed, dragging her feet in the mud, feeling as if her very soul was draining from her.

'Hey, Lizzie Mason! I hear you're waiting for a charming, sophisticated gent like myself to sit with you while your mother's at work.'

The door flew open and Lizzie ran into John's arms. He picked her up and swung her around, showing all her petticoats as he did so.

'You're too old for that sort of carry-on, Lizzie,' said Molly sternly. 'And I expected you to be in bed before John got here.' The devastating impact of John's words

273

had sunk in during the walk home and she had gone into self-protection mode. She would show John Pratt that she didn't need him. After tonight, she'd make it on her own, without any man's help.

'Come on, Molly, we're only playing.' John didn't care for this side to Molly. He'd seen it before: when things weren't going her way she had a tendency to lash out and hurt people, not thinking what she was saying.

'Aye, well, playing leads to other things. Lizzie – bed. John will sleep in the chair until I get home.'

'Moll, stop it! You know I wouldn't lay a finger on Lizzie, else why am I here? Don't be daft.'

'Daft? Aye that's what I've been, all right, falling in love with someone who has no feelings, who can walk away from me when I need him the most.' Tears welled up in Molly's eyes as she walked out the door, closing it sharply behind her.

Inside the hut, the two people she loved stood looking at each other in silence, wondering what they had done.

Molly stroked Florrie's hair, trying to comfort her. The child's fever was out of control, leaving her delirious with pain, writhing and thrashing on the mattress. Her long hair was matted and soaked with sweat and her face was covered with pus-filled blisters. If she survived, the scars would be horrendous. No one would ever look at her again. Her cries of distress mingled with those of the three other smallpox victims in the isolation ward.

'Shh, little one,' Molly told her, leaning into the

candlelight so the child could see her there. 'I'm right here, I won't leave you. And don't you go leaving us – our Lizzie'll miss you. She's not like me, she takes after her father – a right soft lump. Shh, shh, little love, we'll get through this together. And whoever that baby's father is, we'll get even with the bastard and make him stand by you.'

Molly kept vigil over Florrie all night, filling the hours by talking softly, pouring out all her worries. Only when the first grey shards of dawn started creeping across the sky did she leave the bedside, stepping outside to empty the dish of water she'd used to mop the child's fevered brow in an effort to keep her temperature down. As the water trickled away down the drain, Molly gazed out across the dale. The early morning mist mingled with smoke from the huts, casting a veil over Whernside that allowed only occasional glimpses of blue sky. It promised to be a good day, she thought, lifting her head at the sound of someone approaching from the shanties. As he emerged from the darkness, she saw that it was Doctor Thistlethwaite, on his way to carry out the first inspection of the day. Despite the long hours he was putting in, dealing with the epidemic, he seemed a happier man now that he'd married Gladys. She, too, was less of a Starchy Drawers now. The death and devastation brought about by smallpox had made them all realize how lucky they were to be alive, and any animosities had been forgotten as the three of them worked together, battling to keep their patients alive.

'Morning, Molly. How are the patients?' Doctor

Thistlethwaite knocked the mud off his shoes before entering the isolation ward with her.

'No change. But at least there have been no new cases overnight.' Molly led the way to Florrie's bedside, letting out a gasp when she saw the pale arm hanging lifeless from the bed. Gently clasping the hand and tucking it in under the covers, Molly looked into Florrie's face. She'd passed over silently, in the blink of an eye, as if she'd just been waiting for the moment she was on her own. Molly sank into the chair beside the bed, unable to hold back the tears.

Doctor Thistlethwaite put his arm around Molly as she sobbed.

'She didn't have a chance. Don't blame yourself, you did all you could. Come on, Molly, you need to be strong now. There are others who need you. I fear this is just the beginning . . .'

Molly and Nurse Gladys carried Florrie's body into the makeshift mortuary. Another coffin for the carpenter to build; he was going to be a wealthy man at this rate. Molly couldn't help but wonder where this poor soul would be laid to rest. Tomorrow Jim would be buried in the grave next to Rose, leaving Florrie and other smallpox victims with nowhere to go.

'Listen, that sounds like a train!' exclaimed Nurse Gladys. 'I heard they'd almost finished laying the track to where the station will be, but I didn't think there'd be a train on it so soon. How exciting – the first train! I wish I could go and see it, but I'm needed here. You go, Molly. You must be ready for home, you've been here all night. Go on, go – and tell me all about it later.'

Molly was exhausted. She wanted to get home to Lizzie, but she couldn't face her daughter while her mind was on Florrie, lying there in the morgue with no last resting place for her body.

She picked up her shawl. 'I'll go,' she said. 'And then I'll call by the Welcome Inn and tell Helen Parker that her daughter's dead. From what I hear, her father won't be bothered. He doesn't bother about anything, that one, except drink and money.'

Seething with anger at the injustice of it all, Molly reached the platform edge of what was going to be Ribblehead station. The train was just coming to a halt, filling the air with a great cloud of steam. A small crowd of onlookers had gathered to greet the train, and they cheered as the engine driver climbed down from his cabin. As the cloud of steam subsided, Molly spotted John and Lizzie standing near the engine. She made her way through the crowd to join them.

'I'm sorry I haven't been home – there's something I have to do first. I expect you'll be at work by the time I'm done, Lizzie, but I need to tell you . . .' Molly's voice trailed off as she noticed a small man in a bowler hat being helped out of one of the first-class carriages by Lizzie's boss.

'It's all right, Moll. Lizzie and me decided last night to come and watch this. We wouldn't have missed it for the world, would we, Liz?' John was so awestruck by the steam engine that he failed to notice the expression on Molly's face. 'Did you hear the whistle blow and the chuffing that she made when she came around the limestone cutting? What a magnif—'

'I'll be back in a minute,' Molly cut in. 'There's something I must do.' She broke away from them, almost running in her haste to get to the first-class carriages.

'Hey, you!' Molly shouted at the top of her voice, causing the bowler-hatted businessman and Mr Ashwell to turn in astonishment. 'Yes, you – the toff from Leeds.'

'Mrs Mason! Stop this right now. This isn't the time or the place to deal with any problems you may have.' Mr Ashwell turned away, keen to usher the visiting dignitary away from any unpleasantness. 'Come and see me in my hut later, if you must, but this is our director and he hasn't the time—'

'Don't you turn your backs on me! I've sat up all night with a dying lass. Now she's dead and there's nowhere to bury her. I haven't a problem, but he has – ' Molly poked her finger at the speechless director. 'If he doesn't come up with the money to extend that church- yard, I'll see that not another length of track or another brick on that dammed viaduct gets laid.'

Hands on her hips, Molly stood her ground, staring defiantly. Behind her, there were murmurs from the onlookers. Though none of them were prepared to be as openly defiant as Molly, it was obvious the navvies and their families shared her opinion.

'Well, what are you going to do?' Molly demanded.

'Mrs Mason, please . . .'

James Ashwell was interrupted by the director: 'My good lady, I have in my pocket a banker's draft made out to the vicar. It was my intention to present it later today, on behalf of the Midland Railway.' From underneath the brim of his bowler hat, beady eyes peered at the forthright woman standing before him, and the surly-faced navvies gathered behind her.

The news came as a complete surprise to James Ashwell, who had lodged a number of appeals with the Board of Directors to no avail, but he knew better than to show it: 'I'm sure these strong and faithful workers will get to work immediately, clearing a new burial ground,' he declared, gesturing with his walking stick at the crowd of navvies. 'Is that not right, my good men?'

The navvies conferred amongst themselves for a moment, then a spokesman shouted, 'Aye, that's right, Florrie will get her graveyard.' This was followed by a rumble of agreement.

'You see, madam?' said the director. 'The matter is in hand. Now, if you will just leave us to conclude arrangements with the vicar, the graveyard will be extended and blessed by next week, in time for your funeral – my condolences to the young woman's family, by the way.'

Considering Molly dismissed, the director was already walking in the direction of the contractor's hut when her voice rang out again.

'So I have your word on it, sir?' she shouted after him.

Without turning, the director raised his stick in acknowledgement. To his relief, the crowd had begun to disperse. For a while there it had looked as though he'd have an uprising on his hands if he didn't concede to her demands. As soon as they were out of earshot of the navvies, he instructed James Ashwell to find out how much the vicar needed and obtain a banker's draft forthwith.

It was all James Ashwell could do not to smile. Lizzie's mother might have a caustic tongue on her, but she'd succeeded where he had failed, shaming the railway into paying for the extension. Now he knew where young Lizzie got her brains.

'Mam, you didn't half show me up! And why didn't you tell me that Florrie had died? Everyone's seen me crying now.' Lizzie blew her nose, trying to compose herself.

'I hadn't time, love. I didn't want that fat bugger getting away before I'd made him hand over the money so's we can all rest in peace when our time comes.' Molly pulled Lizzie close, wrapping an arm around her as they set off down the track. 'Bloody liar – he'd no intention of paying up. Well, he's got no choice now.'

John walked quietly behind them, watching as navvies approached Molly, patting her on the shoulder to show their gratitude. When they came to the junction, she asked Lizzie, 'You all right, pet? Are you away to your job now? Have you both eaten?'

'Yes, and yes. That is, assuming I've a job to go to. I'm not sure Mr Ashwell will have me back after this morning.' Lizzie bowed her head.

'Go on with you! He'd not sack you – he wouldn't dare.' Molly pulled Lizzie's chin up and kissed her on both cheeks. 'We'll talk tonight.' And then she gently patted her on her bum and sent her on her way.

When the two of them were alone, Molly turned to John, who'd been standing silently waiting for her.

'Are you all right, Moll? I take it it's been a bad night?'

'Aye, it's not been the best. Spending hours sat amongst the dead and dying doesn't do anything for your peace of mind. Thanks for looking after Lizzie. And, John, I'm sorry I snapped last night. I knew it was going to be a bad at the hospital, and your news of moving just put the cap on it.' Molly had regretted her mood swing ever since she'd slammed the hut door the previous night. That was no way to treat the man you loved. 'Come to supper tonight. You'll need company ahead of your father's funeral tomorrow.'

'Aye, go on then. I'm nosy to hear the outcome of the graveyard saga and no doubt Lizzie will be full of it. Besides, happen I can brighten her night up a bit. She'll be broken-hearted that she's lost her best mate.'

'Right, I'll see you tonight, then.' Molly adjusted her shawl and took a deep breath, trying to keep the weariness at bay while she carried out the task that lay ahead of her. 'I'm off to the Welcome Inn to break the news to Helen Parker. God help her, she's not only lost her daughter but her first grandchild. What am I going to say to her?' Molly shook her head.

'I don't know, lass, but you'll do it. She wouldn't want to hear it from anyone else.'

Molly looked on as Helen Parker sobbed into her mucky hankie. She'd arrived to find her with a fresh bruise on her chin, a split lip, and her two youngest clutching at her skirts, looking lost in their filthy rags. Although a good few years younger than Molly, the constant beatings she'd endured had aged Helen. Here she was, running a thriving business, and yet her clothes were shabby and unkempt. The whole time she was talking to Molly, there was a haunted look in her eyes and she seemed constantly on edge, casting glances at the door in case Henry should appear.

'She was a good girl, our Florrie. I'll be lost without her, she was a good hand, helped me keep this place going. What am I going to do now? How am I going to tell the little 'uns that their big sister won't be coming back?' Helen clutched at her lank hair, gazing wretchedly at the toddlers playing with the cat on the sawdust on the floor of the inn.

'Helen, I'm sorry, there's no easy way to say this . . . did you know she was with child? The baby died along with her, but I'd say she looked to be about seven month gone.' Molly's own eyes filled with tears as she watched Helen Parker fighting for breath between the great ragged sobs that shook her body.

'No! That's not possible. She couldn't – our Florrie was a good girl. She'd not let a fella touch her. It wouldn't be her fault, she must have been taken advantage of.'

282

Beside herself with grief, Helen frantically cast her mind back over the last few months. At the time, she'd thought nothing of it – too busy with the younger children and the inn and fending off her bullying husband – but there had been changes in Florrie. She'd become moody and quiet, withdrawing from her mother. Helen had put it down to her age. What kind of mother was she, not to notice her own daughter in that condition?

'I'm afraid there's no doubt about it, love,' said Molly. 'She'd been hiding her belly under her skirts.' Unable to think of anything else to say, Molly rose from her seat. 'Helen, I'll leave you now. If there's anything I can do, let me know. I'll be back at the hospital after dinnertime, and I'll take you to see her in the mortuary, if that's what you want.'

Giving the heartbroken mother a final hug, Molly walked out of the inn. What a state to be in. Molly shook her head; she'd have been up and gone long since if it was her. No man would ever treat her that way. Then she stopped herself, remembering how in the aftermath of Tommy's death she'd allowed Cloggie into her bed. Who was she to judge? If she hadn't come to her senses, she could easily have wound up in as sorry a state as Helen.

Wrapping her shawl tight around her, she stepped out into the harsh daylight. Time to get home and snatch a few hours' sleep before returning to the hospital. All around her, the dale echoed to the sound of work in progress. From high up on the moor came the booming of the blasts as they continued work on the tunnel, from

283

the viaduct and the embankments came the sound of hammers striking stone, horses pulling wagons, visiting traders from Ingleton and Hawes yelling out their wares to the shanty dwellers. One of the traders pulled up on the bridge beside her. She almost waved him on, but then decided to buy some bacon for supper.

As the red-faced trader took her money and handed over the parcel of bacon, Molly reminded herself that, hard as it was getting by on her own, she had proved that she could get by, relying on no one. Perhaps that was the best way to be.

Long after Molly had gone, Helen Parker remained sitting on the bench, her mind in turmoil as her two youngest played unheeded around her feet. She'd cried until she felt completely drained, until it seemed there were no tears left in her. When the doctor had carried Florrie from the inn, part of her had known that she would never come back. It was obvious the girl was deathly ill. Helen thought she'd steeled herself for bad news. But this was worse than she could have imagined. To be told that her fourteen-year-old daughter was expecting, and the baby had died with her ... That was too much to take.

The inn was full of fellas who liked to flirt, but none of them would have dared touch Florrie. Oh, they teased her, all right, same way they teased all the young lasses. But that's as far as they'd go. No, the father wasn't one of the navvies. The bastard who'd done that to Florrie was right there under her roof.

Now Helen understood why she'd not been both-ered since the birth of her last one. She'd been so relieved to find his side of the bed empty, she'd not given a thought to where he was. Until it was too late.

That was why Florrie had withdrawn into herself. That was why she'd not confided in her mother. The bastard! To do that to his own daughter! Well, he'd not do it again. Henry Parker could hit her all he wanted, but never again would he lay a finger on her children. That she'd make certain of.

'So, your mam did it – she made him put his hand in his pocket?' John shovelled in his supper while grin-ning at Lizzie's tale of the director's visit. 'Good lass, Moll!' He raised his fork in acknowledgement of Molly's triumph. He was enjoying every mouthful, he'd barely eaten since his father had died and hadn't realized until now just how hungry he had been.

'Aye, I thought it was too good to be true this morning, all that talk about a banker's draft in his pocket. But it's done now – the vicar's got his money and the graveyard's to be extended.' Molly put another spoonful of potatoes on John's plate to accompany the last rasher of bacon.

'Mr Ashwell's already organized a gang of men to build a wall around the new plot and clear the ground. I wasn't sure how he'd be at first – he took me outside and warned me not to let on whose daughter I was. Not that I was going to anyway – I'm not that daft.' Lizzie chuckled to herself. 'But as soon as the director

285

was gone, Mr Ashwell was laughing and grinning and happy as could be. So was George – he thinks you're marvellous, Mam.'

'Does he now? Well, you can tell that George to behave himself, else I'll be after him and all.'

'Mam, he always does behave. We're just friends.'

Molly narrowed her eyes at her daughter. In another week she'd be fifteen. At that age, Molly had been besotted with a spotty youth, hanging on his every word and gazing lovingly into his eyes. Eighteen months later, they were married with Lizzie on the way. She'd been far too young. She wanted her daughter to take it slower, see life before getting herself entangled in commitments.

'Right, I'm off,' said John, sensing a change in the atmosphere and eager to make himself scarce before the lecture got underway. 'I've a bit of tidying to do before the funeral tomorrow. You will be there, won't you? My father would have wanted it. He always liked you, regardless of what my mother thought.'

Molly assured him that they would and pecked him lightly on the cheek. With a parting wink at Lizzie, he closed the door behind him and set off into the night. He was going to miss suppers like the one they had just shared, but he could make better money if he was lodging in Jerusalem, right next to the tunnel. Hard as it would be, his feelings would have to take second place for a while. Once John had his heart set on something, he'd go all out until he got it.

22

'So you're really off then, we can't change your mind?' Molly watched as John loaded the few things he wanted to take up to Jerusalem with him on the cart.

'No, Moll, I'm off. It'll save me walking that mile or two every day up to my work – why waste time walking when I could be working and getting paid for it? If there's anything you want from my old hut, help yourself before the new tenant moves in.' John tipped the last load of bedding off his shoulder and into the cart. 'There's all my ma's fancy bits still in there – I'd rather you had 'em than anyone else.' He stood fussing over tying things down in the wagon rather than meet her eyes. It was hard to know whether he was doing the right thing, but something told him it was better to go for a while. Maybe then he'd see things a bit clearer.

'We'll miss you, especially Lizzie, she worships you.' Molly really wanted to say, I worship you too, please don't go. But she had her pride.

'Aye, well, I'll be down every weekend. I'm best out

of this spot – too many memories.' John bowed his head.

Molly rushed forward and hugged him with all her strength, looking up into his eyes. 'You know I love you. I just wish things had been different. Don't forget about us, will you?'

'Nay, I'll not do that, not when you're the two bonniest women for miles around. Take care of yourselves – don't you be catching smallpox, and don't be working too hard. It's time you let Starchy Drawers take the strain!' John grinned and kissed Molly on the lips, lingering while he thought how stupid he was, leaving this woman on her own. 'Give Lizzie a kiss from me and tell her to behave herself.' He turned away hurriedly and mounted the buckboard, stirring the horses into action.

Molly watched with tears in her eyes. She kept them focused on the horse and cart as it made its way up the track to Blea Moor and camp Jerusalem. Happen if he had time away from her, he might realize that their lives together could be salvaged from the past. She hoped so, else there was no future for her. She loved that man too much to lose him. She'd realized that as she stood with Lizzie underneath the sprawling yew tree in the old churchyard, watching as Jim Pratt was laid to rest. She was a woman alone with a teenage daughter and no one in the world cared about them except John. And he was so mixed up he didn't know what he wanted.

'Mam, look at this.' Lizzie pulled out a fancy lace table cloth from one of the drawers in John's abandoned hut. 'Did he really say we could have what we wanted?'

'Aye, that's what he said, so we might as well take the lot, rather than leave it for some rough buggers that'd not appreciate it.' Molly was busy taking down the chintz curtains. She'd always made fun of them when Rose was alive, but secretly she had admired them. She had been so jealous of Rose's frills and fancies.

'Look at these doilies, Mam. When will we ever use all this stuff?' Lizzie was loving every moment of ransacking the hut. After the tragedies of the past week, it was a bit of much-needed brightness.

'Stick them in the sheet, Liz, then we'll bundle it all up and carry it home. I think we're going to have to make two journeys with it all. At least if John regrets moving, his stuff will be safe with us.'

Molly hummed a song while she placed everything in the double sheet that she'd brought from home. She was going to have the poshest hut in the shantytown. How things had changed. Now all she needed was a proper home, and she was already thinking of a scheme for that. There was no way she was going back to Bradford when the railway line was finished. It might be wild and rugged at Ribblehead but she loved it, especially on blue-sky days like the last few had been.

'How about we have a ride on the train down to Settle on Saturday? I think I can just about manage the fare – it can be an early birthday treat,' said Molly in a moment of madness, the home improvements going to her head.

'Mam! Mam! Do you mean it, can we really go on a proper train? It's a lot of money.'

'Why not? I don't know about you, but I could do with a break from all this depression. We had some more cases of smallpox admitted this morning. It makes you realize that life's too short to worry about money. We should enjoy ourselves while we can.' Molly tied the curtains back and looked around her now cosy home. She just prayed that neither she nor Lizzie would catch the disfiguring disease. At least these days they were better fed than they had been a year ago. That would give them a better chance of fighting off the disease, though the scars the disease left on the faces of its victims filled Molly with almost as much fear as death itself. She gave a shudder at the thought.

No, whatever the expense, they should make the most of life while they had the chance. Who knew what the future held?

Helen Parker glared with hatred at her husband, drunk behind the bar. He hadn't shed a single tear at the death of his daughter, in fact, he'd seemed quite relieved. But then again, since the baby was no doubt his, it must have come as a huge relief that he'd be spared the shame of exposure. Helen had gone alone to the hospital to see her daughter's body in the morgue. Then she'd come home, beside herself with grief, only for him to kick and punch her because his supper wasn't on the table.

And now he was carrying on like he was cock of the walk, accepting drinks from customers who wanted to extend their sympathy. There wouldn't be much sympathy for him when the truth came out. Nobody had time for a man who had sex with his own daughter. And Helen was seeing to it that the truth about Henry Parker came leaking out with every pint she served. He was already hated for short-changing the navvies and charging extortionate interest on loans, but that would be as nothing compared to the hatred they'd feel once they knew what he'd done to Florrie.

It wouldn't be long now. The silent code of the navvies would see to it that justice would be done. Henry Parker would get his comeuppance, all right. All Helen had to do was wait.

The steam engine stood alongside the platform, water dripping from its pipes and steam like the breath of a dragon puffing out of its chimney and engine. The driver wiped his sweaty brow with a coal-dusted cap and blew the whistle as he watched the first passengers from Ribblehead board his pride and joy.

'All aboard!' the newly appointed stationmaster shouted loud and clear, strutting like a prize cockerel as he herded the people on to the carriages, slamming shut the open-windowed doors. Then he blew a long blast on his whistle and waved his flag, and the train was off. As the first passenger service made its way down the Ribble Valley, he felt as if he would burst with pride. Then he turned to admire his future home, a gothic building adorned with the Midland Railway emblem. He couldn't wait for the roof to be finished so that he could show off their new residence to his wife and young family. He smiled and checked his pocket watch. With a few hours to go before the train returned, he'd have plenty of time to start planning their new garden.

'Oh, Mam, I can't believe it – us on a brand-new train.' Lizzie giggled as she tried to hold on to her shawl as they walked along the corridor, looking in each compartment to see who was in it and if there was room for them.

Molly stopped outside a nearly empty compartment and turned the brass handle on the door. 'In here, Lizzie – there's only a man reading a paper in this one.' The train jolted as she opened the door, almost making her lose her balance, and Lizzie tumbled in and collapsed on the seat beside her. They both slumped giggling on to the patterned upholstery, causing the man opposite to give a disapproving cough and glare over the top of his paper.

Lizzie looked in dismay as she recognized the Reverend Tiplady.

'Good morning, Mrs Mason,' Reverend Tiplady said primly, eyeing them with disfavour. 'I'm surprised to see you here.'

Molly couldn't have wished for a worse fellow passenger. It was on the tip of her tongue to demand what he meant by that, knowing full well that he was questioning how a navvy's widow could afford the price of the tickets.

Lizzie broke the ice for her mother: 'It's my birthday and this is my treat from Mam. We're only going to Settle, but I can't wait.' Eyes wide, she gazed around the compartment, taking in the polished woodwork, the mirror engraved with the Midland Railway emblem, as her fingers stroked the velvet upholstery.

'Indeed,' sniffed the Reverend. 'I'm travelling to Bradford where I'm needed by my colleagues. This dreadful smallpox is rife there. The curate who was with me for a short time at Batty Green sadly died of the disease – the last one of his family. Imagine, a whole family wiped out.'

Molly felt the anger rise within her as she listened to the preacher. Now she knew where the disease had come from.

'No doubt your curate was the one who brought the disease to Batty Green. The doctor has been wondering where Rose Pratt could have caught it. She was cooking and keeping house for you, wasn't she? I'd think twice about returning from Bradford, if I were you.'

'The Lord will look after me and guide me, madam, never fear. He looks after every God-fearing soul.' With a smirk of condescension, he raised his paper and resumed reading.

Molly's eyes burned into the paper, fuming at the ignorance of the man. She felt like knocking the paper out of his hands and asking how come the Lord hadn't done a better job of guiding Rose Pratt. But this was Lizzie's big day and she didn't want to spoil it, so she said nothing.

Lizzie peered out of the window, her nose squashed to the glass. 'Doesn't the dale look lovely, Mam. I love living here, with not a mill chimney in sight – just the rolling fells and the clouds sitting on top of them.'

Molly smiled, sitting back in her seat enjoying the experience swaying with the rattle of the train as it crossed the points on the line. She'd never experienced such comfortable travel.

There was a whistle from the engine and a judder as the brakes went on, and they peered from the window to see Horton-in-Ribblesdale station coming into view. Doors slammed as the passengers boarded, and then the stationmaster blew his whistle and the train puffed on its way.

'You spoke too soon, our Lizzie – look: smoking mill chimneys. Seems they have 'em up here and all.' Molly pointed at Christie's cotton mill on the banks of the River Ribble. 'They make sheets and towels with cotton from America, they even supply the Queen down in London.' Molly enjoyed telling Lizzie about her environment; she felt it was important that she knew about her surroundings. 'Next stop's ours, Lizzie. We'd best get ready.'

Molly stood up and Lizzie followed suit. As she tugged on the handle to open the door on to the passageway, she wondered whether she ought to say goodbye to the horrible Reverend Tiplady. After a moment's hesitation, she decided against it. He'd had the chance to acknowledge them when they got up from their seats, but he'd kept his newspaper in front of his face. Bugger him! Ushering Lizzie out of the compartment, she closed the door behind them and then set off unsteadily along the narrow passageway.

'Mercy me!' she gasped, glancing out of the window. 'Don't you look down, Lizzie Mason – we're on top of a viaduct!'

'Oh, Mam!' said Lizzie, ignoring the advice. 'We're ever such a long way up – and this isn't half as big as the one back at Ribblehead. Just think what it'll be like crossing that.'

Overcoming her nerves, Molly peered out over the market town of Settle. The viaduct spanned the winding road that led out of town, completely dwarfing the church that stood alongside it.

Lizzie laughed with delight at the miniature people and horses and carts going about their business in the streets below. She wasn't the least afraid, and she was enjoying the opportunity to tease her mother, who had gone white.

The train blew its whistle and pulled in to the station, the huge engine letting out steam as the stationmaster bellowed out the station's name and the porter ran about helping people with their luggage and ensuring that those who needed steps had them. Molly and Lizzie gazed in envy at the people alighting from the first-class carriages.

'One day, Liz, we'll be able to travel first-class and have hats with feathers in and fancy coats, I promise you. Then we can look down on others like they are muck on our shoes.' Molly raised her voice as a well-dressed lady gave her a disdainful stare.

'I ain't bothered, Mam. At least I'm here and not dead like Florrie. Come on, let's see what Settle's like.' Lizzie wished her mother wouldn't be so outspoken. It was her birthday and her first ride on a train – she wasn't bothered what anyone else thought of them.

Settle was full of shoppers. Molly had forgotten what it felt like to be amongst ordinary townsfolk. She peered down at the clothes she was wearing; no wonder the snooty woman had given her that look. She was like something from the back of beyond in her metal carckers on her boots and mud along the bottom of her well-worn skirts. She'd forgotten how a proper woman dressed. Catching sight of a woman shaking her head in disapproval, Molly adjusted her hair. Her heart sank at the thought of people staring at her and her daughter. It was all right at Batty Green: there, nobody judged you by the way you dressed. But here in civilization it was a different matter.

Lizzie was oblivious to the stares; she was too busy gazing in shop windows. They walked along Duke Street and both giggled at the pub called The Naked Man with a sign depicting a little naked man holding what appeared to be a pair of trousers with the date the pub was built on them. They gazed across at the houses built on three levels with a walkway on the top row and shops on the second row and another row of houses at basement level. Rising behind the buildings was a huge limestone crag that dominated the market square. They could hardly hear themselves think for the clamour of traders yelling the virtues of their wares.

Exhausted from her shopping, Molly decided it was time for a breather. 'I can run to a cup of tea, Liz, before we go back.' She picked up her shopping basket and waited for Lizzie to answer.

'Can we, Mam? I know that we've not much money, but that'd make the day even more special.'

'Come on then. I saw a little spot down the road we took from the station. If you're good, I might even run to a slice of birthday cake.' Molly put her arm around her daughter. 'Had a good day then?'

'Yes, but it isn't over yet. We've the ride back on the train still to go. I can't wait till tomorrow when I'm back at work – George is going to want to hear all about it.' Lizzie grinned.

'You and that George! Do you never get fed up of him?'

'No, he's a good friend and I like him a lot,' said Lizzie, blushing a deep shade of pink.

'Well, don't get hurt, my love. Men break hearts at the toss of a coin.' She smiled sadly at her grown-up daughter. Having known loss and heartbreak, she wanted only to spare her daughter the pain.

'I know, Mam.'

Molly and Lizzie entered the small tearoom and looked around the room. The place was half-full with people chatting and eating. Everyone fell silent when they entered. The owner approached them.

She looked them both up and down and said, 'I'm sorry, but we are busy at the moment.' She'd come

297

across their sort before: navvies' women who sat down, ordered all sorts, and then did a runner while her back was turned.

'All we want is a pot of tea and a cake. You don't look that busy to me.' Molly stood her ground.

'I'm sorry, I don't serve your sort. I learned my lesson when the railway was being built through here. Now here's the door.' The owner threw open the door, the little bell above it jingling the insult into Molly's ear.

'I'll pay you before we sit down. It's my lass's birthday and I've promised her a cup of tea before we go back up the dale.' Molly was surprisingly calm as she handed the woman the last of her money.

'All right,' she sniffed. 'At least you're not Irish – they cause no end of bother. I'll give you what this pays for. You eat it and then you get out.'

Molly and Lizzie pulled up chairs at the table next to the window and turned to look out on to the street as their fellow diners started to talk in hushed voices.

'Thanks, Mam,' Lizzie whispered.

Molly nodded as she ate her cake and drank her tea. Next time they came to Settle, she'd make sure she had a better dress on and good boots, and Lizzie would look like a princess. She couldn't do with the shame of being talked about; she had her pride.

Dusk was falling fast as Molly and Lizzie boarded the train. As they crossed the viaduct they gazed out of the window, marvelling at the huge green dome of Giggleswick School Chapel and the twinkling gaslights of Settle until the train took them back into the darkness of the dale.

It had been a day to remember for both of them. A day that had reminded Molly she was a female, not a navvy, and perhaps it was time to be more ladylike.

23

John looked around the shabby hut that had become his new home. It was a mess; four men in a small shed with no sanitation, just a designated spot of moorland for ablutions. If the weather was bad at Batty Green, it was even worse up at Jerusalem. On top of Blea Moor the wind howled incessantly and the rain whipped you until it felt as if it would flay your skin. There were times when he wondered what the hell he was doing there. Then he'd remind himself that, if he was to win Molly Mason's hand and rent one of them new railway houses that were being built, he'd need money.

He smiled as he imagined the look on her face when he finally asked her to be his and put the keys to their new home in her hands. She couldn't say no, not to the offer of him and a house with gainful employment all on a plate. Of course, he'd have to make it right with that Ashwell bloke, but he was confident he'd get a house. He was a hard worker and well liked in the offices of the good and great.

Spitting out his baccie, John pulled on his oilskins

– his only protection against the elements until he reached the shelter of the tunnel entrance. He was not looking forward to the long dark trudge through the candlelit tunnel. The first few yards were now bricked and secure, but further towards the Dent Head end blasting was still taking place, cutting deeper and deeper into the huge rolling hillside. He pulled the wooden door to and started down the slope of the railway banking. Horses and carts were lined up waiting for their heavy loads of earth from the bowels of the mountain.

'Now then, John,' said the foreman, 'nobbut a few more yards, then we should be breaking through to the other side. The Dent Head lads are a good way in already. If our lot go quiet, you can hear 'em hammering and braying. Bye, I'll be glad when there's just bricking up to do, then we can get them retaining joists out the way and we'll have a tunnel.'

'Aye, it's getting a move-on now. Us tunnellers are faster than them viaduct builders – precious lot. Is it all right, boss, if I take an hour off this afternoon? I want to put my name down for one of them new Midland houses. I thought the sooner I do it, the better.' John put his hands in his pockets and crossed his fingers as he waited for a reply. The rain was dripping down off his cap and running down the back of his neck under his oilskins. He was looking forward to getting to the shelter of the tunnel.

'Aye, but you'll be wasting your time. I hear they've all gone already. They hired length-men at Settle last week – the railway wanted local folk, not the likes of us. We come and go with the wind, or so they think.' The foreman walked off, shouting at a workman who was whipping an exhausted horse that was struggling to pull away an overloaded cart.

Bugger it! He'd been sure he'd get one of them houses. John kicked out at the wheel of a cart in irritation. Well, he'd go and put his name down anyway. There might be a chance yet. He carried on into the tunnel, past a group of men standing gossiping. He heard Henry Parker's name mentioned. The landlord of the Welcome was the talk of the dale since Florrie's death. As word spread, feelings were running high; what the navvies didn't know, they were making up. John only hoped that her funeral on the coming Sunday would quieten the bad mood about the place.

The Bishop of Bradford sprinkled holy water over the acre of land that ran down to the river and extended the churchyard. The navvies had worked hard all week and now the area was cleared and walled and a mass grave had been dug for the victims of smallpox, one of whom was Florrie. The navvies stood, heads bowed in reverence, as cart after cart unloaded the cheap wooden coffins filled with the pox-ridden bodies ready for lowering into the dark earth of the churchyard. Work on the railway had stopped for the day and even the pompous director was in attendance as prayers were said over the row of coffins. Wives, mothers, husbands and siblings wailed as earth was shovelled over the dead with mourners' eyes searching for Florrie's father, but Henry Parker was nowhere to be seen.

The rain was falling in the little glade as a line of black-clad mourners walked the tree-lined path, which smelled of wild garlic. For Lizzie, it brought back memories of the day she had snuck into the church with Florrie and been accused by the vicar of pinching money from the collection plate. She'd been a sharp 'un, had Florrie, but she'd been such a good friend in the end. Lizzie's eyes filled with tears as she thought about her friend and the good times they'd shared, talking and laughing together. She'd confided in Florrie about George, and the pair of them had giggled at men and talked about what the future might hold. Now she was gone and Lizzie felt very much alone.

The line of mourners made their way across the main road to Ingleton and entered the Hill Inn, a tavern usually frequented by the local farmers and dales folk but today hosting a funeral tea for the navvies and the visiting railway dignitary. In contrast to the Welcome Inn, its whitewashed walls were clean and the floors were polished, and the ale was served in jugs that weren't cracked around the rim. Molly and Lizzie watched as two fat pigs, disturbed by the parade of mourners passing their paddock, ran about emitting shrill squeals of panic.

'This way, gentlemen,' said the landlord of the Hill, doing his best to separate the toffs from the navvies by ushering the bishop, the vicar and railway dignitaries to comfortable chairs in the parlour, where a funeral tea had been laid out. Meanwhile the bar was filling with thirsty navvies, jostling to be served and getting more rowdy by the minute.

'Hold your hosses, I can only serve one person at once,' yelled the sweating barman, becoming increasingly irate as abuse rained down on him, until he finally snapped: 'You can piss off and all, yer fucking navvy.'

A shout went out: 'Where's Helen? Helen, for the love of God open the Welcome up – we aren't wanted here.'

Helen Parker was sitting in a corner with her young family. She'd been grateful to have the day away from the Welcome Inn. Molly and Lizzie sat next to her, Lizzie playing with the two littlest ones.

'Ah! Go on, Helen – we don't belong here. We want to drink to your Florrie's memory, but we can't do that without a pint in our hands.' One of the Welcome's regulars leaned over the table and begged her. 'We don't belong here with these money-grabbing bastards. Let the toffs stop here, but take us home.' He winked and Helen knew in her heart he was right. Even though she was enjoying her day away from the Welcome, it was where she belonged.

'I'll help you,' offered Molly, seeing the look of doubt in Helen's eye. 'I'm with the lads – I don't reckon this spot much.' When Helen gave the nod, she shouted to John, who was looking perplexed at the thought of not getting a pint: 'John, will you run us down in the trap and help us get set up before this lot arrive?'

'Aye, I'll take you – anything to get a pint. We'll have to get a move-on, though – once this lot hear you're opening up, they'll be off. It may be half a mile down the road, but I reckon they're that desperate for a pint they'll cover the distance faster than my horses can.'

'Come on then. Our Florrie would have wanted us at home. I don't suppose her useless lump of a father will have the doors open.' Helen Parker lifted her youngest on to her hip and shouted above the din: 'The Welcome'll be open in ten minutes.'

A cheer went up as John opened the door and held the crowd back so Molly and Lizzie could help Helen and the children out. They mounted the gig and whipped the horses into action, trotting just ahead of the running navvies.

The Hill Inn emptied as fast as it had filled, leaving the sweating barman dumbstruck and short of takings with only the top brass sipping their whisky and eating sandwiches.

As Helen had predicted, the Welcome Inn was closed and in darkness.

'I can pull a gill,' said Molly, putting an apron on and nipping behind the bar. Seeing that Helen was busy lighting lamps and lining up glasses and jugs, Molly took charge: 'Lizzie, you're in charge of looking after them little 'uns. John, bring a barrel in from the yard – we'll need plenty of drink in today.'

'Thanks for this,' said Helen. 'I don't know where my useless lump of a husband is.' She was missing Florrie more than ever. In that past it had been her daughter she'd turned to for help when crowds of mourners flooded the inn, but today it was Florrie they were mourning.

'Happen it's best he's not here. From what I hear, some of them want to string him up.' Molly started pouring pints in readiness for the thirsty crowd.

'Aye, he's not popular at the moment. But folk are scared of him. He still has the ear of the bosses and pays the workers out on a Saturday, and he owns this place and can ban anyone who so much as looks at him funny.' Helen broke off and gave Molly a frightened glance as the first mourners burst in through the door.

Conversation was lost as the inn was rapidly filled to the brim, the oak beams and seats groaning with the weight of people crammed inside.

Molly helped behind the bar while John collected glasses.

'What the hell have you got there, Ted?' John stopped what he was doing and stared in disbelief at what Ted and his mate were carrying through the door.

'I thought Helen could make use of this. I'm sure it'll not be missed.' The carcase of a huge pink-and-black pig was heaved on to the bar. 'I've sticked it,' said Ted cheerfully. 'It just needs shaving and curing. I'll do it, if you like. That'll keep us in bacon for months.' The navvy grinned, showing all his black teeth, as he patted the dead pig on its head. Blood trickled on to the bar from the wound on its neck.

'For God's sake, take it around the back,' hissed John. 'You'll get us all locked up.'

'Nay, I won't,' said Ted calmly. 'The constable from Ingleton caught me at it, but we've come to an understanding: he gets a joint of ham and keeps his gob shut. He wants a bit of pork off the other 'un when I go back and help myself to that.'

A cheer went up as Ted and his mate nudged and wormed their way through the revelling navvies, struggling to carry their burden out to the shed.

John shook his head. It was theft, pure and simple, but Ted's heart was in the right place.

'Come on, lads, get another round in,' shouted one of the railway gangers.

The cry was immediately followed by the slamming of tankards on the tables, and shouts for them to be filled.

'We've only one pair of hands, you know,' said Molly, cuffing one of the navvies round the ear.

While John got to work pulling pints, she swerved through the drunken hordes picking up empty tankards, dodging the hands that tried to pat her on her backside. They grinned at her through cracked and broken teeth, enjoying the way she gave as good as she got, not standing for any cheek.

'Bye, I don't know how you do this every night.' Molly wiped her hands on her skirts and confessed to Helen that she was about ready to drop.

'You just do,' said Helen. 'Either that or risk a good hiding from Henry because the takings are low.' She hung her head in shame at having to admit what she put up with from her husband.

'I'd be giving him a bloody good hiding if he was mine!' Molly said as she served a grinning navvy.

'She would an' all. Our Moll can hold her own with any man.' The elderly navvy gave his four penn'orth to the conversation before retreating back into his corner.

John, listening in, took Molly by the elbow and whispered loudly in her ear: 'Don't you get involved in this, Molly. Henry Parker is a hard man. He'd think nothing of laying into a woman and dumping your dead body under one of those viaduct piers.'

'That's as maybe – he still needs bloody sorting. He's the scum of the earth.' Molly's eyes flashed.

'From what I hear, it's in hand, so keep your mouth shut.' Molly could tell from the worried look on John's face that it was time to stop voicing her thoughts about Henry Parker.

The drink flowed all night and into the early hours with tales being told and songs being sung and tears being shed as memories of home and family were rekindled. The embers in the hearth were glowing their last dying light as the revellers slowly departed, one by one. Helen locked the door behind the last straggler and looked back into the bar to see Molly, fast asleep in the corner next to the fire. She covered her with a horse blanket before winding the chain in the grandfather clock, her last act before bed. It had been a hard day, one she would never forget.

24

Molly and Helen sat warming their hands on mugs of tea, looking around at the beer-swilled flagstone floor strewn with broken glasses. A pile of rags moved in the dim light of the snug, revealing the body of a stirring navvy as the first rays of dawn crept through the murky windows of the Welcome Inn.

'Well, at least the children are asleep, and John saw Lizzie home.' Molly took a long sip of tea and looked at the state of the inn, knowing that she would have to help clean up before starting at the hospital.

'What time did John get away? I didn't see him leave. He was a grand help.' Helen stared thoughtfully into her cup. 'You've a good man there.'

'Nay, some days he's mine, some days he isn't. At the moment he's living up at Jerusalem, wanting time away from me.' Molly could have wept, her heart ached with love for him. She was so tired and emotional after the long hours spent serving people and hiding her emotions, after seeing the people who had died in her care laid into a mass grave.

'That lad loves you. Why, you've only to see the way he is with you to know that. If my bastard of a man looked at me like that, I'd be happy. Instead, he treats me like just another one of his possessions.' Helen gazed out of the window into the grey morning light. 'I wish he was dead. It was him got Florrie in the family way, you know. Her own father! Evil bastard. If I'd known, I'd have tried to stop him, but knowing Henry he'd probably have killed me. And then what would happen to the little 'uns?' Helen was too numb to show emotion. She'd been raped, beaten, kicked and abused so many times that she no longer cried or let her feelings show.

Molly put her arm around her. 'What a bloody pair we are, stuck in this godforsaken hole. But chin up, girl, things can only get better. Let's face it, they can't get much bloody worse! Come on, we need to get this place straightened up. I start work at the hospital in an hour, but I'm not leaving until you are straight.' Molly pulled her long hair back, took hold of a brush and began sweeping, just as the main door's latch went up and the dark figure of Henry Parker walked in.

He was square-set and his shoulders blocked the morning light from creeping in through the doorway.

'Who the fuck are you and why's my pub in this state?' he bellowed at Molly. His face was hard and dark with stubble.

'Henry, Henry, this is Molly, she's helping. We buried Florrie yesterday, along with the rest of the pox victims. Molly's been helping me.' Helen ran to the side of her husband, pulling on his arm.

'Get off me!' He shook Helen loose. 'Fucking well clean up. And you – out of my pub!' Henry Parker pointed his stick at Molly as he pushed Helen to one side.

Molly looked at him. 'You ungrateful bastard! Where were you yesterday?' She didn't care how big he was; no one got away with swearing at her.

Henry lifted his stick into the air threateningly. 'Why, you bitch . . .' An ugly sneer twisted his face as he contemplated striking her across the face with his stick.

'Henry, Henry, she didn't mean it. She helped me, Henry, she helped me when you weren't here.' Helen pawed around him like a helpless puppy.

'Go fuck off, you interfering bitch!' Henry pushed Helen to one side and bellowed that he wanted something to eat.

Molly stood for a moment, watching the menacing hulk stumble into his favourite chair. She was all too aware that he was capable of snapping her neck with a single blow, and if she antagonized him it would only be worse for Helen. Picking up her shawl, she gently touched Helen on the arm as she left, avoiding eye contact with Henry Parker.

She stood outside the inn's entrance, listening to tables being tipped over and Henry's swearing and Helen's screams. The door opened for a second as the pile of rags was thrown out. The elderly navvy picked himself up, shook his head and dragged his weary feet homeward. Molly looked up at the bedroom windows, where a row of frightened children's faces were squeezed up

311

to the glass. There was nothing she could do to help them. Henry Parker would kill her if she interfered. She put her finger her to her lips, urging the children to be quiet, and walked away.

Spring mists clung to the bottom of Whernside as she followed the riverside path back to the huts. All the scaffolding was up now, stretching right the way across the valley. The huge stone piers of the first few arches of the viaduct looked grand; it was going to be an impressive structure when all twenty-four arches were complete.

Molly breathed in the sharp air in and smelled the peat as she mounted the steps to her home. She tried to envisage how the moor would look without the ramshackle shanties on it. One day it would be a sight of great beauty, an engineering wonder of the world. In the meantime it was a place where daily existence was a struggle and you learned to be thankful for what little you had.

She opened the hut door quietly and pulled her new curtains back to let the morning's light in. John was asleep in the chair, snoring loudly, while Lizzie was fast asleep in her bed behind the curtain. There wouldn't be much work done on the railway today, not with the hangovers most of the men were carrying. Molly pulled the curtain back and looked at Lizzie; she was growing up so fast, practically a young lady already. Tears filled her eyes as she thought how proud Lizzie's father would have been if he could see her now. She turned as she heard John stirring.

'You're back then.' John yawned and stretched. 'I kept Lizzie company. She didn't want to be on her own and I couldn't be bothered to walk up the fell in the dark, not when I was the worse for drink.' He opened the stove door and poked the dwindling fire with a kindling stick, then put the kettle on to boil. 'I'll make us a cuppa. I see you've raided the old home like I told you. The place is looking grand.' John yawned again and stumbled to the door, opening it wide. 'You know what I like about this place? The silence, and the smell of the moorland when nobody else is about. Just listen to that – not a sound, just the cry of a curlew. In a few hours there'll be engines running, people shouting, and such a din as you can't hear yourself think, but now it's grand.'

Molly slipped her arms around him. 'I can't stay. I'm working at the hospital today. Lizzie knows to get herself to work. Thanks for stopping with her, I'm glad she didn't stay on at the pub. That bastard Henry Parker came back this morning. God, I'd kill him if he was mine. He'd only hit me the once!'

She kissed John gently on the neck. He smelled of sleep and his reactions were slow. She wished she could curl up in bed with him instead of going to work.

'You wanton hussy, if folk see us they'll think I've slept here with you.' He turned and grinned.

'Let 'em think what they want, I'm past caring.' Molly smiled at him, putting her head on his shoulder.

'Now then, lass, I'm not ready for this yet. I need more time.' He gripped her arms and gazed into her eyes. 'I want things right, lass. This time they have to be right.' He let go of her and walked to the steaming kettle.

Molly stood staring out of the door. Right? What did he mean by right?

'Things will never be "right" here. Look at it – the place is a quagmire, full of outcasts and people struggling to eke out a living. What are you waiting for? You know I love you – or if you don't, you're stupid.' Molly sighed and sat down at the table as John placed a mug of tea in front of her.

'That's just it: I know you love me, but I've got nothing for you. I own nothing, I'll probably wind up following the railway line to Carlisle and end my days drunk in a hostel. I can't even get one of these new houses that are being built because I'm not important enough. You deserve better, lass.' John wiped his face with his hands and stared miserably across the table. Molly looked exhausted and her day hadn't even begun yet.

'Do you think I'm one of those women who follows money? Because I'm not. I love you because you are you, and through all the hard times, the rows and the deaths and the deceit, I never stopped loving you, John Pratt. It makes no difference to me whether we live in a hut, a palace or a cottage by the sea. We could have tuppence or two thousand to our name; so long as I have you, that's all that matters.' She held her hand out across the table. He grasped it and lovingly held it in his.

'But it matters to me, lass. I want to give you every-thing, you and Lizzie. I want a roof over our heads and a wage coming in, and I know you want to stay around here, close to your old man and your baby. I love you, but I want us all to be happy. Give me time and I'll try and get those things for us all.' John bent and kissed her as she pulled her shawl around her, making ready to go to the hospital.

'Nay, save your kisses. I love you for what you are, not what possessions you can give me. You must be more like your mother than I thought – she liked fancy stuff and dreamt of houses, and look where it got her. All I want is you, here with me.' She turned and made her way out of the hut, determined not to let John see the tears in her eyes.

'Molly, my dear, what's wrong?' Doctor Thistlethwaite couldn't help but notice a tear rolling down Molly's cheek as she cleaned the surgical instruments.

'I'm sorry, Doctor Thistlethwaite, I'm just tired. It's been a hard few months and we've had another two deaths this morning.' Molly turned the blame for her tears on to hospital matters but really they were for John.

'My dear, I'm always here if you need someone to talk to, you know that. We were quite close before my marriage to Gladys. I sometimes regret that you turned my proposal down. We would have been better matched.' He put his arm around her shoulders and felt her trem-bling body.

Molly sniffed hard and tried to stifle her sobs. 'Thank you, but you and Gladys look the perfect couple and I'm just tired and acting stupidly.' Molly didn't want to go down that road. She'd noticed that some days the perfect couple seemed anything but happy. She wished that the old doctor would forget his feelings for her.

'As long as you're all right.' He looked into her eyes and squeezed her hand, releasing it quickly as he heard the hospital door open and his wife enter.

Molly mouthed her thanks and went about her business. Here was a man with money and position, and she'd turned him down – a man any sensible woman would want. And yet where did her heart lie? With a man who had hardly any money and no prospects, but she still loved every inch of him.

'That man wants bloody killing.' Molly couldn't contain her anger as she bound Helen Parker's bruised and broken ribs under Doctor Thistlethwaite's supervision. 'If I could get hold of him and bray him like he's brayed you, I'd do a better job and kill him.'

'Now, Molly, it's not for us to comment on a patient's private life.' Doctor Thistlethwaite smiled a knowing smile at his nurse. He admired her outspokenness and honesty.

Gladys Thistlethwaite noted the glance between them. She'd seen them earlier through the window: her husband with his arm around Molly's shoulders. Had he no respect for their marriage, flirting with a common navvy's widow in their own hospital. It was time Molly went. Somehow Gladys had to get rid of her. She didn't know how she was going to manage it, but she was determined that she would.

The wind howled and the rain came down in sheets with the river roaring in full spate as Henry Parker urged his horse on, weighed down with the week's wages for Ribblehead. It was a pig of a day and to make things worse, he was late and the last light of the day was fast fading. He disliked travelling in the dark along the windswept moorland road. One on one, he could take any man on, but the wages provided a powerful incentive for robbery and if a gang of thieves stopped him he wouldn't stand a chance.

'Come on, ya bastard!' He kicked the flanks of his horse to urge it on. The poor animal's ears lay flat against its head as it strained up the incline heading for the lights of the Hill Inn that flickered in the distance. Suddenly the horse stumbled into a rope that had been stretched across the road, tied from tree to tree. Whinnying in terror, it reared up and threw its rider into the wet gutter before disappearing into the night with the money bags.

'Damn and fucking blast!' Henry picked himself up from the ground and realized that he'd been hijacked. His head was spinning and blood dripped from his nose as a cudgel hit him hard on the head, stunning him. Before he could stand up straight, another blow took his legs from under him. He sprawled helpless in the mud as the kicks and blows rained down, curling up with pain as his dark-clothed attackers beat and hit him until he was nearly senseless.

'This 'un's for Florrie,' a familiar voice whispered in his ear before a huge blow hit him on the head, finishing his evil life.

'Not such a big man now, are you?' One of his attackers gave him a final kick. 'Come on, lads, let's get the bastard loaded on the cart. We'll tip him down Batty Wife's Hole, he'll never be found down there, the bastard. That sinkhole goes right to the bowels of the earth, which is where he belongs. He can help the Devil stoke his fires.'

The dead bloodied body was loaded on a waiting cart and horse that immediately began trundling on its way to the deep hole in the limestone that locals knew as Batty Wife's Hole. The place was believed to have been named after the wife of a local cobbler, whose husband had murdered her by throwing her down there.

The four men looked into the cavernous hole as the body plummeted to the depths, bouncing off the sides until it disappeared from sight. Finally they rolled a huge limestone boulder down after him, making sure that the body would not be found.

'Good night's work, lads. We've got rid of the bastard – he'll not be touching any more young 'uns or taking us for mugs with his money-lending. Say nowt to nobody, understood? And don't fret, 'cause he had it coming to him.'

Their work done, the group disbanded and merged into the darkness, unnoticed.

'You say he never returned last night?' The constable from Ingleton pencilled notes in his book as he questioned Helen Parker. He looked at the thin bruised woman with her brood around her. 'His horse was found with the wages still in its saddlebags near White Scar this morning. I've walked the length of the road, but I can't see anything of him. It may be he's had an accident, but until we've found him I can't say.'

Helen held her youngest tight to her. 'He always pays the navvies this morning. He's never missed coming home on a Friday night, he knows that these folk depend on him.' She tried to look worried, but she was glad he was missing. For once there had been no Friday-night drinking, no slaps for her, and the best night's sleep she'd had in years. 'Look at 'em all lined up outside, expecting their pay. What would I have said to them? They'd have been thinking he'd run off with it – and if you hadn't found the wages, I wouldn't have put it past him.' Helen ran her fingers through the hair of her youngest as she painted a lurid picture of her husband.

'I take it your man wasn't well liked, Mrs Parker. I haven't heard a good word for him. Even the folk in the Midland office at Ingleton couldn't stand him. They're sending somebody this afternoon to pay these folk, by the way. I'll go out and inform them in a minute.' The constable stood up. 'Do you think he was hated enough for someone to want him dead?'

'Well, let's put it this way, officer: there will be a lot drinking to his disappearance tonight and few raising a glass to his health. He didn't have many friends.' Helen sent her children into the back room, out of earshot. 'He was a bastard and I won't miss him if he never turns up again.'

'Strong words, Mrs Parker. And I noticed you said *was* – he *was* a bastard. Do you think he's dead, or was it just a slip?' The constable lifted the door latch, waiting for a reply.

'I bloody hope he is! Look at my face. And here – I'll show you my ribs.' Helen started to undo her bodice.

'No, there's no need. I can see that you're in pain.'

'Aye, well, there's only so much you can take. I'll be better off without him. He was or is a bastard.' Helen stood by the bar, looking at the faces peering through the pub's windows, wondering what was going on and if they were going to get their pay.

'Right, I understand,' said the constable. 'I'll be back later.'

He walked out to the anxious crowd and announced that Henry Parker was missing and that their pay would be with them later that day and would be paid from the Midland Railway hut. The crowd were angry. This would put their weekend out, and things had to be done on a Saturday. A cry rang out:

'I hope the bastard's dead! He's never to be trusted.'

'Who said that?' the constable yelled and hurried to where he thought the shout had come from, but the crowd was dispersing, concealing the owner of the voice.

320

A group of four men, one of whom was Ted the pig stealer, stood by as the constable talked to various people. They knew nobody had seen them, and even if they had, nobody would tell. They saw Helen peer out of the window; they'd collect their blood money from her later that night. The cash would be the icing on the cake, but the fact that Henry Parker was off the earth was a big enough payment in itself.

'You sure you're all right, pet?' Molly looked Helen in the eye, she couldn't quite believe that she was taking her husband going missing so well.

'I'm fine, it'd suit me if the bugger never came back.' Helen smiled, she looked more relaxed than she'd ever done in all the time Molly had known her. She'd washed her hair, changed her clothes and even spent time on the children's appearance.

'Now, Mrs Parker, I'm sure you don't mean that.' Both women turned, nearly jumping out of their skins at the voice coming from the other side of the room. 'Mrs Mason? I was told that I'd find you here.' The constable looked at both women, thinking that a woman scorned could be a whole lot of trouble.

'Yes, I'm Mrs Mason.' Molly sniffed and gathered her shawl around her. She wasn't going to be intimidated by the little man who had been sniffing around the camp for days.

'I've been talking to Mrs Thistlethwaite and she told me that while you were bandaging Mrs Parker's ribs she heard you say that you would like to kill Henry

Parker. I'd like you to accompany me down to the cells at Ingleton. I believe you could have something to do with the disappearance of Henry Parker. If you'd accompany me and this officer I've a cart waiting outside.'

'Bugger off. It's nothing to do with me, anyone will tell you that. That stupid bitch will say anything she can think of to get at me!' Molly yelled at the constable and pulled her arm out of the grip of the officer who had appeared from the shadows.

'Now, Mrs Mason, this is only going to make things worse. You were heard saying you'd like to kill him. Come quietly or it'll be the worse for you.' The constable urged the young officer to tighten his grip as Molly was pulled kicking and screaming across the stone floor of the inn and dragged into a waiting cart with the officer cuffing her hands.

'Help me, Helen! Tell them I wouldn't do anything like that, tell them it's that lying bitch of a doctor's wife.'

Helen pulled on the constable's arm. 'She's not done owt. She could never do a thing like that. Let her go!'

The constable pushed her aside, climbing in beside the young officer and the screaming redhead.

'Get John! Tell him what they've done and look after Lizzie for me.' Molly's voice trailed off as the horse was whipped into action and she was forced to be quiet.

A crowd had gathered, wondering what the commotion was and why the constable had arrived with an extra pair of hands. A rumble of discontent went throughout the crowd. They all knew Molly wasn't responsible for Henry's disappearance. She might be mouthy but she'd never kill anyone.

Helen climbed the horse-mounting steps next to the Welcome Inn's door and shouted at the group. 'Go on then, one of you run and get John from up at Jerusalem. I'm off to sort that bloody doctor's wife out, she's the one who's accused her. Jenny, you look after the kids and tell young Lizzie what's happened to her mother.' She looked down at her serving lass, Jenny. 'Tell her not to fret, her mother's done nothing and we'll get her home before nightfall.'

A young lad shouted, 'I'll get John, I know where he's at.' And he flew off like the Devil was on his heels.

Helen stormed through the crowd, which opened like the parting of the Red Sea. Molly had been good to her and she wasn't going to stand for her being accused of Henry's murder when she'd nothing to do with it. She marched all the way to the hospital and up the steps, then barged through the door. Gladys Thistlethwaite was with her husband at the far end of the ward, discussing a patient's notes.

Helen marched down to where they stood and said it as it was:

'The woman that's stood by me through all my troubles has just been taken down to the cells in Ingleton because of you.' She pointed an accusing finger at Gladys. 'Molly's done nowt and you know it.'

'I beg your pardon, Helen, what do you mean by this intrusion?' Doctor Thistlethwaite laid his glasses down and looked at the furious woman.

'Ask her, she knows. Your wife has accused Molly of killing my Henry. She told the police what she said when she was bandaging my ribs, and now they've taken her off to the cells. You lying bitch!'

'I don't know what you are talking about,' said Gladys primly. 'Besides, for all we know, she could have killed him.' She was blushing from head to toe. It was humiliating being spoken to in this manner by a lowly barmaid.

'Mrs Parker, if you could leave us for a minute, please. I want a quiet word with my wife.' Doctor Thistlethwaite, sensing that Gladys knew more than she was prepared to say in Helen's presence, ushered her to the hospital doorway where a crowd had started to gather.

Helen went with him, protesting all the way. When the door was closed behind her she joined the rest of the crowd eavesdropping in the doorway, while others tried to listen under the windows.

Doctor Thistlethwaite pulled up his sleeves and glared at his wife. 'Gladys, tell me you didn't! You know Molly wouldn't do a thing like that – she has a heart of gold. She may be have a fiery tongue but she's too soft to hurt anyone.'

Helen and the others pressed their ears closer to the door, straining to hear the response.

'All right, I did. And I'm glad I did – I wanted rid of her. She's always flirting around you and you're always praising her. You never look at me the way you do that brazen slut.' Gladys flashed her eyes and looked as if she was about to stamp her foot like a child in a tantrum.

324

'Then you must go straight to Ingleton and tell the constable that you said what you did out of jealousy. You know damn well she hasn't killed Henry Parker. And damn and blast, woman, I married you, not her! Although at this moment in time I don't for the life of me know why.'

The door opened suddenly, taking the rowing couple by surprise. 'She can come with me in the trap. I'll take her to Ingleton, and I'll also tell that jumped-up constable that I was with Molly all night on Friday.' John marched down the hospital aisle. 'You always have been a jealous bitch! Did you not know that Molly turned this man down long before you married him? She needs a proper fella like me, not a man lost in books and flowers. What good's one of them on a cold night.' John grabbed Gladys's arm and marched her out through the cheering crowd. 'Sorry, Doc,' he called over his shoulder, 'but it was time she knew she was second best. Happen it'll learn her a bit of humility.' He patted her skirted bottom sarcastically as he pushed her on to his horse and trap. Tears were streaming down her blushing face as she held on for dear life to the buck-board.

Lizzie ran up to the trap as it went past the Welcome's door.

'Fetch my mam back, John! She didn't do it, I know she didn't do it.' She couldn't keep up with the trotting horse.

'She'll be back before dark, Liz. You mind yourself, we'll get this straight. Don't you worry, pet.' John whipped the horse and the dust flew up from the road beneath its galloping hooves.

Helen Parker had remained outside the hospital along with the rest of the crowd that had gathered. All of them were angry about Molly being arrested. Nurse Gladys had never tried to fit in, always acting as if she was too good for them, but this time she had gone too far. The doctor came and stood in the doorway, looking in the direction John's cart had gone and anxiously running his fingers through his hair. When a group of men started to make their way up the steps, he hurriedly closed the door, trying to bar them from the hospital.

'Shutting the door won't close us out, Doc. It's time that wife of yours learned to shut her mouth.' Ted, the ringleader, opened the door and bellowed down the hospital to the table where the doctor was burying his head in his papers. 'You sort her out, else we will – won't we, lads?' A cheer went up outside. 'She needs reminding that she's no better than any of us. Here at Batty Green, all us misfits have to rub along to survive.' Ted slammed his hand on the doctor's table and glared at the quivering doctor. 'Understand?'

Doctor Thistlethwaite nodded his head and whispered, 'I understand. I'll talk to her.'

'Right then, now you know where we stand, that's grand. Isn't it, men?' Ted raised his arm and the men behind him shouted 'Aye' in agreement. 'Nothing more to be said then, long as she's taken in hand.'

Ted and his gang lumbered out of the hospital leaving

the shaken doctor mopping his brow. For a while there he'd been convinced he would end up a patient in his own hospital. It wasn't an experience he would care to repeat.

'You know I could charge you for wasting police time.' The constable glowered at Gladys Thistlethwaite as he unlocked the cell door.

Gladys hung her head and didn't say anything.

Molly pushed the door open and rubbed her wrists where the handcuffs had been. 'Bitch!' She pushed past Gladys and walked out to the trap, not even acknowledging the constable.

'I'd moderate your language in future and think what you're saying,' the constable warned Molly.

'Aye, and I wouldn't listen to idle gossip and jealous wives.' Molly smiled sweetly at the officer, getting in the last word as John flicked the reins and they set off for home.

25

John grinned at his quiet Molly next to him.

'Well, we got you out of there. At least Gladys came clean!'

'Aye, but you told that constable you'd stopped with me all night. There was no need for that.' Molly was annoyed.

'What are you complaining about? Did you want them thinking you spent all night with the doctor and that's why his wife was jealous? That middle-class shrimp would never be enough for you! I gave that plod something to gossip about.' John grinned, watching Molly's face wrinkle as she tried to work out whether it was an insult she'd just been given or a compliment.

'But the truth is, John Pratt, you were on top of Blea Moor with a load of fellas that night, not with me.' Molly turned and looked at him.

'Now don't start. I needed to go and get my mind settled, what with my mother and father dying. Then there was her confession and our Bob . . . my head's all over the spot – no brass and no prospects. Why the hell should you want me?' John blushed and played with the reins of the horse, overwhelmed by his feelings for this woman.

Molly placed her hand on the side of his face and pulled it around so that he was looking at her. 'I love you, John Pratt. How many times do I have to tell you. Let's forget about our families – they're gone now, we can't bring them back. We need to live for us and Lizzie.' She kissed him on the lips. 'Come and join Lizzie and me. We needn't do it legal and get married. Reputation be damned, mine's already shot to hell anyway!' Molly suddenly wanted to throw caution to the winds and be irresponsible. She'd put up with the gossip if it meant catching her fella.

John didn't say a word but he held Molly tightly and kissed her with passion. He did love her, he loved every inch of her, every word she spoke, every smile that crossed her lips. Damn the woman! She was right: the past didn't matter, it was the future that counted. Money or no money, something would turn up. He held her with both arms and the horse neighed as he dropped the reins, sending the trap jolting forward.

'Put her down, you know where she's been!' a gang of workmen shouted at the passionate couple embracing, totally lost in one another.

'Aye, I know where she's been and I know where we're going. And what's more, I don't care if the world knows about it!' John shouted back at the gang.

As the men roared their approval, John grinned and turned back for another kiss.

Molly responded with passion. She'd got her man and she was suddenly happy with life.

When they came up for air, John grasped Molly's hand. 'If we're going to do this, we do it right. I'll not have anyone calling you common, so Molly Mason, like I've asked you before, will you marry me? I know it's not right romantic, but the time's right. And bugger me, I'm not being put off again.' John squeezed her hand and pressed it hard against his heart. Pleading to hear the right answer.

Molly's eyes filled with tears. 'You're not just saying it? You mean it?'

'I should have kept on asking you and not been put off. For God's sake, Moll, please say yes . . .' John held her hands tightly as the horse stepped a pace or two forward and he had to shout a command to halt the inpatient animal.

'Then the answer's yes. Yes, I will marry you, John Pratt! And I promise to always love you and you alone.' Molly kissed him and smiled, her heart beating as if a trapped butterfly was in her chest. She was to be married! She who was down and out and nearly in the gutter over a year ago.

The dusk was falling as she watched John drive away, the arches of the viaduct just visible as he made his way up the fellside to Blea Moor. They'd agreed to take it slow towards their wedding day. Another few weeks and John would have finished work at the tunnel and then they would get married and John would move in.

Lizzie had been over the moon with happiness when they broke the news, nearly strangling John as she hugged him tight to welcome him as her mother's new husband-to-be.

Molly turned and went into her hut. This little home of hers had seen so much hurt in the past year, but now it was going to see love and happiness. She hummed as she washed the pots and helped Lizzie brush her long hair before helping her to twist and tie it in rags for her usual curls to be there come morning.

'Mam, I love you and I love John, but promise you'll not forget my dad, will you?' Lizzie said quietly as her mother pulled and patted her hair.

'No, pet, your dad was special and he'll always be here in my heart. So I promise. But sometimes you have to move on, and John's a good man. He'll be good for us both.'

'We won't ever leave my dad and baby Tommy, will we? They'd be lonely in the churchyard without us near.' Lizzie was thinking of what the future might hold.

'No, Liz, we won't be leaving – not for a long time anyway. The railway's yet to be finished and that viaduct's a long way from being done.' Molly patted the last rag in place and sighed.

'I'm never going to leave. If you go, you'll have to go without me.' Lizzie walked over to her bed and pulled the woollen blanket up to her chin. 'I'll stop with my dad.' She sighed and turned to look at the wooden wall.

'Night, pet.' Molly blew her candle out and pulled

the dividing curtain; with each passing day Lizzie was growing to be more and more like herself – stubborn.

Molly strode out to the hospital. Another smallpox victim was being carried into the isolation ward as she drew near. The sight convinced her that she was making the right decision; money wasn't everything and life was for living. So far she'd been lucky not to have contracted the disease.

She waited patiently at the door as Gladys and Doctor Thistlethwaite comforted the new patient and eased him into what would probably be his deathbed. She watched Gladys glancing nervously up at her, no doubt wondering what she was doing there this morning when it wasn't her shift.

'Molly! I wasn't expecting you. Are you all right after . . . the little misunderstanding?' Doctor Thistlethwaite took her by the arm and guided her back outside.

'Don't worry, I'm not here to cause a scene. I've decided I've had enough, you'll have to find someone to replace me. Gladys can't work with me, knowing what she does. I'll apologize right now on behalf of John – he'd no right to say what he did about you.' Molly had thought about how she was going to say it, but it still came out wrong.

'It's Gladys and I that should be apologizing, not you or John. We have played with people's feelings and we should have known better. Please stay, Molly. We need you – the patients need you.' Doctor Thistlethwaite pressed her hand.

'No, I'm not stopping. I don't know what I am going to do, but I can't play gooseberry between you and Gladys. You'll manage.' Molly started walking down the steps. When she got to the bottom one she stopped and turned. 'Thank you for all you've learned me. You gave me back my pride.'

And then she walked, head held high, up the road towards the newly built railway bridge and the Welcome Inn.

Doctor Thistlethwaite watched her go. She was a beautiful woman; proud, clever and above all gracious. How he wished Gladys was all those things.

'So, you're leaving us, you old bugger!' John's hut-mates hit him on the shoulder as he announced his forthcoming wedding.

'Aye, but not yet. I want to see the tunnel finished, or at least get through to the Dent side and then leave it to you brickies!' He pulled his braces up and laced his boots before putting on his second layer of clothing. 'See you tonight, lads. I'll treat you to a gill or two to celebrate.' Then he set off down the fellside, whistling with happiness at the thought of his upcoming wedding.

'So what are you going to do now then?' Helen Parker looked at Molly staring into her cup of tea.

'I don't know. All I know is I couldn't have worked another minute over there, with the stench of death and that stupid cow Gladys watching my every move.' Molly ran her hands through her hair and took a long slurp of her tea. The two women had grown close since Florrie's death and she felt that she could talk openly with Helen. 'I just need something to make a bit of money with until John finishes up at Blea Moor.'

Helen leaned over the bar, turning for a moment to yell at her children, who were squabbling in the back room. 'Why don't you come and help me? Ever since Henry did a runner, I've been run off my feet. I could do with some help. Besides, the fellas like you behind the bar, I heard one or two of them admiring your assets when it was Florrie's funeral.'

'Give over, Helen, I'm too old in the tooth for any of that. Anyway, I'm about to be married.' Molly grinned, she liked to flirt and wind men up, but that was as far as it went and most of them knew that.

'I'd pay you well and you'd get fed. Are you any good at cooking?' Helen started to think seriously about her proposal. Always a shrewd businesswoman, she was sure Molly's presence behind the bar would boost her takings.

'Cook – me! Happen I can make a good beef sandwich or a tattie stew, but nothing like you can.' Molly laughed, but she was beginning to think it was perhaps a way of making a bob or two.

'Well, you can serve behind the bar then. Will five bob a week do ya?' Helen put her head to one side and smiled at her mate. It would be good to have back-up and someone she could trust; besides, Molly had a reputation of not taking any nonsense and men respected her for that.

334

Molly hesitated for a minute. 'Five bob! Go on then, for pay as good as that I'll give it a try. But what if Henry comes back? He'll not want me here.'

'Don't you bother about him. He'll not be coming back, trust me.' Helen smiled a knowing smile and winked at Molly. She would have liked to tell her friend that she'd seen to it he was deep in the bottom of Batty Wife's Hole, but daren't.

'I've got a new job, Lizzie. I'm going to be helping Helen at the pub.' Molly broke the news to Lizzie while they sat eating their supper. 'I'd had enough at the hospital – and it's only until John comes and lives with us, you'll be all right with that, won't you, pet?'

'Mr Ashwell says Henry Parker won't come back so he's been seeing about the wages with the big bosses from Leeds.' Lizzie spooned broth into her bowl, not looking up at her mother. 'From next weekend everyone's going to be paid partly in tokens and a Midland clerk is going to give them out with a constable on hand in case there's any trouble. So I don't know why you'd want to work at the Welcome.'

'What do you mean, folk are going to be paid by token?'

'One of the snooty bosses was horrified at how much drink was being sold at the Welcome, so he decided on this token system to make sure the men's families were being fed instead of them squandering all their wages on drink.' Lizzie dipped her bread into the last dregs of her broth and sat back to look at her mother. 'Yeah, I'll be fine with you there. I can come and play with Florrie's brothers and sisters, keep them from under your feet.'

Molly, still wrestling with Lizzie's news about the tokens, said, 'But that's not right, Liz. A man earns his money, he should be able to spend it where and how he wants.' She realized this might not be good news for the Welcome Inn.

'Well, all the local traders have been told that they'll get paid direct from the Midland when they hand in the used tokens. And the railway's provisions hut will deal in tokens from now on. You won't be able to get goods on tick there, the way you used to.' Lizzie was surprised at the way her mother was taking the news. When Mr Ashwell explained it to her, it had sounded like a good idea.

'It's another way to make money out of us poor buggers,' Molly sighed. 'It'll be for the good of their pockets, not ours. You can tell your Mr Ashwell there'll be trouble if prices go up with the arrival of his tokens.' She knew why the Midland was reassessing their wage structure and it had nothing to do with the immorality of drink. They had found a way that the railway and local traders could work in league to profit from the workers, and at the same time ensure that the navvies would be more sober when they reported for duty.

'I'll tell him, Mam, but he'll not listen to me. I'd be thinking twice about your new job, though. Florrie's mam might not need you.' Lizzie helped herself to another slice of bread before clearing her dish.

*

To Molly's surprise, Helen Parker wasn't too concerned when she told her about the new token system. Once Henry had gone, she'd wasted no time in searching out his life savings. It turned out they'd made a pretty penny. Another few weeks and she meant to be away from Batty Green.

'We'll be all right, Moll, don't you fret. The fellas will still want their drink, just not as much. Happen I'll be able to get to bed at a decent time.' She pounded her bread dough, flour dust powdering the air. 'Mop the back kitchen floor for me, would you? Then we're about done.' She wiped her brow with the back of her floured hand and watched as Molly grabbed the mop and bucket. She couldn't understand why Molly was so worried about who controlled the navvies' pay; as long as they had enough not to go hungry, with a bit left over for a drink and a smoke, then why should they worry if they got paid in tokens or brass? She was a strange one, was Molly. Wages was man's business, not a woman's affair.

All the traders, the constable and a Midland official were lined up behind the table that had been put out in front of the Midland Railway office. While young George Ashwell opened the token tin, the other official opened the cash tin. The queue of navvies began to get unruly as word spread back down the line that part of their wages would be paid in tokens instead of cash.

'Give me my bloody wages! I don't want any of your

337

bloody tin money.' The outspoken ganger of the length-men banged his fist down hard on the table. 'You bloody thieving lot! I've worked all week and I've a family to feed – what good's this bloody stuff.' He flipped one of the tokens into the air.

The constable pulled his truncheon out, but the Midland official rose from his chair, urging him to put it away. Then he addressed the crowd:

'These tokens can be spent at any of these traders' stores. See, here's Elijah Allen, Ben Lawson, and the clerks from Martindale's and Pickthorn's.' He waved his arm at the traders. 'And the Midland's own provision shop will offer goods at lower prices just for you men and your wives, so you can spend your tokens wisely and keep your family well fed and still have your money for a gill or two. It's no different from money – in fact, it's better, because you get more for your money.'

The official stepped down and quietly took the arm of the ganger, who was still complaining. Leading him out of earshot of the navvies, he whispered, 'You've two choices. Either you take this pay and tell all these it's the best thing you've ever heard of – and I pay you double. Or I get this constable here to arrest you, and him and his pals will break every bone in your body. Do you understand what I'm saying?' The Midland officer's mouth twisted into an ugly grin as he gripped the ganger's arm.

The burly man considered the threat and looked at the constable, clutching his truncheon, ready for action.

He turned to the crowd: 'It's fine, men. Sounds like a good deal – tokens for grub and money for drink, what more do we need?'

The crowd still rumbled with discontent and the ganger glared darkly at the clerks as he held out his hand for his double pay. As he walked away, he shouted at the merchants: 'Get your arses moving then – we'll need to spend these bloody tokens.' He was inwardly furious with himself for being bought so easily, but he'd a wife and five young 'uns to think about. They'd never survive if he was locked up or unable to earn.

Young George Ashwell counted the tokens out and passed them into the rough hands of the working men who were giving their all for the building of the Settle–Carlisle line. It was hard not to shake with fear when they sneered at his lily-white hands and soft nature. He vowed that when he was a older and the viaduct was finished, he was going home to Leeds to get a job in a nice clean office. The Midland was not for him. He wasn't going to follow his father, who'd help plan nearly every railway line in the region, and make it a career. He looked up and saw Lizzie watching him, along with her mother. She was bonny enough and clever for a young woman, but she was a navvy's daughter. He could do better and he knew it.

The token system had taken its toll on trade at the Welcome over the last few weeks and the navvies were growing restless.

'Give us another gill, Moll. I'll trade my wife for

another drink,' pleaded one of the Welcome's regulars, desperate for another mouthful of ale.

'Sorry, mate. No money, no drink.' Molly winked at the disgruntled navvy. 'You can thank the Midland for that.'

'Bloody crooks! Even the bloody flour is full of sawdust! I'd burn that bloody Midland store down if we didn't need it so much, now we can't go to market and buy goods where we like.' The disheartened man picked his cap up and wandered aimlessly out of the pub.

'Something's going to have to be done, else we needn't be here. You can't be making enough to pay me at the moment.' Molly clanked the tankards together as she placed them under the bar.

'I've been meaning to talk to you about that all day, but I haven't had the chance.' Helen slumped down in a wooden chair next to her bar and tapped on the ale-swilled table. 'I'm moving on, Moll. I've decided I've had enough of running this spot. I'm putting it up for sale.' She could hardly bring herself to look Molly in the eye. She hated letting her best friend down.

Molly felt deflated. Not only was she about to lose her friend but also her job. 'I'll miss you,' she said. 'And what if Henry comes back?'

'I'm really sorry, Moll. You really look as if you belong behind that bar. Don't worry about Henry – he'll not be coming back. I've had a letter from him. He's living with another woman, up in the northeast.' Helen could feel her cheeks flush, she hated lying to her friend.

'You never told me!' Molly was upset at all the news Helen seemed to have been keeping from her.

'I only got it this morning.' She quickly changed the subject: 'I'm going to miss your Lizzie; she's good with my little 'uns. She's a good lass.'

'Well, I suppose I'll have to have a rethink about what to do with myself. John says another week and the tunnel will have broken through into Dent, and then he'll be back down with me.' Molly smiled lovingly at the thought of her man coming back to her.

'See, and then you've the wedding to look forward to. That'll be better than helping me out at this hole. I'm off home. My mother's still alive and it'll be good to go back and let her see her grandchildren.' Helen yawned, she'd wound down already, just thinking about going home.

'Where's that at then, Helen?' Molly was beginning to realize how little she knew about her friend.

'I come from Swaledale, a little village called Muker. My mam lives with my brother at a farm called Usher Gap. I've thought of nothing else since Henry left and now I want to go home. It's the bonniest place you can think of in summer: meadows full of buttercups and the babbling river running down the dale. You'd not wish to be anywhere else.' Helen smiled at the memory.

'Sounds grand. Better than the smoky streets of Bradford where I come from.' Molly's memories of Bradford made her cringe. 'I never want to go back there.'

'What will you and John do once the line's finished? Surely you'll not want to stop around here?' Helen was worried about where her friend was going to end up. She'd realized that behind that occasionally caustic tongue there beat a heart of gold.

'Lizzie wants to stay near here for the sake of her dead brother and dad, and I can't see John wanting to stray far, now his brother lives up the road and his parents are in the graveyard. So we have to think of somewhere to live and earn a living after the Midland railway has moved on.'

Helen smiled encouragingly. 'Something will turn up, I'm sure. John's a good worker and a fair man. There's always work in this world if you are prepared to look for it.'

Molly couldn't help but notice how her friend had blossomed since Henry's disappearance. The bruises had gone and the colour had come back to her cheeks, along with a newfound confidence. It didn't surprise her that Helen wanted to make a break from a twenty-four-hour job serving ale to navvies.

'Aye, well, I hope so, because we can't live off thin air and our Lizzie will have to find a job once the railway moves on, or move on with it.'

Molly bade Helen goodnight and set off home, a frown creasing her brow. After all her efforts, she was back to square one: not enough money coming in and without a friend. Then she reminded herself that she still had her John and her health, which was lot more than all those poor buggers with smallpox.

26

The black-capped faces peered through the earth and stone towards Ribblehead.

'Now then, you bastards, we've done it!' John pulled more soil and earth away so the two tunnelling gangs could see each other properly. They reached across the gap to shake hands, laughing with delight as the two lengths of the tunnel were finally connected.

'So that's what you look like.' John patted his Dent colleague on the shoulder and lifted the candle to illuminate his face.

'Aye, lad, here we are – the Dent Head gang to your rescue!' The man grinned a black-faced smile and punched him on the shoulder. 'We thought we'd better help you Ribblehead soft lumps out.'

The two gangs continued exchanging jovial insults for a while, each side claiming the glory for completing the tunnel.

'It's whoever lays the last brick that counts, and that'll be one of my lads.' John led the Dent gang leader to one of the vents that carried air down into the tunnel.

'It's a fair job that we've done. Cost a lot of money and a lot of lives, but the worst bit is over now.' John shook the man's hand.

'Aye, that fell they call Rise Hill is going to be nowt compared to this bugger.'

They both walked on, past the gangs of brick-layers and scaffold-builders, congratulating themselves and laughing. Then suddenly, from deep within the bowels of the tunnel, there was a deafening blast and a huge rush of air filled with debris that almost knocked them off their feet. Grit and dirt filled their lungs, making it almost impossible to breathe. They flung themselves to the floor of the tunnel as dirt and rubble blew over them. The ground under them shook, and the rumbling seemed to go on for ever. John could only lie still, covering his head and praying for it to stop.

Little by little the noise subsided enough for him to hear the coughing and spluttering of tunnel workers. John lifted his head, tried to clear his lungs, and raised himself up to assess the damage. He turned to the leader of the Dent gang, lying alongside him.

'Come on, mate, let's go. There'll be a lot of cas-ualties after that fall.'

There was no response. John shook the man's shoulder: still nothing. He pulled on the shoulder, turning him over. It was then that he saw the spike of scaf-folding wood that had pierced the man's neck. In the dim light of those few oil lamps that had stayed lit, he could see that the man's clothes were drenched in the blood that had flowed from his wound. He was dead.

344

John slumped on his knees, overcome with anguish. Only a minute ago they'd been laughing and celebrating, and now one of them was dead. It could so easily have been his body, lying on the ground. Suddenly the tunnel seemed more like a tomb, its dark walls closing in and what air there was in the chamber so full of dust and debris that he felt he was being smothered. Fear gripped him. He knew he had to get out of this place. Lungs bursting with the effort, he ran the five hundred yards to the entrance, though it seemed more like five hundred miles between him and the daylight and the gentle rain.

Rescue teams were rushing into the tunnel to help the dead and the wounded. In their haste, a couple of the rescuers jostled past, bumping shoulders with John and knocking him to the side of the track. When he finally made it out into the fresh dale air, he collapsed on the ground, gasping to fill his lungs, letting his tears mingle with the raindrops coursing down his face. Never again would he go into the dark bowels of hell. He was finished in the tunnel.

Hands shaking, he wiped the earth from his face, leaving tear-stained streaks on his cheeks. His legs could barely carry him as he climbed the railway bank to the heather-covered fell. He stumbled and tumbled the mile back down to Batty Green, ignoring the men who stopped to ask if he was all right and whether he knew who had been caught in the fall. All he wanted was to get to the safety of Molly's arms.

*

'You're all right, pet, you're with me now.' Molly was on her knees, holding John's hands while he shook and wept openly.

'He was dead, Moll. One minute we were having a laugh, and the next thing I knew, he was dead. That's the second time my number's almost come up. I can't face going back in there again.'

'You don't have to, pet. I'd rather have you than the Midland's blood money.' Molly stroked his dusty blond hair and cradled him in her arms. 'Tell that bloody lot where to put their job. I'm not having another of my men lost for the sake of a bloody railway line.'

'But we need the money. You can't do owt without money.' John wiped his nose and looked up at her. 'Nay, lass, give me a day or two and I'll be all right. What would my mother say if she could see me, bawling like a baby? She'd probably kick my arse good and proper.'

Molly stood back, arms crossed. She'd lived with the fear of what might happen ever since the last time he'd almost been killed. The memory of that day, when she'd wept over a mangled body, believing it to be his, had never left her. No amount of money was worth going through that.

'You'll not be going back, John, not as long as I have breath in my body – and that's final.'

'He was nearly killed, Helen. We can't go on like that – I can't lose him, I can't!' Molly leaned on her broom. She hadn't wanted to leave John on his own after what had happened, but he'd insisted that he'd be all right while she went to work. She turned to her friend, who was wiping the tables down.

'But what else can the pair of you do? There's no other work to be had around here, lass.' Helen resumed wiping the table, but then she pulled up suddenly and turned back to Molly, who was gazing out of the window. 'I think I must be bloody daft! Why didn't I think of this before!' she shrieked.

'What?' Molly was looking bewildered, wondering what had got into her.

'I don't need to sell the pub – I'll be all right living back with my mum. So why don't I rent it to you and John? You know the job, he's had enough working on the railway, and it would mean Lizzie would have a job too, when the railway moves on.' Helen grinned. 'It'd be perfect for you all!' She placed her hands on her hips and waited for Molly to respond.

'You can't afford not to sell – and we can't afford the rent,' said Molly with a shake of her head.

'Listen to me, Molly Mason: you're not to say a word to anyone, but I'm not short of a bob or two. Remember how Henry used to loan the fellas money and charge them interest? He never spent a penny of that on us – the bugger stashed the whole lot away. I found it in the cellar after he'd gone. There's more than enough to see me and the kids right. We won't be going short, the way we did when Henry was around.' She walked over to Molly and touched her arm. 'I owe you more than money can buy for looking after my lass in her last hours, and for helping me out in my hour of need. If you're interested in taking the inn on, the first month's rent is on me – that'll give you a bit of time to get on your feet. Why not see what John says? I know the pair of you could run it with one hand tied behind your backs. You'd be doing me a favour, looking after this place . . .' Her lip trembled and tears began to flow as she added, 'And you could do me a favour and put flowers on our Florrie's grave.'

Molly's response was another shake of the head. 'John will not take charity – you'd have to charge us something. And our takings would be lower than yours because I can't cook. I do appreciate your offer, Helen, but it just wouldn't work.'

Helen ignored her. She was too busy working it all out in her head. 'Just think of the folk that'll come once the railway's finished. They're already taking rides out on a Sunday to look at the viaduct, and it isn't even finished. Once my brood's cleared off, you'll have rooms to spare – you could let them out.' Her enthusiasm for the idea was growing by the minute. At the back of her mind she'd been wondering whether it would be legal for her to sell the pub, seeing as Henry's name was on the deeds and in the eyes of the law he was 'missing' rather than dead. This way she would still own the pub and get an income from it, plus she'd have the comfort of knowing she could trust her tenants.

'I'll talk to him. But there's still the problem of the cooking – and that's what you make your money on.' Molly was uncertain. She looked around the bar-room, picturing herself running it. Helen was right, there would be two spare bedrooms once the Parker family left: that at least would be easy money!

'You'd soon get the hang of it: beef hot-pot, rib of beef with Yorkshire puds, mutton stew – stick to straight-forward grub, that's what people want.' Helen rattled off the menu without even thinking about it. 'And the odd apple pie, if you've time.'

'It might be straightforward to you, but I've never cooked for that many people. As for pastry – the stuff I turn out might as well be cardboard. I can't even do mashed tatties without grey lumps in.'

'Think about it,' Helen said firmly. Then she went about her business, humming under her breath. With a bit of luck, her friend's life would be a little more settled from hereon.

'She offered you what?' John was struggling to take it all in.

Since she'd left the Welcome Inn, Molly had thought of little else. Why shouldn't they take the pub on? John could easily help her, a man behind the bar made it seem more respectable. Ever since Henry had gone missing, folk had commented that it wasn't the same, even though they had hated his guts when he'd been there.

It would also mean that Lizzie would have a home at last and that would be something to be grateful for.

'It could be ours, John. Just think, you could be behind your own bar, like your Mike up the road.'

'Nay, I'll never be like him! He's sold his soul to his

349

in-laws. What would my mother say? Two brothers, brought up strict Methodists, and both of us running pubs! She'd be turning in her grave!' He couldn't help laughing at the thought.

'And Lizzie would have her own bedroom – we'd have a proper roof over our heads, solid brick walls instead of a flimsy shanty. There's even a couple of spare rooms that we could rent out.' She paused, biting her lip. 'There's only one problem. I'm not the best of cooks and the food is where Helen makes her money, especially since the tokens came in. Folk aren't drinking like they used to.'

But Molly's excitement was soon bubbling to the surface again as she tried to imagine all their knick-knacks placed around the rooms, John pulling pints behind the bar . . . She'd manage the cooking somehow.

'Aye, well, there are some good things about it,' said John, nodding. 'It would get me away from the railway, for a start. Then there's the stables behind the pub: we could charge for stabling horses. I don't know why the Parkers never did that. He was an idle bugger, that Henry – made more money through threats than work. Let me sleep on it, lass. I'll let you know in the morning.' He rubbed his head, it was a lot to think about, and his mind was still all over the place with memories of the tunnel collapse flooding his thoughts. He didn't know how many of his workmates had made it out alive. The rescue effort was still ongoing. Some of those who had been brought out were in a bad way and seemed unlikely to survive.

'And where will you be in the morning?' Molly coyly enquired.

'Well, lass, I thought I'd be with you. I'll need a comforting hand through the night.' He grinned.

'Oh, will you now? And what if I don't want you here?' Molly couldn't resist teasing him.

'After all the times you've begged me to stay, you're going to turn me out?' he laughed.

'Well, I suppose you can stay then . . . sleeping in the chair, of course!'

John grabbed her and held her tight. 'Nay, lass. I hope that bed doesn't make a lot of noise, because if it does, Lizzie's not going to get much sleep!'

'Why, John Pratt, you need to watch what you're saying! I'm just thankful she's not back from work yet.'

'Ahh, shut up, woman, and give me a kiss.' He squeezed her tight and kissed her hard and firm on the lips. When he finally released her, he said, 'I've enough saved up to pay for the vicar – how about marrying me quick? You better had if we're going to be running that pub.'

'What did you just say? I thought you wanted to sleep on it?' Molly was flushed and breathless. Could all this really be hers? Marriage and a pub?

'Well, we'd better do it properly if we're going to do it. And I reckon we'd be bloody stupid if we didn't take Helen up on her offer. I can just see myself with an apron on, opening beer casks for my customers while the drunks admire my wife. I don't need the night to sleep on it and anyway I've better things to do in bed with a woman like you than think about business.'

'Oh, John!' Molly hugged him and kissed him all over, only to be interrupted by Lizzie slamming the hut door and bursting into tears.

She stomped past the embracing couple and sat down next to the stove.

'What ever's up, pet? Why all the tears? John's fine – look, he's here, he didn't get hurt in the tunnel collapse.' Molly went to console her daughter.

'It's George, Mam. He's . . . he's going back to Leeds. I'll never see him again! What am I going to do? I love him.' Lizzie sobbed into her hankie, heartbroken that her first crush was leaving her.

'Aye, you wanted nowt to do with him anyway. He's one of them, lass, he's not our sort.' Molly hugged her sobbing daughter.

'Your mother's right. We've our ways and they've theirs. He'd only have used you, lass.' John tousled her hair and looked on helpless as she cried her heart out.

'What do you know? You're both old, you don't know how I feel.' She sobbed and wiped her tears before walking to her bed and throwing herself upon it to bury her head in her pillow.

John took a step towards her but Molly held him back.

'Leave her, John. She'll get over it. I can remember when I lost my first beau. You never forget, your first love is always special.' She pulled the dividing curtain to give Lizzie her privacy. 'Let's go and have a quick stroll before I go back to help Helen with the evening crowd. It's grand out, the days are getting longer. It'll soon be summer.' She grabbed John's hand and urged him outside, threading her arm through his as they strolled down the Hawes Road.

'Would you look at that sunset!' Both turned and gazed at the golden rays of the setting sun filtering through low cloud over the dark shape of the partly built viaduct. The fellside of Whernside was lit up in a blaze of golden light, highlighting the white shapes of sheep as they grazed their last mouthful of moorland feed before nightfall. A lonesome curlew sang its haunting song overhead and the smell of peat and heather filled the air.

'Once all the huts and the navvies have gone it will be a beautiful place. The sort of place where we will all enjoy living, even Lizzie, once she gets over George. It's so hard at that age. She probably feels her whole world is coming to an end. Happen she'll feel different in the morning, poor lass. She's bound to fall in love again before long. Someone usually comes around the corner when you least expect them.'

'Is that what I did?' John sat on an outcrop of limestone and pulled Molly to sit down beside him.

'Nay, I was a lost soul, and you know it. I wasn't coping at all well.' Molly blushed, remembering how she had almost become dependent on drink. 'If it hadn't been for your mother taking Lizzie in, I'd probably be in that churchyard with everybody else. And then you made yourself known, and look where we are now: sitting on a big lump of stone with our whole lives in front of us!' She giggled and kissed John on the cheek.

'Let's do it, lass – let's get married, run the Welcome and start a family.' John hugged Molly tight and kissed her gently on the forehead. 'You're beautiful, Molly Mason, and I'm a lucky man.'

'Family . . . I don't know about family. I've done my bit for children, but perhaps it would be nice to hear the patter of tiny feet again. I miss my Tommy and I wasn't the best of mothers to him.' Molly felt tears coming to her eyes. She was crying too for the baby she'd miscarried and never told anyone about, not even John, the father. She only hoped she could have children after that.

'You'd no choice, lass. This time it'll be different.' He patted her hand. 'Come on, that sun's going down and there's still a nip in the air.' John stood up and pulled her to her feet. 'Time for you to go to work. Tell Helen we'll take her up on her offer. And while you're doing that, I'll go and see our lovelorn Lizzie.'

'Should I tell Helen tonight? Do you really think we can take it on?' Molly was almost trotting to keep up with John's long strides. 'I can't cook, you know.' Waves of doubt kept washing over her every time she thought of that drawback. It was a lot to take on.

'If we don't grab this, we'll be following the railway to Carlisle. I've had enough and I want to settle down.' They were back at the camp now and he stopped walking and turned to her. 'Tell Helen we gratefully accept her offer – we'll worry what to do about your cooking when we're in there!' He winked at her, held her tight and kissed her once again. Catching sight of Doctor

Thistlethwaite watching them from the steps of the hospital, he shouted, 'Go on, lass, this is the beginning of our new future!' as Molly walked away.

Tipping his cap at the doctor, he set off along the track back to the hut whistling a merry tune. He knew he was the better man for Molly, and by gum he liked rubbing the doctor's nose in it.

'Rats were playing dominoes last night,' said Lizzie cheekily, looking over the breakfast table at her mother and John. She'd heard the bed-head knocking against the hut's walls on the other side of the curtain.

'I don't know what you are talking about.' Molly spooned the porridge out and looked slyly at her daughter. 'Anyway, John and I have something to tell you – haven't we, John?

'Aye, that's right. If you're able to face news, after your heartbreak of yesterday.' John tickled her under the chin and smiled.

Lizzie's face dropped, thinking again about her George. 'I know I was upset, and I still am. I'm going to miss him. I think I love him.'

'Never mind, pet. Plenty more fish in the sea – and they'll all be fighting over you, my girl. Now, listen to our news.' Molly couldn't bear to keep it to herself a moment longer. 'John and I are going to get married!'

'Is that all? You told me that before – why tell me again when George is leaving me?' Lizzie sulkily stirred another helping of sugar into her porridge.

'Is that all we get, Miss Misery? Anyway, we've more

to tell you.' Molly drew a deep breath and launched into the news she'd been saving: 'We're going to live and work in the Welcome – Helen's moving back to her family and she's going to rent the place to John and me. Soon you'll soon have your own room and a proper home! You can have first pick of the bedrooms, I promise.'

'Are we really going to live in the pub?' Lizzie beamed. 'And a whole room to myself? Can I help serve on?' The questions came thick and fast and George's imminent departure was forgotten as the move was discussed, and their imaginations ran wild redecorating and furnishing their soon-to-be home.

'Best get yourself off to work, Lizzie, else Mr Ashwell will be docking your wages.' Molly practically had to push the chattering Lizzie out of the door.

'I won't need Mr Ashwell before long, so it won't matter!' Lizzie yelled as her mother watched her running along the track.

'Now, what are you going to do today, John Pratt?' Molly put her arms around her man before she too set off to work.

'First thing I'm going to do is make my way down to the vicarage and see the vicar, set us a date. The sooner the better – will that do for you?'

'That'll be grand, my love.' Molly kissed him on the cheek and wrapped her shawl around her shoulders.

'After that, I'm going to pop my head in on the bonniest two women I know and indulge in a bit of serious flirting, while I'm still single.' John grinned.

'If I find you talking to anyone other than me, John

Pratt, you can forget about getting married!' Molly tossed her hair back as colour rose to her cheeks.

'I meant you and Helen, you idiot. I'd hardly walk from seeing the vicar to another woman's arms. Go on, get a move on, you're going to be late now. There'll be none of this when you're in charge: it'll be a twenty-four-hour job, I hope you know that?' He patted her bottom and winked.

'I do.' Molly grinned and kissed him lightly on the cheek before closing the hut door and humming all the way to the Welcome.

'You'll have to come in early a morning or two, Moll.' Helen, red-faced and sweating, was lifting loaves of bread out of the oven while her two youngest played around at her feet and her oldest teased the pet cat that was sitting on the back of a chair that had seen better days. 'I'll have to show you how to make bread and pastry. Once you've got the hang of that, you can't go far wrong. Cake-making's the extra earner, but without bread and pastry, job's worth nowt.' She wiped her sweaty brow. 'Thomas – leave that cat alone, will you! Take Patsy and Henry into the other room. I can't have them under my feet while I'm working.'

Young Thomas dutifully held the hands of his younger siblings and pulled them into the adjoining room without saying a word.

'Aye, I've had a day and a half already. I've been up all night with young Henry, he's cutting his back teeth, poor little bugger.'

Seeing how exhausted Helen was, Molly volunteered: 'I'll make us a brew, and then you can tell me what you want doing today and what you think I should know. John's coming in later. He's gone to see the vicar to book the church for our wedding. I still can't believe how quickly everything's happening.'

'Believe me, you'll be cursing me this time next year when you're in my shoes – hardly any sleep, a baby round your feet and John sleeping it off 'cause he's taken a liking to the ale!' Helen watched as Molly took the kettle from off the hook above the fire and poured two mugs of tea.

'It'll still beat what I was doing this time last year: up to my armpits in soapy water, mucky laundry every-where and hands that chapped with the cold and wet that I could hardly rub them together! If it means having a proper roof over my head and John and Lizzie by my side, I'll gladly do whatever has to be done.'

Helen took a gulp of tea. 'Right then, you can start by making a rabbit pie. There's rabbits to skin and pastry to make. I'll show you what to do and then you can get on with it. Doors open at ten and close when everyone's gone home. We take no tick, and no one sleeps on the benches. You've to tell 'em how it is from day one, else they'll all take advantage of you.'

Molly had always thought Helen was unsure of herself and easily dominated, but now she was begin-ning to see that her friend was an astute business woman and knew her trade well.

'Any beer you want comes from Samuel Sedgwick

on Lancaster docks – that'll be John's job. Henry used to go for it every Wednesday with his horse and cart, stop overnight and come back the following day. But since he's buggered off, Sedgwick's lad brings it over for me. I've to put him up for nowt, but he's a grand lad so it's no bother. Don't go to the other brewery down there – they water the beer down and charge more, thieving buggers!' Helen rattled on, issuing instruction after instruction until Molly's head was spinning.

The rabbit's innards had made Molly retch and Helen had tutted at her warm hands as she rubbed the lard into the flour before rolling the shortcrust pastry out and placing it on top of the steaming rabbit and potato filling. The huge enamel pie dish was now in the giant oven. Molly hoped that it would be well received by customers. The cooking side of things still filled her with dread and the ordeal with the rabbit carcase had only made her more conscious than ever that this was not her strong point.

Helen stood in the corner of the cold pantry going through all the contents of the stone shelves and telling her where to buy the butter and cheeses that were set out on the cool stone slabs.

'Don't forget to brush the salt off the bacon in a week or two and then hang it up to cure.' Helen pointed at a big zinc bath filled with the two long flitches of bacon covered in salt. 'There's no need to cover them with a pillowcase like I have the hams, but watch for bluebottles later on in the year. They're buggers for laying eggs in food.'

So that was what was in the pillowcases. Molly had been wondering ever since she spotted them hanging from massive iron hooks set into the ceiling. As she looked around her at the jars of pickles and jams Helen had made with loving care, she realized the size of the task she had taken on.

'Anyone home?'

The shout from the bar had both women hurrying out of the pantry to greet John. He was red in the face with a twinkle in his eye. 'Well, Molly Mason, we've got a date when we're to be wed.' He grabbed her waist. 'Next Saturday, one o'clock. I told the vicar we were in a rush.'

'You did what?' Molly's face looked like thunder.

'I told him we were in a hurry. Well, we are, aren't we? You want to get on with it, and Helen will want to be out of here.' John was taken aback by Molly's face and Helen's fit of giggles.

'John Pratt, have you no sense? He'll think I'm . . . you know.' His puzzled expression told her that he didn't know, which made her even more exasperated. 'He'll think I'm having a baby, you silly bugger!' She turned to Helen. 'It's no giggling matter, Helen Parker. I don't want everybody to think I'm in the family way, 'cause I'm not!'

'Oh, don't you go bothering about that, Moll. You know it means nowt up here. And let's face it, lass, you're no angel!' Helen squeezed her friend's hand tightly. 'Congratulations, pet. I'm invited, I hope?'

Molly muttered something under her breath, unheard by both John and Helen.

'Now I know where Lizzie gets her sulks from,' John whispered as Molly stalked off to check her pie. 'Come on, Helen, show us out back and the stables. I'm thinking of doing them up. Happen I could rent them out, if it's all right by you?'

Helen led him through the Welcome's rooms and out to the back yard where the stables were.

'By 'eck, what in blazes is that smell?' John put his neckerchief to his nose.

'That's the privies. I've had no one to empty them since Henry run off, so they do smell a bit.' Helen blushed.

'A bit! Lass, it's enough to knock a grown man down. I reckon that's my first job. Is this where your horse is?' He opened the stable door to reveal a fit enough horse, but its bedding was nearly a quarter way up the stable walls. 'I can see I've some work to do here an' all. You should have said long since that you were struggling. You know I'd have helped.'

John took his jacket off and rolled his sleeves up, lifting the bridle and harness down from the stable wall and encouraging the brown mare out into the cobbled yard.

'Leave me to it, I can manage this,' he said. 'You sort our Moll out.'

Having slipped the bridle over the horse's head, he put her in harness and had her pull the small dirt cart

361

out of the corner of the yard. Not the best job to start with, but the sooner it was done the better the place would smell. And then he'd take a dip in the beck, because by the time he'd finished, he'd certainly need one.

27

The sun shone down and the air was heavy with the scent of meadow grass and balmy herbs as Molly, Lizzie and her followers – an assortment of friends and patrons of the Welcome Inn, many of them already jolly with ale and singing at the tops of their voices – made their way down to the church in the glade. As they followed the trickling stream along the cart track, past the ancient dwellings of Chapel-le-Dale, Molly's dress blew in the slight breeze. She hadn't believed her eyes when Helen had pulled the beautiful cream dress out of a trunk and passed it to her, explaining that Henry had won it in a card game from somebody who was due to be married and it was of no use to her. Molly had tried it on and found that it fitted her perfectly. She'd stood in front of the mirror, gazing in awe at the layers of lace and ribbons, wondering what had become of the woman it was intended for. Had she worn it to get married in, or had her husband-to-be lost it on the eve of their wedding? In her hair was a sprig of wild mountain thyme, matching the pink flush in her cheeks. Lizzie's bouquet was a bunch of bluebells. Their perfume filled the air, and the delicate flowers went beautifully with the cream of her dress.

When they got to the church, Molly stopped sharply outside the porch with Lizzie by her side.

'Lizzie, I just want to say a word or two to your dad, to get his approval.' She smiled at her daughter. 'Stay here, love – I won't be long. Oh, and give me a few of those bluebells, pet.'

Bluebells in hand, she lifted her skirts and walked through the long grass of the churchyard. When she reached the graves of her late husband and baby son, she bowed her head and stood in silence for a moment before tenderly dividing the bluebells and placing a bunch on each grave.

'I love you, pet, I always will, but I need a man. Life's too hard without one. You know me, headstrong and stupid.' A tear rolled down her cheek and she wiped it away quickly. 'And we won't forget you, Tommy. I should have looked after you better, but I did what I could at the time.' She sniffed hard and walked away, turning at the edge of the graveyard for a final look at the graves of her family, before retrieving her bouquet from a smiling Lizzie.

John's head turned to watch his beautiful bride as the vicar stood and the organist played the wedding march. Helen smiled at him and her children giggled as they saw the bride come down the aisle.

Mike, who was best man, whispered into his brother's ear: 'This is a bit drastic for a bet, mate!' He never could resist bringing up that conversation they'd had about Molly, back in the days when they used to dream about her hanging the laundry with her long red hair blowing in the wind.

John gave him a hard kick to shut him up and then Molly was standing at his side, looking more beautiful than he'd ever seen her.

The vicar, who had never forgotten the time he marched Lizzie home and found her mother drunk, was taken aback by the transformation. She might be a little older than most, but she was every inch the perfect bride. As the service progressed, he couldn't stop himself glancing over the top of his prayer book to admire the happy couple. They blushed and smiled and fumbled with the wedding ring, and then embraced and exchanged a kiss when he pronounced them man and wife. As they left the church, he shook their hands and told them he would gladly perform a christening whenever they were ready.

This brought a glint to Molly's eye, and he hastily retracted his words, stammering that of course they wouldn't be needing him for a while yet.

The horse and cart trotted its way to the Welcome, with the wedding party waving at passers-by. The breeze blowing in their hair and the noise of laughter drowned out the cry of the nesting curlews and peewits.

John lifted Molly down from the wagon, grabbing her around her waist and kissing her hard on the lips. Lizzie giggled along with Helen's children at the newly-weds' behaviour.

'Go on then, you big lump! Pick her up and carry her over the threshold, because from tomorrow this is your new home. I'm off in the morning and it'll be all yours, but tonight Lizzie can stop on after the celebrations while you two have the hut to yourselves.' Helen put her arm around Lizzie and held her close for a second or two.

Everyone cheered as John picked up his bride, pretending to struggle to carry her over the threshold while she screamed and giggled, feeling like a sixteen-year-old again.

They entered the pub, which, to Molly's amazement, had been transformed. There were fresh meadow flowers everywhere and enough food had been laid out to feed an army. She turned with tears in her eyes to thank Helen, who was tearful too.

'Well, I had to have a leaving do,' she sniffed.

Molly kissed her closest friend on the cheek and whispered her thanks and 'I'll miss you.' Before she had time to say more, John appeared and pulled her away as a fiddler started to play. Soon everyone was dancing and laughing, drinking toasts and enjoying the food Helen had laid on. The only ones missing were Gladys and the doctor, who had been conspicuous by their absence. John wasn't surprised Roger Thistlethwaite had stayed away: he knew what Molly had meant to him.

The day turned into night and the night turned into early morning. Lizzie curled up in bed with Helen's two youngest and listened as the last revellers set off to walk her mother and John to the hut for their first night as man and wife. This time tomorrow, the inn would be her home and she would be in her own room in her own bed. As her eyelids began to droop and her head settled back on the pillow, she replayed the day's events in her mind. It was a day she vowed she would never forget.

The wedding revellers sang and teased the married couple all the way to their hut. There was raucous laughter as John failed in his attempt to lift his wife over the threshold a second time, and the couple collapsed in a giggling heap before closing the door on the world. As soon as they were alone, he pinned her to the wall and kissed and caressed every inch of her body before pulling her to the bed they had shared in previous nights.

'Lizzie said the rats were playing dominoes last night, it's a good job she's not here tonight! Tonight I've got nothing in my hand to play except you.' He kissed her over and over again and Molly responded. It had been a long time since she had been loved properly by a true loving man and she was going to enjoy every minute of it.

28

'Well, that's it, I'm off. Everything's loaded: bairns' clothes, the dog, all our bits and bobs . . . all the rest is yours – and you're welcome to it, the state that pub's in this morning. I'd close until later on today, if I were you. You'll not get much custom anyway, not after yesterday!' Helen grinned at the hungover couple. They'd survive; a good drink of sweet tea and a bite to eat and they'd soon feel better. She did feel guilty at leaving such a mess behind, but when you ran a pub it was a case of in at the deep end or not at all.

Molly, feeling a bit delicate, filled up with tears as her friend held her arms out for a final hug. 'You take care,' she said. 'I'll miss you and I'll try not to let you down. The Welcome's in good hands – providing I can manage the cooking.'

'You'll manage. Nothing's ever beaten you yet, and you've a good man and Lizzie to help.' Helen smiled. 'And you, John Pratt, mind you behave yourself and look after this woman, else you'll have me to answer to.' She kissed John on the cheek. 'And I've not forgotten you, Miss Lizzie. Here, I've got you something.'

Lizzie grinned and came forward.

'Give us your hand then.' Helen pulled out two florins from her purse. 'That's for looking after my brood. You've kept your eye on them a lot lately.'

Lizzie's eyes glistened. It would have taken her a whole month to make that at the offices of the Midland. 'Thank you, I don't deserve this much.'

'Course you do, lass. Never say no to brass.' Helen pulled her skirts up and hoisted herself up into the seat next to her brother. 'Behave yourselves now. I'll want my rent in two months' time, so I'll see you then.' The cart jolted and the children cheered and then they were off. It was an uphill journey to Swaledale, so it would take them a while to get home.

Molly and John looked at one another and then stepped into the main room of the Welcome. It might be theirs now, but at this moment in time all they really wanted was bed and a few hours' sleep.

'You made a good mess of this spot last night,' said Lizzie, surveying the shambles left by the wedding guests. 'I'll put the kettle on and then I'll start on the bedrooms. I'll leave it to you old married people to tidy up down here.' She smiled to herself as she went out to the pump and filled the kettle. She was going to have first choice of the bedrooms while she had the chance.

'What time did we get to bed, Moll?' John sat with his head in his hands.

'It was breaking light.' Molly took a long sip of the

hot sweet tea that Lizzie had brought her. She could hear Lizzie moving furniture about above her head. At least upstairs was getting straight. 'Do you want to tell Ashwell that there's two huts up for rent now and that Lizzie won't be in for a day or two, just until we get straight.' Molly stood up and pulled her hair back. 'If you can take care of that, and empty our old homes, I'll tidy up here.' She started picking up the empty tankards from the tables and straightening chairs.

'I'm sorry, lass. It's not the easiest start to married life, but it'll get better. I'll take the horse and cart, and start bringing stuff over from the old huts as soon as I've seen Ashwell.' He ran his hand down the length of her back and kissed her.

'Now don't you start! My head's still spinning from last night. Let's get this place square and then we'll have plenty of time for one another.' Molly held the lapel of his jacket and kissed him on his lips.

He patted her bottom, put on his cap, and started whistling as he walked out the back door.

Molly stood at the bottom of the stairs and yelled up to Lizzie, 'The end bedroom's mine and John's, so hands off, young lady. I can hear you moving it about.'

'But, Mam . . .' Lizzie protested.

'But Mam, my arse! It's the main bedroom.' Molly shook her head: give that girl an inch and she'd take a yard. Lizzie reminded her a lot of herself. She turned quickly as the first customer of the day appeared. 'Sorry, we've no food today.'

'No food? But it's dinner time. Helen always has

dinner on the go, and she lets me trade my tokens in for dinner and a gill.' The navvy looked put out.

'Well, have a gill on me, but I can't make you dinner unless you'll settle for bread and cheese?' Molly looked at her first challenge and smiled; she was going to have to get used to these 'But Helen . . .' moments, and she knew it.

'Well, if that's the best you can do.' The tanned wiry man sat down next to the window and waited for his dinner.

Molly went into the kitchen after pouring him a gill. It was no better in here than in the main bar. How she was going to tidy things up today, she didn't know. She carved the man two slices of bread and plated it with a good wedge of Wensleydale cheese and two pickled onions from one of Helen's jars, placing it in front of her first customer with pride.

'I don't want them bloody things, they make me have indigestion, Helen would know that if she was here.' The man poked at the pickled onions and put them on his side of his plate.

Molly bit her lip and wondered just what she had taken on. It was going to be a challenge, keeping her temper in check long enough to get to know all her customers.

Having wolfed down his sandwich, her only customer picked his plate up and licked away the remaining crumbs of cheese. 'Will you have something on in the morning, 'cause I fair like Helen's Lancashire hotpot and I'll come back for it. If not, I'll walk over to the

Cow Dub in Cowgill.' He belched loudly. 'See, I told you that onions gave me wind.'

Molly looked at the man's empty plate as he made his way out of the pub after assuring him that she would attempt a hotpot the following day. It was only as she was wondering why he'd eaten the offending onions that she realized he hadn't paid. The gill might have been on the house, but not the bread and cheese. She was never going to make any money that way.

John came back with his cart laden. The old black mare stood patiently as beds and tables and crockery were unloaded. Rose Pratt's best china took pride of place in the kitchen, making it look like a proper workplace again.

'There's no going back now, lass. Folk are wanting our huts already, so we're here to stay.' John put his arm around her shoulders and rocked her. 'This is our new life. What do you think, Lizzie? Are you happy, have you claimed your bedroom?'

'I had, but Mam chucked me out. I've had to settle for second-best.' Lizzie gave her mother a black look.

'It's better than behind a curtain in a wood hut, lady, so don't you sulk.' Molly pulled her young daughter up.

'I know, but I wanted the view up the fell.'

'Well, it's ours. Besides, that room's over the bar so you'd only be woken all hours with the noise. Trust me, you're better off where you are.'

Molly counted the tokens in the cashbox behind the bar. 'Go and see if you can buy four pounds of mutton off old Lawson – we've had a request for Lancashire hotpot tomorrow.' She handed them to Lizzie. 'And don't let him rob you.'

Lizzie pulled on her hat, grabbed her basket and jangled the tokens in her hand. It would be good to get a breath of fresh air and escape from the two lovebirds.

'Can you make Lancashire hotpot? John asked Molly.

'Never made it in my life. I'll sling some mutton, tatties and onion in a pot and hope for the best.'

While Molly continued getting the kitchen straight, John went to work in the cellar. When he came back up an hour later, there was a handwritten notice in the window:

ROOMS TO LET, ALSO STABLING
ENQUIRE WITHIN

'I take it we're renting the spare rooms and stables as of today,' he said, pulling a glum face. 'I was hoping for a few days with you on my own, without somebody in the next room.'

'It could be weeks before anyone applies,' Molly turned to kiss him.

'Please, you two, not while I'm about!' Lizzie entered with a basket on her arm. 'Here, this is all he's got left.'

John and Molly peered in the basket and saw four pig's trotters.

'What the hell am I going to make with them?' Molly looked dismayed.

'He says get your order in the previous day and it'll be there, providing you pick it up by seven. And he won't take tokens from here – it's cash only, because we're in competition with his pies. I've ordered your mutton for tomorrow.' Lizzie took the basket into the kitchen and picked one of the trotters up gingerly. How could anyone eat pig's feet?

The air was filled with flour as Molly pounded and kneaded her bread. The elastic dough was sticking to her skin, getting brushed into her hair and binding her fingers together. She'd never seen Helen's bread look like this. She added more flour and pounded the dough into loaf shapes, then set it next to the fire to rise. The realization that she would have to do this every day filled her with horror.

Brushing her sticky hands free of the dough, she put the huge brown basin to one side and tackled a dozen onions that needed peeling. As she pulled the skin off the first one, the strong acrid smell stung her eyes and tears started to stream down her face. She chopped and peeled all twelve before adding them to a stockpot that hung over the open fire. All she needed now was the mutton, and John should be coming back with it at any minute. The trotters were already boiling at the side of the fire, the white liquid giving off a pungent smell. She felt sick at the sight of them, without having to breathe in the vapours as well. Some folk liked them, cold and jellied, but at this moment she'd happily have thrown them away, the smell was that horrible.

So – the menu for the day: Lancashire hotpot, jellied trotters, or ham and eggs. That should keep them all happy. Happen she should attempt a pastry . . . then again, perhaps not. She'd put a rice pudding in the side oven instead. Once the bread was out it could cook away all day there, without her having to keep checking it.

Molly sighed and looked around the kitchen. She felt stupid: a woman of her age, with butterflies flitting around in her stomach over a bit of cooking. She'd to remember she was in charge and if they didn't like her food, tough.

She made her way across the flagstone floor of the snug and tried to peer through the mucky brown windows. Once Lizzie was up, her first job would be to clean the glass. She'd not heard a murmur from the girl since they'd said goodnight. It must have been the best night's sleep that she'd had since leaving Bradford.

A welcome blast of fresh air came in when she opened the back door, cooling her red cheeks. John was going to saddle the horse and make the trip to Lancaster later in the day. He'd be gone overnight, but it had to be done. He needed to make himself known to the brewers at Lancaster docks. She didn't want him to go; she'd miss having his warm body next to her. Her cheeks flushed at the thought of their lovemaking these last few nights and she giggled to herself.

'Here you are, woman – four pounds of mutton. And I've ordered four pounds of shin of beef for tomorrow.

The man's a bloody thief, though, his prices are scandalous!' John shouted through from the kitchen, pulling a chair out and sitting down at the table. 'He'll need watching – I'd to tell him to put in a different bit of mutton, in else we'd have had the lump he dropped on the floor. You didn't want it covered in sawdust, did you?'

Molly came in and unwrapped the parcel of meat. 'Do you think that'll be enough?'

'Aye, chop it up into little lumps and it'll go further. Put plenty of tatties in too.'

'It'll have been a bloody old sheep, this 'un – it's all stringy and full of gristle.' She started chopping the meat, practically having to tear some pieces off by hand it was so tough. Then she tossed it in the stockpot. 'I'll put the tatties in later. John, open the front door, time for business – our first day, Mr Pratt, as hosts.'

'Aye, but I've to leave you, remember. I'll not be back from Lancaster until late tomorrow – will you and Lizzie be all right?'

He wasn't happy about leaving the two women on their own, but it was important to make himself known to Samuel Sedgwick. The brewery manager needed to know he was dealing with a man of his word.

'Of course we will, love. I can look after myself, you know I can.' Molly really wanted to say, No, please don't go, I can't cope. But she didn't. After all, what was two days? They'd be fine.

'Good morning, sleepy head.' John put his arm around young Lizzie, who was still rubbing her eyes as she came into the kitchen. She yawned and fell into the chair opposite Molly.

'You'll have to be up earlier in the morning, lady. I'm going to need your help while John's away.' Molly placed a mug of tea and slice of bread and jam in front of her daughter.

'I don't think I can eat anything – not with that horrible smell.' Lizzie wrinkled her nose in disgust.

'Pig's trotters. I'm boiling them up and then leaving them to go cold. Some folk love 'em.'

Molly looked at her bread. It had risen a bit, but nowhere near as much as Helen's. Still, it would have to do. She placed the bread in tins and then into the oven and stoked up the fire. That left only the rice pudding and the tatties to do later. 'Can you clean the snug windows today, Liz? We might even get a bit of light in there if you can get the muck off.'

'I suppose so.' Lizzie toyed with her bread and jam.

'You help your mother, do you hear?' John stood up. 'I'll get the trap and horse ready. Sooner I'm away, the better.'

John swilled his tea down and then went out to harness the horse and cart.

'Come on then, lazy bones. You clean the floors and windows and I'll see to the dinners and customers. I'll need you tonight when the bar gets busy, so you'd better watch what I do through the day.' Molly put a mobcap over her hair and busied herself making the bar ready while Lizzie swept and mopped the floor, getting ready for the first customer of the day. The smell of bread filled the pub and the mutton cooked slowly over the fire. Molly pulled the bread tins out of the oven, emptying one out into her hand the way Helen had shown her. She gently tapped it. It sounded hollow, just like Helen said it should. She felt the weight in her hand; perhaps a bit heavy, but then, this was only her first batch. Gently emptying the tins on to cooling racks, she admired the fruit of her hard work and drank in the uplifting smell of newly baked bread. She replaced the bread in the oven and popped in the rice pudding, adding a few sultanas and some blobs of butter on the top to make it richer. Then she added the tatties to the mutton stew. That was it, everything ready. Now all she needed were a few customers.

John urged the little black mare on. There was no rush, the day was fine and as long as they got there by evening, it would be good enough. He was enjoying the ride out. It was his first trip away from Ribblehead in a long time and it was good to see unfamiliar faces. He passed the medieval outline of Wray Castle and plodded on down the dusty road to Lancaster, pausing to admire the view of the Irish Sea when he turned on to the road to Quermore. The ships' sails looked like white gulls dotted against the azure blue waves. He'd be down at the docks by dusk, just in time to catch Samuel Sedgwick with his order and to make himself known.

'Now then, lad, what can I be doing for you?' Samuel Sedgwick was a portly man, well dressed in a particularly fine embroidered waistcoat. John found him in his office, puffing on a huge cigar.

'Helen Parker's sent me. I've taken on the Welcome Inn at Ribblehead and she says you are the man for my ale.'

'Oh, aye – grand lass, Helen. Her husband was a right bastard, mind. No wonder she had him knocked off.' Samuel took a long drag on his cigar and leaned back on one of his barrels, looking John up and down.

'Did you say what I thought you said?' John was shocked.

'What? That Henry was knocked off? Common knowledge round here, lad. If she hadn't paid someone to do it, he wouldn't have lasted long anyway. That man was hated – and I mean hated.' He had another puff at his cigar and got back to business: 'So, you're after my ale. Forty barrels a month the Welcome goes through, if my sums is right. I'll take my hat off to them navvies, they can sup as well as they dig. They've made me a very rich man.' He rubbed his hands together, eager to do business.

'I didn't know we wanted that much. I thought Helen said twenty.' John thought it must be because he was still in shock after hearing that the quiet landlady was a murderer. Most likely it was just idle gossip; all the same, he couldn't wait to get home and tell Molly.

'Nay, lad, it's forty, else it's not worth my lad coming twice a month with the delivery. I expect prompt payment, mind. The prices per barrel and brew are up there on the wall – you can take it or leave it. I can get a delivery to you beginning of next week.' Samuel Sedgwick looked at his pocket watch, hinting that he'd no patience for time-wasters.

'Right then, it'll have to be forty. Payment on delivery all right?' John prayed under his breath that it would be all right as he'd hardly a florin on him.

'Nay, you don't owe me anything for the first delivery. Helen made it right last time – she said you'd be coming and paying me a visit.' He looked at John's face, knowing damn well that he wouldn't have been able to pay for forty barrels outright. 'Now then, you're to come and have supper with me and th'old lass. I'll introduce you to the family – I've fifteen of 'em, one for every other year of marriage. I think I've called it a day now, but you never know, there could be life in the old stick yet!' He pulled on the black mare's reins and guided John along the quayside. 'I'll have to tell you the tale of Helen over supper and you can make your own mind up, but first a drink – we deserve one.'

'Bloody hell, Moll, what do you call this? The Midland would pay you a fortune for this stuff – they need summat to line Blea Moor tunnel!' The navvy looked at Molly's offering of home-made bread, ham covered with scorch marks, and broken-yolked eggs. 'You can serve a good gill, lass, but your cooking's shit.'

Molly looked at her accuser and bit her lip. She'd been putting up with it all day: not enough salt in the hotpot, bread like bricks and rice pudding with no nutmeg. She should have known better than to take the place on, not when she couldn't cook. It was hopeless.

'Mam, come on, give him a free gill and let it be.' Lizzie pulled her mother away and forced her to sit in the kitchen while she gave the navvy a free gill and apologies. She could see that her mother was going to explode and that would do nobody any good. Lizzie shouted at the top of her voice over the hum of men talking.

'Sorry, gents, there will be no more food served today. But we won't disappoint you tomorrow.'

A cheer went up and a brave voice shouted, 'Thank God for that! I thought I was going to be the next one in the graveyard!' A roar of laughter filled the room and then the chat resumed.

'Listen, Mam, they're happy enough drinking. Why don't I have a go at the cooking tomorrow? Old Rose showed me a thing or two when I was with her. I can soon cobble together a meat-and-tattie pie and a steamed pudding, that'll do them tomorrow.'

Hearing the sound of a tankard being rattled on the bar, Lizzie left her mother to serve the thirsty customer.

Molly sat with her fists tightly clenched. She was more angry with herself than with her customers: they were right, she just didn't have the knack when it came to cooking.

John had the hangover from hell as he climbed the hill out of Lancaster. As he gazed down on the sandstone buildings laid out below him, he spotted Lancaster Moor Asylum and shuddered at the thought of the lunatics within its walls. From the stories he'd been told, many of the inmates weren't really insane, they were just mis-fits who'd fallen foul of polite society.

It had been a very entertaining night at the Sedgwicks. They'd plied him with food and drink until he could take no more. He breathed deep, drawing in the fresh salty sea breeze in the hope of clearing his head for the long ride homewards. The mare knew its way and took no guiding, she must have travelled this route many a time. As he rode, John mulled over the tale that Samuel Sedgwick had told him about Henry Parker's demise. He still found it hard to believe that Helen would have done such a thing. No, he told himself, it can't be true. For a start, surely Henry's body would have been found by now? His mind wandered for a while and then stopped with a jolt: what if Henry was buried under the floorboards at the Welcome? Was that why she'd been in such a hurry to get away?

The sun was setting behind him as John entered Ingleton, the winding narrow streets eventually giving way to open fell and moorland. He passed the place where the little black mare that he was riding was found after Henry Parker's disappearance and he shuddered again at the thought. Suddenly the mare gave a start as something stirred in the darkness of the blackthorn hedge and he caught a glimpse of a body. Or at least it looked like a body. John reined in the horse and shouted at the small dark figure: 'Are you all right? You there, what's wrong?'

A small figure emerged from the hedge, walking unsteadily and wrapped in a dark cloak. John leaned from the horse to see better as a white face looked up at him and whispered in a faint voice, 'I'm fine, thank you, sir.' No sooner had she spoken than her hand went to her brow and she collapsed in a heap in the road.

John dismounted from his horse and lifted the young woman's head into his lap. There was nothing to her but skin and bones, and he was surprised to see that her dark hair was cut short. For a moment he wondered if it was a boy, for it was rare to see a girl with short hair. Her breathing was ragged and she winced as John lifted her on to his mare. Taking the reins, he led the mare past the Hill Inn and on to the lights of Batty Green and the Welcome Inn.

29

'So who do you think she is?' Molly and Lizzie looked down at the small body that John had brought home with him. He'd gently carried her upstairs and laid her in a spare bed in one of the rooms. Molly had washed her face and dressed her in one of Lizzie nightdresses, noticing as she did so the marks on her buttocks.

'Wherever she's come from hasn't done her any favours,' whispered Molly. 'She'd signs of a good hiding on her bottom. She's only a little scrap of a thing, but she looks a bit too old for putting over her father's knee.'

'Is she all right, Mam?' Lizzie peered at the new lodger.

'I think she's just exhausted. Let's leave her to sleep. We might find out more in the morning.' Molly sneaked out of the room, quietly closing the dark oak bedroom door behind her.

Lizzie whispered excitedly all the way down the stairs making up stories about the origin of their unknown guest. 'What if she's run away from the workhouse? Or what if she's from the mental asylum? Perhaps that's why her hair's cut short – do they cut girls' hair like that in the asylum? Maybe she escaped.'

'Quiet, lass. Stop letting your imagination run away with you,' said John. 'She's only young, she can't do any harm. She's built like a sparrow, bless her.' He pulled his chair up to the table.

'I don't know,' said Molly affectionately, 'I send you for some ale and you come home with another woman!' She sat down beside him and watched as he tucked into a plate of warmed-up meat and tattie pie.

'Bye, that's a lovely bit of pie,' he said between mouthfuls. 'I take it we've been busy with dinners.' Molly nodded, she didn't want to tell him that Lizzie was a better cook than his wife.

When his plate was clean, he belched contentedly and said, 'Fetch us a gill, Lizzie. I've some other news to tell you.' He took a long slurp of cold ale and sat back in his chair. 'You'll never guess what I heard down at Lancaster?' He took another slurp.

'Go on then, get on with it!' Molly and Lizzie couldn't wait to hear the gossip.

'Old Sedgwick told me it's common knowledge that your best mate Helen wasn't left for another woman.' John took another swig and leaned back, enjoying his captive audience. 'Henry Parker was knocked off – she killed him. Everybody down there's talking about it.'

'Oh, Mam, we've been friends with a murderer! She could have killed me while I was looking after her little 'uns!' Lizzie was immediately ready to believe the worst of a woman who until a few minutes ago had been the family's best friend.

'Give over, Lizzie, you've been reading too many books! She'd never hurt a fly, not Helen. She was a timid thing really. And Henry was a big brute of a man, she couldn't possibly have killed him,' said Molly.

'They reckon she paid some fellas to do the deed for her.'

'And I reckon they must have been having you on.' Molly shook her head, refusing to believe the gossip. 'I don't believe a word of it. Helen's been good to us, giving me a job, giving Lizzie those florins, and setting us up here – we're the only navvies in these parts with a proper roof over our heads.' Inwardly Molly wasn't so certain of Helen's innocence, but even if she had killed Henry Parker, she wouldn't hold it against her. He'd been a bastard and the world was better without him.

'Did you place the ale order, and did he want money up front? I hope to God not, else we'll be the pub without ale or grub.'

'What do you mean, no grub?' John looked at Molly.

'Nay, nothing,' said Molly. He'd hear the complaints about her fare soon enough. She only hoped that customers would persevere. Determined to stay off the subject for the time being, she demanded, 'The ale – did you get it?'

'That's the other strange thing: Helen's paid for our first forty barrels. Sedgwick said it was for the first month, but it'll last us two, I'm sure. Nothing adds up about that woman. When you think of it, she couldn't get away from here fast enough.'

'She wanted to get back to her family. And I wouldn't be surprised if she got out fast for our benefit. It was right after the tunnel collapse that she suddenly announced she wanted to leave and would rent the place to us. Helen was a kind woman who was appreciative that I was with her daughter on the night she died.'

But even as she was speaking, Molly was recalling the morning Helen told her she'd had a letter from Henry. She'd seemed a little shifty then, right enough. Trying to shrug off her doubts, she employed her usual tactic of changing the subject: 'Anyway, what are we to do with our guest upstairs? Are you sure she didn't say anything to you?'

'Not a word. She was damn lucky she didn't get tangled up with the horse, popping out of a hedge like that. I couldn't leave her half-dead, lying in the road.' John sat back in his chair and tapped the cutlery on the table. 'I'd like to know where she came from, though. I don't like to think of her sleeping under our roof.'

'John! She's a slip of a lass, she's not going to hurt a soul! Besides, from what I've seen she's suffered plenty of hurt herself. Her backside's wealed and bruised – someone's taken their belt to her.' Molly poured John another drink. 'Time for bed, Liz. I want you up early in the morning.'

'Are you working early, Lizzie? I thought Ashwell would be winding down now, not going up a gear?'

Lizzie glanced sheepishly in her mother's direction, then told him: 'I'm helping Mam in the morning. She's told Mr Ashwell that I'm not working for him any more, there's too much to be done here.'

'That's enough, Lizzie! Get yourself to bed, I need to talk to John on my own.' Molly pulled at Lizzie's chair, chivvying her to bed.

'Night, John.' Lizzie kissed him on the cheek and gave her mother a backward glance. She knew that John would not be so suited at her giving up work when hers was the only wage coming in.

'What did you do that for? I know Lizzie doesn't earn a lot, but at least it kept her fed and shod.' John looked angry.

'I need her in the kitchen. I told you I couldn't cook, and it turns out that Lizzie learned a lot when she was with your mother. At least her bread isn't like bricks. It's been a disaster while you've been away, we'll be lucky if anyone will ever eat here again.' Molly hated telling the truth, but it had to be said.

'So what the hell are we going to do? We can make a living with the ale for the next few weeks, but when the day comes we need to pay for more, we're sunk. I'll have to go back to the railway. I can probably pick up work on the viaduct, although it's nearly finished. Another six months and it'll be done. Then I'll have to go and move on with the line men.'

Molly stood behind her fretting husband and rubbed his shoulders. 'Stop fretting, love. Something will turn up, it always does.' She kissed him on the head. 'Come to bed, darling. I missed you last night.' She rubbed her hands down his chest.

'You're right,' he sighed. 'Tomorrow's another day. I'm just tired and fretting over nowt.' He stood up and kissed her tenderly, taking her hand and leading her up the stairs. 'Away, woman – show me what I missed last night.' He pulled harder on her hand and grabbed her by the waist. 'I'm home and ready for a lusty night!'

'That bread needs taking out, Mam,' Lizzie shouted across the steamed-up kitchen. Molly dropped her broom and ran in from the bar. Lizzie was up to her elbows, mixing currants and suet to make a pudding, the way Rose Pratt had shown her.

'Damn! It's a bit brown and hard. I should have grabbed it out ten minutes ago.' Molly dropped the bread tins heavily on the pine table, burning her fingers as she did so.

Agnes made her way shakily down the rickety stairs, the smell of baking bread reminding her of home and making her stomach rumble. She caught the tail-end of the conversation and, without stopping to think, chimed in:

'Rub them with butter while they're still warm. That makes the crust softer and dampens the colour.'

When they turned to look at her, Agnes flushed deep red. What was she thinking, giving an older woman advice?

'Oh, I didn't know you were there! Are you feeling

better?' Molly turned to see her new lodger, who obviously knew something about baking.

'Yes, thank you. I'm so grateful to you for letting me sleep here last night. I doubt I would be alive if it weren't for your kindness. I'm sorry, but I can't remember what happened exactly.'

The frail girl seemed dwarfed by Lizzie's old nightdress. She made to take a step forward but her legs seemed too weak to support her and she wobbled uncertainly and almost fell.

'Here, sit down, you poor mite. You look as if you could do with a good meal inside you. Lizzie, get this young lass a dish of porridge, there's some left in the big pan.'

The dark-haired young woman leaned over the table, her body trembling as she lifted her head to eat.

'Are you sure you're all right, love?' said Molly kindly. 'You look as if you've been through the mill.' She drew up a chair as Lizzie went about her business, getting the dinner menu together while keeping a watchful eye on the young lodger.

'I'm fine, thank you.' Agnes spooned the warm porridge into her mouth, her hand shaking. 'I'm afraid I can't pay for this, but I'll wash the dishes for you.' She blushed with embarrassment.

'You'll do no such thing! When you've eaten that, you can go straight back to bed. You're in no fit state to do anything.' Molly watched as the young lass ate. She was obviously starving, probably hadn't eaten for days. Wherever she'd come, they'd sent her packing without a penny to her name and no means of support, the poor lass. Happen she'd come from the workhouse. No doubt she'd tell them in her own good time.

When she'd finished her porridge, Molly told her, 'Right, young lady, I'll not have you fainting on this stone floor – back to bed with you. And you're to stop in bed until you get your strength back. Lizzie, help this young lass up the stairs. What's your name, pet – can we ask?' Molly's curiosity got the better of her.

'It's Agnes, Agnes Fraser.' She stood up and immediately her legs buckled under her. Lizzie rushed to her side to support her.

'Well, I'm Molly Pratt and this is my daughter Lizzie. My husband brought you home last night. He found you on the road, half-dead, so we put you in the spare room and hoped that you would see morning. Now get yourself upstairs with our Lizzie and don't come down until you're strong enough. We'll fetch you up some dinner when it's ready.'

Molly watched the two girls climb the stairs. Then, remembering what her un-paying guest had said, she took a knob of butter and rubbed it on the warm loaves of bread. The crust immediately softened and shone, making it look more appetizing. Molly raised an eyebrow, impressed. Clearly her guest knew something about cooking.

Customers were scarce and the day went slowly. Molly polished the hearth and Lizzie kept her eye on the dinner that nobody wanted. John had the most profitable morning: Elijah Allen had seen the advertisement in the window and agreed a fee to stable his horses at the inn while he went back and forth around Batty Green selling his produce.

'It's no good, Mam. Word spreads fast, they've all gone to the next dale for their dinners – the opening of that tunnel hasn't done us any favours; now they can just walk through it into Dent. Happen they'll come back tonight when they want a drink.' Lizzie sat with her head in her hands.

'Nay, pet, we don't give in! We just need to come up with something that'll get folk in. Why don't you take our guest a bit of dinner while I have a think.'

Lizzie cut a piece of cheese and bread and placed it on a plate and poured a glass of milk for Agnes. She was dying to find out where their mystery guest had come from.

She pushed the oak bedroom door open with her foot and quietly entered the room. Agnes was lying on her side with the eiderdown over her face. Though her back was turned, Lizzie could hear her sobbing. Placing the dinner on the washstand, Lizzie went to the bed and lightly touched her on the shoulder.

'Agnes, are you all right?'

She flinched as if afraid she was going to be struck, then realized it was Lizzie. Sniffing hard and wiping her eyes, she said, 'I'm fine.' But then she lowered her head, gulping for breath as another wave of tears threatened to envelop her.

'You know, I was once like you,' said Lizzie, sitting

on the edge of the bed. 'I felt all alone and beside myself with sorrow, and I don't know what would have happened if someone hadn't come along and saved me.' She took Agnes's hand in hers. 'You can tell me anything, Agnes. I promise I'll try and help.'

Tears ran down Agnes's cheeks. 'I'm not worth anything to anybody. I wish I could die.' She pulled the covers up.

'You should never say that. I've had my best friend die this year, and we buried my father and my baby brother last year. No matter what your troubles are, at least so long as you're alive you can do something.'

Lizzie remained sitting on the bed, remembering how hard it had been for her. But she hadn't allowed herself to wallow in self-pity.

'You don't know what I've been through,' Agnes sobbed.

'I know someone's brayed you, just like my best friend got brayed, but you're safe now. We'll make sure you're all right while you're here. My mam will do anything for someone who's in bother.' Lizzie looked at the red-eyed lass, only slightly older than her. 'Here, there's some bread and cheese for your dinner. You're our only customer today, so I hope you enjoy it.'

Lizzie was almost at the door when Agnes, struggling to re-gather her thoughts and her pride, said, 'Thank you. I will repay your kindness. And I apologize for feeling sorry for myself. My family disowned me after I got myself into trouble. My father used to belt me nearly every day and then he eventually threw me out to make my own way in the world.'

Agnes managed a wan smile as Lizzie, still angry that someone her own age would say that they wished themselves dead, closed the door quietly behind her.

'Is she all right love?' Molly yelled at Lizzie as she saw her come down the stairs.

'Yeah, Mam, she will be, once she's rested,' Lizzie replied before disappearing out the back door to avoid further questions. Her mam had enough on her plate without a suicidal young woman.

'What the hell was that?' Molly pulled her long white nightdress around her and swung her legs out of bed. 'John, there's somebody downstairs, I can hear them! Someone's in the kitchen – they'll be raiding the stores!'

She shook John into action. He yawned and rubbed his eyes, muttered, 'Give over, woman, you're dreaming.' Then thumped his pillow and buried his head in the soft feathers.

'There it is again!' Molly screeched, making for the bedroom door.

This time there was no doubt. Someone was definitely in the kitchen. John sprang up and armed himself with a candlestick, then led the way downstairs with Molly close behind.

The smell of warm bread was wafting from the kitchen. Molly and John stopped on the stairs and looked at each other in surprise as they sniffed the air, drooling at the delicious aroma. Perhaps it was Lizzie making an early start on the day's cooking, but the sun hadn't even risen, so that was unlikely. As they crept to open the kitchen door the smells grew stronger. Now bacon mingled with the scent of fresh bread. When they opened the door to the kitchen, they found the fire and oven lit and a batch of bread already on the table.

'I'm sorry,' said Agnes. 'I didn't mean to wake you. I just wanted to pay you for my stay and this is the only way I know.' She had Molly's apron on over the shabby dress she'd been wearing the night John found her.

'You frightened us to death, pet. We thought we had burglars! What on earth are you doing up at this time of day? Oh, my Lord, John, look at all this!'

Molly and John gazed in wonder at the rows of bread and buns and a pan full of bacon frying.

Agnes was staring down at her feet, blushing and feeling awkward. 'I'm used to getting up at this time to help my father – he was a baker. I thought that this might help you.'

'What you really mean is, you thought our bread was rubbish.'

Molly's words made Agnes look up in shock, about to protest. But before she could get a word in, Molly smiled and said, 'And, aye, you'd be right! Men have been known to break their teeth on my offerings.'

John meanwhile had sat himself down at the table, glad that there was no burglar to tackle.

'Why's that frying this early?' Molly indicated the pan of bacon.

'There's nothing better than a bacon sandwich in new bread. My father used to go round the lead miners' homes with me and my sister and sell them to the men before they set off to work. It encouraged them to come to you for their dinner at the end of the day, or to buy your bread and things for their lunch.' Agnes blushed, wondering if she'd overstepped the mark. But she'd heard Lizzie and Molly talking about how they had to find some way to attract customers back to the inn.

'By gum, you're a sharp 'un! I bet your father's worth a bob or two!' Molly grinned. Then she went to the door and hollered up the stairs: 'Lizzie – stir your shanks! Me and you have a bit of hawking to do.'

'There's two big baskets in the pantry – help me fill them up, Lizzie. Right, we both know who's wed and who's not on Batty Green, so it's only the huts with single men in that we'll target this morning – they're the ones who can't be bothered with cooking.'

Lizzie joined her mother in loading the baskets with warm bacon sandwiches and bread and fruit buns that Agnes had made.

'Right, girl, let's see how we go,' said Molly, picking up a basket. 'See, I told you tomorrow was another day and not to fret.'

Leaving a busy Agnes and a yawning John in the kitchen, they set off into the cold grey dawn to go knocking on the doors of shanties where men were getting ready to go to work, tempting them to a ready-made breakfast and the promise of a filling dinner later in the day.

All four slumped exhausted in the kitchen. Even in Helen's day, the Welcome had never seen such a rush at dinnertime. Word had rapidly spread that there was a new cook at the inn, and judging from customers' compliments on the food they'd been served, they'd be coming back for more.

'Well, lass, yesterday I hardly took a penny and today . . . well, what can I say.' Molly fanned herself with a newspaper that had been left by a customer.

'I'm glad I paid for my keep. I didn't want to leave without paying the debt I owed you.' Agnes took her apron off and picked her shawl up.

'Well, you certainly did that all right – but what's this about leaving? You still look poorly to me.' Molly pushed her chair back and stood up.

'I've imposed myself upon you long enough, I think it's time for me to go. Thank you for your help, Mrs Pratt. And, Lizzie, your talk did me good.' She drew her shawl around her and quietly made for the door.

'Wait! Where will you go? Where will you sleep tonight, lass? I'll not be having your death on my conscience, so you need not open that door.' Molly's words were stern but her touch was gentle as she laid her hand on Agnes's arm. 'We'll not ask questions of your past, pet, not if you don't want us to. That's none of our business. But I'm making it my business to keep you alive, lass. I'm sure John will back me on this: we'd like you to stay.'

A tear ran down Agnes's cheek as John told her, 'Aye, lass, you can stay. Just don't wake me up so early in the morning!'

'How about you stop in our spare room and we pay you to be our cook? That way we'll all benefit – not to mention the navvies. They'll be that fat after a month of your dinners, they'll not be able to pick up their shovels!' said Molly, putting her arm around the sobbing girl.

'Stay, Agnes. We need you,' pleaded Lizzie.

Agnes, still sobbing into her shawl, nodded her head.

'Good. That's settled then,' said Molly. 'Welcome to your new home. Now let's have no more of these tears. We need to decide what to cook for dinner tomorrow.'

30

Ribblehead Station, 1 May 1876

The Band of Hope's boisterous playing rang out over the dale, trying to rally up support while the directors and railway VIPs strutted up and down Ribblehead station platform. Overhead, bunting fluttered gaily in the breeze. The moorland and tracks were thronged with inquisitive bystanders, watching enthralled as the engine belched clouds of steam into the air as if gathering courage for its first run across the finished viaduct and through the man-made tunnels at the start of its long journey up to the Scottish border. Excited children ran between the grown-ups' legs, pleading to be allowed to ride on the train, while one naughty little boy ran up and down the railings with a stick, making a racket that could be heard even above the playing of the band and the puffing of the train.

'Just look at all these folk, Agnes! And they'll all be wanting something to eat. It's a good job we ordered plenty in. Are we ready to open our doors?' Molly turned away from the window and brushed her hand down the soft velvet pleats of her new dress. It was all she could do to breathe in the tightly laced-up bodice, but it was a dress that befitted her new status and she was wearing it with pride.

'Yes, Mrs Pratt, we're ready. All's cooked – just need the customers now,' yelled Agnes from the kitchen.

'Aye, get 'em in, lass! Let's get some beer sold.' John leaned over the bar, his apron around his waist and a gill in his hand.

'Where's our Lizzie?' Molly scanned the room, wanting to make sure Lizzie was on hand to wait on the customers.

'Where do you think? She's out back, flirting with that Sedgwick lad. Claimed she was nipping out to fetch water, but I heard her giggling with him as he was loading the empty barrels. Poor lad doesn't stand a chance! I should have warned him not to mess with the Mason women.' John wiped his now-empty glass and smiled. 'Go on, open the door, you've folk waiting.'

Molly felt butterflies in her stomach. In addition to the bar and the guest bedrooms, she now had a small tearoom next door in what used to be the barn. Today was the grand opening, not only for the tearooms but the new railway line. It was a day for celebration, in recognition of the labour and the engineering that had gone into building the magnificent line.

Taking a deep breath, Molly threw open the doors, beaming at the crowd of former navvies, all clad in their best suits for the occasion. Then she went to open the doors of the tearoom to the well-dressed ladies making their way down from the station. No longer did she feel uncomfortable in their presence, conscious of the disparity between their finery and her rags and mud-caked boots. She'd come from a navvy's wife to a woman of wealth and property, and her new dress befitted her rise in status. Her future was secure: the signed deeds to the Welcome Inn were safely tucked in a box under her bed.

Their luck had changed the day John brought the nearly dead Agnes into their home. Since then, they hadn't looked back. Lizzie had learned to cook just as well as Agnes, John had settled in behind the bar, while Molly held it all together. The business had flourished to the point that they had been able to buy the Welcome from Helen, who had found herself a farmer and was content settling into her new married life in Swaledale. Henry Parker was long forgotten, along with the ramshackle shanties of Batty Green. The only remaining signs of those days were the tram tracks and sump holes of the workings.

'Molly! We just had to come and sample one of your teas,' said Doctor Thistlethwaite, ushering in Gladys and their two children across the threshold. 'Doesn't the station look magnificent! Who'd have thought all these people would turn out to see the first engine over the new viaduct?'

'Come and sit here by the window. You'll have a good view down the dale from here,' said Molly, escorting them to their table. She was glad to see him with the children, and she'd long since risen above the bitter feelings she'd once felt for Gladys.

'We sail for India at the weekend. I've been offered a practice out there, and you know me – always up for a challenge,' said Doctor Thistlethwaite, unfolding a napkin. 'I'll miss this place, the wild rugged fells and the people.' His hand touched momentarily on Molly's and he smiled.

'I'm sure you'll not be forgotten.' Molly looked at Gladys and thanked God that she'd not married him. Who on earth would want to go to India, and with two children? The poor cow.

Leaving them to it, she went to the back door and yelled, 'Lizzie, stop your flirting with that young Sedgwick and get yourself in here to help Agnes.'

There was a yelp from behind her as the tearoom's newly employed waitress almost dropped a plateful of scones in fright. She was still nervous around the formidable Mrs Pratt.

'I'm coming, I'm coming!' Lizzie pulled her apron straight as she entered the kitchen.

'You'd better have been behaving yourself out there.' Molly fixed her daughter with a stern glare.

'Course I have,' protested Lizzie, embarrassed by her mother's tone of voice. She busied herself picking up a tea tray as her mother hurried back to the inn.

'Your mum's only looking after you, Liz.' Agnes glanced up from buttering her scones. 'You should listen.'

'I am listening, but she should know me better. I won't let anyone near me until I'm married. I know what men are like.' Lizzie turned her nose up and went about her service.

Agnes nodded, she too knew what men were like

402

with their sweet talk. It would have been her undoing, if she hadn't had the good fortune to be rescued by the Pratts.

Silence fell over the Welcome as the train's whistle blew. This was immediately followed by the scraping of chairs and a scramble of customers rushing outside to watch as the first passenger train came shunting over the small bridge next to the inn and then onwards to the twenty-four-arch viaduct. The steam curled around the arches and the whistle blew merrily as the engine and carriages crossed the spectacular granite viaduct on the slow climb towards Blea Moor. The crowds below cheered and threw their hats into the air. After all those years of toil, all the lives lost and the casualties claimed, the Settle to Carlisle line was complete. Passing through some of the remotest moorlands and featuring the highest station above sea level, it would now take its place as one of the greatest railways in England.

John and Molly gazed out at the viaduct, bathed in the glow of the setting sun. They smiled at each other as two courting couples passed by, walking hand in hand down the path to the base of the viaduct.

'I'm glad Agnes has found a good man,' said Molly. 'He may be a lot older than her, but she seems happy with Arthur Dowbiggin. And at least she won't be moving far away when they get married, not with him being signalman at Blea Moor.'

'Aye, he's not a bad man. Did young Dan Sedgwick say anything to you?' John sucked hard on his pipe, he'd wanted to tell Molly his news all day but they'd been rushed off their feet and he'd had no opportunity until now.

'No.' Molly turned to him in alarm. 'He's not putting the price of his ale up, is he?'

'Nope, it's a bit more serious than that. He wants to wed our Lizzie. He'd have asked you first but daren't, so he asked me.' John grinned and put his arm around Molly's waist, pulling her close.

'Our Lizzie? Married?' Molly was frightened of losing her daughter. It made it worse that Lizzie was her only child, and looked set to remain that way.

'She's twenty, Moll. It's time to let her go. Look at them.' John held Molly tight, kissing her neck gently as the outline of Lizzie and Dan could be seen kissing beneath the middle arch of the viaduct. 'Remember what we went through – spare her that heartache. Give them your blessing and put poor Dan out of his misery.'

Molly nestled into John's embrace. 'I hope they'll be as happy as we are. If they are, they'll survive anything.' She looked into his blue eyes. 'I love you, John Pratt. And, aye, let's have a wedding – think of all the ale we can sell! Happen she'll be given a bit of the brewery if she marries old Sam's eldest.'

Happily totting up the potential profits in her head, she bustled back to the inn to serve her customers.

John sat for a moment, watching her, then got to his feet to follow.

What a woman! Wilful, wild and a right handful – but she was his and his alone.

Poor Paddy

Traditional Irish Folk Song

In eighteen hundred and forty-one
The corduroy breeches I put on
Me corduroy breeches I put on
To work upon the railway, the railway
I'm weary of the railway
Poor paddy works on the railway

In eighteen hundred and forty-two
From Hartlepool I moved to Crewe
Found myself a job to do
A working on the railway

I was wearing corduroy breeches
Digging ditches. Pulling switches
Dodging pitches, as I was
Working on the railway

In eighteen hundred and forty-three
I broke the shovel across me knee
I went to work for the company
On the Leeds to Selby railway

In eighteen hundred and forty-four
I landed on the Liverpool shore
My belly was empty, me hands were raw

With working on the railway, the railway
I'm sick to my guts of the railway
Poor paddy works on the railway

In eighteen hundred and forty-five
When Daniel O'Connell he was alive
When Daniel O'Connell he was alive
And working on the railway

In eighteen hundred and forty-six
I changed my trade to carrying bricks
I changed my trade to carrying bricks
To work upon the railway

In eighteen hundred and forty-seven
Poor paddy was thinking of going to Heaven
The old bugger was thinking of going to Heaven
To work upon the railway, the railway
I'm sick to my death of the railway
Poor paddy works on the railway.

Author's Note

The Settle–Carlisle Railway was built by the Midland Railway Company, after a dispute with the London and North Western Railway over access to Scotland via the LNWR route.

It consisted of seventy-two miles of track, with seventeen major viaducts and fourteen tunnels blasted through the seemingly impossible hillsides. Construction began in 1869 and lasted for seven long years with over 6,000 men working on the line, with little to supplement muscle power other than dynamite and temporary tramways to haul materials. Hundreds of navvies and their families died; some were killed in accidents, others in fights and smallpox outbreaks. The building of Batty Green (Ribblehead) Viaduct caused such loss of life that the railway paid for an extension to the local graveyard at St Leonard's, Chapel-le-Dale. Memorials commemorating the deceased can still be seen within the chapel.

The Settle–Carlisle line is one of the most scenic train rides within the UK. The steady ten-mile pull up from Settle Junction to Blea Moor – known to generations of enginemen as 'the Long Drag' – passes between the three peaks of Pen-y-ghent, Ingleborough and Whernside. The line then climbs on, passing through Dentdale and upper Wensleydale to reach its summit at Ais Gill (at a height of 1,169 feet, the highest point in mainline England), before entering the wide valley of the River Eden and reaching its final destination in the busy border town of Carlisle.